TINA BALSER

is "loving, sensitive, brave, craven, worried, humorous, foolish—very human indeed!" She has everything a woman could want. Why then is she going crazy?

Universal Presents

"DIARY OF A MAD HOUSEWIFE"

A Frank Perry Film

Starring

Richard Benjamin
Frank Langella
Carrie Snodgress

Screenplay by
ELEANOR PERRY

From the novel by
SUE KAUFMAN

Produced and Directed by
FRANK PERRY

A Universal Picture
Technicolor®

diary of a
mad housewife

by Sue Kaufman

BANTAM BOOKS · TORONTO · NEW YORK · LONDON ®

A NATIONAL GENERAL COMPANY

DIARY OF A MAD HOUSEWIFE
*A Bantam Book / published by arrangement with
Random House, Inc.*

PRINTING HISTORY
*Random House edition published May 1967
4 printings*
*Bantam edition published November 1968
2nd printing ..... January 1969
3rd printing .... November 1970*

*Bantam Books are published by Bantam Books, Inc., a National
General company. Its trade-mark, consisting of the words "Bantam
Books" and the portrayal of a bantam, is registered in the United
States Patent Office and in other countries. Marca Registrada.
Bantam Books, Inc., 666 Fifth Avenue, New York, N.Y. 10019.*

PRINTED IN THE UNITED STATES OF AMERICA

DIARY OF A MAD HOUSEWIFE

Friday September 22

It is nine-fifteen on this hot September morn, hotter than any summer day we had. All the windows are open and soot, like fallout, is drifting in and settling everywhere. Outside this bedroom door, which I've locked, the apartment is empty and unpleasantly still. The girls went back to school today, a Friday, for what is called Reorientation Day. I've just come back from seeing them off on the school bus and walking Folly on Central Park West, which took forever since Folly hates the gutters, and since I'm afraid to go into the park. Today I swore I'd make myself go in there, and got as far as the entrance when I saw the man in the middle of the path, standing and loonily smiling up at the trees. He was a very old man with white hair, who was probably just somebody's poor old retired Dad, or a senile birdwatcher hoping, perchance, to spot a purple finch—but I wasn't going to risk it. Not these days. Not me.

So it was the dirty gutters with torn pages of the *Daily News*. The minute I got back up here I locked this door—I don't like that silence—opened my middle drawer, and got this pad out from under a pile of nylon slips. It's a wonderful thick pad, one hundred and thirty-two pages. As my hand moves down the first page so white, so new, it leaves damp puffy puckers which make the ink run when I try to write over them. I bought the pad yesterday in the 5&10. I took the girls there for a treat because they'd been so good while we shopped for their new winter underwear and pajamas at Bloomingdale's. The treat was frozen custards and five dollars' worth of school supplies, a pure entertainment since the Bartlett School provides all the supplies they need. But I'd promised and that's what they wanted, so they each took a basket and began to stuff it with things —little spiral notebooks, packs of pencils, pink erasers, boxes of paper clips, plastic rulers, pen nibs, Magic Markers and bottles of glue. As they browsed and grabbed, I stood by watching, wishing the tic in my right eye would stop, and praying that the lump in my throat wasn't going to get any worse, when I spotted a stack of these pads and got the idea. Just like that. I saw them and knew they were what I'd been needing, were what I'd been looking for all along, without knowing I was needing or looking for anything like them, if I make myself clear. And I also knew the idea was right, was sound, because as I stood and stared at the pads the tic in my eye suddenly stopped, the lump in my throat disappeared. A Sign. So I picked up four pads and stuck them under my arm. "Are those for us, Mudther?" asked Liz at the checkout when I put them down to be rung up with their things. "No. They're for me," I said, taking a plastic rainhat out of her hand and putting it back in the stand by the register. "For you?" said Sylvie. "Why do you need all those pads? What are *you* going to do with so many bloody pads?" I took out my wallet to keep from smacking her, hard. "Accounts," I said calmly, counting out bills. "I'm going to do my accounts."

Now Accounts is really a very good word. Accounts in its reportorial not calculative sense. Account, accounting—an account of what is going on. Better than journal or diary by far. *Diary* makes me think of those girls at camp, always fat and damp little girls, who had fake green morocco diaries with locks and keys they wore on chains around their grubby necks. *Journal* makes me think of all those college Lit courses, of Gide or Woolf or Gorky or Baudelaire, though I must admit that something like Baudelaire's "I have felt the wind of the wing of madness pass over me" comes pretty close to what I have in mind.

Anyway, *Accounts* is good. Accounts is best. Yes, Accounts does very well indeed. For an example—an Account of what happened here this morning at 7:22:

Throwing a clean shirt minus two buttons down on his bed with disgust, Jonathan went to his chest for another and said: "Tina. Tina, I'm really very worried about you."

Luckily, he had his back to me and couldn't see my reaction to this. "Really?" I said and finally finished zipping up my slacks. "That's funny. Why on earth are you worried about *me?*"

"It's not at all funny." He turned around as he stuck an arm into a shirt, presumably a shirt with all its buttons on. "In fact, it's downright serious. I'm worried because you aren't yourself and haven't been for weeks."

Wondering if the jig was up, I still managed to stay outwardly calm. I said, "I really have no idea of what you're talking about, Jonathan," and walked to the mirror to comb my hair.

He sighed and went to the tie rack fastened inside his closet door, and began rummaging through the one hundred and seventeen ties hanging there. "I'm *talking* about a lot of things. For a starter, take the way you look. You don't look well, in fact you look just terrible. Your color's rotten, you look exhausted, you seem to be losing weight, and to top it all off you don't seem to *care* how you look. Then along with all this you're touchy as hell. Jumpy and irritable and disorganized. I mean, for example, take a thing like the trunks in the pantry. We've been back from the country for almost two weeks, yet you haven't made a move to unpack those bloody trunks and get them the hell out of here. I could go on, Teen, but I think by now when I say you're not yourself you get the general idea."

I got the general idea. He'd finished dressing and, ready for his breakfast, stood waiting for me to try and vindicate myself. I said: "Railway Express brought those trunks last Friday morning. They've been here one week, not two. Almost one whole trunk is filled with your dirty summer clothes. Since you insist they be put away ironed, as well as laundered, and since you don't like Lottie's ironing and won't let me send them out, I have to get a special laundress, which is something I simply haven't had time to arrange. I haven't had time because until school started today, the girls have been at loose ends. I've had to help keep them amused. For two weeks I've had to run all over town with them in this ungodly heat—taking them shopping, taking them to the doctor and dentist for their yearly checkups, taking them places with friends. If I look tired and pale and somewhat messy, and seem jumpy and disorganized, it's because I can't take all that running around in this heat, and because I haven't had a single minute to myself."

Looking somewhat put off by this elaborate show of circumstantial evidence (which actually, being a lawyer, should have put him wise), Jonathan wearily shook his head. "All right, Teen. All right. I grant you all that is true, but I'm still worried about you. What I'd like you to do is go to Max Simon and get a complete checkup —it could be you're anemic or something like that without knowing it. And I think after the checkup it might be a good idea to go and see Popkin, go and have a talk."

"Popkin. Why in God's name should I see Popkin?"

Jonathan gave another long-suffering sigh. "Why. Because he helped you enormously when you were in such a state two years ago. That's why."

"May I remind you," I said loudly, "that I was *in* 'such a state' because my father was expected to die at any moment. I am not in any kind of state now!"

"Okay, okay. Take it easy, for God's sake— That's just what I mean. You're touchy as hell." And he went clacketing off down the hall in his brand-new $65.00 Peal shoes.

End of Account. Comment: That was close. Close shave. Poor Jonathan. Touchy and disorganized he thinks I am. Jumpy and irritable. What I really am and have been since midsummer is paralyzed. What I am is paranoid as a coot. What I am at times is so depressed I can't talk, so low I have to lock myself in the bathroom and run all the faucets to cover the sound of my crying. What I am at other times is so jazzed up with nerves I can't stand still and everything shakes, and I end up either having to take a pill or a quick sneaky shot of vodka—it depends which is available. What I am is suddenly afraid of most everything you could name. I'll name a few. I'm afraid of:

elevators
subways
bridges
tunnels
high places
low places
tightly enclosed places
boats
cars
planes
trains
crowds
deserted parks
dentists
bees
spiders
fuzzy moths
cockroaches
teen-age gangs
muggers
rapists
sharks
fires
tidal waves
fatal diseases—every one
known to man

The list could go on, but I can't. I've never had to face it in black and white before. It's a trifle off-putting, as they say. The thing is that though it all started in early August in the country, it didn't really get going full-speed-ahead until we moved back to the city the week-

end after Labor Day. How I've managed to hide it is
beyond me, but even before Jonathan's little speech this
morning, I knew I wasn't going to be able to keep it up
without help. But by help I didn't mean Popkin. Long
before Jonathan brought him up I'd decided against it,
the main reason being that I simply couldn't face the
prospect of going through all that again. Supposing one
even could. I mean I was shrunk, thoroughly, and presumably with success; for eleven years I've been func-
tioning beautifully, and I can't help but feel that I've just
gotten temporarily Out of Order, and that what's gone
wrong is something only I can fix. Not wig-picker material at all. The other reason I'm not going to go see
Popkin is that though I never told Jonathan, I'm still annoyed as hell about that little reprise Popkin and I had
two years ago. While it's true that I was "in a state," as
Jonathan points out—I couldn't stop crying—there was
a damned good reason: my father had had a coronary
occlusion and lay in an oxygen tent in the hospital, On
the Brink of Death. I cried day and night, which is
pretty exhausting. Finally I called Popkin and went to
see him, prepared for a brush-up of sorts, perhaps a re-
hash of the whole Electra thing, with some snappy new
flap like The King Must Die thrown in to liven things
up. Ha. For two sessions Popkin didn't speak, just listened to me weep and ramble on. In the third session he
finally spoke up. He said I wasn't crying about my father but about myself. He said: "I could never get you
to come to grips with the whole concept of mortality
during your analysis. But you did so well in spite of it
that I decided to let it pass. One must do that in therapy
—let certain issues pass—otherwise certain patients
would be endlessly detained. However, here it is at last.
And you are crying because you see now that you too
must die. You are crying because the imminence of your
father's death has made you see the inevitability of your
own, has made you see at last that no one is immortal,
above all, yourself." Though I'd wept a little in the beginning of the third session, I'd stopped crying by the
time he said all this. To my mind I'd stopped crying
simply because my father was off the critical list by then

—out of the oxygen tent, out of danger, well enough to be making plans to sell his business and retire to Florida. But of course I thanked Doctor Popkin, who said he'd mail me a bill (for $120.00) and said I should call and come in any time I felt the need, and left him putting a fresh paper towel on the headrest of his couch.

Which is where I'll leave him. Not only do I think I can fix what's the matter with me, but I also think it will turn out to be a fluke. Something environmental. Or something way out that hasn't been documented yet, like a Pre-Menopausal Agitation, a little preview of what's coming. Or because I turned thirty-six in early August: the timing is certainly right. Thirty-sixitis. I'll never forget that summer we spent three weeks in Wellfleet, the same summer Marilyn Monroe died, when some analyst's wife sat on the beach one afternoon holding forth on the horrors of turning thirty-six. Claimed that thirty-six was a significant and dangerous age for a woman—like fifty for a man. Claimed *she* thought that the fact that MM had just turned thirty-six had a lot to do with her suicide. At the time all I wanted to do was bop her on her thick skull with Liz's sand shovel, but maybe she had something after all. Thirty-sixitis. Is that what I have?

I don't think so. But whatever it is that's wrong with me, I think it will be a big help to write in here. Proof of how good my hunch was, of how therapeutic it's already been: my hands are dry and warm—I haven't made the paper pucker since the second page—and I'm hungry enough to want to eat some lunch for the first time in weeks. Yes. I think it would not only be a good place to let off steam, but also might help me see things more clearly: if I made it my aim to set things down objectively, as they happen, and then at some later time reread it, I might be able to spot some trend, some key that will help explain why I've gotten in this state. If I do decide to go on with it, the big problem will be a safe hiding place, a place safer than my underwear drawer or the storage box for purses on my closet shelf, since Lottie puts my clean laundry away, and the girls rummage in my closet from time to time. But that's a bit

premature. I'll have to stop for today. It's 11:45, much
later than I thought, and Lottie's been in for three quarters of an hour. As I write this, I can hear her moving
the girls' beds as she makes them in the room next door,
which means she'll want to get in here soon. So while
there's still time, I'll stop and hide this in my stocking
drawer, and go in the kitchen and get some lunch. Then
I'll phone Doctor ("call-me-Max") Simon and make an
appointment for a checkup—not just to appease Jonathan, but to see if I can con him into giving me more
pills: the supply I got from that quack in Sag Harbor is
running dangerously low. After that I suppose I really
should phone for a laundress to come and do the things
in the trunks, phone for a man to come and wax the
floors while the rugs are still up, phone for a window-
washer . . . and phone for God knows who else. But,
somehow, the idea of making all those calls doesn't ap-
peal to me, speak to me. So I'll put on a dress and take
Folly over to that Poodle Parlor on Lexington Avenue
for a clip. Better her than me.

Wednesday September 27

"OH, MUDTHER," say the girls. "Oh, Mudther, *really*," and I can hardly keep from slapping them, hard, snarling, "Don't you dare oh-Mudther me!" "Oh, Mudther," says Sylvie when I ask what she had for lunch at school. "Oh, Mudther, *really*," says Liz when I ask her when she last moved her bowels. "Oh, Mudther," said Sylvie at 7:56 this morning in the front hall. "Are you going to see us off on the school bus every morning this year? I mean for heaven's sake we're not babies any more—Liz is seven, I'm nine—and what do you think can *happen* at eight in the morning on Central Park West?"

Since I wasn't about to go into my visions of obscene old men with slobbery lips, or fresh-faced boys with Krafft-Ebing minds waiting to Lure little girls like themselves to rooftops or basements, I silently bent to hook Folly onto her leash.

"Mudther," said Liz, coming up behind me, "are you going to wear those pants downstairs?"

Never bright at that hour, I snapped, "What's wrong with these pants?"

"They're too tight across your bottom. And ladies your age just don't *wear* jeans."

Grim but still silent—I'd asked for that, after all—I went out and punched the elevator bell and they followed me out. The elevator came, run by Sven the drunken Swede, and in a hostile silence, down we went, gagging on the fumes of Sven's breakfast of gin. As we walked across the lobby I saw in a mirror that I *did* look particularly seedy today—quite the old vintage Gel from Smith. The loafers, the jeans, the Brooks Brothers shirt, the long straight hair with bangs were the same; the pale haggard face beneath the bangs was not. Yet this reflection pleased me, soothed me, being the reverse image of the one I'd had to look at for months, Ella Cinders instead of Cinderella, you might say.

When we came out of the dim lobby the sun was blinding, the sidewalks already giving off blasts of heat. Another scorcher. Cool, unruffled, satchels in hand, Sylvie and Liz lined up at the curb, all sass and starch—two flossy little girls with impossibly clean dark blond hair. In the rush I'd forgotten my sunglasses, so I moved back under the shade of the canopy to get out of the painfully brilliant light, where I watched the girls as if they weren't mine. Dreamily smiling and humming to herself, Sylvie stood smoothing her smooth hair with her free hand; after one minute Liz, who copies everything Big Sister does, assumed the exact same pose. They reminded me of something, but I couldn't think what. They also annoyed me beyond belief, and I was telling myself how Unnatural I was when the wee sleekit blue Bartlett School bus pulled up at the curb. The door opened, the driver called good morning, the girls turned and airily waved goodbye and climbed aboard—and I knew then who they'd reminded me of: Meg and Lillibet from my childhood newsreels, waving to their loyal subjects as they boarded the royal yacht.

Mercilessly examined by nine little pairs of eyes behind glass, I waited until the bus had gone to light a cigarette—a token gesture to the girls to make up for the jeans. For a few minutes then I just stood there smoking, feeling my palms grow wet, feeling the awful shakes starting somewhere in the backs of my knees. Across the street was the dusty jungle of the park where I knew I had to make myself go. I knew that the first step in proving that I'm not really crazy, in proving that I can be the one to set myself straight, was to start facing up to some of my loony fears, call their bluff, and the best place to

start was to cross the damned street and walk Folly in
the park. Perspiring heavily, I put it off a few more minutes. Then I finally threw away the cigarette and
crossed the street, squinting in the glare. Directly on the
other side, a young tramp lay on a bench against the
wall bordering the park, his mouth open and drooling
spittle, his face a toxic blue. Six months ago I would have
kept on going. This morning I stopped and stared. I
wondered if he was dead or had had a stroke; shouldn't I
do something, shouldn't I prove that I wasn't the heart-
less kind of New Yorker you read about in the papers,
the kind of person who lets someone else die rather than
get Involved? Shaking, Folly tugging at my wrist, I stood
there pondering these imponderables, until the tramp
rolled over, a bottle crashed, and the smell of Gallo bur-
gundy filled the air. I walked on and turned into the
park.

The path was deserted, the benches empty, the still-
ness so deep I could hear a squirrel gnawing a nut, sitting hidden in the leaves hanging motionless over my
head. This very air I breathed seemed unnatural—heavy,
loaded with something that made my throat tickle and
eyes itch, that diffused the outlines of objects. It's only
Air Pollution, Stupid, not the Russians, I told myself—
get *on* with it. I did, briskly marching about twelve
yards down the path, but suddenly losing my nerve
when I saw that the path twisted out of sight about
forty feet ahead. I stopped and tried to interest Folly in
a patch of parched grass covered with turds and swarming with flies, but she was so excited to be back in the
park again that she had other ideas. Tugging, throttling
herself on her collar, she strained for a place farther
down the path, so I reluctantly shuffled along about another fifteen feet and she finally veered off onto the
grass. As she daintily began sniffing around in some
leaves, at last maneuvering herself into her ridiculous
squat, I ran my sweaty hands down the legs of my jeans
and turned to look idly off down the path just as the rat
came sliding out. Now, for the record: I am not afraid
of rats. Jonathan is afraid of rats, but I am not. I wasn't
afraid of this rat either, but he was the most disgusting

rat I have ever seen. Huge, red-brown, strangely wet-looking, with a grizzled wolf-like face and a long hairless tail of a pale and obscene pink. What he did was pop from some bushes on my side of the path and slither across to the grass on the other side, where he stopped and turned his head and stared. Yes, stared. Though I realize that it sounds like more of my current craziness talking—that rat stared at me, and I back at it, and we exchanged a look of hatred so pure and intense you could almost hear it, grinding like knives, in the air. I'll also admit that I *know* that part of my new looniness is the need to see signs and symbols in everything, everywhere —but once again, my current compulsions aside, that revolting rat seemed to stand for more than itself. Don't ask me what—I wouldn't want to put myself out on any limb by offering a few suggestions. All I know is that while I stood there, a person who literally hates to step on an ant, my arms ached to swing a big stick or heave a rock, to fill the turdy grass with blood and mangled guts. And as I stood there, seeing and needing all that, a whiff of his own death must have gotten to that rat, because he suddenly turned and scrambled across the grass and disappeared down a hole between the roots of some bushes.

For a minute I had the decency to be shaken. I began to think I really *was* crazy. I couldn't imagine what in God's name I'd wanted from that poor old rat, and was reminding myself that Jonathan was the one who hated them—when it happened: something inside me suddenly switched off, like a motor, and I felt better. It was as though that little imaginary murder had purged me. I not only felt better, I felt marvelous. So when Folly had finished with that spot and started tugging forward to find another, I walked on without a thought. Soon I was deeper in the park than I'd ever gone in my normal days, but I wasn't afraid, not even when I heard gritty footsteps coming around the sharp bend dead ahead. A good thing too, because in another second a tall skinny boy of about fifteen rounded the corner, a boy with a lot of thick bright yellow hair and an early-Van Johnson sort of face, so happy to be playing hooky he was whistling.

I smiled as he passed, but the round blue eyes gave no sign of even seeing me, and he ambled on, hands in pockets, cheerily whistling what sounded like "John Peel." I stopped to let Folly hop off onto the grass again, and as she went into her second routine, I looked dreamily off through a gap in the trees at the towers of Fifth Avenue across the park. I was noticing how the heavy if Polluted air did marvelous things to the light, making it a thick Impressionist peachy-gold, when I suddenly noticed myself noticing. I mean it was the first time in weeks I'd noticed anything, anything that wasn't sinister, that is, and it seemed to me to be proof of what would happen when I faced up to *all* my nutty fears. Happy, congratulating myself—I was going to beat this after all—I looked down and saw that Folly was done, kicking up dirt, and turned to go home.

He was standing smack in the middle of the path about six yards away, hands still in his pockets, but lumpy-bunched now, his shoulders back and a wildly evil smile on his round pink face. I froze. How long had he been standing there? And what—oh, what—did he *want?* Two seconds ticked by. Stupefied, I saw how broad the skinny shoulders were and how his eyes glittered crazily in the sunlight. Then at last I knew that whatever he wanted I was in for it. Well, here it is, I thought, and wondered if it was all right to scream. I realize that sounds pretty funny now, but I found out that probably the worst part of suddenly finding yourself a "victim" is the state of paralysis you get in during the first few seconds—you just can't believe or be sure that what's happening is really happening, and you're too damned embarrassed to open your mouth and start yelling. So three more seconds went by. He just stood there. And I just stood there, dimly wondering was it going to be for money, rape, or the thrill of what the papers call an "assault." I was finally about to make a break for it, to try and run and get past him, when I saw what he couldn't: a man with two huge Weimaraners coming through the entrance to the park.

At last he stirred. As he gave a sort of shudder and took one of the fists from his pocket, the Weimaraners began barking at a squirrel. He turned his head slowly. Then in one movement the rest of his body turned, the other hand came out of the pocket, and he began to walk rapidly towards the entrance to the park. When he came abreast of the man and the dogs he gave them a wide berth, and the man frowned and said something inaudible. The boy kept right on going, and once past the dogs, broke into a run. As he disappeared through the entrance, I finally began to move in slow motion, shuffling towards the man who'd saved me. As we got nearer, I recognized him as the scenic designer who lived in the penthouse of our building—Jonathan, who keeps track of all the building's celebrities, had once pointed him out in the lobby. His name is Edmund Pear. Edmund Pear is tall and frail, with curly black hair, and this morning wore a blue pin-stripe suit with a red carnation in his buttonhole and horn-rimmed glasses the size of a Baby Ben's face. He was the most beautiful sight I've ever seen. He stopped when there were a good five feet between us, and apparently not frail at all, powerfully reined in the silvery dogs, signaling me to stop. "They hate poodles," he explained. Then he put his head to one side. "My dear . . . was that young man bothering you in any way?"

It was simply too much. I began to laugh and laugh, shaking my head. "Yes," I finally managed. "Yes, he was."

Mr. Pear stared at me, appalled. "How frightful," he murmured, covering both my hysteria and the incident itself. "And not a policeman in sight. Isn't that just typical." He paused, embarrassed. "Ah, just what did he do to you, my dear?"

Folly, cringing out of the Weimaraners' sight behind my legs, began to whimper. "Nothing," I said. "That is, he was just getting ready to do whatever he was going to do when you came."

"Well, *that's* a blessing," sighed Mr. Pear and said something sharp to the dogs, who were moaning low in their throats at Folly. He glanced at his watch. "I'd dearly love to help you . . . escort you to your door or help you find a policeman so you can report the little monster, but I've a nine-thirty appointment downtown. As it is, I shan't make it."

"I'll be all right," I said, meaning it. "I can't thank you enough."

Mr. Pear acted as though he hadn't heard me. "I'm sure he isn't lurking about still. He wouldn't dare— If you need me in helping to make any sort of report to the police, my name is Edmund Pear. My number isn't listed, but I do believe we live in the same building, and you could always send up a note via the elevator."

I thanked him again. "Please go ahead. I'm really fine."

"*Ciao!*" he said, smiling and waving, and was immediately dragged off down the path by his dogs.

A little apprehensive, I ventured back out onto Central Park West. Neither the boy nor a policeman was anywhere in sight. I bolted for our building, went upstairs and headed for the bathroom, where I threw up, quick and neat. Then, after rinsing my mouth and splashing cold water on my face, I went into the kitchen to stack the breakfast dishes for Lottie. I was tapping coffee grounds into the garbage when the kitchen wall phone rang.

"For God's sake, Tina," shouted Jonathan, "I've been trying to reach you for half an hour. Where the hell have you been?"

Calmly I said, "I've been walking Folly in the park. Where I almost got assaulted—whatever that means."

There was complete silence. Jonathan seemed to have stopped breathing. Finally he said, "Tina. Are you serious?"

"I never could tell a joke."

Jonathan sighed, and in a voice I'm getting to know better every day, a voice just loaded with Patience and Forbearance, he said, "You'd better tell me what happened."

"I'll tell you tonight."

"You can't. That's just the point. That's why I've been trying to reach you. The minute I walked through the door down here I found out I have to leave for Wichita. Late this morning. A turbine blew up at one of the power companies we handle. I've got to get down there and help prepare local counsel for a hearing, and since that'll take a couple of days I need some things. If you pack me a bag, Miss Brekker will come over and get it in about half an hour. Have you got a pencil? I'll tell you what I need."

"Yes. I have a pencil."

"Good. *Okay.* First of all, I want to take my tan cowhide two-suiter, not the one from Mark Cross, the new one from T. Anthony. It's on my closet shelf. Then I'll need two suits—the grey Glen-plaid dacron-and-worsted from Brooks, and the oxford-grey basket-weave polyester-worsted from Press. I'll need six pairs of grey lisle socks, the ones with clocks, and six shirts: give me three white oxford voiles and three Sea Island cotton stripes, two grey, one tan. Then six ties, use your own judgment, keeping the suits in mind . . . you know, some small-patterned reds and golds. Maybe one green. Then I'll need my toilet kit—it's in my bottom drawer—with toothpaste, shaving cream, razor, deodorant, *you* know. I don't want to have to waste time buying any of that there. Then a pair of pajamas, make them batiste, I don't know if the goddamn hotel is air-conditioned, and my madras robe. And slippers, and oh my God shoes—the black wing-tips on the top rung of my shoe rack. And that clothes brush hanging above my tie rack . . . I guess that's all. I'm taking so much because it will probably be hot as hell there and I'll need changes. I'll probably only be gone four days . . . Did you get all that down?"

I had, but I had something else to say. "Jonathan, do you think you could manage to walk Folly in the mornings before you leave?"

"For God's sake, Tina!" shouted Jonathan. "Did you listen to anything I just said?"

"I listened and I've got it all down," I said calmly. "Just when did you say Miss Brekker would come by?"

"In about half an hour, depends on what luck she has with cabs. Listen, Tina, are you all right? You really sound very strange. If what you said about this attempted assault is true, you'd better call the police and file a complaint. And maybe you should even go take a slug of whiskey to calm your nerves before packing my bag. I'm sorry I haven't time to hear all about it, but Hoddison wants to go over some things before I leave, and my plane leaves Kennedy at noon . . . Kiss the girls for me. I'll try and call tomorrow, if not then as soon as I can. I'll probably be back by Saturday at the latest. In any case, I'll let you know."

Despite this more or less official sanction to take a drink, and despite the fact I had a dentist appointment at noon, I didn't. I felt just fine after hanging up on Jonathan. Once the initial shock about the incident in the park had worn off, it seemed that the whole thing had proved to be a sort of tonic for my nerves. Efficient and cheerful, I packed Jonathan's bag, using a technique for folding things he had taught me last year, even adding things he forgot—underwear, handkerchiefs, a belt, after-shave cologne. Once I'd handed the bag out to poor distracted Miss Brekker, who had a cab waiting downstairs, I showered and dressed and went to Dr. Gorley, our dentist, across town. I did not call the police.

I'd made the appointment to see Dr. Gorley because even I could see that the toothache I'd had for a month was only going to get worse. My lovely calm left me the minute I sat down in that white plastic chair. In fact, my hands under the plastic apron were so drenched, and I began to shake so uncontrollably, that I was certain Gorley would make some comment, but he didn't seem to notice a thing. Smelling of mayonnaise and pepsin gum, he happily picked, poked, and scraped away, and took an X-ray of my whole mouth. Finished, he examined the developed films and stood there, smiling, enchanted with himself. "Well, I'm sorry to have to tell you, Tina," he said, all beamish, "that there's a lot going on under that old inlay—the one you had made before coming to me. You also have quite a cavity in your second rear molar on the lower right, and an erosion on your upper left lateral incisor which may or may not require a cap. You'll have to have a new inlay, of course, which *is* expensive, I'll admit, but it has to be done and I'm sure Jonathan will understand. It sounds like a lot of work, but I think we can wrap it all up in five or six visits, and since we should start at once, stop by Miss Sallit's desk and make the first few appointments on your way out. My calendar is filling up—my busy season's starting now." Climbing out of the chair, I thanked him, and once out in the waiting room, rushed past Miss Sallit, saying, "I'll have to call you after I get home and check. My calendar is filling up—my busy season's starting now."

Shaken, limp, I came back here, and since Lottie had finished cleaning my room, I got this out of my stocking drawer, where it's been since Friday, and sat on my bed and wrote this all down. It is now 2:30, and I'm going back downtown to Goldsmith's to buy some sort of thing with a lock to keep this in: since I've definitely decided to keep it awhile, I *have* to have a safer hiding place.

Before I go, here is a sort of Thought for the Day. I came across it during last night's reading stint (it took me two hours to read myself sleepy last night), and instead of copying it out and sticking it on my closet door as an object lesson, I put it in here:

> "Then I am as particular as an Englishman. I keep myself in hand, as they say, my dear, and am always dressed and have my hair done *comme il faut*. Do I allow myself to go out of the house even into the garden in a dressing-gown, or without my hair being done? Never! What has preserved me is that I have never been a dowdy, I have never let myself go, as some women do . . ."
>
> Madame Arkadin, *The Sea-Gull*

YESTERDAY AT GOLDSMITH'S I bought what is called a storage vault: an asbestos-lined steel box, a little larger than legal size, with a "tamper proof" combination dial lock. Though the salesman (perceptive man) thought I was out of my mind, I insisted on taking it home with me in a cab. I did this because I knew that what with my luck, United Parcel would bring a huge Goldsmith box at a time when the girls or Jonathan were home, and I'd have to explain what was in it. As it was, luck was with me for a change: when I got home the girls were downstairs visiting the Jocelyn girls and Lottie was in the kitchen ironing. I lugged the storage vault into the bedroom, locked the door, took it out of the carton, and put it on the floor of my closet behind the long chintz garment bag. I unlocked the door, took the carton out back to the garbage, chatted with Lottie a bit, then came back up here and put the slip of paper with the combination for the lock in a brocade evening bag on the top shelf of my closet. It will stay there until I have it memorized. Then I'll burn it.

Last night, with Jonathan in Wichita, I had a surprisingly pleasant, relaxed time with the girls. I mean you would have thought that being here all alone, I'd have been just terrified—but it was just the reverse. The girls were almost abnormally sweet, and after a quiet dinner without any comments about the lamb stew, they did their homework, took their baths and went to bed with-

out the usual fuss. Though I have to admit that I dou-
ble-checked the locks on the doors and the window to
the fire escape, I wasn't at all uneasy and took *my* bath
and got into bed and finished *Buddenbrooks*. This made
me so sleepy without a pill that I turned off my light at
eleven, and just before dozing off into the best sleep in
weeks, I thought for a few minutes about what I call
This Thing, for lack of a better name. It struck me, as I
lay there, that having decided to keep at this for a while,
I ought to do it properly. I'd just put down *Buddenbrooks*, and maybe it was simply the influence of Mann,
with his Germanic passion for order and the documentary fact, but it seemed to me that This Thing should
have a beginning of sorts, and since I might even reread it
at some point to see if I can get a more objective look at
myself and what's going on, the best place to begin was
with some facts. "Let's take a look at the facts," says Jonathan. Counselor-at-Law, when he wants to work something out.

So, let's. I think last night's reasoning was correct.
Let's make a proper beginning and let's take a look at
some facts. Today, being Thursday, is a perfect day to
tackle the job; with Lottie off, I won't have to worry
about her getting suspicious, about her wondering what
in God's name I'm doing locked up in here for hours.

Here we go then. The plunge:

I am Bettina Munvies Balser, thirty-six. I am tall, thin,
and have dark blond or light brown hair, and one of
those faces that keep changing: I can look hard, soft,
plain, almost-pretty, and at times—when I'm tense or
sick or posing for a snapshot—so ugly I look like Alice
the Goon. I am the only child of Blanche and Jules
Munvies and was born and grew up in White Plains,
New York. Until I was twelve we lived in the ugliest
brick house ever built, a house with no real garden to
speak of, no trees; during the war we moved to a white
Colonial house set well back on three acres of lawn and
trees, and I was much happier. I love trees. This move
gave rise to the rumor that my father was a Black
Marketeer, but it was a vicious rumor and completely
untrue. Up until the time he had the coronary two years

ago, my father manufactured men's and women's shirts, and during the war had the luck to get a perfectly legitimate government contract to make Army uniforms instead of shirts. The horrible brick house aside, there had always been money enough before—enough for my father to belong to a club where he could play golf, and for my mother to hire the full-time maids needed to take care of the house and me while she played cards. That's the hooker about dear old Ma. She was, and is, a bridge fanatic. One of those women who take all of what they call the Normal Feminine Drives and channel them into a deck of cards. Darling Mums. She was playing bridge the afternoon I had the croup and turned blue and a maid rushed me to the hospital in a taxicab. She was playing bridge the day I stepped on broken glass at day camp and had six stitches put in my foot, while another maid held my hand and dried my tears. (There was, as you can imagine, a fast turnover in maids.) She was playing bridge the day I won the debate for our school debating society, the night I had the lead in the high school play. She was playing bridge on every single Mother's Visiting Day the school had. She was playing . . . Oh, well. No need to overdo it. Mudther Dear. There you have her. I hated her until I had my head shrunk, at which time I learned to "understand" her and be tolerant—which simply means I learned how to think of her without getting overwrought or blind with rage. Trying to picture her now, as I write this, I get a thin sandy-haired woman, well-dressed, groomed to the nines, sitting at a card table; her eyes are narrowed against the smoke drifting up from the cigarette in her mouth, a cigarette which stays stuck to her lower lip as she opens her mouth to say "I pass." She did just that. Pass. Pass everything else up. I had maids, and thank God, playmates. My father had shirts and golf and mistresses. They never divorced, though nobody could ever figure out why.

Mudther aside, I still somehow managed to grow up a nice, apparently normal if somewhat docile girl who was bright enough to get into Smith. I bloomed at college. I made a lot of friends and did well in my work, which

for the first two years was focused on Literature. Then
in my junior year, I switched to Art. On the academic
side I studied the History of Art, on the practical side I
began to paint and sculpt. By the middle of my senior
year I'd decided that I was going To Paint, give my all
for Art. It's rather depressing, writing that—to think
there was a time when it was considered unusual and
original and even courageous to go to college a Nice Middle Class Girl and come out a Rebel for Art, but there
was such a time and it wasn't that long ago. So, feeling
very daring, I graduated and, drunk on defiance, deaf to
Dear Daddy's alternate pleas and threats ("if you come
home to live I'll buy you a car" vs. "I'll never give you a
cent, you can starve for all I care"), I went to live in a
one-room apartment on Sullivan Street, which I shared
with a girl named Tibby Larson from Ardmore, Pa.,
who was doing her own version of the rebellion bit.
Mornings and evenings I worked in a Village bookstore,
and went to classes at the League in the afternoons;
Tibby sold stockings at Hearn's all day and wrote another *Nightwood* at night. After six months my father,
having gotten over his initial reactions, and having resigned himself to the fact that I wasn't about to get a job
as a receptionist in some elegant Fifty-seventh Street gallery and commute from White Plains (where on week-
ends I'd ultimately meet some Nice Boy at his country
club), finally got in touch with me and took me out to
dinner at the Thirteenth Street Schrafft's. It turned out
to be so pleasant that soon we were having dinner there
the first Wednesday of every month, a dinner which
would start with his discreetly inquiring after Tibby and
about the progress of my work, and would end with
him furtively pushing a check across the table between
the paper doilies. Though it pains me to admit it now, I
always took it.

   This life (?) went on for two years. The first year I
lost my virginity to a cousin of Tibby's from Siwickly,
Pa., who had just graduated from Princeton and was
selling barometers at Abercrombie & Fitch. I then slept
with two painters from the League, a bisexual fashion
photographer and a man who owned an elegant gallery

on Fifty-seventh Street. The second year I became the mistress (meaning I saw him regularly, three mornings a week) of a rather crazy fifty-five-year-old sculptor with a very rich wife and six children. All this time I was painting, of course, being told by my instructors that I was on the verge of a "vital breakthrough"; I was determined that until that happened—until I broke through—no one except Tibby would see my work. Then suddenly, by the middle of the second year, I was all alone in the apartment on Sullivan Street, and Tibby was locked up in some place in upper Connecticut called Clearwater Farms. By the time summer came I'd begun to have itchy crusts on my elbows, knuckles and neck, blockbusting headaches and complete loss of appetite. Or, to put it technically, eczema, migraines, anorexia. Needless to say, I was not very appealing, and after having talked for months about the "abandoned" July we would have while his wife and children were off in Montecatini, my sculptor penned me a two-word note —"Goodbye. Regrets."—and hopped on a plane for Rome.

On the first hot Wednesday night in July, at our usual corner table in Schrafft's, my father put down his fork and in a strangled voice said: "Tina, I can't stand it any more. You're killing me, honest to God. You look like something out of a concentration camp. Won't you tell me what's wrong? Won't you let me help? Do you want to give me a heart attack?" I began to cry on my chicken-salad-on-toasted-cheese-bread sandwich and didn't stop crying for days, not even when I found myself back in the white Colonial house in White Plains. Darling Mums, after discreetly ascertaining that I wasn't pregnant ("Tina, I know we've never discussed these things, but . . ."), relegated me to the care of my father and the family doctor who'd known me all my life, and went back to her bridge games at the club. By then my weight had dropped to ninety-six pounds, so after several private conferences with the family doctor, my father put me in the car and drove me into the city to the office of Doctor Leonard Popkin on Ninety-sixth and Fifth.

And so it began. The long haul. Three years. For the

first six months I lived in White Plains and commuted daily into New York, just to stretch for fifty minutes on a green plastic couch that smelled like the upholstery in a new car. At the end of six months Doctor Popkin announced that I was strong enough to take a big and necessary step—to leave White Plains for my own apartment in the city, and to take a small job that would be the start of my self-support. So I rented what is called an Efficiency Apartment in Tudor City and got a job as a dentist's receptionist. No sooner had I done that than Doctor Popkin said he wanted to see some of my paintings. Now. When I'd moved, or rather, *been* moved back out to White Plains, I'd destroyed all but six of my canvases. Wrapped in heavy brown paper, those six had come along with me to White Plains, where I'd stuck them in an unused cedar closet in the attic: my Time Capsule. The first Sunday after Popkin's little injunction, I journeyed out to White Plains. I returned to the city with a full-blown migraine and three of the paintings, which I brought to Popkin's office the next day, and which he propped against a chair and the wall, the better to study them. For five interminable minutes I lay stretched on the couch while he sat behind me in his chair, a faint rumbling in his stomach the only sound. Then, just when I had decided there wasn't going to be any comment, and that perhaps I ought to start talking about a dream I'd had that morning, he sighed. He sighed again. Then he said: "Those dibs. Those daubs. Those fecal smears. They are a graphic expression of all the conflicts, aggressions and hostilities you had repressed for so long. These so-called paintings are not art, or even excuses for art. They are excuses. Period. For not facing, not coming to grips with what you really feel and are. Now, for a start, let us consider those foetal shapes that occur in each ah painting like a leitmotiv . . ." At this point I did an unheard-of thing: I sat up on the couch and turned around to look at him. "Foetal shapes! Fecal smears!" I cried in a strangled voice. "I'm goddamn sick and tired of having everything reduced to the bathroom or sex!" His bald head gleaming in the gloaming, Popkin gave a dry little cough. "Your paint-

ings have already diagrammatically expressed your anger,
Bettina. It is now our job to uncover the source of that
anger and deal with it, and so doing, eliminate the need
for such elaborate dissimulations." "But I don't *want* to
eliminate the need," I wailed, in a last upheaval of defiance or what they call Resistance, "I want to be a
painter!" Popkin gave me a long sobering look. "But that
is precisely what you cannot be. You must be what you
are, not so?"

Quite so. And I lay back down, the first big step—a
symbolic one you might say—in acquiescing, in prepar-
ing to face and accept just what I was. That took a lot
of doing and in terms of time took another year and a
half, but I finally learned to accept the fact that I was a
bright but quite ordinary young woman, somewhat passive and shy, who was equipped with powerful Feminine
Drives—which simply means I badly wanted a husband
and children and a Happy Home. As I said, it took a lot
of doing: in view of earlier aspirations it wasn't the
greatest news in the world, and my pride took a bit of a
beating, but once I'd gotten it all straight, and bought it,
the search for a man was on. That sounds pretty cut-
and-dried now, but the truth is that when you're in analysis and are given sudden Insights, you don't stand
around mulling them over—you take those Insights and
translate them into action right away.

Now, during the time it had taken to find out what I
was, my life hadn't been standing still. While it was ac-
knowledged I couldn't possibly ever pay for the analysis
all by myself, I was supposed to be making an effort to
help pay my father for at least part of it. That, of
course, meant a job with decent pay. After about a year
of further Resistance—of first trying to be a reader in a
publishing house, then trying to be a researcher on a
news magazine, (my explanation to Popkin, being that I
was trying to utilize my college Lit training), and barely
getting paid for any of it—I finally gave in and listened
to Popkin. (Popkin: "A college degree alone means
nothing nowadays. You must have something, some talent, some commodity besides yourself you can sell.") I
took an intensive secretarial course at night, and when I

had completed it, got a job as a secretary to one of the section chiefs at Memorial Hospital. So that by the time I was straightened out on the score of who I was and what I wanted, I was not only earning a respectable salary, but was also in a field supposedly rife with eligible men. Supposedly. Though I liked my job, I never met any of the Nice Young Doctor types Popkin had hinted I might. I met only married or unmarried doctors who wanted just one thing and wanted it fast—a thing I wasn't supposed to give anyone, fast or slow, what with my brand-new Insights: Femininity = Discretion = No Jumping Into Bed. I was all for Femininity, but my social life got pretty drab. The few men I saw, men who didn't want one thing fast, were dull, often creeps, and the few women friends I had were nice intellectual girls I'd either met at the news magazine or publishing house, girls whose idea of excitement was dinner at Longchamps and a poetry reading at the YMHA.

It was all pretty grim. A hiatus. Or an impasse of sorts. I mean there I was, all ready and eager to start being what I was cut out to be, with none of the essential props in sight. It was just about that time that Popkin began to chide me on another score: it was appalling that I, a bright young woman with varied interests, should be so politically in*active*, so apath*etic*. Why didn't I keep up with things, read more, take a more active part in things; why didn't I do something simple and constructive like joining my local Democratic club? Who knows, added the indefatigable doctor, I might even be pleasantly surprised, I might even meet some interesting young men. As always, being *In Analysis*, I did exactly what I was told to do. I joined my local Democratic club, and for the longest time I wasn't at all surprised. Then one hot September night I attended a meeting of ardent Adlai supporters like myself, and a tall sandy-haired young man took the floor. He stood up in front of us, loosened his tie, gave a Gary Cooper sort of "shucks" shrug, and, apologizing, took off his seersucker jacket. He had on brilliant red suspenders.

Okay, I blush. In fact, looking back now I get the crawls all over, but it's an inescapable fact that those red

suspenders got to poor old Bettina Munvies sitting
slumped and wilted on her hard folding chair. Suddenly
there she was, sitting up straight, smoothing her skirts
and hair, stretching her neck the better to see around the
woman in front of her, listening and watching, hypnotized. Skinny yet brawny, he lit a lot of cigarettes, ran a
nervous hand continually through his hair, and Earnestly
furrowing tufty red-gold eyebrows, talked of Tricky
Dick and Ike in what sounded like a faint Boston accent.
Witty, charming, he went on to talk of Adlai as if he
knew him (he did), and all the while Bettina Munvies sat
glued to her chair. Who *is* he? *What* is he? Why hadn't
he been at any of the other meetings? He was, she found
out that very same night, Jonathan Edward Balser from
Brookline, Mass. He'd gone to Harvard and then to Yale
Law School, where his studies had been interrupted by
Korea. At the present he was halfway through his first
year of clerking for the DA. He was a "brilliant" young
lawyer, with political ambitions of his own, a sort of
forerunner of the New Frontier type before it ever *was*
a type.

Oh God. We bog down here. SENTIMENT, as thick
and gluey and sickeningly sweet as that damned Irish
honey Jonathan eats on Swedish flatbread, is seeping in
and covering everything. Even as I write this my idiot
eyes are so filled with tears I can barely see, and a Billie
Holiday kind of voice in my head is wailing But I *did*
love him and he *did* love me and our love was True. And
that's really how it was. Sweet and True. Right off the
bat. For him I was the Smith Girl he'd never had time to
date at Harvard, being too busy studying and working
to put himself through. For him I was a phenomenon—a
gay, bright, pretty (o God) girl who didn't drink too
much or fall right into bed or want to be the best adver-
tising copywriter in New York or an editor on a fashion
magazine. For me he was the Harvard Boy I'd never
dated at Smith, having only had a pipeline to my class-
mates' dreary brothers at Swarthmore, Williams, Brown
and West Point. He had read Proust and Joyce and
Levin on Joyce and Kafka and Flaubert and Gerard
Manley Hopkins and Yeats and Hart Crane; he knew all

the painters of the Quattrocento, could describe each of Picasso's periods and owned a Matisse drawing and a Klee lithograph. All of this besides having been editor of the *Law Review*, and being an expert on the Civil War, and being an assistant the DA was said to consider "remarkably brilliant" with a "tremendous future" in politics. And sweet and gentle, yet strong and masterful and sexy to boot. How could a girl resist? I didn't. I was sane then.

After a slow start, things went off like clockwork. At first we went out to dinner and the movies or theater and didn't go to bed. Finally we went to bed. We then had dinner out and went to bed. Then we mostly went to bed, not bothering with dinner at all, and talked of getting engaged. Yes, engaged. We had this terrible compulsion to be Proper. One weekend I flew up to Brookline to meet his father, who was a CPA, a sweet, completely ineffectual man with beautiful manners; his mother had died while he was in Korea. Another weekend we rented a car and drove up to White Plains, and he met my mother and father, whom—miracles never cease—he seemed to like. In fact, that was the prevailing attitude: everybody seemed to like everybody else. Everybody seemed to *love* everybody else. Even Doctor Popkin, without ever actually meeting Jonathan, let himself get a bit carried away: he said that Jonathan sounded like that great rarity—a completely normal, forceful, effective man —and just in case I was "interested," the way things were going my analysis could be terminated by spring. "Interested": I said goodbye to Popkin in April and at the end of May Jonathan and I were married on the back lawn of the house in White Plains. We had wanted a tiny civil ceremony, but my father, overjoyed by my cure and what he clearly saw as its Reward, had other ideas. So we were married on the lawn, where a huge tent was set up and two bands alternately played sambas and fox trots while the guests ate squabs and wild rice washed down with Dom Perignon, after which Jonathan and I sneaked off for a two-day honeymoon at an inn in the Berkshires—all we could afford.

Of course we had no money, and of course that didn't matter. I gave up my two-room apartment on East Thirty-third Street and moved into Jonathan's two-room apartment on West Ninth Street. I kept my job, which by then was secretary to the chief of the medical service, and Jonathan started his second year with the DA. For a month I kept telling myself it was impossible to be so happy, and before you could say prognostication, had the thrill of having that turn out to be absolutely true. In July I discovered I was pregnant, which wasn't exactly what we'd had in mind. We certainly wanted children, several children, but we had a plan to wait at least a year or two before Starting a child. But there we were. And no sooner had we finally adjusted ourselves to that than September brought another setback: Jonathan didn't get the nomination to run for the Assembly, a thing we'd both worked for, a thing that Jonathan had wanted badly. Though he was very good about it and said he didn't mind, said that in two years he *would* get it, I could see he *did* mind—very much. But I pretended I didn't see, and we both threw ourselves into the campaign for Adlai, another loser. Meanwhile, there I was, getting bigger by the minute, trudging up four flights of stairs several times a day (I kept on working until my seventh month), until it finally became clear that we'd have to move. Through someone in the DA's office we got ourselves put at the top of a Peter Cooper waiting list, but even so it was months before an apartment came through, and by then Sylvie was born. Also by then there had been an even greater change in our lives: Jonathan had left the DA's office and taken a job with a huge corporate law firm called Hoddison and Marks.

In short, everything was changing, but as someone once said, Change is Growth and Growth is Life, which makes a pretty neat equation. Though it took a while for me to adjust to the idea of Jonathan, the Corporation Lawyer—I'd never been warned this was something he might become—it was a role he slipped into with the greatest of ease, and from the start seemed tremendously excited about his new job. Of course I finally did get used to it, and once we'd settled into our four sun-filled rooms with their view of the river, it was Happy Time again. Jonathan threw himself into his work, and I threw myself into the Feminine Role, being all Popkin had said I was cut out to be. My days were spent between the Peter Cooper playground, the A&P and the laundromat, and my nights doing anything I hadn't had time to do in the day, anything from cleaning the apartment to reading the morning paper to getting a sitter and going out. Sometimes I fell asleep while reading the paper on the couch after dinner, but I didn't mind and Jonathan certainly didn't; if he was home, he'd pick me up and gently put me on my bed. I'd never even heard of Nembutal.

Then, one night when Sylvie was almost a year old, Jonathan said, right out of the blue, that he thought it was time to start another child. He said that since we wanted at least three children, it seemed to him that it was time Child Number 2 was under way. He said—and I can quote, because I'll never forget it: "You spend about ninety per cent of your time taking care of one child, so why not be practical and spend ninety per cent of your time taking care of two?" Though I must confess I found that a trifle cool, I also saw that like most of Jonathan's suggestions, it made sense, so I agreed. We Started Liz, but unlike the first time it wasn't that easy, and it was several months before her Start was really started and I was pregnant again. Also unlike the first time, it was a "difficult" pregnancy in the beginning, and I had to spend the first few months off my feet; when once again Jonathan began his campaign to get the nomination to run for the Assembly, I couldn't help him to ring doorbells and pass out handbills. Once again he failed to get the nomination, only this time he didn't bother to say that he didn't mind. He minded terribly, more than I ever knew at the time. And I guess it was then, though I didn't realize it until much later, that the New Frontier light went out in Jonathan's eyes for good. All I saw was that he got much too thin, something I attributed to the incredible hours he kept at Hoddison and Marks, and that he suddenly began to pay a lot of attention to his appearance and his clothes. But I chalked that up to the job too: in dealing with the stockholders of those large corporations and all the other well-heeled clients of the firm, he *had* to look impeccable.

As always, Jonathan had been right about having Liz when we did, and once she was born life hardly changed. There was a little more to do, but not that much; ninety per cent is ninety per cent, after all. The only really noticeable change was that I began to see less and less of Jonathan. He drove himself at a terrifying pace, and when I thought about it, it seemed to me this might be his way of drowning his sorrows about his political career. But I really didn't think about it too often; I was much too busy.

And so, as they say in the story books, The Years Passed. Though they're just a blur now, I know they were happy years. When Sylvie was five and a half and Liz three and a half, we left our four bright rooms overlooking the river, and moved to five dark cramped rooms overlooking a courtyard on Seventy-seventh Street off Madison Avenue. We moved because Hoddison and Marks had moved from downtown to the upper Fifties on Madison Avenue, and Jonathan naturally wanted to be closer to work. He was the one who found us the new apartment. He was very excited about it. He said what a *difference* it made, how wonderful it was to finally live in a civilized neighborhood! He said that since he had no time for organized exercise like squash or tennis or a workout in a gym, it was just marvelous to be able to walk twenty blocks to work on a nice day, with the added bonus of seeing, while he walked, windows filled with paintings and sculpture and antiques, and well-dressed interesting-looking people. Though these remarks were an Augury of sorts, I could hardly have

been expected to know it. He just kept saying over
and over that the move had made him very happy, and
I believe this was true for the simple reason that he
was hardly ever *in* the new apartment, which was
horrible. It was so dark that we had to burn lights all
day long, and so short of closets we had to put one of .
those rattling portable Kraftboard things in every
room, even the living room. The whole building was
infested with roaches and giant water bugs, the
plumbing was always breaking down, and every man
who worked in the building, the super included, was
a hopeless drunk. When I complained, which was
often, Jonathan had a little set piece he'd recite. In-
dulgently smiling, he'd say: "There's bound to be
drawbacks when you have a rent-controlled building
in such a terrific location, Teen. What you have to do
is think of the assets. Think of Central Park. Think of
the Metropolitan Museum. Think of what we save in
cab fares and will save in tuition. Think of P.S. 6!" So
for about eight months I thought of the Assets. Think
of Central Park, I'd tell myself, housebound with a
croupy Liz on a snowy morning. Think of the Metropolitan Museum, I'd tell myself on a rainy Saturday when Jonathan was working, as I tried without
success to interest the girls in a visit to the Egyptian
mummies. Think of P.S. 6! I'd mutter, heading to that
very place to pick up Sylvie, who had thrown up in
kindergarten. By the end of eight months it didn't
work any more, and I'd just gotten myself revved up
to the point where I was determined to have an enormous showdown with Jonathan, when he came down
with a terrible case of flu which kept him home for a
change. For three days he lay in our gloomy bedroom, where the radiators were stone-cold (it was
early March) and the roaches came out to investigate
the remnants on his lunch tray. The fourth day, when
there was no hot water for his shave, he tried to reach
the super by phone all morning. That failing, he
threw an overcoat over his pajamas and, pale and
weak, went down to the basement, where he found
the super and the so-called handyman dead drunk in

the boiler room, and where a rat came dashing out of the laundry room and ran between his legs. Jonathan is mortally afraid of rats. The search for a new apartment began.

From the outset we both agreed that the only sensible thing was to make this a semi-permanent move, to try to find an apartment that would be big and pleasant enough to accommodate us for the next ten or fifteen years. Though we hadn't talked about it in quite a while, it was understood (I thought) that we would have another child, soon, and would need room for it. Jonathan was working harder than ever, so I undertook the search, about which Jonathan made one firm stipulation: the apartment had to be on the East Side. For weeks I hired sitters to pick up Liz at nursery school and Sylvie at P.S. 6, while I investigated misleading ads in the paper, or the even more misleading listings of real estate agents. Of course it finally became blindingly clear that we could never find eight or even six rooms on the East Side at a rent we could afford, Jonathan's ever-increasing income aside. So once again I was steeling myself for a showdown with Jonathan—he *had* to give up his little dream of living on the East Side—when I bumped into a girl I'd known on the news magazine. In the years since we'd last seen each other, she'd married and had two children. She had also, for a once-shy girl, grown extremely talkative. Her husband, she babbled on, was a television producer who was just about to transfer operations to the Coast, and did I by any chance know of someone who might be interested in an eight-room apartment on upper Central Park West?

Did I. I climbed into the cab with her, and for half an hour walked in a trance through eight large, light, high-ceilinged rooms. I wanted to move in that afternoon. After she'd given me a drink and the assurance that the apartment could be acquired by making certain "arrangements" with the building agent, a friend of theirs, I left, telling her I'd call her the next day.

That night was one of Jonathan's rare nights home. I waited until the girls were in bed and he was sitting in our one comfortable armchair, before I timidly broached the subject. Grudgingly putting aside the paper, he listened to everything I had to say about the apartment. "I'm sorry, Teen," he said when I'd finished. "I won't live on the West Side." He opened the paper again.

"You're not sorry," I said, "so don't give me that. And you'd damned well better give me at least one good reason why you won't live over there."

His paper fell into his lap. He stared. "Does there *have* to be a reason?"

"Yes. Yes, there does. My feet are sore, I've spent God knows how much on cabs and sitters in the last month or two, and I never get to see the girls. Give me one good reason why you won't live over there."

"It's too far from work."

"That just won't do."

Though he was startled, he was also getting angry. To demonstrate this, he flared his nostrils and thinned his lips. "It's dangerous over there on the upper West Side. It's the borderline of the Negro and Puerto Rican neighborhood. It isn't even safe to go in the park over there in broad daylight."

This from Jonathan Edward Balser, Democratic liberal. As I stared at him, he flushed and got up and went to the bookcase where we'd made a little makeshift bar. For a few minutes he made a great clatter with ice as he fixed himself a drink. "That's not bigotry," he finally said, going back to his chair. "It's just plain reason, common sense. It's not safe over there, which is a fact everybody in New York knows." He gulped at his drink.

"Give me one more reason. A better one."

He glared, pale with rage. "I *hate* it over there!" he shouted. "Is that what you wanted? Is that enough?"

No, it wasn't, but at last we were getting somewhere. I said quietly, "How could you hate it when you've never lived there, never been there, really, except the times we've visited friends."

"How the hell do *you* know I haven't spent time over there?"

"That's just it. I don't know," I said with deadly calm, and thinking of those eight rooms across town, added, "But if you have you'd better tell me all about it, Jonathan."

Jonathan stared: Was this Sweet old Reasonable old Docile old Teen? No. No, it was not. And finally seeing that, Jonathan told his little tale. When he was a boy of nine and lived in Brookline, his father was found to have a "nodule" on his prostate gland which some Boston doctor told him would have to be removed. Before consenting to the operation, Jonathan's father phoned his sister Tessie's husband in New York, her husband being an internist who was the Oracle the family consulted in all graver matters of health. After many phone calls back and forth (which Little Jonathan overheard), Jonathan's father was persuaded to come down to New York and see a famous urologist, since matters were grave indeed. It seemed there was something Mr. Balser hadn't been told: if the "nodule" proved malignant poor old Mr. Balser might also have to have his testicles removed. So down they came to New York, bringing Little Jonathan along. Because they couldn't afford a hotel they stayed at Tessie's apartment on Central Park West. That is, Jonathan and his mother did, and since his mother was at the hospital most of the time, Jonathan was left alone with Aunt Tessie all day.

Draining his glass, Jonathan said: "They—Irwin and Tessie—didn't have any kids, and they didn't like kids, especially me. I'd get up in the morning and both my mother and Uncle Irwin would be gone, and I'd go in the kitchen for some breakfast and there would be Tessie, standing at the stove. Nine o'clock and she'd already be cooking. In her goddamn ratty bathrobe, cooking up some awful-smelling mess. Goulash. Stuffed cabbage. Mushroom-and-*barley* soup. Chicken fricassee. At nine in the morning. I could hardly get my orange juice down. Because my mother told her to, she made me eat a big breakfast, but she made me eat it in the dining room by the light of an awful crystal chandelier. And while I tried to eat, she'd come in and start bumping a carpet sweeper over the rug, all around my feet, as if I was making a mountain of crumbs. God knows why she didn't have a maid or somebody in to clean, Uncle Irwin made enough, but she insisted on doing it all herself. Tessie the Martyr. After breakfast, while she did the dishes, and put the twenty-thousandth coat of Johnson's Glo-Coat on the dining-room table, and dragged a Hoover through all the rooms, I'd lock myself in the bathroom with one of Irwin's medical books. After a day or two she must have decided I was masturbating in there, because she suddenly began pounding on the door and yelling for me to come out. In fact, the whole thing shook her up so much she forgot the Hoover, took off the bathrobe and put on a dress and took me to the Museum of Natural History, which was just a couple of blocks from where they lived. I liked it so much and it was so near that she let me go there by myself every afternoon for the rest of my stay. It saved my life. My two favorite things were the big stuffed whale and a petrified man, some Inca-type who'd gotten trapped in a landslide hundreds of years ago. I used to just stand there and stare at his bashed-in face, imagining how it had been in that cave—the rocks, the pain, the screams —putting off going back to Tessie's as long as I could."

Jonathan shuddered. "God. The West Side. You know what Central Park West *means* to me?" I shook my head. "It means rooms with the lights on all day long and velvet furniture with tassels and fake oriental rugs. It's the smell of goulash and mushroom-and-barley soup, and a bedroom window that looks out on a Sing Sing sort of courtyard, that's dark all day, hemmed in by walls so steep not a single goddamn sparrow or pigeon ever flies down into it . . ."

As his voice drifted off and he stared morosely down into his empty glass, I felt an overwhelming desire to laugh and a terrible sort of tenderness. Luckily the tenderness won out. "Poor darling," I said. "The petrified man and mushroom-and-barley soup. It does sound pretty horrible. Are they . . . are Tessie and Irwin still alive?"

Jonathan shook his head.

"And your father. Whatever happened?"

"They took off the nodule. It wasn't malignant, thank God."

"And if it had been . . . would they *really* have had to take his testicles off?"

"How the hell should I know! And why the morbid interest in such ghoulish details?"

"It's not 'morbid' interest, and it seems to me a very relevant detail."

"Relevant to what?"

"Your aversion to the West Side." By then I knew I'd made a mistake, but it was too late to stop, so I barreled on: "I mean, though there was all that dreary business at Tessie's, it isn't what really counts. I think the West Side is synonymous with the threat of castration in your mind."

I got what I deserved. For a minute Jonathan just looked at me with disgust. Then in a tired voice he said, "What a cheap, lousy thing to do. I guess having had your head shrunk it's a miracle you've never done it before, but I warn you, Bettina, never play Freud to me again."

Apologizing, I began to weep. Then Jonathan apologized and I stopped weeping and we both got up and made ourselves a drink. All brave resolve, I decided to get things straight about moving, once and for all. I said: "All right, the West Side is out. And so is the upper East Side. That leaves the Village or the country."

"I hate the Village, and the country—where?"

"Oh, not really country. Not country-country. One of those places like Greenwich or Rye or Pelham or Teaneck or Stamford or even Riverdale . . . some place close enough for an easy commute."

"I'd die before I became a commuter," said Jonathan.

Slowly, slowly I emptied the glass.

Across the room, Jonathan coughed. "You say those rooms are high-ceilinged and get plenty of light . . . ?"

And that's how we moved to the West Side.

It's strange how often one drastic change in your life seems to be a signal for a lot of other changes to cut loose—a sort of chain reaction of changes gets under

way. We moved and hadn't been here two days—crates,
barrels and trunks still stood around unpacked—when
Jonathan's father had a stroke and died in Massachusetts
General. With things chaotic here, there was no question of my being able to leave, so Jonathan flew alone to
Boston to bury his father and settle his affairs. He went
to Boston in a state of shock (he'd clearly been more devoted to his father than he'd ever let on), and when he
came back six days later he was still in a state of shock,
but, as it soon became apparent, of quite a different
order: For thirty years Henry Balser, that CPA, that
gentle and seemingly ineffectual man, had been taking
his earnings and quietly buying blue chip stocks, stocks
which were now worth about $90,000 and which he had
bequeathed to Jonathan, his sole heir.

Jonathan's numbness gave way to wild, euphoric excitement, but there was a terrible bitterness mixed in
with it. The bitterness came from remembering the terrible struggle he'd had putting himself through college
and law school, and from thinking of all the sacrifices
he'd had to make—when all the while his father could
have helped him instead of putting his money into
stocks. Of course this reaction didn't last very long: the
stocks were there *now*, by God, and just the dividends
from them were enough to pay the girls' tuition at a private school plus a goodly hunk of the rent, all of which
made Jonathan a rich man. The bitterness couldn't have
lasted long in any case; the thing had started, the chain
reaction of changes was under way, and about a month
after his father died Jonathan was made a partner at
Hoddison and Marks.

This was the real turning point, and because it was, I
remember it well; I remember every damned detail:

It's a hot late-August evening, sometime after eight.
The girls have just been put to bed, and Jonathan and I
are sitting in our new living room. Though we've placed
a few odd pieces of our old furniture here and there, the
room looks cavernous, unfurnished, and is full of echoes.
But we don't notice. Without turning on the lights, we
sit looking through our curtainless windows at the dark-
ening park, sipping the champagne Jonathan has picked

up on his way home. We're celebrating the partnership. We haven't eaten dinner, and when we finally do, it will be the caviar sandwiches Jonathan has also picked up on his way home. This constitutes another Augury, but again I can hardly be expected to know it at the time. Though we're both silent, we are—I think—happily, peacefully silent, and it's only when I finally get up and snap on the glaring overhead light that I see the excitement on Jonathan's face, see that under the cover of darkness he's undergone a transformation. He is not himself. Wary now, I come back and sit down next to him on the worn couch, and as I do, he turns and gives me a brilliant manic smile. My heart sinking, I watch him drain his wet glass and set it down with a flourish on the walnut coffee table I've waxed for years, a table that has never known a coasterless glass, and I have no trouble getting the message: There are going to be coffee tables and *coffee* tables from this point on, old girl! Deliberately not looking at me, he takes up a pack of cigarettes, puts one between my lips, one between his own, and lights them both with a shaking hand. "Well now, Teen," he finally says, luxuriously blowing out billows of smoke and settling back: "Let's begin."

"Begin?"

"Begin to talk."

"Talk?" echoes Stupid-on-Champagne.

"Yes, talk. We've got a lot of plans to make. Big plans. We've got to get started, and right away, and the only way to do that is talk."

He talks. I listen. Before getting launched he opens another bottle of champagne. Which is a mistake as far as I am concerned, because it is one of those days where I haven't had time for lunch. So though I listen, I don't quite grasp all I hear. But my vision doesn't seem to be impaired, since I can see that Jonathan is more excited than I've ever seen him before. His face has a ripe, pink, bursting look that I'll get to know very well later on. What he says—his Plans—does not really penetrate except to make me dimly wonder how long he's had all this seething away in his mind. I am also dimly aware that this is an opportune time to bring up a little Plan of

my own—the other child I want to have—but this somehow gets lost. The champagne finished, we eat the caviar
sandwiches, and then, instead of making love as Jonathan
wants, I get violently sick and have to be put to bed.

It would now seem that I stayed rather dazed for a long
time after that night, and with no thanks to champagne,
for while Jonathan immediately started to put some of
his Plans into action, I just drifted dopily along, accepting everything. His first step was to use some high-powered connection to get Sylvie accepted and enrolled in
the Bartlett School in time for the fall term—a nearly
impossible feat, but this was the beginning of the time
when Jonathan accomplished the impossible. Though I
was happy we could now afford a private school for the
girls, I'd had something more relaxed and progressive
than the Bartlett School in mind. But I acceded to Jonathan's wishes (he was very set on the Bartlett School),
playing Passive Female to Jonathan's Dominant Male
right up to the hilt. Because that's what Jonathan suddenly was with a vengeance—The Forceful Dominant
Male. Of course he'd always been strong and effective,
but now he was Forceful to a fault—was, in fact, often
just downright overbearing—and his brain seemed to be
teeming with all sorts of schemes I found more than a
little grandiose. Though I knew we were now rich by
certain standards, I also thought that what with taxes
and the cost of living we weren't anywhere near as rich
as Jonathan apparently thought we were. Which only
goes to show you how blind I was to everything that
was going on. Oh, I did things Jonathan wanted—I hired
Lottie, but not full-time as he'd requested, and I slowly
started to buy some new furniture, but on a very modest
scale. And things went on like that for a while, until Jonathan finally stopped spinning long enough to take
stock of what I was doing and set me straight.
     He said apparently he hadn't made himself clear that
hot late-August night (he probably had, but how was I
to know?), though he thought he'd talked pretty graph-
ically about one of the changes that was to be in my
province, namely, the furnishing of the apartment. He

said that he'd said he wanted it done with style, really
Done. He said he'd told me he didn't want a decorator
because they gave a place a "stiff, decorated look," and
also because I had perfectly marvelous taste which I'd
never had a chance to *utilize*. He said: "Maybe it's the
frustrated painter in you, but you've got a perfectly
great feeling for color and form, Teen. You've also got a
great sense of style, and all you need is a little boning up
on technicalities. That can be done by a book or two on
antiques and periods, which I'll buy you at Brentano's
this week." While I sat clutching this armload of unexpected bouquets, he grew more specific. He said: "What
I want is a place that is a mixture of things—antiques,
but real antiques, no reproductions, the best of the modern designer's, like a Barcelona chair, only not a Barcelona chair because everybody has them, and a lot of
really first-rate art—a place that has that great, rich,
eclectic look the Barkers' place has . . . if you know
what I mean." I knew. And when I'd recovered, I said
very quietly that while I thought the sort of apartment
he had in mind sounded charming, it was really quite
unfeasible. I said that what with the girls' schools, the
maid, the new rent, the taxes on his new income, etc.,
there wouldn't be enough money for that sort of thing
unless we sold off some of the stocks, which of course
was an utterly insane idea.

Quietly, with that damned ripe, pink, bursting look I
was getting to know better all the time, Jonathan said it
could hardly be called insane, since he'd already sold off
some of the stocks. He'd sold some of the General Mo-
tors, and with the money he'd bought, on a tip, twenty-
thousand shares of some Canadian oil stock called Boswego at a dollar a share—a stock which, he had it on the
best authority, was to quadruple in value within months.
I burst into hysterical tears. I demanded to know what
he, a lawyer, thought he was *doing*, Speculating, taking
our new-found security and gambling it away on the tip
of some cheap tout? All the time I ranted, Jonathan just
sat there getting pinker and puffier by the minute, and
when I'd done he smiled and shook his head. He said it
just so happened that his source had been impeccable,

that Boswego had already gone to 1⅞ths and was supposed to go to 3 before the month was out. When it went to 3 he would sell, and taxes aside, there would then be enough money to furnish the whole damned apartment in style.

Infected by the fever (or maybe just plain greed), he didn't sell until Boswego reached 4, which took several months. From that point on we were off to the races, or at least, hell-bent-for-leather, Jonathan was, because that's the point at which I really fell off . . . to carry this metaphor through to the bitter end. I simply stopped wondering or asking what Jonathan was up to, and since he volunteered very little on his own, I had no idea of what was going on. Oh, I knew a few things. I knew that he sold the Boswego and promptly bought something else another Impeccable Source put him on to —stock in some engineering company that was about to convert to the manufacture of color-television tubes. I also knew that within half a year he had become as deeply involved with Wall Street as he was with his job at Hoddison and Marks, and that on half the evenings he was home and closeted in the den to "work," he was on the phone with his broker or one of the Impeccable Sources. Actually, his work didn't seem to suffer. In fact, it was quite the reverse: he seemed to meet the demands of his new role as a partner with magnificent ease. I suppose it's that old saw that claims the more you live up to your potential, the greater your potential becomes. Or that other old chestnut: the busier you are, the more you seem to be able to find time for. Certainly that seemed to be true of Jonathan, who, in spite of the pressures and demands of his job and Wall Street, still managed to find time to embark on his Culture Kick.

Now, in my own defense, I must say that this particular time I was doing pretty well myself. Having undertaken the job of decorating the apartment in just the way Jonathan had specified, I was rushing around New York, attending auctions, tramping up and down Second and Third avenues, visiting showrooms, my purse bulging with swatches of fabrics and cards of paint samples, my head bursting with facts about French and English furniture, carpet piling and wood stains. And while I was distractedly bidding on twelve Regency chairs for the dining room (I got them), Jonathan was buying paintings and sculpture and books and reams of records for the stereo he was having installed. It was also at that time that he began to take an interest in still another art form, The Theater, which later gave him another outlet for his gambling fever. By which I simply mean he invested a lot of money in a play. As with the stocks, I didn't know what he was up to until it was too late. Oh, there were some clues—we seemed to be going to a lot of plays, and he suddenly was reading everything from George Kelly to Anouilh—but none of that really prepared me for the night he confessed (with that same old look) that he had put some money in a play that was a cinch to be a "smash," and that he wanted me to go out and get something appropriately "smashing" to wear on opening night.

Yes. He really said that. And of course the play *was* a smash. The Midas Touch, don't you know. And with that, life changed again. Within weeks we'd begun to drop a lot of the people we had seen for years and were seeing more and more of what I call The New People, for lack of a better name. It's almost impossible to give them a name, because they come from so many worlds. Some come from the theater (producers, actors, playwrights—the lot), some from the art world (painters, sculptors and their dealers), and some from that mixed-bag world of fashion and magazines (editors, photographers, the most famous of the models). Then still others, the sort of filler, come from that world without any real name, that stratum of society that isn't Society at all, and isn't even quite what they used to call Café Society, then The Jet Set, and now is called only God knows what. The Beautiful People? Whatever they're called, the people I mean don't quite make that top set, but make a set all their own just beneath it. Aside from a few loners, it's made up of couples, mostly youngish, like us, but about twenty times richer than we are, whose only aim in life seems to be to climb out of the set they're in and make it into the one above, and who try to do it by surrounding themselves with as much Cultural Schmear and as many celebrities as they can lay their hands on.

The New People. Though it sounds as if I hate them, that's not quite right. While I don't exactly love them, it's more a case of that old Abner Dean thing "Who *are* all those people?" plus my own little addition of "And what the hell am I doing with them?" I'm certainly not afraid of them or intimidated by them, and if I were coping on my own I think things would be different. I've always liked bright and talented and amusing people, and have always been able to hold my own with them. But I'm not on my own. In fact, the real un-beauty part about The New People is that a lot of them patronize Jonathan and try to use him, and since he doesn't see it, and since I can hardly point it out to him, it puts me in a rather peculiar position. At the dinners and parties and openings we now go to all the time, where I am more-often-than-not "Balser's wife . . . whatsername," and where I often find myself stuck off alone on the side-lines, forced to watch Jonathan getting put down without his knowing it, how can I be anything but stiff or tense or resentful, how can I loosen up and start Swinging or Getting with It, as Jonathan puts it? Of course we still see some of the old people, especially the ones from Hoddison and Marks, but it's mostly The New People, clear and away. And when from time to time Jonathan asks me don't I think it's marvelous that we've developed such an interesting, exciting social life, I always quickly say, Yes, I certainly do think it's marvelous! . . . What else can I say?

In fact, what *more* can I say? Here and now. I seem to have mucked up my chronology, so that all of a sudden we're up to the present. I also seem to have bogged down again, nerves instead of sentiment this time (my hands are leaving snail-trails again), seem to have reached an impasse in this little Account. But then, as I said, what more is there to say? Shall I say the obvious, the thing I've told myself every day for weeks—that I know I'm a Very Lucky Girl, and really *must* be crazy to get into the state I'm in these days, when I have everything

A Girl Could Want? I have two bright, healthy, attractive children. (Just two. Jonathan didn't want any more, said we'd waited too long.) I have a "brilliant," successful husband, and every material thing I could possibly want, A Beautiful Home included. Outside this bedroom (20 x 15, two windows overlooking the park) there are seven large, airy, high-ceilinged rooms filled with light and colors and textures and objects that dazzle the eye. The petrified man and goulash have been outshouted, over-lived. In the living room the walls are covered with paintings, the best of the current crop, and the mantel, coffee table, Directoire Palissandre table, Louis XVI Harlequin table and built-in shelves between the windows are covered with sculpture: a tiny gold wire horse, little greened-copper figures, things that look like icicles and sand castles of brass. There are hi-fi speakers concealed in the pelmets of the drapes, in the innards of a Chinese Chippendale secretary-cabinet and the broken-pediment molding over the door. (The turntable and all the records, Palestrina through Cage, are in the four-wall bookcase in the den.) As Jonathan specified, the furniture is an "eclectic" mixture of French and English and Modern, although the glass-and-steel coffee table is actually the only Modern thing in that room. Jonathan is particularly fond of the coffee table, which holds a Careless Clutter that he personally weeds out and rearranges from time to time, and which at the moment is composed of a tiny Vermeil fish, a Pre-Columbian gold bird with turquoise eyes, a massive Steuben ashtray, several thick art books, and *The New Republic*, *Réalités*, *Punch*, *Financial World* and *The Partisan Review*. Even our Clutter is eclectic.

So much for The Beautiful Home. Let's move on to something else material—like clothes. Since I don't much feel like going into mine, let's take Jonathan's. Jonathan has 23 suits, 7 sport jackets, 9 pairs of slacks, 2 raincoats, 5 overcoats, and a plum-colored velvet smoking jacket he rarely wears, thank God. He has 35 shirts and 11 pairs of pajamas (2 are silk), 3 robes, 15 pairs of shoes, 12 pairs of gloves, and God knows how many pairs of socks and handkerchiefs and underwear shorts. He has 9 sweaters,

3 dinner jackets with trousers, a suit of tails he's never worn, and a striped-ticking butler's apron he wears as a "gag" when he makes the dressing and tosses the salad at small dinners for friends. Though he never wears hats, he owns 4, and last year he bought a fuzzy green Alpine sort of one with a pheasant-feather cockade, which, unlike the others, he wears, but only on Saturday afternoons, either when he is setting out on one of his rare jaunts with the girls, or is setting out, alone, for his favorite kind of Saturday afternoon—a leisurely stroll across the park to Madison Avenue, where he drops in at "his" gallery, or into Parke-Bernet to watch the bidding, or to Sherry-Lehmann to pick up some Montrachet on sale, or to one of his gourmet havens for a jar of Damson Plum preserves or a tin of Earl Grey's . . .

I could have kept that up forever, only I suddenly felt violently ill. I know that Clothes Don't Make the Man, but I suddenly realized that I couldn't even figure out who the man in all those clothes was. I mean just who *is* that bird whose idea of fun on a crisp autumn Saturday afternoon is a walk to Fraser Morris for a pound of Scotch salmon or a whole Brie cheese, in an outfit that is only lacking a shooting stick? Who is that wonder in worsted, that marvel in madras, that dirge in serge? Jonathan. Are you *in* there, Jonathan? If you are, come out. Please. Come out, come out wherever you are.

Well, now I've really gone and done it. My damned wet hands are puckering this page so badly it looks like a box for eggs. I've also got that charming peach-pit kind of lump starting in my throat, and it's getting so big so fast I may end up having to have Sven the drunken Swede do a tracheotomy on me with the passkey from his belt. Before I get to that point I'll stop for today. I have to stop anyway—it's a quarter past *two*. I've been at this for hours, yet wasn't aware of time passing. I didn't even get hungry or writer's cramp, which must be proof of something, but I'll have to consider just what it is later: the girls get home around four, and between now and then I have all the beds to make, dishes to wash, and Folly to feed and walk. Poor baby . . . she's sitting over in the armchair, all forlorn and glassy-eyed. And she isn't the only thing I forgot. I also forgot to phone for an order of groceries from the Nieuw Amsterdam Market. Since it's much too late to call now, and since there's nothing in the house for dinner, I'll have to have some chow mein sent in from The White Jade. Which brings us to the Department of Small Blessings: Thank God Jonathan is out of town and can't come home and ask why I couldn't find the time to fix a decent home-cooked meal.

"The full teapot
  makes no sound"

"Sorrow is the child
  of too much joy"

"Friend, do not try
  to borrow combs
  from shaven monks"

"Beware of too much laughter
  for it deadens the mind
  and produces oblivion"

"To lock up mischief
  shut your mouth"

> Messages from the fortune cookies that
> came with last night's chow mein from
> The White Jade; obviously they have
> Lao-tse locked up in the bakery

LAST NIGHT at 10:43 Jonathan called from Wichita, just
as I was about to turn out the light and go to sleep.
Though we talked less than the allotted three minutes,
the call left me so strangely jazzed up, I had to read
Flaubert for an hour before I got sleepy again. I didn't

take a Nembutal, because I've only about seven or eight left, and thought I'd better hold off until I see if old Doc Simon comes through with a prescription for more this afternoon.

Last night I also realized that my bedside table is a dead giveaway of the state of my mind. I suppose it's stupid to leave such damning evidence lying around, but Jonathan doesn't seem to notice a thing beyond the fact that I read about an hour each night before going to sleep. At the moment, stacked around the lamp are:

> *The Collected Plays of Chekhov*
> *Buddenbrooks*
> *Three Tales* by Flaubert
> *The Collected Works of Jane Austen*
> *The Poems of Andrew Marvell*
> *Howard's End*
> Auden's *Age of Anxiety*
> *Lady Chatterley's Lover*

On the shelf underneath are some fashion magazines, American and French, some back issues of *Art News* and the editorial pages of several daily editions of the *Times*. This shelf represents my Required Reading, things Jonathan insists I read, but I never touch it except to weed out the stack from the *Times* when it gets too high.

Perhaps one of the reasons Jonathan hasn't noticed what I'm reading is that on the nights he's home and isn't working in the den or on the phone and isn't in the mood for sex, he's got some Required Reading of his own. He sits propped up with three pillows against the headboard, smoking one of those smelly little cigars he's taken up since he quit smoking cigarettes last year, reading, reading away. And what does he read, this Brilliant Lawyer? Alan Nevins? Shelby Foote? Benjamin Thomas? *Foreign Affairs? The Reporter? The Yale Law Journal* or *The Political Science Quarterly?* No, he reads the pages of two evening papers with the closing prices. He reads *Financial World* and *The Illustrated London News*. He reads *Variety* and the current *Art*

News and *Gourmet Magazine* and seven gossip columns in three different papers, chuckling and clucking to himself.

My own reading could be a reaction to his, but I think more simply it's a way of calming myself without pills or booze, and on nights I'm permitted to read for an hour I can usually fall asleep without a Nembutal. I say "permitted" because Jonathan often interrupts; in fact, it seems that on the nights I'm most absorbed and far away I hear that bored yawn coming from the next bed, hear the rustle of newspapers or the smack of a magazine hitting the floor before "Hey, Teen— How's about a little ole roll in the hay?"

It's only fair to say that Jonathan has never gone in for four-letter words when dealing directly with sex— either during it, or talking about it afterwards or before. He's always said things like "let's make love" or "let's go to bed," and though I like things more graphic than that, I've never minded—it was part of the package, red suspenders and all. But this—God, this makes me go all dead inside, and it doesn't help to look at his face, which is bland and smooth like a nice boiled egg, the eyes like buttons on a Brooks Brothers shirt. It's odd, because along with this new Buddy Ebsen approach to sex, he seems to want it a lot more than he used to, but it doesn't seem to have anything to do with me. I mean I would respond, could respond, with a different approach, but as it is I have a pretty hard time. Of course I don't show what I feel, and if I can't get away with those oldies "I'm too tired" or "Not tonight . . . I had a terrible day," I get up and go in the bathroom, and like some fastidious plumber, fix up. The sex itself I don't want to go into except to say that twelve years ago Doctor Popkin once talked about what he called The Regularity Theory of Sex, and I laughed like hell. I don't remember any more just why it came up—maybe someone I'd slept with at the time—but I'll never forget how funny I thought it was that there were men who were convinced that for the sake of their health, they had to "relieve" themselves in sex a certain number of times a week. I laughed like hell then, but I'm not laughing now. And it's not that I'm particularly naïve. Ten years are ten years. But it doesn't have to be like that, and wasn't until a few months ago, and still isn't when we make up after a fight or when we've both had a lot to drink.

But to get back to those books on my night table, which I picked at random off the shelves in the den the second day we got back from the country: escape, pure and simple, a source of peace, nothing more. Frosty English parks, melancholy Russian gardens, stuffy German parlors—how far away can you get? Last year at this time I was reading best-sellers from Rachman's lending library and the paperbacks of Ian Fleming, Rex Stout and Margery Allingham. But then last year at this time I was supposedly sane. Last year at this time I was doing everything I had to do (running this place efficiently, still furnishing it, going to parties, being a Model Mother), and what I didn't like I overlooked, repressed. If at times I couldn't listen to The New People talk, or couldn't look straight at Jonathan in his new $200.00 evening suit and bowed patent leather pumps, I accused myself of provincialism and inverse snobbism and kept on going. In short, I managed to keep one step ahead of myself until this July, when I found myself stranded in that ratty little house in Easthampton with Liz and Sylvie and a Mother's Helper for company all week long. For the last two summers we'd rented a house in Rowayton. We went to Easthampton this year because some of The New People—the same people who managed to forget his existence the minute we were there—convinced Jonathan it was a Mad Fun Place to be. Oh, on the weekends we were invited to *some* parties, but never the ones Jonathan wanted to be at, and though during the two weeks he took off he played a lot of tennis and swam, it was never on the courts he wanted to be on, never in the pools of the people he longed for. During the week, when I was alone, there was no problem. I spent the days shuttling the girls and the Mother's Helper to and from the beach, or to the occasional dates they had with New People children. At night I read Agatha Christie or Simenon or Ngaio Marsh and watched old movies on TV, and though at times I was swamped by an almost unbearable loneliness, I would tell myself I was being childish and wait for it to pass.

Then, toward the end of July, it began. Mild shakes in Bohack's. Sweaty hands on the steering wheel when I was driving to the beach. A sleepless night here and there. And the beginning of the fears—a fear of sharks if I swam out beyond the breakers, a fear of the bees buzzing in the ramblers that climbed our rotting porch railing (I'd be stung, be allergic to the sting, and without the necessary antitoxin serum, would swell up and die), a fear of prowlers and Peeping Toms at night. And then in August the sickest fear of all: at night, while we slept, a tidal wave as tall as the Empire State Building would come rustling in from mid-ocean, and sweep us and our cottage and half of old Long Island out to sea . . . Well, I saw it coming. Not the tidal wave, but Trouble, and finally took myself off to some doctor in Sag Harbor who I suppose was used to the hippy Summer Colony because he wrote me prescriptions for tranquilizers and sleeping pills without a qualm. It was only when I got back to town that it all got going full speed. . . . Damn. The phone.

Back from the phone. It was, so help me, someone named Carter Livingston, an off-Broadway producer, inviting us to a cocktail party next week. I said we'd be pleased to come. *Pleased.* Jonathan will be as thrilled as a high school freshman asked to the prom by the captain of the football team. No double-entendres intended, but now that I think of it that *is* a funny thought. Anyway, no sooner had I hung up than Lottie was knocking on the door. Forgetting I'd locked it, I told her to come in. The handle turned as far as it could, then stopped: Nov Shmoz Kapop? As the handle spun back, Lottie, obviously very embarrassed, called through the door that she couldn't find any *Fab* powder for the washing machine. Not wanting to make the damned door more of an issue than it already was, I left it locked and shouted back that I'd forgotten to order *Fab*, to try *Cheer* in the machine instead. As I heard her go back down the hall, I

cursed myself for being so stupid and wondered what
she was thinking about my locking myself up in here.

Being who and what she is, nothing. Part of the whole
Gestalt of Lottie Masters is to have no thoughts or curiosity about what goes on here. Before I was on to that,
her attitude unnerved me. In fact, when she first came to
work for us and my gushy ZaSu Pitts tries at Friendship
and Rapport were spurned, I thought she might be a
Muslim. Yes, I really gave that a whirl. Now, after almost three years, I finally understand her and respect
her for what she is: a damned hard-working Negro
woman who wants privacy—yours and hers. In the beginning she worked for us only three half-days a week,
just cleaning. Then Jonathan insisted we hire a full-time
maid. I knew he had something other than Lottie-ex-
tended in mind, a sort of combination of a Mary Petty
maid and Dione Lucas and Katinka (or was it Hefty
Helga?) from "The Toonerville Trolley," but I had my
own ideas. I liked Lottie very much. I knew how badly
she needed the money, and I was damned if I was going
to fire her without warning and then go out and try to
find Jonathan's impossible idea of a maid. So Lottie and I
worked things out. She is completely devoted to her husband, who works as a porter in a rectory uptown. Because he isn't well, she goes home in time to get his dinner for him, and only sleeps in on the nights we go out.
(Needless to say, this created certain problems when our
new social life really got under way last year.) She
comes in at 11:00 and leaves at 6:00 five days a week, and
does not work on Thursdays or Sundays. She cleans,
does what is called light laundry, and cooks our dinner
and leaves it warming on the stove. I think she's a very
good cook and an excellent laundress. Jonathan, however, is not of the same mind: after Lottie had a go at his
shirts for a while, he told me that she wasn't to touch
them, and now has me send them out to some incredible
French hand laundry which charges 70, yes, SEV-
ENTY, cents a shirt; he also insists we hire outside
cooks whenever we have guests—French ladies, Finnish
ladies, Haitian ladies—which is all right when there are
more than four guests, but when there are only two it's

rather . . . trying. My only quarrel with Lottie is her excessive sense of Duty. If I try to do any of the things she considers "her" work, if I so much as make a bed or wash a dish on the days she comes in, she gets angry. She's better about the times when I have an urge to cook something special for our dinner. Though it's gotten rather lost in the recent shuffle, I like to cook, and was well on my way to becoming a fairly good one until we moved here and I was told not only to decorate this apartment, but to get someone to do the cooking for me. Naturally that put a damper . . .

Phone again. It was another invitation for a party, this one being for the 28th of October. It seemed to me that that was overdoing it, inviting people to a party a month and a half in advance, but when I hung up and went to write it down in the new appointment book Jonathan bought at Gucci last week, I saw that today was the 29th of September. Which makes Sunday the 1st of October and which explains both of today's calls. The 1st of October signifies the beginning of the fall season, and its arrival seems to be a sort of signal for all The New People to come pouring out of the ground like Army Ants and start their fall rampage. This particular invitation will fill Jonathan with rapture. (*sic*) Rapture. It was tendered by a lady I loathe named Charlotte Rady. She is tall, blond, pushing fifty, and in the early forties was a minor movie queen—she was the Wicked Sexy Blonde who had somebody like John Garfield or Joel McCrea climbing the walls with mad passion, until he finally came to his senses and deserted her for the Good Girl. Around the end of the war she married Rady and his millions, and after someone did a Professor Higgins on her, after she learned to talk with a marbelized voice and to forget all that white fox, she entered Society. She has skin like a gardenia that's been in the icebox one day too long, and a fantastic figure she no longer puts to any use. Though she's had nothing to do with men since Rady died, she doesn't dig women either—it's just drugs, alcohol and celebrities. She runs a Salon, or what used to be called a Salon—I don't know any of the new names for things. On the phone just now she had the gall to say, "I heard you were out at the Beach, and I kept meaning to phone, but I got *so* involved with visiting firemen from Europe I never had a chance to call anybody." *Eheu.*

The thing I want to know as I sit here on this hot end-of-September morning, beginning to shake again, is whatever happened to Shirley and Harold Glick? Shirley and Harold, the first friends of Jonathan I ever met. Harold, who had gone to Harvard with Jonathan and become an anthropologist; Shirley, who had gone to Radcliffe and worked for some child welfare organization. When I said I didn't like them, Jonathan accused me of being a snob. I didn't think I was, I just thought I knew a phony when I saw one. Of course I see now that as always I was wrong and Jonathan was right. He used to love them, Shirley and Harold, Jonathan did. Said they were Salt of the Earth and Real. Real People. Real Folks. (Jonathan lapsed into quaint phrases way back then.) And I see now they were. Real, that is. And that's why I want to know whatever happened to them, these Real Folks so Salt of the Earth. O Harold, O Shirley—what has become of you? You, Shirley, do you still wear those stretch pants with the stirrups pulled over your moccasins, and the dingle-dangle earrings and peekaboo lace blouses bought in Yucatán when Harold was studying some lost Indian tribe on a sabbatical? And you, Harold, do you still take off your professorial tweeds the minute you're home, and put on those workmen's shirts that Shirley had bleached with Chlorox to white-blue, and those corduroy pants and suede desert boots of a matching olive-green? Do you still, O Harold and Shirley, give those little din-dins where everyone sits so *gemütlich* on the floor, eating their tacos and chili and shouting brilliant, provocative things above The Goldberg Variations? Yes. I have this overpowering need to see you, Shirley and Harold Glick, so Real, so True, so Salt of the Earth. I definitely have to know how you are, so I will talk to Jonathan when he gets back from Wichita and we will arrange things so that you can come to dinner and meet some of our exciting new friends and we can talk about old times and . . .

The noon siren just went off, and Lottie is timidly rattling pails in the girls' bathroom, her way of letting me know she has to get in here next. And since I have a 1:30 appointment for a checkup with Max Simon, that wraps it up for today. Question: Will he or won't he come through with a prescription for more pills?

ANSWER TO QUESTION at end of last entry: No more pills.

On Saturday Jonathan got back from Wichita at twenty to six. Up until then I'd had a remarkably good day with the girls, first taking them out to lunch, then on to Jean Louis for haircuts (all the girls at Bartlett have their mothers' hairdressers cut their hair), then on to finish shopping for their winter clothes. We got home at 5:20 to find Lottie sitting in the front hall with her hat on: her husband had phoned to say he was home early from the rectory, feeling sick, but she hadn't wanted to leave without my permission. *Permission.* Recovering from that, I told her to go, adding that in the future she was to go any time she was needed without asking me, and while the girls went into the den to watch TV, I started to fix a horseradish sauce for the tongue she'd left simmering on the stove. While I was making a great clatter with whisks and pots, Jonathan quietly let himself in, set his suitcase down by the door, and made straight for the pantry, where he poured himself a drink. But it wasn't until he gave one of the trunks a swift kick that I heard him. It's a singular sound. However, just for the face of things, I called, "Jonathan . . . is that *you?*" and after another strangled sort of noise he came into the kitchen, carrying half an old-fashioned glass of bourbon without ice, and kissed me on the cheek. He gave off a stale sickish smell and looked just

57

terrible. He was a deadly white, his eyes were sunken into his head, and he had the look of a man who's just had the fright of his life. He had: his plane had developed trouble with its landing gear just outside New York; after circling Kennedy for an hour, their pilot had decided to "try it" (his very words, via the stewardess), and they finally landed, safely, to find the whole Emergency Squad out to greet them. "Even the foam trucks," concluded Jonathan, draining his glass.

"You poor darling," I said. "It sounds like a nightmare." One of my favorites, I forbore to add. As I stared at him, limp, haggard, I mentally followed him from the front door, down the hall to the pantry, to the kitchen where we stood. "Did you say hello to the girls?"

"No. I didn't want them to see the shape I was in. I'm better now," he said, setting down his empty glass with a flourish, and with that, went out to see the girls in the den. By the time he'd said hello, and given them some little presents he'd brought them from Wichita, I'd finished the horseradish sauce and was at the sink washing salad greens. He came back in, and going straight to the stove, lifted the lid of the pot and sniffed. "Do we have to have that?"

"What."

"That crummy tongue. You know I hate tongue. Besides, I'd like to go out tonight."

I was determined not to have a fight. He'd been home exactly fifteen minutes and had been away four days. "Jonathan," I said gently. "You said on the phone that if you did get in today, it wouldn't be in time for dinner and not to expect you. The girls love tongue and so do I. But just because we're having it doesn't mean you have to go out. I can fix you a tuna salad or an omelette. It will be much better than going out—you look just exhausted. Besides, you've been eating in restaurants for four days. I should think you'd be tired of them."

"Restaurants in Wichita are not restaurants in New York. I don't want a tuna salad or an omelette and I'm not as tired as I look. I'm just *ment*ally tired. Besides, it's Saturday night. A good dinner out with some friends

and a movie afterwards would make me forget the whole
thing on the plane."

I turned off the lights under the tongue and horseradish sauce. "If that's what you want to do, we'll do it. But
you must realize it's six o'clock. Everyone is probably all
tied up now, and I might have a terrible time getting a
sitter."

"Why a sitter? Where the hell is Lottie?"

"She went home. Her husband is sick."

"Christ. Is she *ever* here? . . . Well, never mind. Before we start worrying about a sitter, let's see if we can
dig up someone to come out with us. Let's try the
Langs."

"The Langs are up in Ridgefield. They go every
weekend until there's snow."

"Well then, try the Franklins."

"They're in London. Don't you remember they left
on Labor Day?"

"Yah, now I do." Jonathan rubbed his bloodshot eyes.
In spite of what he said, he looked completely done in.
"Hell . . . is anybody we know in town? Is there any-
one *you* can think of calling?"

"Why," I said slowly, "don't we call the Glicks?"

"The Glicks. Harold and *Shirley* Glick? What made
you think of *them?*"

"I don't know. I was thinking of them just the other
day."

"We haven't seen them in seven or eight years, for
God's sake."

"That doesn't mean we couldn't call them. I'm sure
they'd be just delighted to hear from you. They loved
you. And you used to love them."

"Seven or eight years ago. I've changed my mind since
then. I always thought she was pretty much of a slob
anyway, never shaving under her arms and wearing those
pointy brassieres under sweaters. Besides, though I never
told you, I bumped into Harold on the street two years
ago and it depressed the hell out of me for days. I didn't
even recognize him—he's going bald and he's gained
about twenty pounds. He's given up anthropology and
gone into his father's stocking business. Shirley had just

given birth to *twins*." Shuddering, Jonathan gave me a suspicious look. "But you never liked them. What the hell do *you* want to see them for?"

"I don't know," I said vaguely. "As I said, I just happened to think about them the other day and I wondered how they were."

"Well, now you know, so forget them." Jonathan loosened the knot of his tie and undid the two top buttons of his shirt. "Listen, Teen, I've got to get a shower. I sweated like a pig during that hour we circled Kennedy. While I'm inside freshening up, why don't you try the Willards, and if they're busy, try the Barrs. If the Barrs are tied up, we'll go out anyway, so line up a sitter no matter what."

With that he took off, first stopping in the pantry to fix himself another drink, then looking in again on the girls. Following suit, I fixed myself a drink, then got our address book and carried it to the kitchen phone, where I first tried the Willards. Sally Willard said: "Oh, Tina, what a *shame*. We'd love to join you, but I seem to have these perfectly beastly curse cramps. I plan to spend the evening eating Empirin and watching *Casablanca* on TV." Next I called the Barrs. Peter Barr said: "Gee, Tina, Joanie's in the tub. We're getting ready to go out with the Willards—just to get some dinner and see a flick—why don't you and Jonathan join us?" I mumbled something about not wanting to intrude, put down his feeble protests, and hung up. I then called a Barnard student who sometimes sits for us, but she was in bed with the flu. I tried three other women who also sometimes sit for us, and when none of them could come, called a woman named Mrs. Prinz who lives in our building. I feel sorry for Mrs. Prinz, who is a lonely widow, but Jonathan and the girls don't like her. Of course she was free, so I told her to come up in an hour and went to break the news to the girls. The reaction was worse than I had expected.

"Why don't you like her?"

"She smells like wet dog," said Liz.

"She always reads us that bloody old Kipling book just because her daughter loved it," said Sylvie.

"She always makes us turn off our lights on the dot of eight, even on Saturdays. Just so she can go and eat up all the ice cream in the freezer while she watches some movie on TV."

"She was the only sitter I could get," I said grimly. "Now if you'll please go inside and wash up, I'll give you your dinner before I get dressed."

When the doorbell rang at seven-thirty, I had just gotten out of the tub. Jonathan was on the phone with Hoddison, giving him a long involved report about Wichita, so I threw on a robe and went to open the door for Mrs. Prinz. Mrs. Prinz is that New York phenomenon, the Widow of a Certain Age, who, like Madame Arkadin, is always *comme il faut*, always formidably equipped against the onslaughts of the cruel world with intricate make-up, dyes and expensive clothes. To spend an evening baby-sitting with two little girls, Mrs. Prinz had rigged herself out in a black crêpe dress, a pearl choker and matching pearl earrings, and had poured half a bottle of *Quelques Fleurs* over herself. Thinking that the latter would at least camouflage any traces of Wet Dog, I ushered her into the den, where the girls were watching *The Wizard of Oz*, and fled. Jonathan was finally off the phone and stood retying his tie at the mirror. With one glance I saw how depressed he was that we hadn't been able to get anybody to go out with us. For that reason I didn't rise to the occasion when he turned and looked at me still in my robe, and said, "How much longer are you going to be? What's taking you so long, what the hell have you been *doing?*"

"What I've been doing is giving the girls their supper," I said quietly, pulling some things from a drawer. "I've also been taking a bath. Is there any reason we should be in a rush? Is there somewhere special we have to be?"

"Yes, there is. While you were inside, I made a reservation at Emma's for eight. I made it then because it seemed to me we could get there in plenty of time."

"We can," I said, rushing for the bathroom. "I'll be ready in ten minutes."

I was ready in eight. I came out of our bedroom into the hall to find Jonathan and Mrs. Prinz standing outside

the door to the den. From the den came the sound of
Judy Garland belting out "Over the Rainbow." Mrs.
Prinz had the skirt of her black crêpe dress hiked up,
and was treating Jonathan to a view of an Ace-bandaged
knee and about ten inches of mottled thigh mapped with
blue veins. Jonathan was not looking at all well again.
Pointing to a purple Rorschach splotch of broken blood
vessels, pitching her voice above Judy Garland's, Mrs.
Prinz was trying to explain a fall she had taken on some
cracked pavement in front of Rachman's Stationery
Store on Broadway—the upshot of course being, could
she sue?

I extricated Jonathan, gave Mrs. Prinz explicit instructions that the girls were to stay up until the end of *The
Wizard of Oz*, no matter how late it turned out to be,
that there was to be no bed-time reading—and we left.

"God, what a pig!" said Jonathan the minute we were
in a taxi. "What unmitigated *gall*, making me look at that
obscenity of a leg, trying to cop free legal advice. I hate
leaving the girls alone with her."

Because I felt the same way, I didn't say anything. In
fact, with one word of encouragement from him, I'd
have turned and gone back. But after a final, disgusted
"*God*," he sat back and talked about Wichita for the
rest of the ride.

Though I hadn't let him know it, I was unhappy that
we were going to Emma's. I adore Italian food and
Emma's has the best I've ever eaten, but it's also the most
outrageously expensive and stupidly overdecorated restaurant I've ever been in. I hadn't asked him to go somewhere else because I saw that his depression was getting
worse by the minute, and I didn't want to add to it. In
fact, by the time we got to the restaurant I was so concerned about him that I didn't even mind when he pulled
one of his newest stunts, which is to refuse any table
that's been reserved for him, and insist that the headwait-
er give him a "better" one. When we were finally settled at a "better" table and were waiting for our drinks,
I tried not to look at his glum face and made nervous
tries at small talk, until I suddenly remembered the one
thing that was sure to bring him out of his gloom.

"Charlotte Rady. Charlotte *Rady*. Well, well, what d'you know." His face was transfigured. Rapture, as I'd predicted. "What else did she have to say?"

"What do you mean 'what else'?"

"I mean did she say anything . . . personal?"

"Only that she was looking forward to seeing us," I lied.

Jonathan snorted. "That's a formula, for God's sake. Everybody says that." The waiter brought our drinks, and after a few thoughtful sips, Jonathan said: "Why do you suppose she invited us now? I mean we first met her about a year and a half ago. I wonder what suddenly made her decide we were . . . ah . . . eligible."

Though I'd wondered the same thing, I hadn't put it to myself in quite the same way. Eligible.

"Why do you think?" persisted Jonathan.

"I don't know."

"I don't either. Maybe it has to do with the fact that she's seen us around at everything, all the parties and openings she goes to. I mean maybe the fact that we're at all the right places at the right time finally made an impression—the old success-begets-success thing . . . You think that might be it?"

I'd been trying, without any luck, to swallow past the lovely lump that had suddenly bloomed in my throat. Desperate, I picked up my glass and polished off my drink.

"Well, *do* you?"

"Yes," I finally managed. "Yes, I think that might be it."

Later, as we were eating our main course, Jonathan said, "Well, one thing's clear. We've got to give a big party."

I stared down at my veal. "Why is it so clear?"

"Because we have so many obligations, that's why. Because it isn't enough to go to parties; you have to give them too. Those crummy little dinners we gave last year don't mean a thing. In fact, I see now they were really a mistake. Now that the apartment is really finished we can make it a sort of big housewarming."

"Just how big a party did you have in mind?"

"Oh, about a hundred people."

"For *dinner?*"

Jonathan shrugged. "Not a real dinner, more a cocktail-buffet sort of thing. Nobody asks people in just for cocktails any more. It just isn't done."

I pushed my glass towards Jonathan. "Could I please have some more wine?"

Giving me a quick, shrewd look, Jonathan lifted the bottle from its wicker cradle and poured. "If you're worried about all the work involved, relax. You won't have to do a thing. I'm planning to get someone like that man—Beaumont?—the Willards and Barrs use."

"But he's so expensive. And . . . well, pretentious."

"Pretentious. What the hell does that mean?"

"Just what the dictionary says."

For a moment we just sat there glaring at each other, until it became clear that Jonathan was really seeing me for the first time since he'd gotten back from Wichita. It's an understatement to say that what with the rush and the events of the last two hours, I was not looking my best. "You know," Jonathan said slowly, "I completely forgot. What was all that business on the phone the day I left—about someone almost attacking you in the park. What was all that?"

Bending my head, I worked to extricate my fork from a long chewing-gummy strand of Mozarella cheese. "Oh, it was nothing much."

"Nothing much. You were *beside* yourself."

"Well, it might have sounded like I was at the time, but I've almost forgotten it by now." Aware that Jonathan was watching me closely, waiting, I plowed on: "I mean, looking back I can see now where it was the sort of thing that's completely commonplace, the sort of thing you have to expect in a big city like New York with all the crackpots and loonies around."

"Crackpots. Loonies." By now Jonathan had completely given up on his *vitello tonnato*, which he loves. His face had the same look it had had that morning he'd told me he was so "worried" about me. "Tina," he said gently, indulgent. "What the hell are you talking about?"

I also gave up on my veal *parmigiana*; my hands were wet and shaking and I hid them in my lap. "I'm talking about what goes on in this city, or any big city like it nowadays. It's all a sign of the times, the terrible pressures we live under. The exhibitionists in the park and subways, the rapists in elevators, the muggers on the streets—why, even those telephone perverts who call and say obscene things—they're all a sign of the times."

"And just exactly what does *that* mean," asked Jonathan, Counselor-at-Law, stickler for facts.

"It means that some people just can't take all the pressures we live under—the Russians, the Chinese, the war in Vietnam, the Negro Revolution, and of course The Bomb—some people just crack."

Crack. I listened to the word that Idiot-Girl had used all by herself.

"You don't really believe all that?" asked Jonathan softly, still indulgent, but hopeful.

With a gigantic effort I pulled myself together: in two seconds we'd be on to the subject of Popkin again. With cold fury I said, "Stop patronizing me, Jonathan. I refuse to submit to this cross-examination. You're not a trial lawyer, you know."

Fixing me in a long fishy stare, Jonathan said, "I wasn't aware of any patronization on my part. And I found it a highly illuminating conversation. In fact, I'd like to go on with it."

"I have nothing more to say."

And I was as good as my word. We ate in silence until the *caffè espresso*, when I decided I had to get something straight. "Are you serious about giving a big party?"

"You're damned right I am!"

"And just exactly when were you thinking of giving it?"

"It depends. I probably won't be able to get Beaumont until Christmastime. He's booked months ahead." Signaling the waiter, he casually added, "Do you think you can manage to have those trunks out of the pantry by Christmastime?"

The waiter came with the check; Jonathan put down bills; I fumbled with the purse in my lap.

As the waiter went away, Jonathan said, "All right, I'm sorry. It's only that . . . oh, for God's sake, Tina! People are *staring* at you."

We went to an Italian movie in a theater near the restaurant. It was our Italian evening. It was only 10:15, much too early to go home, where we'd only have to be alone with each other. The movie was terrible, even though Mastroianni had the male lead, and I came out with a splitting headache. When we got home we found Mrs. Prinz stretched out asleep on the couch in the den, her skirt hiked way up, while across the room a rerun of *Casablanca* flickered on the TV. Bergman was saying to Bogart, "Kiss me! Kiss me as if it were the last time!" and while that epic embrace took place, Mrs. Prinz rolled over and let out a volley of snores, completely drowning out "As Time Goes By."

"Christ, what a sight!" hissed Jonathan, coming up behind me in the doorway. "Get her out of here and see that she never comes back!"

I reluctantly went in and turned off the TV. Though I'd seen *Casablanca* six times in my lifetime, I was ready to sit down and see it a seventh. Gently, I shook Mrs. Prinz, who came out of her sleep saying, "Gog. Nub. Ack," and burst into tears. "It's my daughter I never see," she sobbed. "I don't sleep nights for thinking about her cruelty. My son I've gotten over, but a daughter's a whole other thing . . ."

After I'd paid her, or rather, overpaid her—I always overpay or overtip when upset—I looked in on the girls, whose room seemed very hot. Jonathan was already undressed and in bed, smoking one of those damned tiny cigars and reading the October issue of *Art News* that had come while he was away. "The windows in the girls' room were shut," he said without looking up. "It's a wonder they fell asleep. It's a wonder they didn't *suffocate*."

Exhausted, I threw off my clothes. "She won't sit for us again," I said and walked stark naked to my closet and put on my pajamas. When I came out of the bath-

room after washing up, Jonathan was still deep in his
magazine. I said goodnight and turned out my light, so
utterly weary that all my bones ached. No sooner had I
shut my eyes than I heard the rustle of pages, the yawn.
Then one second later: "Hey. Teen. How's about a little
ole roll in the hay."

"No," I said without even rolling over to face him.
"Not tonight. I'm much too tired."

Art News hit the floor in a furious thwack of splayed
pages. "And you wonder," said Jonathan, "why I want
you to go and see a doctor! Christ. Do you realize that
we've gone to bed just once in the last three weeks?
Christ. Is there *any*thing you can do any more?"

I rolled over and looked at Jonathan. Jonathan looked
at me. I got out of bed and went into the bathroom and
fixed up. I am not completely mad.

Wednesday October 4

Yesterday afternoon there was a tea for new mothers at the Bartlett School. As an ex-new mother, I'd received a phone call asking me to come. To help me get through it I took one Equanil—I only have about six left—and a shot of vodka. The combination backfired; instead of calming me down, it jazzed me up into an ideal candidate for the PTA: animated, gay, smiling, I did the girls proud; I was "that charming Mrs. Balser, the mother of Sylvie and Liz." Wearing a plastic badge with my name pinned to my last clean linen dress (the heat wave is still on), I smiled and smiled, shook hands that were as cold and clammy as mine would have been without the Nerve Tonic, and poured endless cups of cranberry-orange punch. I even had a long if somewhat baffling conversation with Sylvie's teacher, a trim little hockey-captain-type blonde who kept telling me how "sensitive" and "gifted" Sylvie was. In short, I got through the whole thing with banners flying, and on reaching home I was so reluctant to lose the lovely jazzy feeling that I took a drink before I had dinner alone with the girls. Jonathan was working. This drink seemed to work in the same way: the banners flew until about eight o'clock, when another kind of delayed action set in. Thanking my lucky stars that Jonathan wasn't home, I barely made it to bed in time.

My sleep was so thick and doped that I didn't even

hear Jonathan come in. Then at 3:00 I woke up with a
violent twitch. My hands were clenched into fists, my
teeth were grinding against each other so hard my si-
nuses ached, my heart was racing, my pajamas were
stuck to me with a cold sweat that had nothing to do
with the heat and stuffiness of the room. And I realized
that there I was again, in for one of the worst phases of
my new looniness—middle-of-the-night insomnia.

I've never in my life had insomnia before this summer,
and this isn't normal insomnia, coming as it does at the
tail end of the night or beginning of the morning. It's
sheer hell, and it's always the same. It always happens on
a night when I've fallen asleep without trouble, helped
by pills or not, and I sleep soundly until 2:00, 3:00, 4:00,
when I suddenly wake up Bang with the whole syndrome—the cold sweat, racing heart, et cetera. As I lie
there breathing hard, unknotting my hands, wondering
what woke me up, the Guilt and Shame hit me like a ton
of bricks—Guilt and Shame without any rational focus,
which of course is the worst part of it. Just what in
God's name have you *done* to make yourself feel so stupid and worthless and terrible? I ask myself. You haven't
been unfaithful to Jonathan, you haven't stolen or
cheated or murdered or been cruel. What *is* it? And
then slowly, by way of answering, the little review begins:

At first it's Humiliating Moments and Wicked Deeds
from childhood: the time I wet my pants in first grade;
the time I stole a manicure set from the 5&10 and the
manager collared me; the time I forgot my part in the
Thanksgiving Pageant and was led, sobbing, from the
stage; the time I was caught with a pony translation
copied into my Virgil. These go on and on until I run
out of them and have to move on to a fresh supply, Humiliating Moments and Wicked Deeds from the present:
the time the bakery gave me $5.00 too much in change
and I didn't give it back; the time I gave the cab driver a
twenty-dollar bill, thinking it was a single, and *he* didn't
give it back; the time we went to the Langs' for dinner
and I started splashing in the finger bowl, while everyone else set theirs aside; the time I came out of the ocean

in Easthampton and the top of my suit popped its straps
and fell down. Like that. On and on it goes, making me
toss and writhe in my bed, until finally the parade of objects begins. I see tarnished flatware and streaky windows, I see burnt-out light bulbs, cracked cups and sau-
cers and dinner plates and unwaxed floors; I see shirts
and pajamas without buttons, shoes that need reheeling,
shoes without laces, socks with holes in the toes, worn-
thin sheets, squeezed-out tubes of toothpaste, slivers of
soap, a toaster with a dangerously frayed cord, an iron
with a broken plug . . .

Of course this cyclone of things is at least valid, a re-
minder of the one place where I really have cause for
Guilt these days—the way I've let this place go. And in
the past few weeks I've discovered a simple enough way
to stop the cyclone and get back to sleep: I shut my
eyes and conjure up a vision of myself as a paragon-
housewife, a model of efficiency. The funny thing is the
way I have myself looking in this soothing little fantasy
that gets me back to sleep: my hair is neatly bunned and
shining; my dress, which is made of something quaint
like calico or dimity, has skirts to the floor, and is covered by an apron, dazzlingly clean and starched, of
course; and sometimes there is even a bunch of keys at
my waist. I'm a sort of Victorian Chatelaine, or a
cross between Tabitha Twitchit and Mrs. Danvers—
an unsinister Mrs. Danvers, all sweetened and lightened
up. But funny as it seems in daylight, in those terrible
predawn hours she does the trick, this paragon-me, and
as I lie there, under closed lids watching her rustle about
a house which isn't quite this one—sun seems to be
streaming in everywhere—taking a sort of glorified in-
ventory, checking to see that everything is in its place, a
delicious calm comes over me. I watch her open the door
to a linen closet where on the top shelves towels and
sheets lie in pastel stacks, and the bottom shelves are
loaded with rolls of toilet paper, boxes of Kleenex and
boxes of lanolized bath soap, all in colors to match the
linens, and all bought, thriftily and efficiently, at some
department store's January White Sale. Finding all well
there, Mrs. Tabitha-Twitchit-Danvers shuts the door,

and I watch her proceed to a pantry where she opens cabinet doors on rows of sparkling glasses, stacks of un-cracked plates, and scores of cups hanging from unbro-ken handles. Since clearly everything is in order there too, she shuts the doors and goes into the kitchen and checks all the closets and cabinets there. In the big walk-in broom closet, the broom has all its whiskers, there's a bagful of soft linen rags (old torn sheets re-placed in the White Sale), a brand-new vacuum cleaner, and on the shelves is every kind of wax and polish and soap that one could need. Also on the shelves are honey-combs of boxed light bulbs in every wattage from 25 to 150, neatly coiled extension cords, a box of fuses, and a tool box equipped with everything from a saw to a tog-gle bolt. After the broom closet there's the grocery closet, but by then I'm usually back to sleep, thank God.

Of course it's actually just a variant of the old Count-ing Sheep Trick, with me counting bars of soap and cans of peas instead of the woolly hindquarters of sheep. And as I said, it usually works like a charm. This morn-ing it did not. I'd gotten Mrs. Twitchit-Danvers as far as the grocery cabinets with their boxes of every kind of pasta made—spaghetti, broad noodles, green noodles, linguine, lasagne, maccaroncelli, spiedini, rigatoni, can-nelloni—when I saw that it wasn't going to work and got up and went to the bathroom. By the time I got back into bed I was wide awake. As usual, Jonathan had pulled the blinds all the way down with the slats tightly shut (he says the sun wakes him too early otherwise), and the room was unbearably hot and stuffy. It was also very noisy. Jonathan was lying with all his covers kicked off, making loud smacking sounds with his lips; though a faint breeze had sprung up outside, it couldn't enter the room, and only made a clatter as it rocked the lowered blinds; and to round things off, Folly, who always sleeps at the foot of my bed, seemed to be having some terrible dog-nightmare, for she gave off high-pitched little yips and scrabbled at the sheets with her paws.

I gave up and lit a cigarette and by the flare of the match saw it was a quarter past four. The cigarette tasted peculiar—it had that strange fresh-roasted-nuts sort of taste that cigarettes have on the beach—and suddenly remembering my new fear of fire (I would fall asleep, set fire to the mattress, and die a Human Torch), I put it out after only four or five puffs. Then I was really in for it. Not Guilt any more, just loneliness, a loneliness so acute and overwhelming, I suddenly understood why dogs put back their heads and howl when left alone. I felt like doing the same. But after a minute of picturing Jonathan sitting up in his bed, blinking at me howling with my head thrown back, I reconsidered, and contented myself with reaching over and taking his hand, which was lying, Napoleon-style, on his chest. Jonathan has good hands, big, strong, long-fingered, always dry and warm, and the minute I had one of them in mine I felt better, anchored, less alone. After a while I began to feel something else. It was so unexpected and such a relief—it was so *normal* of me—that I was about to disregard Jonathan's one big idiosyncrasy (he insists on being the Aggressor) and climb over into his bed, when he muttered something like "Cabbot" or "cabbage" in his sleep, and rolling over on his other side, took his hand along with him to scratch an itch. That stopped me cold. But for a while I just lay there having some nice, graphic erotic thoughts, remembering just how it had been in the beginning, so great and hot and urgent that we did it anywhere—on the floor of a public bathhouse, in the back of a rented car pulled up on the Taconic Parkway, under a weekend host's basement pool table, once even between the coats in an upstairs closet at a party—and, strangely enough, thinking about all that soothed me so much that I got sleepy.

Maybe it wasn't so strange. Because I suppose it squashed all the doubts I've begun to have about whether I should have ever married Jonathan in the first place. It made me remember just how right and good we were, not just in sex, but in everything, made me see how wise and full of good judgment I was in those days, as opposed to now, and made me realize that my current trick of thinking he doesn't love me any more is one more indication of my new inability to face facts. With the biggest fact of all being that Jonathan has changed

and grown (those words again), and that I haven't
changed and grown apace, haven't tried to keep up with
him, haven't followed through on the precepts set forth
in my analysis. It's all very well to keep running off at
the mouth about the Feminine Passive Role, and to con-
gratulate oneself on having accepted it, but the truth is
that there's a second phase to that role, a logical se-
quence to be followed, a transition to be made—and I
haven't made it. Women like me, after a certain number
of years of Fulfilling themselves in domestic necessities,
are supposed to leave the seclusion of the lair and re-en-
ter The Great World, where they're supposed to snap-
to and get *with* it right away. They're supposed to go
back to a job they once had and left, or, never having
had a job, get a job; they can join committees and do
good works, they can go back to school and get a Ph.D.,
they can open an art gallery or an antique store or a
bookstore or a jazzy boutique; they can even just become high-powered social types and run charity balls
and give endless parties—it doesn't matter what, as long
as it's Action. Which of course is the reverse of this paralysis I'm in. And as soon as I can pull myself out of it,
snap out of it and snap to, start getting with it, things
will fall into line and get better, maybe better than
they've ever been . . .

That was the line of positive thinking that put me
right back to sleep at twenty to five this morning. When
I woke up two and a half hours later my eyes opened on
Jonathan's empty bed. I heard the shower drumming on
the plastic shower curtain, which happens to have a big
tear in the middle that lets the water leak onto the floor
and which I have been asked, ten times, to replace. My
first waking thought was: You forgot to change the
towels again. (Clean towels are put out every Monday;
this was Wednesday.) My second waking thought was:
You forgot to get the girls that awful cereal. Groaning,
I put on my slippers and robe and went in to wake the
girls, then came back to our bathroom to wash up. The
steam was so thick I could hardly breathe. As I stationed
myself at the sink, I said good morning to Jonathan
standing four feet away in the tub, his chest and stom-

ach white with suds, his hair plastered to his forehead in Stan Laurel bangs. Startled, I noticed he was getting a small pot. "*Good* morning!" he bellowed, very Cheery-Deary. "You certainly had yourself a sleep—you were dead to the world when I came in at ten." Nodding, smiling, I bent to rinse my face. "Hey, Teen," he continued, spitting water like a surfacing seal, "has my navy pin-stripe featherweight dacron-and-worsted come back from the cleaners yet?" His navy pin-stripe featherweight dacron-and-worsted was still hanging in the closet in Lottie's room. "Not yet," I said and buried my face in a towel which smelled like a mildewed bathhouse. "Damn," said Jonathan almost merrily as I took off for the kitchen, where I found a huge dead cockroach lying in the sink.

Everything was ready by the time the girls came in, all crisp and glowing, Liz carrying the *Times*, which she dutifully put at Jonathan's place.

"Mudther," said Sylvie from our walk-in grocery closet. "Didn't you get any Maple Crispies yesterday?"

"The market was out of them," I lied, and thought of Tabitha-Twitchit-Danvers. "How about some scrambled eggs?"

Sylvie came out of the closet clutching a box of Wild Rice Pancake Mix. Jonathan had bought it at Bloomingdale's gourmet shop one Saturday last spring. "Can we have these?" she asked, squinting at the directions. "They sound just yummy, and we can eat them with that great Real Maple Syrup Daddy gets from Vermont."

"Darling, they're not normal pancakes. I mean I think they may be rather lumpy and I just know you won't eat them."

"Of *course* they'll eat them!" said Jonathan, still irrepressibly cheery, bouncing in.

Of course they didn't. After one bite apiece, they had cornflakes and toast. Because I was still in my bathrobe and it was late, I let them go down to wait for the bus alone. Once they'd gone, I excused myself from the table, where Jonathan was finishing his coffee and reading the editorial page, and locked myself in our bathroom, where I turned on all the sink taps and had a short cry. I was splashing cold water on my face, planning to stay in there until Jonathan called goodbye and left, when he suddenly called through the door: "Tina. Are you all right?"

"Of course I'm all right— Goodbye. Have a nice day!"

"I'm not leaving yet. I don't have anything until a meeting at ten. Are you coming out soon? I want to talk to you."

Knowing the jig was up this time and that it was idiotic to stay in there, I tensed all my stomach muscles like someone expecting a kick, unlocked the door and went out. Jonathan was sitting in the armchair, smoking a cigar. As he motioned me to sit down on my rumpled bed, the smoke made an arabesque in the heavy air. His face, pink and faintly shiny, was furrowed with kindness and concern.

I sat down. "What is it you want to talk to me about?"

Giving a weighty sigh, he considered the tiny glowing tip of his cigar. "Tina. I don't want to upset you any more than you already seem to be, but the fact is I think you simply have to call Doctor Popkin and arrange for a series of sessions."

My heart pounding, I said, bored, weary: "Oh God. So we're back to *that*. Ten days ago you told me to go and check up. Well, though I forgot to tell you, Friday I did just that. Max Simon found me fine, 'in splendid shape,' to quote him exactly." I saw no point in adding that having indeed found me so fine, Dear Old Max had refused to give me prescriptions for either tranquilizers or sleeping pills, and to quote him on that. (Dear Old Max: "I'm old-fashioned, Bettina. That's why my practice is so big. I don't believe in any of that stuff. All you need is some simple old-fashioned *e*xercise. Get out and walk twenty or thirty blocks a day. Join a local Y and swim fifteen laps twice a week. Take up horseback riding or play tennis at the Armory. Or just stay home and get down on your knees and scrub some floors. You'll see how quickly those 'nerves' of yours will disappear!")

"I made a mistake," said Jonathan quietly, tapping ash into an ashtray. "I've begun to see that what's the matter isn't physical."

"Matter," I said through clenched teeth. "*Matter*. Just what the hell makes you think anything's the matter wih me?"

Jonathan gave me a look glimmering with warnings. "Tina. I don't want to have a fight. And I don't want to have to go through all that again. As I said ten days ago, I'm worried about you, don't you understand?"

"Why?" A pathetic attempt to gain time.

"Why. That's the word I ought to use. You were crying in the can just now. Suppose I ask you why you were. Or take those books on your night table. Suppose I ask you why the hell you're reading them. What are you doing—taking some mail-order course in Great Books?"

"I'm brushing up, improving my mind. You yourself said I ought to read more."

"More things that would keep you informed about what's going on in the world."

"I know what's going on in the world."

"How could you when you never sit down and read a newspaper through?"

"The newspapers depress me."

Jonathan wet his lips. "I suppose you know where this country would be, where the *world* would be, if everyone who got depressed by the papers stopped reading them."

"I'm not trying to run this country. Or the world."

This time he flinched. And then, as people often do when dealing with the insane, he gave up and went all steely inside, at the same time trying to cover up the shift by talking in a soft, Earnest voice, and by displaying as much patience and logic as possible. "Tina, dear. Let's not get sidetracked. Let's not get involved in sweeping generalties. Let's stick to things at hand, to specific . . . ah . . . indications or examples of the sort of thing I mean. For a starter, let's take a look at this place. Do you realize that it's the 4th of October today? Do you realize those damn trunks have been sitting in the pantry over three weeks? Do you realize that this place is filthy, that the windows are so dirty you can hardly see out? That the ice bucket and all the flatware is tarnished, that the kitchen floor hasn't been waxed since late June? At the rate you're going we'll be lucky if the drapes and rugs are back before next spring!"

He'd worked himself right through his determinedly reasonable "handling" of me, right back to rage. But of course he was right. And because I knew his anger was justified, and that I was guilty, I got frightened and began to lie. Rapidly. "As it just so happens, a special laundress is coming to do the things in the trunk next week. It can't be until next week because the agency was all booked up until then. The same goes for the window-washer and a man to do the floors. Everybody's fixing up for fall at the same time, and the agencies are swamped with orders. Which also proves that I'm not as late as you seem to think."

Like all liars, I thought I had to account for everything. I'd left out the silver. Realizing this, I nervously waited for him to ask why Lottie hadn't polished the silver (she hadn't because I'd forgotten to buy silver polish for two and a half weeks), but he had more important things on his mind. He waved my lies aside with a flapping hand. "Okay. Ok*ay*. So maybe you've finally begun to pull yourself together as far as the house is concerned. What about yourself? The way you look? I mean just like you've always taken pride in the way you ran your home, you've always taken great pains with yourself, the way you looked. I mean you've always been a neat, attractive, well-groomed woman, and you were finally, with my help, really learning how to dress. Now all of a sudden you've let yourself go, and you don't seem to give a damn. In fact, at times you just look a goddamn mess."

Though once again I'd been guilty—the Ella Cinders complex had been at work—my feelings were hurt. "All right. So I've been a little careless about my appearance. Are those grounds for going and seeing a shrink?"

" 'Careless.' You must be kidding."

I returned his dour glare.

"And it's not just 'a shrink' or any shrink. It's an analyst who helped you enormously once and can help you again— *Will* you go see him?"

"No, I will not."

Now I know what they really mean by If-looks-could-kill. Redfaced, fed up with Reason and Kindness, Jonathan got up out of the chair and went to his bed, where he had left the neatly folded jacket to his suit. His face growing redder by the second, he put it on, picked up his attaché case and started through the door, then turned and said in a choking voice: "Of course I can't force you to go. Even if I could, it would have no point. But I'll tell you some things I *can* make you do, things that I, as a husband and the provider around here, have every right to expect, to demand, and you, as my wife, have a duty to do. I want this place pulled together, put in shape, and the same goes for yourself. I believe we're going to Carter Livingston's Friday night. I want you to do something with that godawful hair of yours. I want, by Friday, to see you looking human again."

"Now you're the one who's kidding."

"Hardly," he said and turned and went crashing out the front door.

For a while I just went on sitting on my bed, violently shaking, and staring through my tears at the dusty trees and the reservoir, wondering if I was crazy, or he was. But of course I knew which twin really had The Toni, so I got up and took an Equanil (which leaves me five) and then sat down on Jonathan's bed by the phone and made several calls. The lies I'd told turned out to be true: everybody *was* fixing up for fall at the same time, and it was impossible to get a laundress or window-washer until next week. I couldn't even get through to the agency for a man to wax the floors and wash the walls, because all the lines were busy, and the same went for the cleaners, where Jonathan's winter suits have been in storage since late June. By the time I'd finally gotten the cleaners and finished making an appointment at Jean Louis' to have my hair restyled, it was pouring outside. I put down papers for Folly in our bathroom, left a note in the kitchen for Lottie that I was doing some "work" in my room and wasn't to be disturbed, to please go ahead with her other chores and I'd do this room myself today. Then I came in here and got this out and by now have written myself back to sanity. I know it isn't just the Equanil. It's now a quarter past one and the rain has stopped, but the air is thick with a kind of steam you can see rising from the wet pavements outside.

Well. This room. Then Folly's pee-papers in the bathroom. Then off I go. First to take Jonathan's navy pinstripe featherweight dacron-and-worsted to that rapid-service cleaner on Broadway: if they don't tear off all the buttons, none-the-wiser, he'll have it tonight. From there, on to the market to buy some silver polish, some Maple Crispies and *Fab*.

"DIFFERENT, WOT? And why? Your hair is now the chicque, the style," said Jean Louis, dragging his comb across my wet scalp like Mister McGregor using his rake.

"My husband wants me to try something different. He's tired of it the way it is."

"O. Heugh. That is another story," said Jean Louis, reaching for his scissors. "That already is serious. We will take care of *that*."

An hour later as he was combing me out, I dared to look in the mirror at last. "But I look like Shirley Temple, Jean Louis. Nobody wears curls any more. And it's so *short*—how much did you take off?"

Jean Louis gave some hair a vicious tug. "Wot you know. Here is the straight. But in Paris is coming back. More curl. The Laidy Look. Only two inches is gone." He reached for the hair spray. "Wait. You will see."

When the clouds of hair spray had settled, I saw: Alice the Goon with Theda Bara hair.

"*La*," said Jean Louis, posing a cupped hand in the air on either side of my head. "Is very sexy. And gamine, that look. Your husband will fall in love with you all over again. You will thank Jean Louis."

I thanked him, and rising from the chair, overtipped him—a thing I always do when upset, as I said—and fled home. It was almost five. The girls had each brought a

80

playmate home from school and barely looked up when I called hello from the doorway to their room. I started for the kitchen to talk to Lottie, and passing through the dining room, almost broke my neck on a huge wooden crate. Oh God, *now* what? I thought, bending over to rub my shin and peer at it. On top of the two trunks in the pantry, it could prove to be the straw that broke Jonathan's back. It was a giant crate of oranges and grapefruits, bearing the label of some Miami fruit-packing firm. I knew from experience that there wouldn't be a card inside. Just "J. Munvies" after the printed word "Sender" on the label. That was all. Orange and yellow globes and bits of crinkled green paper peeped out through the spaces between the slats: "Why haven't you written?" they asked; "You haven't written since late last spring." "Next week," I mumbled, and giving the crate a wide berth, went into the kitchen.

Lottie was cooking supper for the girls; she was staying overnight because we were going out. "Mrs. Balser, I'm terribly sorry about that crate in the dining room," she said as soon as I came in. "I told that expressman to leave it here, but he just went on like he was deaf and dumped it inside. It was too heavy for me to budge it, but maybe you and I could move it between us into my room now, before Mr. Balser gets home."

Astonished, I stared at her, hard, trying to make sure I'd heard right, but she placidly went on turning the chicken she was frying. In the lightest tone I could manage, I finally said, "It's really just fine where it is—Mr. Balser won't mind at *all*," and rushed off to take a bath.

In recent weeks I've begun using showers and baths as a form of hydrotherapy. It works. My new hairdo, the crate, the crate's message and the guilt it brought, my dread of the party ahead—all that floated away in water thick with bath oil. As I lay there, idly turning the hot-water tap on and off with water-puckered toes, the doorbell rang twice (the girls' friends being picked up), the phone rang three times, the girls had a screaming fight. When I finally came out, Jonathan was standing at the bureau loosening his tie, reading the closing prices in the paper opened on the bureau's marble top.

"Hi! How are you?" I was on a new campaign to be Cheery At All Times.

"Hi!" He bent close to the paper to read a tiny number. "What time does this thing of Livingston's start?"

"He said six-to-eight." Like someone unveiling a statue, I slowly lifted the puffy showercap off my hair.

"That means we should get there at seven." Still not looking up, Jonathan sighed at something on the financial page. Finally he straightened up, and rubbing his eyes, headed for the door. "It's been quite a day. Think I'll get a drink."

I was sitting on my bed, putting on my stockings, when he came back. From behind me there was a mirthless laugh and the sound of drawers being opened and shut: "Boyohboy. All we *needed* in this place was a crate of fruit. Last time your old man sent some, it was around rotting in the icebox and on windowsills for a *month*. I thought you were going to write him not to send us any more."

"I couldn't. I didn't want to hurt his feelings. Besides, it's his substitute for letters."

"Why can't he just write a letter? Or for that matter why can't *you?*"

I got up and went into my closet. "He does. And so do I."

"Yeah. About twice a year. I never have dug the relationship between the two of you, but then I guess that's one of the reasons why you had to have your head shrunk in the first place." On that profound note, he went into the bathroom to shower and shave.

I finished dressing and went to the kitchen, where the girls were happily eating their favorite dinner of southern fried chicken and corn pudding. They stopped eating when I came in. There was a stifled little silence while they took in Mudther's new hairdo and stunning *toilette*. "My, you look lovely, Missus Balser," said Loyal Lottie from the sink. The girls made several small noises and went back to their dinner. They answered my questions between bites and swallows, neither of them looking up at me again: Yes, they would take their baths after supper. Yes, they would remember to brush their teeth. *Yes*, they would turn off their lights at nine.

On my way back to the bedroom I stopped in the pantry, where I stood in the little aisle left by the trunks and poured myself a drink. The ice bucket, polished that morning, shone with a blinding light.

Jonathan was standing at the mirror in his shorts and a shirt, fixing his tie. As I passed behind him to settle in the armchair, I was reflected in the mirror. He slowly turned. ". . . Well. Well. That's an improvement, Teen. It looks kind of French. And it makes you look years younger, it really does. But if you don't mind my asking . . . where did you get that dress?"

"You bought it for me last November. Don't you remember? You saw it in some magazine."

Delicately blushing, Jonathan reached for the pants on his bed and put them on. "Oh. Yah. Now I remember." He tucked in his shirt and zipped up the pants. "And the truth is . . . I'm sorry, Teen . . . I see now I made a big mistake. I mean you've got a terrific figure, Teen. That's one thing you really *do* have, old girl. And that dress makes you look like a goddamn Druid. Don't you have anything else to wear?"

Solemn, I shook my head. "Nothing that would be comfortable in this heat, and still look autumnal, if you know what I mean."

He knew, as I knew he would: it was he who'd dinned such stuff into me. Sighing, nodding, he gave up and quickly finished dressing.

For all his recent success, Carter Livingston lived in a modest three-room apartment on the fourth floor of a very old and what I thought rather ratty brownstone in the East Fifties. As we climbed the rickety stairs, I tried not to notice how flimsy the risers were, how warped and dry the banisters were, how the whole damned building, aside from the plaster, seemed a tinderbox. Supposing someone drops a lit cigarette in a corner? I wondered, rounding the second landing. Is there a fire escape? Could forty or fifty people get down these stairs without the whole staircase collapsing? — There's nothing like a little pyrophobia.

On the fourth-floor landing a door stood open and about three or four people holding glasses were standing in the hall, the overflow from the three jammed rooms inside. As we pushed through the solidly packed mass of people in the front room, looking for our host, two more of my new and charming fears—agoraphobia and claustrophobia—came to the fore. I broke out into a nice cold sweat. It appeared that both the bar and our host were in the back room, which was just as crowded as the front room. In the corner, several people were lolling on a gigantic bed covered with a tiger-skin throw and leopard pillows. After we greeted our host, Jonathan went to get us drinks, and I stood staring out the back windows, unable to believe my eyes: though it didn't seem possible, there appeared to be no fire escape. Soon I saw that it was not only possible, it was a hard fact: there was no fire escape. And so I stood there, in the grip of three of my pet phobias—pyro, agora, claustro —until I finally realized that the only way I could stay at that party was to go back up front and station myself near the front door.

Actually, this wasn't so hard to do. As can be expected, Jonathan hates me hanging onto him at parties; separate-and-circulate is his policy. Once we had our drinks, we stopped and chatted with our host for a few minutes—he really is a very sweet man—and when he left us to greet some new arrivals, Jonathan said, "Well, *I'm* going over to talk to Graham Tilson . . ." and took off. Taking my cue, I began pushing my way through the crowd. Breathless, my heart pounding, I finally got through the crush in the front room, and glued myself to the wall opposite the door standing open to the stairs. If someone shouted Fire! I could be out of there in three seconds; if I suddenly got too dizzy or faint from the heat, the confinement or the simple presence of all those people, I could walk down four flights and stand on the sidewalk until space and fresh air revived me. Reassured, I slowly finished my drink, and soon felt heartened enough to look around. Aside from my host, I didn't know a soul. But this was a blessing, for it meant that I could stand there alone without feeling at all self-conscious, and as long as I kept my eye on the little hallway connecting the two rooms so that I could spot Jonathan before he could spot *me*, I was in pretty good shape.

The walls in the front room were covered with beautiful sketches of costumes and drawings of stage sets from plays that Carter Livingston had done. After examining these as long as I could, I steeled myself and pushed back into the other room for another drink. Jonathan stood jammed into a corner, talking to some people I didn't know. When he finally saw me, I gaily waved, and with the air of someone who has left people waiting elsewhere, busily shouldered my way back up front. In just those few minutes the crowd in the front room had thinned out considerably, and I finally began to feel conspicuous standing against the wall. Asking someone the way to the bathroom, I went in, locked the door; putting the lid down on the toilet, I sat down and leisurely sipped at my drink while I smoked two cigarettes. My phobias receded. Except for the one time someone urgently knocked and rattled the doorknob (I ignored it, and presently it subsided), everyone's bladder seemed to be holding up, and I sat there almost fifteen minutes without being disturbed. Finally, when there was a second, discreet knock, I unlocked the door for a thin timid-looking girl, and went out.

Out of habit I went back to the wall opposite the door. We'd been there almost an hour, which meant that very soon I could go and find Jonathan and say that I was hungry and wanted to leave. By now the front room was almost empty, and I was telling myself that I'd better not let Jonathan find me alone, I'd better go barging up to those people by the window, when out of the corner of my right eye I saw a man bearing down on me. The impossible had happened: someone was coming to talk to me. Slowly, assuming what I hoped was a languid expression of curiosity, I turned. The man, without so much as a glance at me, stopped three feet away, looked at his watch, and scowling, crossed his arms and settled back to wait against the wall. *My* wall. As he stood

glowering at the door, I stared at his profile, faintly
bothered: Where had I seen that face before? It was an
unnaturally pale face with regular features, topped by a
lot of straight black hair coarsely threaded with grey—
all of which sounds Byronic, but wasn't. He merely
looked unhealthy and quite unpleasant, and if he also
looked familiar, I realized, it was only because I'd seen
his picture in the papers on and off two years ago. He
was some off-Broadway playwright, whose name I
couldn't remember, even though I'd seen his awful play.

Overwhelmed by weariness and boredom, I turned
away: I had absolutely *had* it, I was going to go and get
Jonathan that very minute, and, if necessary, drag him
out of there by the collar of his navy pin-stripe featherweight dacron-and-worsted suit. Suddenly I heard a
stagey cough, and turning, found the playwright examining me. Jesus Christ! I heard him think, as he got a full
view of my Theda Bara hair and Druid dress. What he
said was: "I noticed you standing by this door on and off
all night. Did you by any chance see a tall, skinny blonde
with horn-rims come in or go out?"

"What makes you think," I said icily, "that I have
been standing by this door all night."

He blinked. His eyes were terrible—all cold, blank,
grey-white iris with tiny black holes for pupils—the
eyes of a marble statue. "You were standing here when I
came in about an hour ago, before I got trapped in back.
You were standing here when I came out, once, and
you're standing here now. Did you see her? The tall
skinny blonde."

"No."

"The horn-rims are green."

"No."

"Skinny as hell. About six foot. You couldn't miss
her."

That was clear. "*No.*"

"The lying cunt," remarked he, and walked off.

Like musical chairs, the minute he left, Jonathan came
up—beaming proudly. "*Well.* I see you were talking to
George Prager. What's he like?"

"Charming. Just fascinating— Jonathan, I'd like to

leave now. I'm starved. I'd like to go and get something to eat."

"That's why I came to find you," said Jonathan, and I finally noticed the telltale pink bursting look. "Frank Gaylord asked us to go to Sardi's with him and his . . . ah . . . assistant, this sort of Girl Friday he has."

"I'm hungry, but not that hungry, Jonathan." Frank Gaylord was a fairly well-known producer. "I mean I only wanted a sandwich, or something light like that."

"You can get a sandwich at Sardi's, for God's sake. You can get any damned thing there you want!"

At Sardi's Frank Gaylord was given the kind of table Jonathan dreams about, and this effortless coup brought a look of such awe and envy to Jonathan's face that I immediately lost my appetite. In fact, as we sat there, bathed in that refractive sort of glow the faces of the famous seem to give off, Jonathan looked so feverishly happy I began to feel ill. But a drink helped, and by the time the food came, I was able to eat my chicken sandwich. The others hungrily dug into heaps of chicken *tetrazzini* and steak *tartare*, while Gaylord, a sleek grey-haired man in his late fifties, made clear what he wanted from Jonathan: tips on the market, and some sort of avowal about investing in his new play. While he and Jonathan did all the talking, his "assistant" and I stared at each other with that perfection of loathing that can spring up between women on first sight. She was a tall olive-skinned girl named Margo, with long lank black hair and the kind of eyes that are called Sultry and seem to promise many things—things that clearly didn't all materialize in her particular case, since during coffee Frank Gaylord put a hot sweaty hand on my knee. I took it off.

When we finally reached home, it was only eleven o'clock. I got undressed and made straight for the bathroom, where I stood for fifteen minutes under the shower, letting the hot water soothe my nerves (hydrotherapy again), letting it wash fourteen dollars' worth of "styling" and hair spray down the drain. When I came out, Jonathan was sitting up in bed read-

ing what looked suspiciously like a plastic-covered playscript. As I padded past him on bare feet, leaving wet
tracks on the floor, and went into my closet for my pajamas and slippers, he said without looking up, "Don't you
think it's amazing how simple and unaffected Gaylord is,
despite all his success?"

I made a low, inarticulate sound from my closet.

"I thought she was very nice too," he continued.
"Very sweet and outgoing and bright. Do you suppose
he sleeps with her?"

I came out of the closet in my pajamas, toweling my
hair. "Are you going to invest in his play?"

"I don't know. He just gave me the script."

"So I see. Exactly when did he give it to you?"

"When we were waiting for taxis outside Sardi's.
Why? It sounds as though you don't approve."

"Approve is not the word," I said slowly, for the first
time in months saying what I really meant. "Understand
is much better. I don't understand this whole theater
kick you're on. I don't understand what you're doing. I
mean you're considered a brilliant lawyer, who has more
than enough responsibilities in his work, and yet here
you are, going off on this *tangent*, running after these
people, lapping it all up, acting in a way that I find de-
meaning, that I think belittles what you are."

Having steeled myself for a big reaction to this little
speech, I was astonished when Jonathan merely sighed,
and putting the playscript face-down on his bed,
reached for the box of smelly little cigars on his bedside
table. "Yes, I know you think all that," he said sorrow-
fully (of all things), lighting a cigar. "I know you don't
understand, and the truth is, it deeply bothers me. I
mean implicit in your not understanding are so many
other things—like your own terrible timidity, like your
inability to comprehend the dynamics of men. You don't
seem to understand that there are certain kinds of men
who can't be satisfied with being just one thing, who
have to express and fulfill themselves in many ways . . .
In the last few years I've finally let myself acknowledge
this terrific creative *urge* in myself, an urge I always
made myself ignore, put down. At first I thought that

my interest in painting and sculpture would help funnel
it off—be an outlet, so to speak—I mean if I couldn't
create such things myself I could at least *appreciate* in a
more active sort of way the creativity of others. But that
didn't quite pan out the way I'd hoped. I still felt I had
to be more involved. I happen to think the theater is one
of the few truly creative art forms left. I've discovered I
have a real feeling for the theater—and I don't mean as a
spectator enjoying a play. In fact, I must confess that
there have been times lately when I've had to ask myself
if perhaps I didn't take a wrong turning way, way back
there, if maybe I shouldn't have gone to Europe after
graduating Harvard, or just come down to New York
and messed around a year or two, trying my hand at a
few things, giving myself a chance, before I went on to
law school. Of course that kind of thinking is unproduc-
tive . . . but I'd like to think it's not too late to do something about it now. Which is what this is all about. I
mean I have this idea that maybe if I start out in the
theater on the financial end, backing a few things, I
might slowly work my way into the more active end of
things, into production . . . into all sorts of exciting
things."

All the time Jonathan had been delivering himself of
this little allocution, I'd just stood there, the towel in my
hands, water dripping off the ends of my hair and plas-
tering my pajamas to my shoulders. I was afraid that if I
opened my mouth, like Gerald McBoing-Boing, terrible
inhuman sounds would come out—brakes screeching,
metal clashing, tires skidding, trains roaring past in the
night.

Staring, Jonathan broke the silence: "What the hell
did you do to your hair?"

The power of human speech returned. "Isn't it obvious?"

Jonathan grinned. So help me, g-r-i-n-n-e-d. Yes, Boy-
ishly. "It really was pretty terrible. And I'm perfectly
willing to admit I'm wrong when I'm wrong. You look
better the old way. You have your own sort of style
which is right for you . . . Are you sore at me?"

"Don't be silly, Jonathan." I went to the bureau mirror and began combing out the tangle. As soon as I had, it was clear that the two inches Jean Louis had taken were not disastrous, in fact, they were just what was needed to get rid of the Baggy-Old-Gel-from-Smith look.

"How long is it going to take to dry?"

"About half an hour. Why?"

"I thought when it was dry we might have a little ole roll in the hay."

A WEEK AGO quoth Jonathan: ". . . things that I, as a husband and the provider around here, have every right to expect, to demand, and you, as my wife, have a duty to do."

So be it. Today was the day. All systems Go—or at least beginning to Go—laundry, trunks out, vacuuming, windows.

The day began with another quotable quote:

"Well, at last we're in business!" said Jonathan at 7:36, stepping over the piles of clothes on the kitchen floor and giving me an Approving smile. With that he poured himself some coffee and carried it into the dining room, where I'd set the table because of the mess. It was an unusually pleasant breakfast.

The agency had told me that the laundress would arrive at eight sharp, so I'd gotten up at 6:30 to unlock the trunks and sort things into piles. By the time the back doorbell rang at 9:30 I was furious. Determined to say something to that effect, I opened the door on a perfectly enormous woman, all dressed in black and carrying an equally enormous shopping bag. "How do, Missus," she said in a charming singsong Jamaican voice, smiling dazzlingly: "I am the laundress."

"Good morning," I said, and decided not to mention the time. "I'm Mrs. Balser. Won't you come in?"

Trying to match her smile, I showed her into Lottie's

91

room to change. She shut the door and locked it. I nervously began rooting around through the heaps of things on the floor. After fourteen minutes by the clock above the sink, she came out looking like a character dressed by Cecil Beaton for a musical set in the West Indies. The black coat was replaced by a tentlike brilliantly flowered sort of muu-muu, the trim black oxfords by bunion-bulgy old tennis sneakers, the staid black hat by a stocking-pink scarf, tied Aunt Jemimy-style about her head. "Can I have a cup of coffee, Missus?" she asked, smiling that smile, having apparently forgotten my name. "I didn't have time for breakfast this day."

"Of course," I said and wildly clattered out a cup and saucer, telling myself not to get excited, I could explain what had to be done while she drank her coffee. But when she was finally seated at the formica table, coffee and honey-buns in front of her, she left her coffee to cool and opened her black purse and lit a cigarette. Her attitude was so forbidding, and the look she gave me so plainly demanded privacy, that I got out of there, fast. For fifteen minutes I sat on my bed, trying to ignore the faint heat-lightning sort of flickers on one side of my head, and the way my hands were beginning to twitch. Finally I stood up, announced "This is *crazy!*" to Folly, who still hadn't been walked, and went back to the kitchen.

As I came in, the laundress gave a massive sigh and pushed back her chair. She set her cup, saucer and plate on the edge of the sink. Then she slowly turned, and putting her hands on her riotously-flowered hips, cased the piles of what were mostly Jonathan's summer clothes on the floor. "Missus," she finally said, looking up at me and smiling that smile. "Missus, you expect me to get through all that today?"

I did. "Well. It really isn't as much as it looks. And of course that pile near the door, those woolen things, are going out to the cleaners. I thought I'd put out everything and let you do as much as you could."

Giving a grunt, she bent down and began to pick through the clothes with such a strange finicky air, I felt ashamed. It made me think the clothes reeked of perspir-

ation and BO and I'd missed it—I'd sorted them myself,
and they'd only smelled faintly of the sea and beach to
me. While she poked with just two fingers through a
pile of madras things belonging to Jonathan, I explained
how the washing machine and dryer worked. I also explained that though the madras pile and another pile by
the icebox could go in the machine, the madras pile had
to be done on Lukewarm, so the clothes wouldn't
"bleed" too much, and that the small pile by the stove
(Jonathan's Lacoste shirts, some washable white flannel
tennis shorts, a Swiss cotton robe) were to be rinsed out
by hand and hung on the drying rack in Lottie's bath-
tub, and would be ironed some other time by "someone
else." Of course I hadn't the least idea who I meant. Beginning to stutter by that point, I also explained that
though it did look like a lot to do, it really wasn't: none
of the bathing trunks needed ironing, for instance, and
there were a lot of bathing trunks. Thoroughly unnerved by her glum silence, I then showed her where the
ironing board and iron were kept and fled to the bathroom to take two aspirins. The flickering sensations in
my head were beginning to feel exactly like the first
phase of my old migraines.

When I came out, Folly was barking hysterically and
the back doorbell was ringing without letup as someone
leaned on the button. I burst breathlessly into the
kitchen, where the laundress was calmly stuffing clothes
into the machine. "I never opens other people's doors,"
she explained while I dashed past to open the back door.

A tall, surly-looking dark-haired boy holding a pailful
of equipment stood by the garbage can and empty soda
bottles. The window-washer I'd engaged for today and
forgotten. Smiling, I said good morning, but he wordlessly strode past me in grimy high-laced work boots,
trampling sweaters and flannel slacks and summer blankets underfoot. He filled his pail in Lottie's bathroom
and I showed him into the dining room. While he
pushed up the right-hand window and began to unlock
the safety bar, I explained that I wanted him to do this
part of the apartment first and slowly work his way up
front. Looking surlier than ever, he put the window bar

on the floor, stepped onto the sill and began hooking himself outside. Though I had more instructions, I was overcome by a huge dizzying wave of hypsophobia as I stared at him, his boots balanced on the narrow sill, his rear end dangling in outer space. When he leaned back, testing his belt, I rushed to the bedroom and took an Equanil (which leaves only four), then collapsed in the armchair. Folly gave me a long begging look from the foot of my bed. "Soon, baby, soon," I promised and guiltily shut my eyes. Not only was I too damned dizzy to walk her—I was also afraid to go out and leave those two types alone in the apartment. It was sheer paranoia and I knew it, but in a leap of the imagination that out-soared any agency clauses about "Bonded Help," I saw the laundress (who by now terrified me) going into the pantry and stuffing Jonathan's beloved James Robinson silver into her enormous shopping bag, saw the window-washer going to Jonathan's chest of drawers and stuffing Jonathan's gold cuff links, gold lighter and gold cigarette case into the pockets of his stained coverall.

I was so ashamed of myself I opened my eyes. The room had stopped spinning. Sobered, I was forced to admit that Jonathan was probably right: I had damned well better go and "see" someone—Popkin, anyone—because I'd never pull myself out of this without help. But no sooner had I thought this than I was furious. I jumped out of the armchair, and still ignoring Folly's pleading looks—Lottie would be arriving in twenty minutes—went to the phone. In a grim mood I made the rest of the calls I'd put off, making the necessary arrangements for the drapes to be rehung, the rugs relaid, the walls washed, et cetera. By the time I'd finished I was no longer shaking, which I attributed to the lucky combination of Equanil and Resolve, and I was just about to start getting dressed when the phone rang. It was Sally Willard, who'd had the excruciating "curse cramps" the night Jonathan got back from Wichita. Her wry-dry tone undid all the little amenities (". . . been so long," "meant to call long before this") and I could hear Jack Willard saying wearily, "Yes, we've *got* to have them."

"Eight o'clock, semi-dressy," Sally concluded.

"Just what does that mean, Sally?" I asked timidly.

"It means not black tie but almost."

I hung up and cried for five minutes, and when I was done, my eyes were so swollen I looked Oriental, looked quite the Mongolian Idiot. I splashed cold water on my face and began to dress. I was in my brassiere and a pair of pants when there was a knock at the door. "Who is it?" I called above Folly's barking.

"Window-cleaner."

"Don't come in!" I shrieked and stared at the key in the lock: if I turned it he would hear me. I had a flash vision of myself being shoved back on Jonathan's bed and raped, and I stepped forward and turned the key with a loud click. "What do you want?"

"Newspapers, lady," he said with sublime disgust. "The guardrails you have on the windows up front here are too rusty to lay on the floor."

This from someone I'd seen as a potential rapist and thief. I looked at the clock. Lottie would be in. "Go in the kitchen," I called through the door. "A lady there —not the laundress—will give you all the newspapers you need."

Mumbling something I couldn't hear, he went away. I quickly finished dressing, unlocked the door, and headed for the kitchen to say good morning to Lottie and tell her I was going to walk Folly. The laundress stood at the sink, violently rubbing one of Jonathan's Lacoste shirts up and down on a zinc scrubboard I had deliberately not put out. Lottie was at the broom closet, taking out our battered old Electrolux (Jonathan has promised to give me money for a new one for over a year). The washing machine was making a loud threshing noise. "Good morning, Lottie," I shouted, and she straightened up and turned, wanly smiling and murmuring a good morning that was drowned out by the washing machine.

"Lottie," I said, still shouting, gesturing towards the laundress at the sink, "this is, this is . . ."

"Nina," said the laundress in a normal voice, for the washing machine had shifted cycles with a click. Now it was making the peculiar humming it went into before pouring rinse water out. "We already introduced ourselves, Missus," said the laundress, not turning to face us, rub-a-dubbing away.

"How nice," said I, noting there was nothing nice in the air of that room; there was, in fact, a hostility so thick it almost had a smell.

Lottie wordlessly picked up the vacuum and went into the dining room. I stared at the broad flowered back where the muscles were bunched with the exertion involved in rubbing the balled-up shirt. I took a deep breath. "Nina. I have a . . . favor to ask."

"Yes, Missus?" The rub-a-dub stopped; the smile under the bandanna flashed radiantly.

". . . I wonder if you'd mind not using that board for those shirts. I mean they're awfully delicate and stretch out of shape so easily. I mean I washed them myself all summer, and only used lukewarm water and never even wrung them out."

The laundress chuckled. "That explain the spots. Missus, these shirts they full of spots. Rubbing's the only way you get at the spots."

"Yes. Well," I said, raising my voice above the whine of the vacuum in the dining room. "My husband's very fussy and will be very upset if those shirts are stretched."

"He very fussy, he don't want any spots. I know my business, Missus," she continued, resuming her rubbing as a torrential roar from the washing machine drowned out the rest of what she said.

Trembling, I went to find Folly. Behind me the vacuum droned. As I passed the den, the window-washer was swaying on his belt outside the window, his squeegee making a high squeak on the glass. I'd planned to spend the day at home, doing some work myself—cleaning closets, drawers—while these major chores were getting done, but I suddenly knew that I had to get out of that nuthouse, even if it was for just an hour.

I walked Folly in a record five minutes, the poor dog being too desperate by then to be choosy about the dusty gutters of Central Park West. Back upstairs, I went to tell Lottie I was going out for a while, but the vacuum lay silent in the dining room. I found her in the kitchen, where the laundress had finished with the sink, and she was stacking the breakfast dishes for washing—a chore she always does first. The laundress was taking things out of the washing machine and stuffing them in the dryer. After explaining that I was going out (I still had no idea where I was going to go), I asked Lottie to sign the window-washer's receipt and fix the laundress some lunch.

"I always bring my own lunch, Missus," said the laundress, slamming the dryer door. "All I'll be needing is a cup of tea."

"Fine. Then Lottie will show you where the cups and teabags are," I said and quickly got out of there. On my way to the front door, I saw the window-washer in the den, standing and looking down at the clutter on Jonathan's desk as he wiped his squeegee with a rag. I'd already noticed what a good job he'd done on the windows in the kitchen and dining room, and in a sudden spasm of remorse for those sick little rape-and-robbery fantasies, I rushed in and pressed several singles into his hand—the same old overtip-when-upset tic. To my horror, he looked slowly from the bills to me, and faintly smiling, slipped them into his pocket without so much as a thank-you: naturally he had heard the key turn in the lock.

Once on the street, I stood blinking around. It was close to noon and nearly ninety degrees. I was hardly dressed for downtown in my cotton dress and sandals, but I couldn't think of any cool and restful place uptown where I could spend an hour. An air-conditioned movie was out: I was sure that at that time of day all the movie houses would be just crawling with the dregs of humanity—junkies, perverts, lady-molester types. But where? I stared at the park, and suddenly, just as if I'd been given X-ray vision and could see through all those dense, parched trees, I "saw" the Metropolitan Museum. I considered the idea of going there without any enthusiasm. I hadn't been there since the days we'd lived on Seventy-seventh Street, when I'd dragged the girls there on boring rainy or snowy afternoons to look at the mummies or suits of armor. (That little prescription of Jonathan's: "Think of the assets! Think of the Metropol-

itan Museum!") I hadn't been there to really look at
paintings since my Sullivan Street days, which made it
about fourteen years. In fact, I suddenly realized, aside
from my more or less social excursions to openings at
the Guggenheim and the Modern Museum and a few
galleries with Jonathan, I hadn't voluntarily gone *any*-
where to look at paintings for fourteen years. I put up
my hand and hailed a cab.

It was an inspired choice. The museum was cool as a
cave, and after the loony din of the washing machine and
vacuum cleaner and Folly's barking, it was as hushed as a
cathedral, the soft pittering of feet on stone the only
sound. The clopping of my sandals seemed to make a
tremendous racket, and I thought a few people stared at
me, but I soon forgot it as I roamed from room to room,
happy when I came on some old favorites—Rembrandt's
Lady with a Pink, the Vermeer, the Patinir with the
quiet corners—just as happy when I didn't. After about
three-quarters of an hour of this I was human again,
calm and tired enough to want to sit down and smoke a
cigarette. I remembered a little smoking room on the
museum's south end, and set off in search of it. After a
lot of false turns, I finally found it, a pleasant airy place
with big ceiling-to-floor windows overlooking the park.
When I'd last been there, two worn velvet couches,
placed at right angles to the windows, had faced each
other across a distance of twenty feet; re-covered in
plastic, the couches were now placed at right angles to
each other, so that one had its back to the view. To my
great annoyance, someone was sitting smack in the middle of each couch. On the one with its back to the window, a stocky woman with clipped white hair sat busily
writing in a spiral notebook. On the other, a small balding grey-haired man sat fighting off sleep, the eyes behind his steel-rimmed glasses blinking heavily. Though I
was tired, I wasn't tired enough to want to sit next to
either of them, so I stationed myself at the window
where the casement was opened to the air, and lit a cigarette.

In the parking lot below, cars burningly refracted
sunlight. Beyond, on the path leading in from Fifth Ave-

nue, all the benches were filled with men in shirtsleeves, women in summer dresses, nurses rocking baby carriages with hoods up against the midday glare. And beyond the path, in the park, the grass was swarming with children and dogs, the steep slope of a hill was covered with people lying stretched out on the ground—lovers, girls sunbathing, men sleeping with tents of newspapers over their heads.

It struck me as being such an agreeable, cheerful scene that I stood there, smiling—a thing I am not exactly given to doing nowadays—feeling almost happy, until I finally smelled my cigarette, which had burned right down to the filter. Sighing, I turned to look for an urn, and finding one just behind me, bent to bury the smoldering cork tip in the sand. When I straightened up I saw that the white-haired schoolteacher-type had gone, and that the little man had fallen completely asleep, his head thrown back, eyes closed, the hands plunged in his jacket pockets, pulling the jacket about him as if he were cold. At least that's what an idle glance showed. But something jarring made me take another look, and then I saw. Saw the glitter of the eyes behind the slitted lids, the seeping red of his face, saw what he had taken from his unzipped pants and had framed between the flaps of his jacket.

I blinked. I looked again. I blinked and looked again. No, no mistaking that. And then, instead of gasping or screaming, instead of becoming frightened or enraged—either being a reaction the poor little man needed, had worked for—I burst out laughing. I couldn't help it. Something clicked in my head, *clicked*, mind you, not snapped. Rembrandt and Vermeer and Uncle Pee Pee: yes. It all fit, made sense. In the mad world my new perceptions made me inhabit, they complemented each other, were necessary parts of the whole, and I was laughing at the sheer rightness of it all. Well. As I said, the little man had obviously counted on quite another reaction, which he needed for his poor sick kick; when, still laughing, I left the window and headed, he thought, for him, he slumped down, cringing, covering himself up, clearly terrified—as if I were the one who were mad and possibly dangerous. But of course I merely walked on past him, and graciously inclining my head like a dowager at a tea party, said, "Congratulations!" and continued on out through the galleries, out of the museum.

Utterly lucid and calm and cheerful (it was a world I was beginning to understand), I took a taxi home. It was twenty-five past one and I was starved. Letting myself into the apartment with my key, I headed straight for the kitchen to make a sandwich, but as I pushed at the closed swinging door to the pantry, it slammed up against something and there was a muffled exclamation. Since I'd sent the emptied trunks down to the storeroom first thing that morning, I couldn't imagine what was in there, blocking my way. What it turned out to be was Lottie standing on a stepladder. Once she'd opened the door from the inside, I stared, bewildered, at the stacks of china and glassware she'd taken down off the cupboard shelves and put on the counter; the shelves were all wet and bubbly with soap. "You didn't have to do this today, Lottie," I said slowly, as she climbed back up the ladder, sponge in hand. "I only meant for you to vacuum today."

"Well, I finished the vacuuming early and thought I'd start on this today," she said firmly. Puzzled by something unusual in her face and manner, I decided not to interfere, and went on into the kitchen.

Nina, the laundress, was sitting at the table, reading the morning *Times* and eating the largest hero sandwich I have ever seen. In front of her was an empty soup bowl, the quart thermos from which the soup had been poured, and a chocolate éclair on a plate. "My, that looks delicious," I said, trying to ignore the baleful look she gave me. I went to the icebox.

"I always bring my own food," she said behind me. "You never believe what some people gives a day-worker to eat."

Supposing her to mean something like the ham and Swiss cheese I had taken out of the icebox, I said nothing, and began to make my sandwich as quickly as I could. As I set myself a tray, I tried not to notice the bundle of dry madras clothes balled-up on top of the washing machine. Two pairs of madras shorts and one madras shirt lay finished on the ironing board, and what was to have been the second load for the washing machine was still lying where I'd left it, in a heap on the floor. She's probably taking great pains with Jonathan's white flannel tennis shorts, I told myself. She's probably finishing up the hand laundry, I added, and in a silence broken only by the rattle of dishes on my tray, went to my room. There, at least, all was dazzle and order. Sun poured through the sparklingly clean windows onto spotless floors and sills, and the air was filled with the sweet resinous smell of furniture polish. How had marvelous Lottie managed to get it all done? Feeling better again, I ate my lunch, and read the telephone messages Lottie had left for me. One was from Miss Brekker, Jonathan's secretary, saying that Jonathan had had to go to Philadelphia for the day, and would not be home until late that night. One was from Mrs. Jocelyn downstairs, inviting the girls to go to Jones Beach on Saturday with her and her girls. (Jones Beach in October!) And the third was from Mrs. Marks, the wife of Mr. Marks of Hoddison and Marks, inviting us to dinner sometime in November—light-years away, thank God.

Passing through the pantry with my tray, I told Lottie how wonderful the place looked. "Did you ever take time off for some lunch?" I asked.

"I'm not hungry today, Mrs. Balser," she said, muffled, her head inside the top shelf.

What the hell is going *on*? I wondered, and went on into the kitchen, which was deserted, the laundress nowhere in sight. All the dirty plates from her lunch still sat on the table, and the madras pile still lay dry, unsprinkled for ironing—in short, all was as I'd left it twenty minutes ago. Mind your own business, she knows her business, I grimly told myself, and went about the job of freezing the leg of lamb I had planned for our dinner; now that Jonathan wasn't coming I would take the girls out. As I tried to make room for it in a freezer jammed with Jonathan's latest Saturday gourmet-shopping (frozen *coq au vin*, frozen *blanquette de veau*, etc.) the toilet flushed in Lottie's bathroom, the sink taps ran interminably, and Nina the laundress finally came out. Without so much as a look at me, she plugged in the iron, took a handful of things from the top of the dryer, sprinkled them at the sink, and then began to iron a madras shirt. Finding the iron not hot enough, she put it upend on the board, and stood, arms crossed, waiting, watching me clear her dishes off the table.

"Nina," I said, my shaking hands clattering the dishes. "Do you think you'll get to run a second load today?"

Wetting her finger with her tongue, the laundress poked it at the iron where it went s-s-s-t. "I do that, Missus, and I never leave here till eight o'clock."

"Oh dear," I said. "I'm sorry to hear that. I mean the last laundress we had managed to do two loads by five o'clock."

She extended a massive arm and savagely yanked out the iron plug, but the face she turned to me was utterly bland. "Missus," she said, setting the iron flat on its asbestos stand, "I think I be going now."

My heart began to whir like the refrigerator motor, which had just started up. "Yes," I said faintly. "Yes, I think that would be best."

From under her gay and kindly Aunt Jemimy bandanna, she suddenly glowered at me. "You still has to pay the agency for the full day. And my carfare. You has to give me that."

"I have every intention of paying what I owe," I said coldly, growing more enraged by the minute.

She grunted, chuckled, shook her head, and then, giving that terrifyingly radiant smile, went into Lottie's room and shut the door, turning the key in the lock. Trembling, not wanting to encounter Lottie, I went through the dining room to get my wallet, and returned the same way. My legs were so rubbery I had to sit down at the kitchen table. As I sat there, looking at the heap of dirty clothes in the middle of the floor, at the unironed things near the sink, wondering how I would ever get them finished and put away for next summer, the key scrabbled in the lock and the laundress came out. She was back in her sober black clothes, carrying the

enormous shopping bag, and was now so filled with fury
that her breath came in short gasps. "You people think
we are cattle. Arnimals. You think you can treat us any
way, but one day soon they come a reckoning and you
will *see.*"

A pure calm descended: here at least was one thing I
was clear on. "You have no right to talk to me like that.
You have no idea what I think, and this has nothing to
do with the issues you're trying to drag in. This has to
do with one thing and one thing only—doing a job you
have contracted to do properly. You have not done
that."

Huffing, she said, "I never worked for a lady before
keep hanging and snooping around like you. You been
spying on me ever since I came through that door. You
and that ole lady you got working for you."

And you, I told myself, think *you're* paranoid. "The
agency always bills me. How much do I owe you for
carfare?"

"Two dollars. I live way up in the Bronx."

Weary of this, I handed her two dollars, and after a
terrible moment when I thought she might smash me in
the head with the shopping bag or spit in my face, she
snatched the money and slammed out the back door.

When I finally heard the back elevator come and take
her away, I picked the dirty clothes off the floor and
stuffed them in the washing machine: I would put everything, unironed, into storage boxes, and not think
about them until next spring. As I was sprinkling soap
into the machine, Lottie came in from the pantry for a
drink of water, perspiring heavily from her work in the
airless shelves. I shut the door, but before turning on the
machine with all its noise, said, embarrassed: "The laundress left. We had a little disagreement. I thought I'd
finish up myself." Looking enormously relieved, Lottie
put down her glass of water and wiped her face with a
Kleenex. "That woman was a terrible crook, Mrs. Balser."

I smiled. "Well, I did feel she was taking advantage of
me. I mean I know how some laundresses eke out the
time, but she . . . well, she was ludicrous."

"More than that. She was a thief."

"Thief? What on earth do you mean, Lottie?"

"I mean I caught her stealing. I was up front, cleaning your room, when I ran out of fresh rags for the furniture polish. I came back here for some, and there she was, stuffing things in that ee-normous old shopping bag."

"Things. What kinds of things?"

"Oh, some boxes of soap powders, some of those fancy canned goods Mr. Balser buys, some of those brand-new huck towels you got for the good china. Nothing much, I guess, but enough."

Indeed. "But what did you *do?*"

"I told her to put those things straight back, else I'd call the police."

"But weren't you afraid? I mean she was twice your size, and ugly, and there you were in the kitchen with all those knives."

Lottie burst out laughing. "No, I wasn't afraid, Mrs. Balser. Not of *her*. I had her number the minute I came in and saw her with all her Island airs. Time I said about the police she started crying and whimpering, saying she had this sick husband to support, calling me Sister all the time, telling me we had to stick together. *Sister.*" Now it was quiet Lottie who looked about to spit. "After all those airs, trying to pull that on me. As if her color would make me forget what she was—rotten, evil through and through. Her skin be white as snow and she be what she is."

Speechless, I stared at this Lottie who had never said so much, and who I knew would never say so much again. Then I said, slowly smiling, "And that's why you're doing the pantry shelves. You were guarding the silver."

Smiling too, Lottie nodded. Then, strangely embarrassed, reading my mind, she said, "I guess you're wondering why I didn't say anything when you came in—tell you, so you could send her away."

Also embarrassed, but clearly for different reasons, I confessed, "Well, yes . . . why didn't you?"

By now Lottie's embarrassment was so great she

couldn't look at me, and she bent her head to rub at a nonexistent spot on her uniform. "Well, you see, I know that Mr. Balser's been wanting those trunks out of here. I guess I know because one night he came home early when I was cooking in here, and I couldn't help but hear him when he was in the pantry getting himself a drink, kicking at those trunks and talking to himself . . ."

Oh my *God*.

". . . I wanted to offer to do those things myself," continued Lottie-of-the-bent-head, "but I know that Mr. Balser doesn't like my ironing and you would probably only have to get someone in to do them all over next spring. Well, that woman came today, and I figured that as long as she was here, thief or not, she might as well stay on and be of some help to you—help you get these things out—while I kept my eye on her."

I was so mortified I was near tears. I went for the pack of cigarettes I always keep by the toaster. There were two cigarettes left. It had been a full pack that morning. Lottie doesn't smoke. "It isn't that he doesn't like your ironing, Lottie," I finally said, exhaling smoke. "I wish you wouldn't think of it that way. I mean I wish you would think of it more as just the fact that he's got a thing about his clothes, that he's just a man who's unusually fussy about his clothes."

"I don't mind, Mrs. Balser. I never have. My husband's the same way about what he eats. The only thing is all this laundry. Tomorrow's my day off, but what I'd like to do is come in anyway and get all this finished for you. I could get that done and all the silver too."

The silver. Had she overheard Jonathan on *that?* Briskly I said, "I won't hear of it, Lottie. What I'll do now is help you finish those pantry shelves, and all these things are going, unironed, into boxes until next spring."

And that was what we did. For two and a half hours we scrubbed and rubbed and washed plates and glassware and put things in boxes and carted them to the basement storeroom downstairs. The girls, arriving home, were a bit bewildered by all this, but I put them to work on their homework so that it would be done before we went out to dinner. We ate at Dillman's Delicatessen on Seventy-second Street, a place we all love but Jonathan has grown to loathe. Happy, stuffed with pastrami and pickles, they were in bed and asleep by nine. Strangely jazzed up and not tired from the housework, I got this from the storage vault and brought it into the den, the one cool room in the house. It's now 11:00, and I'd better stop before Jonathan returns from Philadelphia and finds me scribbling away at what I would tell him was a letter to my parents—the one so long overdue.

I've been writing this at Jonathan's desk, with its elegant clutter of Things. His silver perpetual calendar and silver thermometer from Tiffany's are gone. There's no way of telling whether it was the laundress or the window-washer, though when I left for the museum the window-washer was standing and looking at this desk. Whoever, whichever, I'm simply going to dash down to Tiffany's tomorrow and replace them both—much easier and less painful than the fuss with the agencies Jonathan would make me go through. Now I really am exhausted and completely limp from the heat. It must be in the eighties. Will normal autumn weather *ever* come?

IT CAME. The cold weather. Three days after the last entry in here, too soon, too abruptly, from Indian Summer to bitter cold. Luckily I'd gotten Jonathan's things out of storage in the nick of time, but on Monday, the second day of the changed weather, he took one look at the girls setting off for school in thin cotton dresses covered with sweaters and raincoats for warmth, and Thundered, "Why the hell didn't you get their warm stuff up from the basement yesterday afternoon?" Why indeed: "yesterday" had been a Sunday, and though I could easily have gone down there while he was out with the girls, I'd been too damned frightened to go alone. Even on weekdays our basement is a spooky place with endless dark crannies—storerooms, a laundry room with defunct machines, and a furnace room that looks like a set for *The Hairy Ape*. No one's ever around, not even the super or a handyman. And ever since that gory murder this summer, where some poor Bronx woman was raped and stabbed in the basement of her building, and stuffed in the cold furnace with her feet dangling out ("The badly decomposed nude body was discovered by Mr. Otto Gruzenhauser, the superintendent, who told this reporter . . ."), wild horses couldn't drag me down to our basement alone.

This being something I couldn't exactly tell Jonathan, I said as authoritatively as I could, "I'm going to bring up all their warm clothes today. Since there's too much to carry, I had it scheduled for today, when Lottie could help me. And since everything else is *scheduled* to get done this week and next, I'll thank you to drop that critical tone and leave me alone, Jonathan."

Once committed, I was as good as my word. Two weeks have passed since I last wrote in here. The drapes have been hung, the rugs relaid, the floors waxed, the walls washed down, the closets cleaned and filled with everybody's winter clothes. And I managed all sorts of extras besides. I attended a meeting at the Bartlett School to help plan the annual Christmas Fair. I took the girls shopping for winter coats. Because there was a case of hepatitis at their school, I took the girls to Doctor Miller for shots of gamma globulin, and to make up for that, took them and two friends to lunch and the movies the next day, a Saturday. I wrote a letter to my parents, enclosing snaps of me and the girls taken in one of those machines at Woolworth's. I even went to the dentist, but that didn't go off as smoothly as everything else. I made the mistake of taking two Equanils (leaving me two), and when he injected the novocaine it occurred to me that Equanil and novocaine might be incompatible, that the combination might produce a lethal toxicity that would stop my heart. Luckily that didn't happen, but I sat there with a rubberized cheek while he pried off the old inlay and began to drill, entertaining a new possibility: the supersonic drill would hit the nerve, I'd scream and jump and the drill would rip my whole mouth apart. I finally left with a temporary filling and an appointment for the following week (yesterday), wrung out, but damned proud of myself—like everything else, I was getting it *done*. And, I may add, on top of getting everything done, I went to two parties and three openings with Jonathan, and managed to look so *comme il faut* for all of them that he remarked, "It's wonderful to see you coming around, Teen. It's a relief to see you beginning to look and act like your old self!"

Which of course was what this was all about. I'd thought that if I made a gigantic effort for a while (and it was gigantic, taking all my pills and strength), I might get let off the hook, have time to coast and collect my really still-shattered nerves.

Ha.

Two nights ago we spent our first quiet evening home together in weeks. That is, Jonathan wasn't working, we all had dinner together like a normal family, and afterwards, for the first time in God knows how long, he didn't lock himself in the den to work or make phone calls. Though he did end up in the den, it was to watch some old Jimmy Stewart movie, which I watched too, a little unnerved by the novelty of sitting quietly side by side with my husband on a couch in our own home, just staring at a TV screen, as moronically content as a couple of million other Americans. Or so I thought. I had no idea how bored and restless he'd really been until we were getting ready for bed.

"I thought we had so many dates," he said as he undressed.

"We do, but they don't really get started until the end of this week. After Saturday things get under way."

"What's Saturday?"

"Charlotte Rady's party."

"Ah. I forgot all about that." Warming himself at this like someone at a fire, Jonathan smiled and went to his closet for his pajamas. Coming back out, he put them on the bed, and finished undressing, a bemused, thoughtful expression on his face. "I want you to go out and get a new dress for her party," he said, stepping out of his underwear shorts.

I was already in bed, and had been trying, without success, to read *Lady Chatterley's Lover*, which, for some reason, I'd never read. The book was Jonathan's, bought back in his Harvard days. I lowered the book and stared at him, naked, stepping into his pajama pants. The small pot I had noticed the other day seemed a little bigger. "I don't need a new dress, Jonathan," I said quietly.

He stood balanced on one leg, poking the other into his pants, and glared at me like an angry stork. "Now you can't tell me that's normal," he said softly, and, swaying, put down the leg even though it was just halfway in the pajamas. "Nobody can tell me that's a normal feminine reaction. Why, most women would jump for joy if their husbands told them to go out and buy a new dress. But you . . . you act like I'd insulted you, like I'd attacked your goddamn integrity."

"I'm only being practical." I spoke quietly, but I was shaking with anger. "I should think you'd appreciate a wife who doesn't want to waste your money. I have several perfectly good dresses you told me to buy last year."

"Well, this is *this* year, and you let me be the one to worry about the lousy money." He pulled up his pajama pants, almost bisecting himself when he tied the drawstring. "I'm asking you to do a very simple thing. I'm asking you to go out and get a new dress for Charlotte Rady's party. I want you to do it. You understand?"

I understood. I understood that unless I wanted to divorce Jonathan, or have Jonathan divorce me, I had to jump when he said Jump. Since the very word divorce brought on an avalanche of bewilderment (Why? How did we *get* here? What happened? etc.), and since I went into a tailspin at just the very thought of trying, in my current condition, to go it alone with the girls (provided, that is, I got them) and to cope with all the problems of existence by myself, I knew I would jump. And jump and jump. Until maybe, by some miracle, Jonathan stopped saying Jump. So I assured Jonathan that I'd get a new dress the very next day, and while he went into the bathroom, I went back to D. H. Lawrence, and presently came upon this:

> What is more, she felt she had always really disliked him. Not hate: there was no passion in it. But a profound physical dislike. Almost it seemed to her, she married him because she disliked him, in a secret, physical sort of way. But of course, she had married him really because in a mental way he attracted her and excited her. He had seemed, in some way, her master, beyond her.

I read it three times, and was going over it a fourth when Jonathan came out of the bathroom and got into bed. I sat gripping the book, waiting: it was exactly the sort of ironic moment for him to propose a Roll in the Hay. It never failed. But incredibly it did: "That movie made me so sleepy I can't even keep my eyes open," he said, and turning out his light, rolled over so that he faced the door. I went back and read the passage once more. I then went on, until I reached a passage where Connie Chatterley and Mellors spend a lovely afternoon in the leaves; suddenly unable to keep my eyes open myself, I dropped the book, turned off the light, and sank into a deep marvelous sleep.

I woke up to a beautiful day. (Yesterday.) It was a typical October day, all brilliant golds and blues, with a humming sort of excitement and snap in the air, the kind of day that has every radio disc jockey playing Cy Walters' "Autumn in New York." It was a day to walk in the park, to sit in the open-air cafeteria by the boat basin, sipping a lemonade and watching the rowers on the water—a day that would find me rooting around in stuffy stores for a new dress. It was also, as it turned out, the day I had a dentist appointment to take the impression for my new inlay. When I called to cancel it, Miss Sallit acidly said that I would have to pay for the time anyway, and since I only had a temporary filling I'd better make another appointment right away. Sweetly demurring, I hung up and set about walking Folly and cleaning the house—yesterday, being a Thursday, was also Lottie's day off. By the time I got everything done, lunched, and walked Folly again, it was a quarter past one. But since each of the girls had arranged to visit a new friend after school, that still left me about three hours to find a dress before I picked them up—two hours and twenty minutes too much.

I set out. Because I was shaking, and had no pills to take, I thought that a look at some scenery might help, and told my driver to go downtown through the park. "Anything the little lady's heart desires!" said he, which ought to have warned me, but I was too busy drying my hands on a handkerchief and telling myself that any Normal Woman would jump for joy at the prospect of the afternoon ahead. Like everyone who lives in New

York and rides in cabs, I've evolved a defense against talk-ative drivers, a little system of grunts and nods that al-lows me to go on thinking my own thoughts. Dimly aware that my driver had been talking about a Negro family that had moved onto his block in Rego Park, I was concentrating on the job of lighting a cigarette with my shaking hand when we came to a red light. "The trouble is," he went on, swerving to avoid hitting a rear bumper, "they don't know their place any more. They're out to take over this whole town. The whole country—like the goddamn Jews."

A year ago, even six months ago, I would have taken my purse and slammed it down on Mr. Alvin Comfort's thick skull. I would have called him an ignoramus, a fas-cist, made speeches, and, if necessary, called the police. Yesterday, paralyzed, I blinked out at a lady astride a splendid chestnut gelding, cantering under the yellow razzle-dazzle of the leaves, and told myself it was a waste of time and breath to even try to talk to such a preju-diced moron.

The light changed; the cab started rolling. "I cried like a baby when Goldwater lost," said Mr. Comfort. "There was a man this country *needed*."

I threw my cigarette out the window. "Will you please turn in at the Tavern on the Green."

With slitted pig-eyes Mr. Comfort studied me in his rear-view mirror. "I thought you said Fifty-seventh and Fifth."

"I've changed my mind."

"Ladies," he said as the Tavern on the Green came into sight. "All day long I hafta ride ladies who change their minds every four blocks."

"And would you please shut up for the last minute of this ride."

Mr. Comfort was busy turning into the driveway of the restaurant. But as he swung the cab in an arc to pull up at the door, he swiveled his head around, glaring: "Whasamatter? You dint like what I said?" By some miracle the cab came to a lurching stop, just avoiding climbing the curb and knocking over one of the canopy's stanchions.

"That's the idea," I said through my teeth, counting out the exact amount on the meter. A doorman was coming to open the door.

With his head still screwed around on his thick red neck, Mr. Comfort showered me with spittle: "It's people like you who are ruining this country!"

I threw an assortment of coins into the front seat and climbed out of the cab.

"*Communist cunt!*" shrieked Mr. Comfort through the rolled-down front window. Then, true to type, he took off with a roar of his motor and a squeal of tires.

People lunching behind the plate-glass window of the restaurant sat gaping, knives and forks poised midair.

"I got his number, Miss," the doorman said softly. "Would you like to write it down?"

"All I'd like," I said, shaking my head and turning my back on all those faces, "is another cab."

Luck was with me this time. The next driver wore a hearing aid, and I drove in blessed silence all the way to Fifth Avenue and Fifty-seventh Street.

To save time, I'd picked a few stores within a two-block radius. Steeling myself, I pushed through the nearest revolving door and the nightmare began. In every store the same lady came crawling out of the zinced *boiserie,* or reluctantly hauled herself out of a gilt bandy-legged chair: spiritual cousins of Mrs. Prinz but possessed of more gristle, Widow Ladies of a Certain Age, they all had the same gimlet eyes, carefully made-up hatchet faces, dyed hair, and Basic Black dresses worn with one Good Jewel. To each I would murmur my little set piece about the very simple sort of dress I wanted, adding "anything except black." After hours in the stockroom each would reappear carrying drifts of beaded, spangled, feathered dresses in violent purples, greens and reds. Despairing—it was getting later and later—I would timidly retire to the dressing rooms, where, trying on the least obnoxious offering, ignoring the croony hard-sell "It *does* something for you, could've been *made* for you," I would finally dispatch old Widow Lady out for some more. When she'd gone, I would sit down on the bandy-legged chair, trying to ignore the three-way reflection of Alice the Goon, whose skin sickly glimmered, and who had on a nylon slip with lace so worn it was fuzzy and a brassiere that looked too small. Finally I would realize W. L. wasn't coming back, and would put on my clothes and go.

At 4:32, in the fifth store, I was looking at a three-way reflection of myself in a very low-cut black dress and W. L. was crooning, "It *does* something for you"—when I suddenly broke out into a thick cold sweat and my ears began to tweetily sing. "I'll take it," I mumbled, and getting out of the dress as fast as I could, sat down. "We have no returns in this department," snappishly warned W. L., all business now. "I know," I said, and gave her the charge and asked her to wrap it up so I could take it along: after going through all this, it was crazy to risk not getting it in time for Charlotte Rady's party Saturday night.

Of course the minute I was out on the wind-swept sidewalk, the bulky box under my arm, I knew that I loathed the dress and might just as well have flushed $150.00 down the toilet. The temperature had undergone a violent change in the hours I'd been shopping. Buffeted by freezing wind, I stood on the street corner thinking of some of the things $150.00 would buy: six CARE packages, ten months' support for a Foster Child in South Korea or Hong Kong—or even, coming closer to home, a new Electrolux with all the latest attachments. I clenched my chattering teeth and wondered if I had the nerve to go back upstairs; the policy of no-returns could hardly apply to a ten-minute interval. I not only did not have the nerve, I also saw by the clock across the avenue that it was five to five, and that I'd be late getting the girls as it was: Liz was to be picked up at five at Eighty-third and Park, Sylvie at five-fifteen at Eighty-ninth and East End.

After ten minutes I saw I wasn't going to get a cab, and walked over to Madison Avenue and fought my way onto a crowded bus, only to be ordered off by the swearing driver, who wouldn't break my five-dollar bill. I walked seven blocks before I found a stationery store that would give me change. There were still no cabs, so I climbed aboard another jammed Madison Avenue bus, where my huge box knocked off a lady's mink hat and she stood up and began to scream at me in French.

At twenty-five past five, I was shown into a sumptuous hexagonal hall by a starchy maid and told to wait. Finally there were footsteps, and Liz appeared in one of the endless doorways off the hall, accompanied by a tall gaunt woman in tweeds. Clutching my box, I got to my feet and put out a hand. "Hello, Mrs. Grimes, I'm Mrs. Balser. I'm terribly sorry I'm so late."

"How d'you do," said the woman, ignoring my hand and looking from my box to my wild wind-blown hair. "I'm Melissa's nurse, Mrs. Haverstock. We talked the other day on the phone." As Liz buttoned her coat she gave her a proprietary pat on the rear. "Such a lovely girl. Such good manners. I hope you will let her visit our Melissa soon again."

"Did you have a nice time?" I asked once we were in the cab.

"Melissa has a doll's house with running water and electric lights."

"What's Melissa like?"

"She doesn't come to school in the bus. She comes in a Rolls."

Soon the cab pulled up at the house of Sylvie's friend on Eighty-ninth Street and East End. While Liz hopped out, I explained to the driver that we would only be a minute and asked if he would keep his meter running.

"Not a chance, lady. I was heading into the garage when I picked you up."

I paid him, but as I climbed out I couldn't resist: "If you were heading into the garage why didn't you have your OFF DUTY lights on?"

"Ah shiy-ut!" he answered, and yanking the door from my hand, slammed it shut, punched down the lock and zoomed away, his OFF DUTY lights springing brilliantly on.

"What did that man say to you, Mudther?" asked Liz as I came up. "Nothing, love," I said and rang the bell. After three rings the door was opened by a small red-headed boy of about four; holding it wide, he just stood and glared at us. In the dim narrow hall behind him there was a flight of uncarpeted steps, down which came piano chords, shrieks, and a marmalade cat with all its back hair on end. Reaching the bottom, the cat shot through an open door on the right; there was a startled scream and a tinny crash. After an eloquent little silence a woman called, "*Timmy?* Timmy, did you get the door?"

"Yeah. Yeah, I did," said Timmy in a hoarse basso, still glowering at us.

"Who is it?"

"How should *I* know." Timmy now focused balefully on Liz alone.

"Oh God," moaned the woman, and a second later rushed through the door—tall, skinny, about thirty-five, wearing jeans that were covered with flour. When she saw us she came to an abrupt stop, and stood tweaking back lank blond hair from a tired face, blinking at us with dazed blue eyes.

I blinked back, just as dazed: It's *ma semblable, ma soeur*, I thought, inspired.

All this time we were still outside on the doormat. "I'm Tina Balser, Sylvie's mother," I finally said. "I'm sorry I'm so late, but I had a lot of trouble getting cabs."

"Oh. Come in," she cried, bodily removing Timmy and ushering us into the dim warm hall. "I'm Sally Goodman." She stuck out a flour-coated hand, then dropped it, laughing. "Your being late was a blessing. It kept the girls busy while I tried to make a beef pie . . . You look absolutely frozen. Would you like a drink?"

I refused, saying I had to get home to cook *our* dinner, and she looked immensely relieved. She turned and bellowed up the stairs, "Florence, *Flor*-r-ence! Sylvie's mother is here!" When this didn't carry above the uproar, she swore and went bounding up the stairs, taking them three at a time with her long skinny legs. As the piano and shrieks subsided overhead, I quickly took in the lower hall where we stood. Dead ahead, a bicycle with mud-caked wheels leaned against the newel post; there was a mountain of sweaters, gloves, coats on a bench; three pairs of roller skates lay under a tiny console stacked with unopened mail; and above the console a Bonnard poster hung crazily askew. Who and what was *Mr.* Goodman, I wondered with feelings I didn't want to classify, as Mrs. G. came bounding back down the stairs. She was followed by a tall homely blond girl, Florence, and a dirty-looking Sylvie, who smiled happily and said, "Hi, Ma, hi, Lizzie," like a perfectly normal child, and got her coat from the heap on the bench.

"What a nice family," I said in the cab going home; we'd walked to Doctors Hospital around the corner and gotten one right away. "Are there just Timmy and Florence?"

"No, two more. Brian and Solange. Brian goes away to school, but Solange was upstairs. She's in Liz's class. She wouldn't come down because she says Liz hates her."

"That's not true! She hates *me*," shouted Liz, and it was only then I saw how stupid I'd been, going on about the Goodmans.

"You're wrong," said Sylvie, very high and mighty. "She'd like to be your friend. Only she says you hang around with that Melissa Grimes and the two of you laugh at her because she wears some of Florence's old clothes."

"That's not true!" Liz screamed again (I believed her), and bursting into tears, fell on Sylvie, pummeling her with knobby little fists.

"*Lady!* Lady, if you don't stop those brats of yours I'm gonna put you outa this cab!"

He put us out at Ninety-sixth and Fifth.

By the time we got another cab, the girls were so frozen they'd forgotten their quarrel, and we rode home in silence. It was 6:30 when I unlocked our door. "What stinks so?" said Sylvie as I groped for the light, and turning it on, saw that Folly had let go both barrels on the pale gold hall rug—the rug just returned from the cleaners. Folly was nowhere in sight. Holding their noses, the girls went inside while I set about cleaning up. It was my fault: though I'd walked her before leaving, I'd forgotten to turn on a light. Folly is afraid of the dark, afraid of being alone, and her reactions upon finding herself in either situation are somewhat visceral. I sprayed the hall with Jasmine air spray, coaxed Folly out from under the bed, patted her reassuringly, then washed and went to the kitchen to cook.

We were having a simple steak-and-salad dinner, and I was at the sink washing the romaine lettuce when Jonathan came in. "We're going to have to get rid of that dog. That damned neurotic dog. D'you realize the rug in the hall will have to be cleaned all over again?"

"Good evening, Jonathan," I said calmly, and began shaking and swinging the lettuce basket with more vigor than was necessary.

Jonathan backed off from the shower of drops. "Why *did* she go in the hall? Did you forget to walk her this afternoon?"

"I walked her early, before I went out to look for a dress." I swung the basket in a wider arc. "What I forgot to do was leave a light, so she was alone in the dark."

Jonathan retreated a little further back from the spray. "Why alone? Where was Lottie *this* time?"

"Off. Today being Thursday."

Looking only faintly set back, Jonathan muttered, "Well, she's still not a normal dog, she needs a dog shrink or a dog training school," and sauntered over to inspect the sirloin I'd put on a wooden cutting board. "You find a dress?"

"Yes."

"What's it like?" Bending low, he closely inspected the steak, even lifting a corner of it with two fingers.

"I can't describe it. I suppose you could call it a sexy dress."

Jonathan gave a little grunt and straightened up, wiping his fingers on his handkerchief. "That's a very nice sirloin, beautifully marbleized. In fact, it's so nice I think I'll make a Caesar Salad out of that romaine you've got there . . . D'you have all the fixings?"

"Yes."

"Anchovies and croutons?"

"*All* the fixings, Jonathan."

"Well, well. Things are looking up. So much so I'm going to break out a bottle of Chambertin to celebrate."

He started for the pantry, where the wine is stored, and turned at the door. "I didn't hear you, what did you say the dress was like?"

"Pretty. I said it's a pretty dress," I lied.

"I hope not *too* pretty. Pretty dresses are seldom smart." With that, he left to get the Chambertin.

"MUDTHER," said Sylvie, appearing in the door to our room. "You're not going to wear that dress?"

"Apparently I am," I said absently, working on my bangs at the mirror. "What's wrong with this dress."

"It shows all your buhz."

"My what?"

"Buhz. Boozums. *You* know."

"Breasts. The word for them is breasts." Satisfied with my hair—it was my old, normal hair, clean and shining, looking very nice—I put down the hairbrush, and began to load my purse with compact, lipstick, keys, comb. "I can't understand," I said, impulsively tucking in a five-dollar bill, "why you and Liz persist in those silly words, when I've told you both a hundred times to call things by their proper names."

"Because they're disgusting."

"What's disgusting?" Distractedly rummaging for some gloves, I came upon a pair, miraculously new, still in cellophane, bought last year and never used.

"The names for things you want us to use."

Ready to go, I sighed and turned to Sylvie, standing rigid and pink-faced in the doorway. "They're not disgusting. You mustn't be ashamed of natural, functional things. I suppose you think 'po-po' and 'poo-poo' and 'Thing' and 'down there' are nicer?"

"Nicer than yours!" Sylvie burst out. "It's just like
120

that dress. I mean I suppose you think that's a nice and *natural* dress, cut so low your *breasts* are hanging out!"

Choking, she turned and ran, apparently colliding with Jonathan in the little hall; after a muffled exclamation he came in, readjusting his overcoat. "Have you been fighting again?"

"Not at all. We were just having a little discussion about semantics." I gave myself a final check in the mirror.

"Ah. *I* see," he said, dry, not seeing, and after a resigned sigh, glanced at his watch. "I hope to God you're ready now—it's almost seven o'clock!"

Charlotte Rady lives in a large old building right on the river at East End Avenue, exactly the sort of location Jonathan once wanted for us, still wants, and will, I'm afraid, insist on having once our lease here is up. In fact, as we went up in the wood-paneled elevator, I could actually hear his thoughts—Co-op? Restricted? Purchase Price? Maintenance?—and was so afraid he'd start cross-examining the elevator operator that I'd begun to shake by the time we reached the eleventh floor.

After handing our coats over to a butler, we were shown down a long hallway, over gorgeous Kirman rugs, to a huge room where our hostess stood receiving just inside the tall doors. She looked very splendid, hair piled high, simply dressed without the usual blaze of jewels, and for one horrible moment clearly had no idea who on earth we were. She stared at us with those green eyes (made all iris by some drug), then finally gave a fluttery little cry and kissed us both on the cheek. "There are too many people for introductions," she said, giving off gusts of bourbon and *Joy*, "so be good little lambs and get yourselves a drink and madly circulate. You know most everyone anyway."

This of course wasn't true. As we stood at the long bar waiting for our drinks, we both shyly turned and looked around, and in one glance I saw I didn't know a soul. I also saw that amongst the eighty-odd people in that room alone (a door behind us opened into another), there were enough celebrities to keep Jonathan happy for months. *Please* don't leave me just yet, I wanted to beg him once we had our drinks, but before I could get up the nerve, Jonathan said, "Hey, look who's here!" and took off. It was too soon; I simply wasn't ready to fend for myself. Doggedly I set out after him.

I found him with the director of the first play he'd invested in, and three other people. The director, a tall, balding, notoriously temperamental European, didn't look enchanted to see Jonathan, or me bringing up the rear. But naturally Jonathan didn't notice this or the strained, heavily ironic air with which the director finally introduced us to the three other people. Jonathan just stood there beaming. Slowly, with much twitching of the nostrils, the director resumed a monologue about the troubles he and the producer were having casting their new play, a play poor Jonathan had obviously never heard of until now, because he looked absolutely crushed: why hadn't he been asked in? As the director went on and on—though odious, he had an undeniable sort of overworked Viennese charm—Jonathan's face grew longer and longer. I quietly finished off my drink.

"Of course she'll eventually come round," said the director of a certain actress. "It's just a matter of waiting her out."

"But she's such a bitch, Kurt!" Jonathan burst out, trying to assert himself for the sake of his wounded pride. "Why do you want to let yourself in for that?"

"Kurt" gave Jonathan a long pained look, and after a little cough, turned back to the other three: "Now I ask you . . . have you ever heard of such a price, such *hootz*-pah?"

The others gravely shook their heads. Fumbling, Jonathan lit up a little cigar.

"Excuse me," I said to no one, and went back to the bar and had my glass refilled. Afterwards I stood and desperately cased the room, hoping to see a group big enough to attach myself to inconspicuously. I didn't see any—everyone stood in forbiddingly cozy twos or threes—but I did see Charlotte Rady standing with some people by the door, thoughtfully watching me. I also saw George Prager, the playwright with whom I'd had that world-shaking exchange at Carter Livingston's, standing and talking to a fat pasty-faced man by the windows at the other end of the room. You're not *that* desperate, old girl, I told myself, and grimly headed back to Jonathan and Friends. As I reattached myself, Jonathan glared at me: *Can't you make out on your own?* Answering with a sweet and vapid smile, I stationed myself at his elbow and started sipping my second drink. Kurt the Raconteur was now telling a long detailed story about a famous actor who'd once worked for him. It was the most vicious, irresponsible and unethical story I'd ever heard, yet Jonathan and the others listened, rapt: this, after all, was straight from the horse's mouth. As they all began laughing at a particularly sordid detail concerning the poor actor's love life, I said "Excuse me" to no one again, and started pushing through the crowd, heading for George Prager and the fat man: I *was* that desperate, it seemed.

I knew I was wrong when I was still several feet away from them. As they glanced up and saw me relentlessly bearing down on them, they exchanged a look which made me wonder why I hadn't just gone and locked myself in the bathroom again. But there was no turning back by then, so I traveled the remaining distance and came to a shuddering stop in front of them. "Hi, there," I said to George Prager, trying for something like the bumbling breeziness of Doris Day.

George Prager blinked at me. I'd forgotten those eyes.

"I'm Tina Balser. We met at Carter Livingston's. At least we *chatted* for a bit. You were looking for somebody, a tall, skinny blonde with green horn-rims, I think . . ." Out of breath and nerve, I ran down.

Raising his eyebrows, Mr. Prager glanced from my face to my buhz (???), then turned to his fat friend with a pleading look: For God's sake, Sam, it's not *my* fault! "Mrs. . . . ah . . . Balser. Samuel Keefer."

"How d'you do, Mr. Keefer." Mr. Keefer was the drama critic on a weekly news magazine.

"How d'ye do," Mr. Keefer murmured icily, and turning to Mr. Prager, wildly rolled his eyes.

There was a long silence. Mr. Prager studied the ice

cubes in his glass. Mr. Keefer chewed the insides of his cheeks and studied the patterns in the Samarkand rug. Mr. Keefer looked like Oscar Wilde. Mr. Prager's face was an unhealthy grey-white, his hair needed cutting, his navy blue suit needed pressing. A charming pair. However, when, with the air of people who've been praying for a miracle, they both finally looked up, I was still there, calmly lighting my own cigarette. I'd decided to dig in.

Seeing that there was only one way to handle this, Mr. Prager sighed and turned to Mr. Keefer. "So. That's really what you think I oughta do, Sam?"

After a long and withering look at me—Will you go a-*way!*—Mr. Keefer said through his teeth, "Yes, it is. There's no other way."

"But he and I've been buddies for over twelve years," said Mr. Prager with an absent look at my buhz.

"You? Sentimental? Don't make me laugh." Mr. Keefer threw back his head and laughed. He had very crooked nicotine-stained teeth and the hairiest nostrils I'd ever seen. Mr. Prager smiled and took a swallow of his drink. He had very white, even teeth, but the fingers around his glass were brown with nicotine.

"Though you may find it hard to believe, I'm not without loyalty," said Mr. Prager.

"You're also not without ambition. In fact, you're the most ambitious prick I know. Because of that, you've got to do what I told you, like it or not. Though you swing it with the broads, you can't play it both ways in *this* racket." By now Mr. Keefer had worked himself around so that his back was to me. His hound's-tooth jacket reached only halfway down his fat rear end. He had a boil on the back of his neck.

"Yeah, I guess you're right," Mr. Prager said almost humbly, and took another gulp of his drink.

"Excuse me," I said and turned and walked away to the nearby window. I walked to the window because I was going to cry, and that was something I wasn't about to let those two bastards, or anyone else there, see. The window reached from ceiling to floor and was a good place to hide. Faintly recessed, it was hung with heavy draperies and even had a shallow little window seat. I stood and stared out at the red and blue *Pearlwick Hamper* sign, a violet blur. I'll finish this drink and go home alone, I told myself, remembering the five-dollar bill I'd "impulsively" tucked in my purse. I won't even tell Jonathan I'm going. Later I'll have it out with him once and for all. I'll tell him point-blank that these people use him, laugh at him, that as an appendage I come in for the same treatment, and I simply won't take it any more.

As soon as I thought this I felt better. Sipping my drink to get up the rest of the courage needed to walk out of there, I stared out at the view with dry eyes. Directly below swirled the black water of the river; it was like being on a ship. Across, on Welfare Island, a few dim lights shone cheerlessly, but beyond, across more black water, the lighted windows of Long Island City twinkled cozily. I was imagining how nice it would be to be sitting on a couch in one of those rooms behind the windows, eating a TV Dinner on a tray and watching the Million Dollar Movie, when I heard a burst of laughter from Messrs. Prager and Keefer, behind me. Cruel, nasty laughter. Paranoia said: they're laughing at *you*. Sanity said: they're laughing at one of their rotten private jokes. Paranoia won out and I swung around, glaring.

Mr. Keefer's back was still turned, but Mr. Prager faced me and was looking right at me. He stopped laughing and nudged his friend, who swiveled about, frowning.

Literally wishing I were dead, I whipped around and faced the view again. Behind me I could hear Mr. Keefer's hissing whisper: ". . . not serious, George . . . draw the line *some*where . . . no taste . . . hopeless."

"We weren't laughing at you, you know," Mr. Prager said suddenly, so close behind me that I jumped.

"I didn't think you *were*," I finally managed to say to Welfare Island.

"Oh, yes you did, and in case you didn't know it, that's pretty sick."

"Oh, go to hell," I said over my shoulder.

"Now that's what I call a witty retort, snappy repar-

tee— What's *bugging* you, baby? You're in perfectly
terrible shape. I mean I'll admit we weren't exactly
*aff*able before, but the truth is you did come barging in
on a very private conversation. But even so, you didn't
have to come marching up to this window, looking like
you were going to throw yourself out. You been watching Joan Crawford on the Late Late Show?"

"I'm not at all interested in having this discussion," I
said, fully turning and trying to get past him, but he
reached out and grabbed my wrist.

"Stand *still*, for God's sake. Can't you relax?"

"If you don't let go my wrist, I'll scream."

"I believe you would," he said and laughed, but kept
an iron grip on my wrist.

"What is it you want? Did you come over to have
yourself more fun? Why don't you go away and leave
me alone?"

Disgusted, he now dropped my wrist. "Jesus H., are
you ever worked up! I come all the way over to try and
be nice, to give you a compliment, in fact, and you act as
if I'd come over to insult you. If that isn't paranoid, I
don't know what is."

"Compliment?" I repeated vaguely, having spotted Jonathan at the bar, a fresh drink in hand, restlessly casing
the room for his next stop, his eyes moving our way.

"Yes. *Comp*liment," said Mr. Prager, doubly annoyed
because I wouldn't look at him. "I really didn't recognize you before when you first came up, I wasn't putting you down. I didn't recognize you because you look
like a different woman. A woman, period. That night at
Livingston's you looked like someone in drag."

I burst out laughing. It was too much—Jonathan's
double take, followed by a congratulatory smile ("Atta
girl!"), plus Mr. Prager's idea of a compliment.

"Are you slaphappy or just drunk?" asked Mr. Prager,
watching all of me shake as I laughed.

Subsiding, I shook my head. "Just mad. Paranoid, like
you said."

He studied me carefully. "No, you're not crazy. Just
all worked up. And I owe you an apology for that para-

noid bit. We *were* laughing at you before—indirectly, that is."

I froze. "You were?"

He nodded, trying to suppress a smile. "After you walked off before, Keefer wanted to know where in hell we'd met. I'd remembered you by then, and told him what you'd said was right. I also told him how you locked yourself in the can for an hour or so, and how some poor slob who needed to get in finally lost his cookies all over Livingston's kitchen floor— Did you know that?"

I shook my head, and remembering the urgent knock I'd ignored, began to laugh. Strange things were happening to me.

While I laughed, Mr. Prager watched me closely again. "That's better. Much better."

I stopped laughing.

"You're married to Whoosis Balser, aren't you?"

"His name is Jonathan."

"Easy, baby, easy. How long have you been married to him?"

"Him?"

"Jon-a-than. Balser. You married to someone else?"

"Ten years."

"Ah." He smiled. It was not a nice smile, nor was the look he gave me afterwards. "How old are you? About thirty-five?"

"Why are you cross-examining me?"

"Let's just say you interest me."

"Why. Because I'm in Terrible Shape?"

"Not bad. Not bad at all. Actually, you're not in such terrible shape. What's the matter with you couldn't be clearer, in fact."

As he stared, I felt a Lady Blush start way up under my bangs, and travel down into the V of my dress, following the path of his eyes.

"What's the matter," he said softly, taunting. "Are you afraid of him? Or doesn't fucking interest you?"

"I see," I said slowly, "that you try to talk like the characters in your plays."

"Let's leave my plays out of this. And stand *still*, for

God's sake. I haven't finished, things are just beginning
to get interesting."

"I find this very boring."

"You're not bored, so cut that crap. In fact, in just a
few minutes you've thawed, begun to come to life."

Much as I hated to hear it, this was true. I hadn't felt
so alive in years. I might be bristling and fuming with
anger and Lady Outrage, but I also was humming with
vibrations that had nothing to do with nerves.

"I don't dig it," he continued. "You're really not my
type at all, yet even when you stood there with Keefer
and me I got this funny thing—I call it the-kick-in-the-
gut syndrome, a feeling I get when the sex wave length
is right. You interest me, or, to be more accurate, you
excite me like hell, and it isn't just those gorgeous
knockers of yours. No, it's something else, that sex wave
length thing you get right away—powee! pam! And I'll
tell you something—I excite the hell out of you too, so
don't start any of that righteous indignation crap I can
see you're getting ready to pull. In fact, right this minute there's something in the air between us so thick you
could cut it with a knife."

This again being true, I stood there hypnotized, paralyzed.

Suddenly he burst out laughing and sat down on the
window seat. "Man," he said, shaking his head as he
laughed up at me, "Man, that hasn't happened to me in
public in *years*. Not since I was a horny teen-ager.
You'd better just stand there a minute—unless of course
you want to come sit on my lap."

"Congratulations," I said (I never throw away a good
line). Then, becoming a combination of Gladys Cooper
and Cathleen Nesbitt, I added, "You are the most dis-
*gust*ing man I have ever met," and went huffy-puffing
off, leaving him to his problem. I found Jonathan in a
corner of the other room, talking to Frank Gaylord,
Margo, and two men I didn't know. After a spectacu-
larly flat greeting, Jonathan introduced me to the men.
"You know Frank and Margo," he said smoothly. Ah
yes, indeed I did. Frank Gaylord gave me a big wet
wink; silent as usual, Margo sullenly glared. The conver-

sation resumed, this time being about Frank Gaylord's new play. Sidling up to Jonathan, I whispered in his ear, "I want to go home," but he scowled and moved away, pretending he hadn't heard. Several minutes later George Prager appeared in the doorway. Searching, he found me, grinned, blew a Bea Lillie kiss and waggled his fingers (ta! ta!) goodbye. With his back to the door, Jonathan missed this, but Frank Gaylord didn't; he looked at me hard and began to leer: *So!* I glared back at him: So *noth*ing, you worm!

It took a half-hour, but I finally got Jonathan to leave. Since one of his great concerns these days is what kind of figure he cuts in the eyes of doormen, elevator men and waiters, he didn't say a word until we were alone in the building's pillared carport downstairs. While the doorman whistled for a taxi out on the cold and windy street, Jonathan hissed: "And what was it *this* time? What was the reason for all the rush tonight?"

"Since we'd been there almost two hours, I'd hardly call it a rush," I answered with dignity.

"We were there exactly an hour and a half. What do you suppose people thought . . . Charlotte Rady, or Gaylord and Margo . . . our rushing off like that?"

"That we're very much in demand. I distinctly heard you tell them all we had to go on to dinner somewhere."

Riding the cab he'd gotten two blocks away, the doorman hopped out. Jonathan tipped him, and when we got in, gave the driver the address of a steak house on Third Avenue. "I'm not very hungry," I said. "Why don't we go home and I'll fix something light, an omelette, a soufflé."

"Because *I'm* hungry and I don't want any bloody omelettes or soufflés. I don't want to go home." Then, since cab drivers aren't among the public retainers whose opinions he cares about, he added, "In fact, I don't know why I let you con me into leaving that party at all. I'm tempted to go on back and let you go home alone and eat an omelette."

"That would suit me fine." I meant it.

But Jonathan merely settled back into the corner and

glumly stared out the window until we reached the restaurant.

Once we were settled at a table and had given our orders, Jonathan resumed. "Now. Suppose you try to tell me just why you wanted to leave that party."

"I was bored."

"That's a lie. You were just feeling inse*cure*. It was written all over you. And that's what gets me, old girl—you, who used to be so good at parties, be such a good mixer, turning into such a clinging vine, a shrinking violet! My *God!*" Finished with such niceties as botanical metaphors, he shifted into high gear: he'd been a magnificently patient and tolerant man, but now his patience was at an end; it was abundantly clear that I was undergoing some sort of character-breakdown or crisis of the personality, and my "pigheaded" refusal to acknowledge it was more than he could bear. Since all this had begun to happen at a time when he'd really begun to find himself, fully utilize all his Po*ten*tial, it had begun to occur to him that there might even be something sinister here, might be some sort of subconscious hostility working in me, working to hold him back . . . On and on he went, gulping down oysters between theories, while hot salty tears began to run down my cheeks, dripping off my chin into my untouched tomato juice. Pushing a plateful of empty shells away, Jonathan turned. "For God's sake," he whispered, horrified. "Get ahold of yourself. People are staring at you."

People. Along with doormen, elevator men and headwaiters, the opinions of People matter greatly to Jonathan these days. And who are People? His great secret public—strangers, anybody he doesn't know. An old lady knitting on a park bench when he walks Folly, a man reading the papers on the stoop of a brownstone when he climbs out of a taxi, a woman walking a dachshund up Madison Avenue as he comes out of Parke-Bernet in his fuzzy green hat. Tonight it was a poor old palsied man at a table just across from us, desperately trying to get his soup spoon to his mouth without a spill. Or the not-so-young lovers at the table next to the old man, doing intense things under the table with their hands and legs, thinking the tablecloth longer than it was. Our audience.

"Here, take this," whispered Jonathan, handing me his handkerchief. "And if you can't stop, go to the ladies' room. You're making an absolute spectacle of yourself."

If he'd looked closer, he'd have seen I'd already stopped. "Jonathan. If you don't shut up I *will* make a spectacle of myself. I'll stand up on this damned banquette and throw back my head and scream. And *scream*."

It was the second time that night I'd threatened that, but unlike George Prager, Jonathan neither laughed nor jauntily said, "I believe you would." Seeing that I would, he turned pale and shut up, and once the waiter had cleared the plates, said he wanted to go home. But I said I didn't want to go home now, I was suddenly very hungry, which wasn't just a try at evening the score. I *was* hungry, and when the waiter brought my ground steak platter, I began to eat with great appetite, lavishly buttering rolls, tasting salad, even eating some of the French fried onions which I normally loathe. Meanwhile Jonathan silently cut into the steak he'd ordered rare, and which turned out to be well-done, but instead of making a big fuss and sending it back (another one of his charming new restaurant compulsions), he stoically began to eat it.

After a long silence, during which he'd apparently worked out the best way to handle me, he gave up on the steak, pushing the plate away. In a soft solicitous voice he said, "I'm not starting in again, I promise. But I've been doing a lot of thinking sitting here, and there's one more thing I have to say, one positive thing: you're a damned attractive woman, Tina. Damned attractive. And you have a very good mind. You even have a pretty good sense of humor when you don't take yourself so seriously. With all that working for you, I can't understand how you can feel insecure. Your children love you, I love you. People find you bright and charming. Why, Mrs. Marks tells me all the time how lucky I am to have found a girl like you. And for another example, take tonight. I noticed George Prager talking to you again. If I remember correctly he went out of his way to talk to you at Carter Livingston's. A thing like that ought to prove *some*thing to you. I mean I happen to know that Prager has a reputation for being quite a man with the ladies, for being quite selective. He wouldn't have given you the time of day unless he'd found you attractive or amusing in some way. Further-more, it seemed a very animated discussion—I noticed you both were laughing a lot—and I was damned proud to think you could hold your own with someone like that. What were you talking about, the theater?"

I pushed my empty plate away. "Sex," I said, patting my mouth with my napkin. "We were talking about Sex."

"Sex?"

"That's right," I said, taking out my compact.

For a minute Jonathan watched me calmly powder my nose. Then, signaling the waiter, he began to chuckle with relief. "You're all right, Teen, you really are. I take it all back. If you can banter about sex with someone like Prager, you're not as bad off as I thought."

AT SIX THIS MORNING I woke up to find the radiators hissing and filling the room with hot dry air; Jonathan, who has a thing about cold night air as well as light, had only opened the windows a crack. Perspiring, licking dry lips, I jumped out of bed and turned both radiators off, and after quietly raising the windows, peered through a blind to see what the weather was like. For the first time in days there wasn't any frost on the ground. A fine mist hung over the park and the sky was a heavy rainy grey.

"For God's sake, Tina, it's only five past six! What the hell are you making such a racket for?"

I turned and found Jonathan glaring at me with one round yellow eye, the rest of his face shrouded by covers. "It was too hot in here and I was letting in some air."

"Well, now it's too cold. Shut those damned windows and come back to bed. How's a person supposed to get any rest with such a bloody racket going on."

As he rolled over and covered his head with the pillow, I closed one window, but didn't go back to bed. Inspired by the idea of a peaceful, solitary breakfast for a change, I went into the bathroom to wash. I was tiptoeing past the girls' room when a tight dry cough stopped me in my tracks. It was a cough I'd gotten to know well over the years.

133

"Mommy? . . . *Mom*-mee?" called Liz.

With a sinking feeling I went to their open door and put a finger to my lips. "Yes?" I whispered.

"*Please* come in here, Mommy," wailed Liz.

If possible, their room was hotter than ours, and I remembered I'd asked Jonathan to go in and check their windows before we went to sleep. Sylvie was still asleep, tightly rolled in a cocoon of blankets. Liz lay with all her covers kicked off, her pajamas stuck to her legs with perspiration, her face glimmering with what I call The White Rabbit Look—the red-eyed white-faced look of the city child on the verge of coming down with something terrible.

I sat down heavily on the edge of her bed. "What's the matter, darling?" I whispered.

"I feel just *horrible*. Everything hurts. My knees hurt, my head hurts, and my throat is so sore I can't even swallow."

I put my hand on her burning forehead. "You do feel a little warm. I think I'll take your temperature."

I left her with the thermometer in her mouth and dashed to the kitchen to put on the coffee. When I came back I carried the thermometer to the light. It read one hundred and three. As I tiptoed back to her bed I told myself not to panic. In a whisper I told her that since she had a little fever she wouldn't be going to school; I'd get her an aspirin and then she could go back to sleep.

"How can I sleep when everything hurts? My head, my arms, my neck, even my teeth!"

"Oh, for God's *sake!*" Exploding covers, Sylvie sat up. "How's a person supposed to get any rest with such a bloody racket going on!"

Even the yellow eyes were the same. "Be quiet, Sylvie. Your sister's sick."

"That's obvious. What's the matter with her?"

"I think it's just a little cold," I lied, for my morale as much as theirs. Grumbling, Sylvie flopped back down and pulled her pillow over her head: was it genes or mimicry? "I'll get you an aspirin," I said to Liz, who warned as I went out the door, "I won't take it unless it's mashed up in a strawberry milkshake."

An hour later I was in the girls' bathroom, cleaning the pink curdy lumps of Liz's throw-up off the tiled floor; she hadn't made it to the toilet in time. Jonathan and Sylvie were having breakfast in the kitchen. I'd only managed a cup of black coffee, which was a mistake, because as I crouched, gagging, swabbing at the tiles with paper toweling, my poor empty stomach rebelled. Unlike Liz, I made it to the toilet in time. I had washed and was groping for one of the girls' towels when I saw that Folly had come in while I'd been bent over the sink. Unable to believe my eyes, I watched her sniff the pink mess still on the tiles, and with a thoughtful air stick out her curly tongue. It was too much. I began to scream and lash out with the towel. No one hits Folly—ever. Frightened out of her wits, she started snarling and baring her teeth; equally frightened, I started flapping my towel like Clyde Beatty and finally chased her under Sylvie's bed. Leaving her growling and moaning under there, I backed off and turned around. Liz was sitting up and goggling with huge red eyes, and Jonathan was standing in the doorway, his lips shiny with melted butter, the folded *Times* under his arm.

"May I ask," he said slowly, "what the hell is going on? Don't you realize this child is sick? Why were you screaming like that? Have you completely lost your mind?"

I stared at him, freshly showered and shaved, spruce and pink in a monogrammed shirt. "Folly was eating Liz's throw-up."

Paling, Jonathan shook his head. "My God. Can't a child even get sick in this house without a crisis coming of it?"

I gave a warning little cough and tried to smile reassuringly at Liz, who was glassily watching her Dear Mums and Dads.

Jonathan looked at Liz, then turned and went back to his hot buttered scones.

Doctor Miller's office opens at nine. At two minutes past nine I called, and after ten rings the answering service picked up and said that on Fridays Doctor Miller didn't get in the office until 10:30, but if I left my name and number he would call me as soon as he arrived. I left my name and number and went to look in on Liz, who, thanks to a second aspirin, was back asleep. I showered and dressed and was in the kitchen stacking the breakfast dishes, when the wall phone rang. I put down a plate and went to pick it up, thinking: It's Lottie, to say she can't come in today.

"Good morning, Mrs. Balser. This is Lottie."

"Yes, Lottie." I shut my eyes. "Is anything wrong?"

"I'm afraid so, Mrs. Balser," she said faintly. "I was up all night with a tooth, and this morning my face is swollen out to here. I'm sorry, but I just don't think I can make it in today."

"How *awful* for you, Lottie. You'd better go see a dentist right away."

"That's what I'm about to do soon's I hang up this phone, and that's why I can't come in. This dental clinic I go to, there's a terrible wait. Last time I waited almost four hours." She concluded by saying that no matter what happened, she'd be in tomorrow, but I told her to wait and see how she felt; after I hung up I put down papers for Folly in the bathroom.

By 11:30 Doctor Miller still hadn't called. At 11:45 Liz woke up and began to weep; her temperature, only temporarily brought down by the aspirin, was back to one hundred and three. I called Doctor Miller's office again, and after listening to me, the nurse crisply said, "Just one moment, Mrs. Balser. I'll see if he can come to the phone." A button clicked, and after three minutes of deafening silence there was another click and the dial tone began buzzing.

With trembling fingers I dialed again. "I'm sorry we were cut off, Mrs. Balser," said the nurse, "but Doctor Miller's all tied up now. Can you give me your number and I'll have him call you back?" When, in a choking voice, I gave her a piece of my mind instead of my number, there was another click and three seconds later Doctor Miller was angrily shouting "*Yes*, Mrs. Balser?" in my ear. In the background a baby was screaming with the rhythmic rise and fall of hysteria. Intimidated, I began. "I can't hear you, Mrs. Balser. Speak a little louder, please." Trying to be as brief as I could, I told him about Liz while the baby screeched and he suffed and sighed with exasperation, waiting for me to bring my tale to an end. "Listen, Mrs. Balser," he bellowed above the screaming. "This Thing is all over New York. I've been swamped with calls. In some cases the fever runs as high as a hundred and *five*, and *still* it's nothing to worry about. There's absolutely no point in my coming to see Elizabeth since there's absolutely nothing I can do. This Thing has to run its own course—no antibiotics touch it. All we can do, *you* can do, is keep her quiet and warm, see that she gets plenty of fluids and plenty of rest. Feed her lightly, give her aspirin every four hours and give me a call tomorrow and let me know how she is."

He hung up with a crash.

For a while I just sat on the edge of Jonathan's bed, staring with fascination at my hands: dangling between my slacks-covered legs, they were doing a spastic little dance on their own. Then Liz called, "Mommy? Mommee, where *are* you?" and I dashed into her room and found her sitting up in bed, her face swollen and turned an ugly mottled red.

"Mommy," she gasped, tears rolling down her cheeks, "I have to throw up again," and promptly did so all over the paisley quilt.

This time I managed to clean up and change her without following her example. After I'd put the quilt in the washing machine, I went back to her room with some ginger ale and ice. As sometimes happens, the second bout of vomiting had left her feeling weak but better; propped up on pillows, she sipped thirstily, while I pulled a chair alongside and sat down next to her. She drank with one hand cupping the glass, and when suddenly the other stole out across the clean sheets, palm upturned, asking to be taken, something enormous turned over inside of me: this hadn't happened in years. I took the hand, hot and limp and dry, in mine, and felt knots untying, giving way. The rain, which had started at eleven, quietly threaded down in the streets outside, a lulling autumn downfall. To complete the picture, Folly came in and curled up at my feet. It was all so power-fully seductive, so overwhelming, really—the helpless softness of the sick child, the lamplight, the rain picking and ticking on the windowpanes, the pouffy fluff of dog at my feet—that I stared down at the hand in mine, hyp-notized, utterly at peace.

The phone rang, shattering the silence.

I reluctantly put down Liz's hand and went to answer it.

"Hello?" I said.

Silence.

"Hel-*lo?*"

Breathy silence.

"*Hel*lo!" I was angry now.

A man—his voice high, disguised, thickly distorted with excitement—proposed explicitly and pervertedly what he had in mind for me. He called me by my name. Tina.

Stupefied, I listened to every obscene detail, then hung up. The receiver glistened with cold sweat from my hand. George Prager. Like someone releasing a depth charge, I let that name out of some locked hatch in my mind, where it detonated dully. No. *No.* I knew that whatever else he was, he wasn't sick in that way, wasn't the type to get so bottled up he had to do *that* for kicks. Who, then? I was turning over possibilities, not coming up with anyone remotely likely, when Liz called from her room.

Looking infinitely better, she said that she was hungry and asked for some chicken noodle soup and crackers. It was such good news I immediately forgot the telephone maniac. I moved Lottie's portable television set into her room so that she could look at cartoons while I was cooking. Leaving her happily watching Mr. Magoo fly a space capsule he thought was his car, I went back to the kitchen. In the grocery closet there were cans of Wild Duck soup with sherry from Scotland, cans of *Petite Marmite*, *Potage St. Germain*, mushroom bisque and *bouillabaisse* from France. There was even a can of Kangaroo Tail Soup from Australia, but there wasn't a single can or package of chicken noodle soup.

I sat down on the floor of the grocery closet and started to cry.

Since even I can see that this sounds a bit excessive—sounds like what Jonathan calls Over-Reacting—an explanation is in order. At about the same time he was getting his first tips on the market, someone (maybe one of the same people) tipped Jonathan off to the fact that there was a "quality" market in our neighborhood, the Nieuw Amsterdam Market, which carried Choice beef and S. S. Pierce canned goods and fresh dill and tarragon and out-of-season fruits. Jonathan immediately opened a charge and insisted that I do all our shopping there, by phone; naturally I did and have ever since. I've always gotten a small shock when I open the bills from the Nieuw Amsterdam Market, but when I open them and find them a month overdue it's even worse. (Jonathan pays all the bills; I only go over them; I don't have a checking account of my own.) Though Jonathan is almost fanatic about paying certain bills promptly—the rent, the girls' school, the phone, doctors, dentists—he has a block about bills from the market, the milkman, the cleaners, the electrician. It's like his block about buying a new vacuum cleaner. Yesterday, when I'd opened the bill from the Nieuw Amsterdam Market—a staggering bill for September and October, with a curt notice at the bottom—I'd almost died of shame. It was the second time it had happened in five months and about the tenth time in two and a half years. Being me, I'd sworn not to order anything from them until they received Jonathan's check, which he promised would go out in the mail today. Which left me without a market, in need of groceries. I may not be Tabitha-Twitchit-Danvers, but even I had seen we needed a lot of things, and before Liz's getting sick had made me forget it, I'd intended to ask Jonathan for some extra cash this morning so I could go to a supermarket. I'd run terribly short this week; Jonathan gives me my household allowance on Saturday.

I finally stopped crying, picked myself off the floor of

the grocery closet, and went to the phone. Bracing my-self, I called the Nieuw Amsterdam Market, and Sam, the manager, picked up. "Mrs. Who?" he said. "Balser, Sam. How are you this morning?" ". . . Mrs. *Who?*" I hung up, got the Yellow Pages and phoned a market on Broadway I'd never used before. "We don't open charges by phone, lady," said the man at the other end, "the order'll hafta be COD." Rattled, I agreed, telling him for the third time to send the order out immedi-ately, and was on my way back to Liz's room when I remembered that I had exactly four dollars and thirty-seven cents in my wallet.

I went into Liz's room and lowered the sound on Mighty Mouse. "Liz, darling, how much money do you have in your red schoolhouse bank?"

Keeping her eyes on the screen, Liz frowned. "Thir-teen dollars and eighty-five cents. Why? Can you please turn that sound back up?"

"I'll turn it up when I'm through talking. I'd like to borrow ten dollars to pay for some groceries. And since it may be a while before they come, is there anything else you might like besides chicken noodle soup?"

Giving up on Mighty Mouse, Liz stared at me with Jonathan's yellow-brown eyes. Like Sylvie's they change and are sometimes pure brown like mine, sometimes pale amber like Jonathan's. "Sylvie's got *twenty-three* dollars hidden in that old Lord & Taylor shoebox on her closet shelf. Why don't you borrow ten dollars from her?"

"Because she's in school, Elizabeth, and you're here. Where's the key to your bank?"

"In my underwear drawer, beneath my socks."

Trembling—I knew whose genes *those* were—I turned the sound back up on the television, got the key, unlocked the bank and took out ten dollars. Returning everything to its place, I paused in the doorway. "Thank you," I said loudly above Little Lulu. "Would you like me to bring you some tea and crackers, or would you rather wait for the noodle soup?"

"I'll wait," said Liz. "I'm not so hungry any more."

At 1:48 Liz threw up all the chicken noodle soup and crackers she had managed to get down.

At 2:12 the phone rang. After letting it ring twice, I steeled myself for the nut again and picked it up. It was Miss Brekker, calling to say that Jonathan wouldn't be home to supper, and that he wanted to know how Elizabeth was feeling. In a shaking voice I told poor Miss Brekker, the innocent go-between, that if Jonathan wanted any information about his daughter he'd damned well better phone himself, and hung up.

At 2:37 Liz's fever was back up to one hundred and three. She was convulsively coughing, complained of terrible pains in her stomach and chest, and her eyes were almost swollen shut.

At 2:41 I called Doctor Miller's office and the answering service informed me that Doctor Miller had gone for the day. In a lethal voice I informed the answering service that I had a very sick child on my hands, and that if they didn't reach Doctor Miller and have him call me back within ten minutes, I would report him to the AMA. "Just a moment, Madame," said the breathless lady from the answering service, "please hold on." She clicked off, and several minutes later clicked back on: "Doctor Miller has signed out to young Doctor Bookman for the rest of today. I have Doctor Bookman on the other line now, and if you give me your name and address, he'll be at your house sometime before five o'clock." I was going to shout that I wanted Young Doctor Bookman at my house *now*, or at most within the next half-hour, but I knew when I was licked, and gave her my name and address and hung up.

At 4:07 Sylvie came home from school. Doubly dosed with aspirin, Liz had finally fallen asleep, and I was seated by the window in her room when Sylvie appeared in the doorway. Even in the dusk I could see The White Rabbit Look on her face. She slowly looked round at the empty glasses and cups on trays, the balled-up Kleenexes, the sleeping Liz, and beckoned me out into the little hall. "Mudther, can I go lie down on your bed? It's awful in there," she whispered hoarsely. "I have to lie down because I have the bloodiest headache," she added, and burst into tears.

At 4:23 I was in the kitchen fixing Sylvie a cup of hot tea when the phone rang. I'd completely forgotten the telephone madman by then, and picked it up after the first ring. It was Lottie. They had pulled out her tooth at the dental clinic. Over their protests she had insisted on gas, and had been so dizzy ever since, she couldn't stand up. She was also beginning to itch all over and her wrists and ankles were swelling up, which she thought might be a reaction to the penicillin shot they'd given her afterwards. As she began to stammer doubt about being able to get in the next day, I told her severely not to think of coming in, and to call a doctor *immediately* —a penicillin reaction was nothing to fool around with.

When I brought Sylvie her tea, the bedroom was in darkness; she'd fallen asleep. Blessedly, Liz was also still sleeping in her room. I set the tea tray down in the pantry and took out one of the Baccarat old-fashioned glasses Jonathan bought last winter and poured it half full of bourbon. I didn't bother with ice. Forgetting that I hadn't had any breakfast, and that my lunch had been three saltines and half a cup of soup, I carried the glass into the kitchen, where I sat down and lit a cigarette. I'd been too busy to smoke all day, and for a while I just sat there, all of me focused on the simple pleasures of orality—drawing in smoke and letting it out, rolling the warming bourbon around my tongue. When the doorbell rang and Folly began to bark, I wondered, pleasantly dazed, Now who can that be? When I got to my feet, all the pleasure vanished: *That* was the doctor and I was half looped.

I opened the door on a sturdy young man with rumpled hair taking his rubbers off. Young Doctor Bookman. He straightened up, a bright smile on his pugnosed baby face. It was a face that looked oddly familiar. Oh *God*, I foggily thought. "Would you like me to leave these out here?" he asked, gingerly holding out a dripping raincoat and a hat with a plastic cover. Taking care to enunciate clearly, I told him to bring them in and I'd hang them in the girls' bathroom, where he could wash his hands.

While he was washing off any remnants of measle and mump and whooping-cough germs, I snapped on a lamp and unsteadily tiptoed to the bed where Liz still lay in a comalike sleep. I gently shook her by the shoulder, and she finally stirred, her swollen eyelids fluttering, then opening, on the face of Young Doctor Bookman, who was now standing behind me.

Liz sat up and began to scream. Young Doctor Bookman, I finally realized, looked familiar only because he was a dead ringer for the ear-nose-and-throat specialist who had lanced Liz's ear when she was five.

Above the screams I tried to explain the unfortunate resemblance to Young Doctor Bookman. He'd grown very pale. I was having trouble with my consonants. The smell of 90 proof sourmash filled the stuffy room.

"Oh sure. Josh Manulis. A great ENT man, old Josh. I know him well. Everyone says we look alike." He gave a loud sniff and stared at me with round blue eyes. "Uh. Mrs. Balser, I think I could get Liz calmed down a lot quicker if you left us alone."

I left the room on stork legs. The screaming stopped the minute the door closed behind me. I lurched into my room, where Sylvie, awake now, was lying on Jonathan's bed with a wrung-out washcloth on her forehead, looking like Garbo in *Camille*. She announced that her headache was Positively Beastly, and there was a terrible taste in her mouth, a taste like the smell of an exploded cap pistol . . . did I know what she meant? Oddly enough, I did. I gave her an aspirin, told her that the doctor was here and that he'd examine her when he was through with Liz. To my horror, I seemed to be getting drunker by the minute.

I went back and knocked on the door to the girls' room and was told to come in. Young Doctor Bookman was looking in Liz's ear with one of those long black instruments, saying, "Hey! Did you know you had a big white pigeon roosting in here?"

"S'cold," giggled Liz.

I leaned against the wall for support.

Young Doctor Bookman removed the instrument and patted Liz on the arm. "You're a grand girl, Lizzie!"

"How is she?" I asked from the wall.

"She's just fine," he said heartily. "Though the symptoms are alarming, it's not at all serious, as I believe Doctor Miller told you on the phone. This Thing is all over New York. I've been swamped with calls. In some cases the fever runs as high as a hundred and *five*, and *still* it's nothing to worry about. There was really no point in my coming to see Elizabeth, since there's absolutely nothing I can do. This Thing has to run its own course, no antibiotics touch it. All we can do, *you* can do, is keep her quiet and warm, see that she gets plenty of fluids and plenty of rest. Feed her lightly, give her aspirin every four hours, and give me a call tomorrow and let me know how she is."

During his speech the bourbon fog had miraculously lifted, my head had cleared. "Can't you at least prescribe something for the nausea?" I briskly asked Young Doctor Bookman, who was buckling shut a shiny new black doctor's bag. "I can hardly feed her lightly if she doesn't keep anything down."

Looking somewhat sheepish, Young Doctor Bookman said yes, he guessed he could prescribe something for the nausea, and went into my room to phone our pharmacy. Before he called, he gave Sylvie a quick going-over. "Well now, Sylvia, I don't see a thing. But if you're going to get it, you're going to get it, that's all. We'll just have to wait and see." Brightly smiling, he picked up the phone and dialed.

As he talked to the druggist, Sylvie appealed to me. "It? What does he mean, *It?*"

"A Thing that's all over New York. They've been swamped with calls. In some cases the fever runs as high as a hundred and *five*, and *still* it's nothing to worry about. There is absolutely nothing they can do. The Thing has to run its own course, no antibiotics touch it. All we can do, *I* can do, is keep you quiet and warm, see that you get plenty of fluids and plenty of rest."

Having hung up in time to catch the end of this, Young Doctor Bookman stood blinking at me in my slacks and a shirt splattered with Welch's Grape Juice that I hadn't had time to change: What kind of a Mother *was* this?

Ah, if he only knew! I thought, returning a stare so like Jonathan's that I had a terrible impulse to do or say something lewd, obscene. What I said, and sweetly, was: "Thank you so much for coming by, Doctor Bookman. I know you're a busy man." With that I fetched his coat and hat and saw him to the door.

As he put on his rubbers and rang for the elevator, I stood in the door. "How long does this Thing usually last?"

"Anywhere from five to eight days."

"And my husband and I? Will we catch it too?"

"You might, Mrs. Balser. You might!" And with a tip of his hat, which seemed to be covered by one of those plastic icebox-left-over things, he disappeared into the elevator run by Sven the drunken Swede.

At 6:47 I was in the kitchen, scraping the barely touched Sick Child's Meal I'd compulsively cooked (broiled lamb chops, baked potatoes) off plates into the garbage, when Jonathan called.

He said: "I'm really awfully sorry, Teen. It's been one helluva day. Miss Brekker said you sounded very upset, but I honestly couldn't get free until now. As it is, I'm late for where I'm going—I was supposed to meet Marks and this client of ours in the Oak Bar fifteen minutes ago . . . How is Liz? What did Doctor Miller say?"

"Doctor Bookman says she's just fine. She's just got this Thing that's all over New York. In some cases the fever runs as high as a hundred and *five* and *still* it's nothing to worry about."

There was a long singing silence. "Did *she* have one hundred and five?"

"One hundred and four. But she's much better now."

"Whew. For a minute there I almost pushed the panic button. I've really been worried as hell about her all day, and hearing she's better takes a big load off my mind . . . And you. How are you bearing up?"

"Just fine."

"Atta girl, I'm glad to hear it. I knew you'd rally round . . . I've gotta run. Don't wait up for me—I'll be very late."

It is now 11:12 P.M. Both girls, dosed with aspirin and Compazine (antinauseant) have been asleep since eight. Sylvie woke once around nine and asked for a cold drink, but outside of that I've had a completely peaceful three hours. I've been sitting at Jonathan's desk in the den, writing, smoking, drinking No-Cal ginger ale. I've written all this down like someone writing a note, putting it in a bottle and pitching it into the sea: HELP! HELP! HELP! is what this entry says. Of course I don't expect the call to be answered. We will all get this Thing, I see it clearly—two shipwreck weeks dead ahead.

RIGHT AGAIN: exactly two weeks.

I remember hearing somewhere that one of the clearest indications of a Paranoid-Schiz is their claim to prescience—which makes me a guess-what. Two weeks: Liz, Sylvie, me. Lottie seems to have escaped, but, as of a few hours ago, I'm not sure about Jonathan. But if he's going to get it, he's going to get it, as Young Doctor Bookman so incisively put it. It hit me—and hit me hardest of all, naturally—when Liz was back at school but Sylvie was still home. I lost seven pounds and still feel weak and bruised.

The thing that saved me was Rediscovering Proust. It happened one afternoon when I was lying in bed feeling too weak and giddy to read, and bored beyond belief. Things were drifting in and out of my head in that wispy way they do when you're sick, and I suddenly found myself thinking of a crazy Irish poet I'd seen for a while in my Sullivan Street days. It had been a very short while, because I wouldn't go to bed and he wasn't about to waste his time. But while he was still making the Big Pitch, I came down with a bad old-fashioned cold, and he called and asked if he could come over and cheer me up. Since it obviously was the idea of me lying in bed, with Tibby off at Hearn's, that prompted this kindness, I politely demurred, saying I was too sick. "A visit from me would do you more good than ten doctors,

old bean," he said. "H'w'ver, since you won't avail yourself of thet, I'll offer some advice in my stead: make
yourself a nice hut tuddy, and while you sip it, read
Proust. Proust is the only thing when you're sick." I
didn't take the advice at the time, but on that dreary
cold afternoon about a week ago, remembering that poet
(who, in retrospect, seemed fascinating), I got up and
went staggering into the den, where Lottie was polishing
Jonathan's desk with lemon oil according to Jonathan's
instructions. While she fussed at me for not having
called her, I pulled down the first volume of Proust and
went tottering back to bed. I skipped the hut tuddy, but
by God it worked. Saved me. Was the antibiotic which
wouldn't "touch" the Thing I had. Marvelous crazy
poet. Marvelous Proust. Marvelous Swann. Marvelous
Odette.

*Any*way—hawthorns, cattleyas, church spires, Balbec
—all that lovely stuff aside, I got up two days ago, and as
of today started to go about my business again. First on
my agenda was my tooth: on Tuesday night my temporary filling had finally given way and fallen out. The exposed tooth was agonizingly sensitive to hot and cold,
and after a day of horror, I arranged to go to the dentist
this afternoon. About one o'clock I was in my bathroom, shaving my legs, when Lottie came to the closed
door. "Mrs. Balser, can you come to the phone? There's
a man wants to speak with you."

I knew at once who it was. I was halfway down one
leg, but I said, "Yes, Lottie. I'll take it. I'll be right out."
As soon as I heard her start for the kitchen, I came out,
hopping, so my wet foot wouldn't stain the rug.
"Hello?" I said into the bedroom extension, breathless
from hopping—I told myself.

"Hello." The voice was the one I knew it would be.
Mr. Telephone Pervert hadn't entered my mind.

"Just one minute, please," I said, and covering the
mouthpiece with my hand, shouted, "I've got it, Lottie.
You can hang up now." In the earpiece I listened to
heavy steps on linoleum, and then the click of the receiver being replaced.

There was a laugh from the other end. "You *sure* she's hung up?"

"Yes," I said, and suddenly not giving a damn about the rug, put my wet foot down and kicked the bedroom door shut with the other one.

"Christ. You really *are* paranoid."

"I thought we'd settled that," I said and wondered, Is this conversation ever going to have an official start?

It immediately did. He said: "Well. How are you? Recovered from my shocking behavior yet? I gave you a lot of time. Three weeks."

"I'm just fine," I said, Miss Prissy Prunes.

"Okay. That's over. Let's get to the point. Can I see you sometime soon? Like this afternoon? It took me three weeks to make up my mind to call, but now that I have, I'd like to see you right away. That's the way I operate."

The way he operated was too much for me. Stalling, trying to collect my wits, I said: "Did you call once before today? Did you call about two weeks ago and . . . try to be cute?"

"Cute? What d'you mean by 'cute'? You mean say things? Jerk off into the phone?"

I made an affirmative noise.

"Do I seem like the type to do that?"

He didn't, and wasn't, and I'd known it. I'd just been trying to gain some time.

"It must have been some poor guy driven clonkers by your charms . . . So. What about it? When do I see you?"

Oh God, I thought, and still stalling, said, "What do you mean by 'see'? Do you mean you'd like to meet me for a drink or lunch?"

He burst out laughing. "Jesus, baby. You expect me to go through all that?"

I said nothing. I felt too peculiar, and knew if I spoke I would sound that way. Besides, I wasn't sure how I wanted to be, what sort of thing I wanted to say. It had been three weeks. I had thought of him once—on a conscious level. But from the way I felt I knew that subconsciously I'd been thinking of him steadily.

"I'd give you a drink if you came by here," he said, breaking the heavy silence on the line.

"Where is here?"

"My apartment. Pad. Best view of the Hudson in town. We're practically neighbors, you know—it's about a seven-block walk from there to here. You could drop by some afternoon on your way home from marketing."

"I do my marketing by phone."

"Shit. Come on, baby, be a big brave girl and play it clean and straight."

"I can't be brave. I'm a coward through and through. I'm afraid of most everything you could name."

"Yah, and I'll name one: me."

"And if I am, what's wrong with that?"

"Nothing. In fact, it's exciting as hell."

And so it was. Even over the phone. How *sick*.

"Come over now. This afternoon," he said after another silence.

Decided at last, I said, "I have to go to the dentist. My appointment's in an hour."

"Tomorrow. No, tomorrow's Saturday. Monday."

"Monday I promised Jonathan I'd go downtown and pick out our Christmas cards for this year."

He made an indescribably obscene noise. "If you ever change your mind, I'm in the phone book. If you do call, you'd better leave all that crap at home." He crashed down the phone.

I hobbled back to the bathroom and finished shaving my legs, nicking myself so badly in the process that I had to put on a Band-Aid—a charming sight through nylon mesh. Since I'd been out of pills for weeks and couldn't face the prospect of the dentist chair without any fortification, I took a small shot of vodka before I left the house. It was a mistake. Not only did the alcohol hit my poor convalescent stomach like a pickaxe, but Gorley smelled it, as only he would. "*Well*, Bettina," he said, beamish as usual as he tied the plastic apron around my neck, "you've set a record, making a temporary filling last a month." "It was just a little over three weeks," I corrected him, nervously watching him take out instruments, "and I've been sick." That was all I was able to say, because he pried my mouth open and began, first taking a deep sniff. "It Leaves You Breathless," I assured myself, squeezing my eyes shut and trying to ignore the vodka-burns in my stomach, "he can't smell it." From the endless sniffs he took, it was apparent he could; but that and the burning aside, it was worth it, for I managed to stay relatively calm until he took the impression for the new inlay. Then, my mouth held open with clamps, jammed with things—cotton cylinders, wax, a tube for sucking up saliva—I felt my throat closing and prepared to die. Making faint gurgling sounds which neither he nor his nurse appeared to hear, I waited for it to close completely, in a sort of swoon seeing Gorley doing a tracheotomy with that curved pick, missing the windpipe and hitting the jugular, seeing my blood spurting out and splattering his white-and-gold vinyl *terrazzo* floor . . .

Still alive, another temporary filling in my mouth, I finally climbed out of the chair, and after making a next appointment two weeks away, fled home. The Willards were giving a huge party. They'd invited us weeks ago, but I'd already begged off, telling Jonathan I was still not well enough to go. Naturally he planned to go without me, and when I got home I thought with relief of the quiet evening ahead. Looking into their room, I said hello to the girls and the Jocelyn girls from downstairs and walked Folly. When I came back up, I sent Lottie home and happily began making a pilaff to go with the pot roast she'd cooked. The vodka had apparently burned out the last vestiges of my disease: I was starved.

Still wearing his coat, Jonathan came into the kitchen. "I better not kiss you," he croaked hoarsely. "Even though I think what I'm getting is that damned Thing you all had."

I put the lid back on the bubbling pilaff, turned down the flame and said brightly, "You'd have caught it long ago if it's what we had. What makes you think it's the same Thing?"

"What makes me *think* so," he said, furious, "is that I've got a sore throat, all my goddamn joints ache, and

the smell of whatever muck it is you're cooking makes
me want to throw up."

"It could be just the start of a cold," I said, determined not to knuckle under. "But whatever it is, you can
probably head it off by taking some aspirin and going to
bed."

"And skip the Willards' party?"

And skip the Willards' party. "Well, of course it's up
to you."

It was, and so he lay down for an hour, and then,
looking terrible, got up, groomed himself to the nines
and went to the Willards' party. It is now 10:30, and exhausted by what I shall call a trying day, I'm going to
take a bath and go to bed and read Proust. I've been
whipping along so fast I'm in the second volume. With
Albertine.

THIS IS THE fourth day Jonathan has been home sick. Having come in from the Willards' at a quarter past two, he managed to stagger around for one more day, before collapsing into bed on Sunday. He's now been home from work for three days, and this, the third, finds me so wild, so desperate, that I'm risking writing in here while he's in the house. Actually, there's not that much risk: It's 2:08 P.M., the girls are in school, Jonathan's sleeping, Lottie's in the kitchen, and I'm seated here at the desk in the den, this pad hidden by stacks of little boxes which make a high wall between me and the door. The boxes hold party invitations, and from the doorway it looks as though I'm busily filling them out and addressing them—something I actually *have* been doing for the last hour and a half. The invitations are to a large party we seem to be giving on December 16th. Jonathan casually gave me this information when I lay sick with the Thing, adding that he'd engaged Beaumont and his staff over a month ago, but hadn't wanted to upset me at that time. Since he finally did tell me at a time when I had a fever of one hundred and two, I couldn't have cared less. Now, today, at a cool 98.6, I care very much, but won't go into it. I'm wild enough as it is.

I'm wild because Jonathan sick is not to be believed, not to be borne. I think the Thing has softened his brain.

He is overbearing, plaintive, vile-tempered, lachrymose, demanding, hypochondriacal to the point of hysteria, steeped in self-pity, infantile. To top it all off, he takes a perverse pleasure in looking as horrible as he can, refusing to shave or comb his hair, and just lies there, glaring out of a stubbled face with bloodshot eyes. A device aimed at getting pity, no doubt, but one which ends up getting him the reverse. In spades. But what I mind most is the way he orders Lottie and me around. Nothing is asked for. It's never "Tina, could I please have an aspirin?" or "Lottie, would you mind bringing me some pineapple juice"—but "Bring me a Sucret, Tina," and "Lottie, I want a glass of ginger ale with lots of cracked ice, cracked, mind you, not cubes, and a piece of that Holland Rusk." All day long trays go back and forth from the kitchen. And it's not just trays of tea-and-toast, either. If it *is* tea, it's Major Grey or Lapsang Soughong, on a tray with some *gaufrettes* or Cornish Ginger Bread Biscuits. It's trays of four-minute eggs and Carr's Wheatmeal Biscuits, trays of Baxter's Scotch Broth and Bent's Cold Water Crackers, trays of hot madrilène and French *biscottes*. The room smells of soup and mandarin oranges and Vicks VapoRub (some throwback to his Brookline childhood, I suppose). At this very moment there are cracker crumbs all over the bed and floor, but he claims he's having a relapse, and won't let Lottie in to vacuum them up.

Before this "relapse," when he was beginning to feel better, and wasn't sleeping or lying around looking martyred, he was reading every newspaper and magazine that Rachman's had in their store. As he finished them he'd drop them, *splat*, on the floor, and by the end of each day the bed was adrift on a sea of paper: *Playboy*, *Esquire*, *Holiday*, *Mad Magazine*, *The Enquirer*, *The Daily News*, *The Guardian*. When he wasn't reading, he was on the phone with his office, or his broker, or someone involved with that play of Gaylord's—which I gather he's going to invest in, though he hasn't said as much. By now he's given up phoning Max Simon, but the first two days he called him several times. Like Doctors Miller and Bookman, Simon said he saw no point in coming by. After listening to a detailed recital of his symptoms, he told Jonathan that he had "this Thing that's all over New York," and told him to keep warm, drink plenty of fluids and get a lot of rest. "That bastard. That bloody *bast*ard," Jonathan would whisper upon hanging up, but several hours later, having popped a thermometer into his mouth and finding that it read one hundred and one, he would pick up the phone and call That Bastard again.

Twice yesterday I looked up George Prager in the phone book in the den. He was still in there the second time. You won't call him, I said to myself. The man is a monster. Frying pan into the fire. You want proof that you've really gone mad? And what kind of a woman goes and hops into bed with another man, just because her husband is sick and temperamental?

That was yesterday. This morning, around 11:30, I was sitting in the living room with a cookbook open in my lap, looking for an interesting new turkey stuffing. With Thanksgiving only a week away, I thought I'd better get busy. Suddenly Jonathan came shuffling in like a refugee from an old men's rest home. His hair was wildly tangled and he didn't have on a bathrobe or slippers.

"Are you getting up?" I asked brightly. "Are you feeling well enough to be up and around today?"

"God no, I feel perfectly lousy. I only got up because I suddenly remembered something very important, and came to see what you were doing. What *are* you doing? What's that you're reading?"

"A cookbook. Is there something you wanted, or wanted me to do?"

"There sure is. My brain's been so affected by this Thing that I completely forgot about the invitations to our party. They've got to go out right away."

I closed the cookbook on a recipe for turkey stuffing made, so help me, of pine nuts and prunes. "I don't see what's so urgent. The party's still a month away."

"A month really isn't enough advance notice for a party this time of year. Don't you realize most of these people make their plans two, sometimes even three months ahead?"

"I'm afraid it isn't something I've given much thought to."

"Well, they do, and we'll be damned lucky if a lot of them aren't all booked up . . . You'll find the invitations and guest list on the shelf of the hall closet. They're not really what I wanted—they were out of the engraved kind the Barrs always use, but Dempsey and Carroll assured me these were good form. Would you mind doing them right away, Teen? I'd help you if I didn't feel so goddamn rotten, but I'm so weak I can hardly stand up. And you don't have anything else to do, do you? I mean there you are, reading a cookbook. Why, if I may ask, *are* you reading a cookbook?"

"I'm looking for a new turkey stuffing."

"Turkey?"

"Thanksgiving turkey."

"Thanksgiving. Christ. When's *that*?"

"A week from tomorrow."

"God. It's even later than I thought! I've lost all track of time with this damn Thing. God. Listen, Teen, do you think you could put everything else aside and get those invitations out in the mail today?"

"I suppose I could get them filled out and addressed, but I'll have to mail them tomorrow. I don't have any stamps in the house."

"The post office is only four bloody blocks away, and it doesn't close until five or five-thirty!"

"That's true." I put the cookbook aside. "What you say has a certain ring of truth."

"I'm sorry, Teen. My nerves aren't in the greatest shape. And I'm sorry to interrupt your recipe hunt. I think a new stuffing would be great. In fact, I think it would be just great if you did a whole different kind of Thanksgiving dinner this year. Not that your Thanksgiving dinners aren't always great, but it would be fun to jazz it up, have it more gourmet and . . . less classic American, y'know."

I knew. "Could you possibly stay up for a while? I'd

like Lottie to go in and change the sheets on your bed, and air and freshen up the room."

"I'm sorry Teen, but I've got to go straight back to bed. I'm weak as a kitten. And I've got to rest because no matter what, I've got to get up and go to work Friday." He was almost out of the room when he stopped and turned. "Do we have any lemons?"

"I suppose. Why?"

"I have this terrible thirst, this terrible craving for a big tall lemonade."

"There's a can of frozen lemonade in the freezer. Ask Lottie to mix it up for you."

"I'd really rather have fresh lemonade, if you don't mind. And I don't feel well enough to go all the way to the kitchen. Tell Lottie to make me the real old-fashioned kind, tart, with plenty of cracked ice and sliced lemons, and maybe just a touch of grenadine."

Since I wasn't about to go into the kitchen, where Lottie was doing the breakfast dishes, and ask her to start squeezing lemons and cracking ice in a dishtowel with a hammer, I made the lemonade myself. When I brought it to Jonathan, I told him that because it looked like it might rain or snow, I was going out to the post office for the stamps now, before I started on the invitations; if he wanted anything while I was gone, Lottie would get it for him. I then put on my coat and went into the den and got the phone book out of the closet. I copied George Prager's phone number onto a piece of scratch pad, jammed it into the pocket of my camel's-hair coat along with my wallet and left.

It was a freezing, grey, windy day. I walked three of the four blocks to the post office and then ducked into an outdoor phone booth. It smelled like every tramp on the West Side had been using it for a urinal. The smell was so overpowering that I had to hold my nose while I dialed, a neat trick.

"*Yes?*" George Prager shouted angrily after it had rung four times.

"Were you working?" I let go my nose, not the only reason I was having trouble breathing.

"Would I answer if I was working? So. It's you."

It was me all right. "That's right."

"What's up? You want a drink?"

"I thought that might be nice."

"Conditional?"

"I would like a drink."

"Better. It'll have to be the day after tomorrow. To-morrow's out. Friday, the day after tomorrow, at three?"

"All right," I said, remembering that Jonathan had announced he was going back to work no matter what, come Friday.

"You going to change your mind? Chicken out? Not show?"

"No."

"Ok*ay*." He hung up.

I went to the post office, came home, fixed Jonathan a lunch tray, then came in here and addressed invitations for an hour and a half. The timing was just right: Jonathan is awake now and calling "Tina? *Tina!*"—peevish, like Clifton Webb. Until the coast is clear enough for me to lock these pages in my storage vault I'll put them in the big Skira book on Rubens that I bought way back in my Art Major days, and which now sits in the book-shelf to my left. The pages will be perfectly safe there until Jonathan goes back to work. Jonathan long ago announced that he couldn't stomach Rubens, that he thought him a bad painter, a thoroughly Vulgar man. And so he was. Not a bad painter. But Vulgar. So he was. The dear sweet man.

"I'M A NANIMAL," he said to the ceiling.

I didn't say a word.

"And you. You're a nanimal too."

We lay with the covers pulled up to our noses, like the kittens in the old Chesapeake-Ohio ads: Nanimals?

He sighed and stirred and patted me under the covers. "Baby, you're a terrific piece of ass. Are you always that good?"

"No."

He laughed and got up. "So much for the compliments. I'll go inside and fix up our drinks."

"Inside" was his living room, huge, barely furnished, with a big uncurtained window overlooking the Hudson and Palisades. Light, the color of the river and the sky which threatened snow, poured in, making the room seem colder and barer than it was.

When I'd arrived an hour earlier, that light had blinded me. His face pale and grave, he had taken my coat, and while he hung it up in a closet inside the door, I made straight for the window, wincing at the brilliant whiteness. "What a marvelous view!"

Behind me I heard the closet door shut, heard him laugh. "Barbara Bel Geddes couldn't have made a better entrance, Pussycat— What're you drinking?"

"Vodka and tonic," I said to the windowpane where my warm breath made a round cloud. I thought: If Jonathan gets home before I do, he won't smell the vodka; he won't be inside my mouth like Gorley was . . . at least not if I can help it, by God.

While he rattled around in the kitchen, I took a few deep breaths to compose myself, and turned to steal a quick look at the room. Against the wall to my right was a long black foam-rubber couch; in front of it was a marble coffee table, with a canvas chair off to each side, and covering the floor was a worn but spotless white cotton rug. There wasn't a picture on the wall, or any other sort of ornament in the room, and the only other furniture was a card table and bridge chair by the window. It wasn't only austere, yes, monastic, but almost fanatically clean and neat. Hearing him coming, I quickly turned back to the bleak view.

He brought the drinks to the window, and after handing me mine, studied me, while I sipped and studied the grey Palisades. "You've gotten thinner. In fact, you don't look well."

"I've had a virus since I last saw you. We all had it . . . Is this the table where you work?"

He gave a loud sigh, and I turned to look at him at last. Like the room, he was extraordinarily neat and clean. He'd had a haircut, he wore a handsome dark blue flannel shirt and grey flannel slacks with knife-sharp creases, and there was a fresh nick from a razor on the jawbone near his ear. The effort behind all this momentarily threw me off: all this for *me?*

But the eyes were the same stony grey-white with black pin-points, and they stared at me expressionlessly while my question about the table went unanswered.

"Well, if it's where you work, you've got a marvelous view to inspire you," I said, disconcerted. "Are you working on a new play?"

He sighed again, bored. "I never talk about my work. *Ever.* So forget it from now on— Are you going to come and sit down, or are you going to stay glued to this damned window all afternoon?"

"Don't start. Please."

"Don't start what?"

"Being impossible."

He grinned. "Baby, that's the way I am. Don't *you* start."

"Me? Start what?"

"Getting all nerved up."

"I'm not nerved up. You just . . . antagonize me."

He gave a soft laugh. "That isn't exactly the word for it." With that he went and sat down on one end of the couch. Not wanting to feel any more foolish than I already did, I went and sat down on the other end. From a distance of about five and a half feet, we warily watched each other breathe. "What changed your mind?" he finally asked. "About coming here, I mean."

"I'm not clear on that."

"It's becoming clearer by the minute, isn't it?"

When I didn't answer, he faintly smiled and with narrowed eyes watched the rapid rise and fall of my chest.

"Interesting . . . isn't it?" he finally said in a deeper, changed voice.

"That isn't exactly the word for it."

He laughed, relieved: I was beginning to play ball. He got up and went over to the window for a pack of cigarettes lying on the sill. He lit one for each of us, then slowly headed back to the couch, skirting the coffee table, coming to the end where I sat. For a second he stood looming over me, looking much taller than he actually was, then moved so that his legs, apart, straddled and enclosed my primly locked knees. For a moment the legs, hard-muscled and strong, held me tightly, tensely. Then suddenly they relaxed their grip, and he bent down and put the cigarette in my mouth, sliding his hand away from my lips until it cupped my cheek. It was such an unexpectedly gentle gesture, almost tender, and the coldness of the hand on my burning cheek was such a giveaway to the real state of his nerves that for a moment I couldn't breathe. Apparently he had the same problem, for he suddenly drew in a sharp racking breath, and dropping his hand, walked abruptly back to the other end of the couch. He sat down heavily, and sprawling back, legs outstretched, not looking at me, smoked fiercely for several minutes.

"You know anything about me, aside from my plays?" he said finally.

"Enough."

"Everything they say is true. Except the bit about my being on the stuff. I was for a while, but not long enough to get hooked."

"I gather this is The Warning, which I must say I find quite presumptuous. I can take care of myself."

Still lolling back, with his face tilted to the ceiling, he wearily shut his eyes. "Don't start that lah-de-dah shit with me. It makes me want to puke. Save it for your husband and your charming crew of friends."

"The Big Virile Playwright," I said through my teeth. "Only you work too hard at it, it's so *obv*ious. It's like that thing Sinclair Lewis said to Hemingway about the hair on his chest."

Opening his eyes, he said to the ceiling: "Christ! There she goes again!"

I got up. "This is ridiculous. I'm going home."

"For God's sake, sit down and *relax!*" he roared.

"I can't possibly relax. You make me too mad."

"You're not mad. You're scared to death!" His glare fading, he smiled and added softly, "And goddamn it, so am I. So am I."

I just stood there, looking down at him. His face was drawn and deadly pale, the eyes all pupil, black. We stared at each other God knows how long, neither of us moving a muscle or batting an eye. Then he got to his feet and said softly, "Come on, baby. Come on. Come *on*."

And so I did. Oh yes. I did. And now, as I watched him come back, naked, into his bedroom where we had finally ended up, I stared, my skin prickling with goose-flesh. After so many years of Jonathan's long loose body covered with its furze of pinky-blond hairs, looking at this one was like seeing a man's naked body for the first time. Compact, powerful, flatly muscled, almost hairless and startlingly white, it made me shudder—and not from pure pleasure either, or the memory of what it could do.

He handed me my glass and climbed into bed. **Punch-**

ing his pillow against the headboard for support, he finally sat back: "So. Now. Let's discuss it. What the hell is going on?"

"What do you mean?"

"I mean, what the hell do we do? I thought you'd be good for a couple of screws. But this could get out of hand."

"It won't get out of hand. I won't let it." I gave him my drink to put on the night table next to him. I didn't want it. "I have no intention of getting involved with you."

" 'Involved.' " He burst out laughing. "I might've known. You think I want to get 'involved' with a dizzy mixed-up broad like you? I may be greedy, almost a pig about sex, but that doesn't mean I lose my head. I've had a pretty shitty life. About two years ago things started changing, and now, when things are really finally beginning to break for me, I'm not going to let anything fuck it up, especially a broad. Broads like you always get hung up: sex, particularly great sex, has got to be love."

"I couldn't love you, ever." I threw back the covers. It was a tiny room. The head of the bed was against the wall, and a black lacquer Chinesy sort of chest of drawers was pushed against the other end, making a high footboard. To get out of bed I would have to climb over him, a bit of suggestive acrobatics I didn't feel like risking.

"I won't argue with you," he said amiably, and turned to see me sitting on my haunches, trying to figure out a way of getting by him. "Hey. What's the big idea?"

"If you'll get up, I'll be able to get out of this bed."

"For what?"

"To get dressed and go home."

"It's only ten past four. You just came."

As he chuckled at his great wit, I decided the hell with it, and started to scramble over him. My hunch had been right. He grabbed me with his free hand, just where I'd known he would. "Please, George. Let me go."

"Why?" He still held me, but his grip was changing.

Slowly he put the drink in his other hand on the night table.

"You're hurting me," I lied; he wasn't hurting me any more. "And I'm so mad and upset my teeth are chattering."

"So you're mad and upset. You're alive, aren't you?" He put the hand still cold from the drink on my left breast, and slowly, thoughtfully, checked my heartbeat. "Oh yeah, you're alive. Alive and *kick*ing . . ."

Later, to the circle of lamplight on the ceiling, he said, "Goddamn. Now what?"

"Now I'm going home," I said, and nimbly climbed over him. It had suddenly gotten dark, and I turned on a lamp when I went into the cold living room for my clothes. When I'd finished dressing, and was checking my face and combing my hair, he appeared in the door to the living room, still naked and drink in hand. "The thing it all hangs on," he said, effortlessly picking up where we'd left off ten minutes earlier, "is do you think you can have a straight sex thing or not?"

The truth was I couldn't think. At all. I sighed, put my compact away, and giving a half-shrug, went to the closet for my coat.

"Well, can you or can't you?"

I started to shrug again, but then, changing my mind, gave my head a little shake.

"I thought so," he said and scowled. "Since I'm not sure I feel like coping with the *stuss* you're bound to make, let's say we play this by ear for a while."

"And what does *that* mean?" I said, buttoning my coat.

"It means we don't see each other awhile. Say, about a week. Nobody calls anybody else—and don't give me that smile, you'll *want* to call. Let's say we have a date a week from today, here, same time, and during that week we both think things over. *Carefully.* You think about whether or not you can swing this for what it is, pure and incredible Sex, and I'll think about just what I can or can't take. If during the week you've found you kicked it, or don't want to play it my way, don't show. If during the week I find that I've kicked it, or decided the high isn't worth the cost of the fix in *any* case, I'll either call and tell you not to come, or not be here when you show."

I couldn't help it. My hand on the doorknob, I bust out laughing. Never in my life had I been exposed to such pure gall.

"It's not that funny," he said, refusing to get angry. "What about it. Is it a deal?"

"Deal," I said, and still laughing, went out—Barbara Bel Geddes on the exit too.

By the time I got home it was five past five. I was out of breath and my ears and nose were numb. I hadn't been able to get a cab and so had walked the seven windy blocks, running when I hit the dark side streets between Columbus and West End. I unlocked the door on a frantic Folly. The lamp on the table was the only light. The hall smelled of O'Cedar polish and roasting veal and the silence was deafening, absolute.

Alarmed, I called out for Lottie and the girls, and even for Jonathan, but no one answered. Folly put her head to one side and began to whine. Had they all just vanished? Was I paying some terrible price for my afternoon? Beginning to shake, I, a likely candidate for a Straight Sex Thing, stood twitching in the dim hall until finally, like someone thinking back ten years, I remembered the plans I'd made for that afternoon—elaborate plans: novice that I am, I'd just discovered how much arranging and lying it took to get free for a few hours. For the first Friday afternoon in weeks, the girls hadn't had dates. Though Lottie is very fond of the girls and sits with them evenings, playing nursemaid has never been part of her job. Since I couldn't, with a clear conscience, leave the girls rattling around alone in the apartment with Lottie while I was at George's, and since I had no intention of *not* going to George's, I'd done an extraordinarily aggressive thing for me—I'd called Mrs. Goodman and asked if the girls could go there, mumbling something about having to go to the dentist. Being what she'd seemed, Mrs. Goodman had naturally said they could.

Remembering this wheeling and dealing, I started to sweat. I was still in my coat. At that very moment, I realized, Lottie was picking up the girls at the Goodmans', and Jonathan was at the meeting he'd hied himself out of bed to attend. For one more minute I stood in the hall with its wholesome domestic smells of roasting meat and wax, and allowed myself the luxury of feeling like some Sullying Presence. Then I rushed off to our bedroom to wash. And wash and wash. Tina Macbeth.

When I came out, the girls were just walking in the door. After Lottie had gone home, I sent the girls into their room to do their homework (if it isn't done Friday, it never gets done), and went back to the kitchen. Within half an hour I was myself again.

The phone rang while I was basting the veal, and it was Jonathan. "It doesn't look like I'm going to be able to get home for dinner, Teen. In fact, it doesn't look like I'll get home till rather late. But I have this nagging feeling . . . isn't there something we're supposed to be doing tonight?"

"There's a late party at Graham Tilson's, starting around ten, but I called him two days ago and told him you weren't well and we couldn't come. Which is a point, Jonathan. I mean it's your first day up and out . . . don't you think you're overdoing it? You'll have a relapse. How do you feel?"

"I have to overdo it, like it or not. When these stockholders hit town, old Hoddison expects me to sweat blood. And actually I feel all right, but it's really very sweet of you to be so concerned, Teen."

Ashamed, I shut my eyes.

"I tried to call earlier to let you know I wasn't coming, but nobody answered. Where the hell *was* everybody, anyway?"

Smoothly, as though I'd been at this for years, I said, "Lottie was out picking up the girls, who were visiting friends, and I was at the dentist." Easy as pie.

It's now five after eleven, and he still isn't home, thank God. I'll lock this and the last entry, which I've just rescued from the Skira Rubens, in the storage vault, then get into bed and turn out the light fast. I won't wait up. All I *need* is for him to come in, find me awake and say, "Hey, Teen. How's about a little ole roll in the hay?"

Friday December 1

IT'S EXACTLY A WEEK since I've written here, a week in which I didn't want to write because it would have meant putting down in black and white what was on my mind. I tried to dispense with what was on my mind early in the week. You can't have a Straight Sex Thing, Bettina Munvies Balser, I told myself: you will not call or go there next Friday, you will not go there ever again. That decided, I then kept myself too busy to think. It wasn't hard because there was so much to do, and though I never thought I'd see the day, I continually blessed our new social life. Starting on Saturday we went out every night—museum openings, parties, theater, ballet. During the days I did things like finish shopping for the girls' clothes, get my hair done at Jean Louis, attend the Pilgrim Festival at the Bartlett School and shop for Thanksgiving, which was yesterday. Wednesday night, Thanksgiving Eve, there was a "party" at Frank Gaylord's, a backer's audition for the new play, which turns out to be a musical, but I didn't go. I was able to swing that because Jonathan forgot to tell me about it far enough in advance; I'd promised Lottie she could leave mid-Wednesday to spend Thanksgiving with her family in Philadelphia, and was unable to get another sitter, even Mrs. Prinz. So though Jonathan was annoyed, it was only at himself. At my insistence he finally went to the party alone, while I happily stayed home and made cranberry-and-kumquat relish; I couldn't have planned it better myself.

Thanksgiving was the biggest help in keeping my mind off George. I've always had a big sentimental thing about Thanksgiving, and using Jonathan's repeated request for a different sort of meal this year as an excuse, I really went overboard.

God. The phone just rang and I almost jumped out of my skin. It wasn't him. It was someone accepting the invitation to our party. I might as well come off it and confess: every time the phone has rung in the last five days I've almost jumped out of my skin. It's never been him. But since it's now only 10:35 A.M. he could still call and tell me not to come. Which is really why I'm sitting here on Jonathan's bed, pad on my knees, next to the phone: I want to be sure to be here if he *does* call. In other words, in my typical spineless fashion, I'm hoping he'll relieve me of the burden of decision. For I've undergone a change of heart, and now want to go, but hate myself for it. If he doesn't call I still have four hours to make up my stupid mind.

Luckily, I'm here all alone. Liz was picked up by the Grimes' limousine, and is off to lunch and the Thanksgiving show at the Music Hall with Melissa and Nurse. Sylvie is at some Bowling Club outing organized by the school. Jonathan is at work, and Lottie isn't due back from Philadelphia until early afternoon. I've straightened the house and walked Folly, taking the phone off the hook before I went down. I want to stay right by the phone, but since I'm wild with nerves and without a pill, I've taken this out to help calm me and sweat out the time.

Thanksgiving. As I was saying, ever since childhood I've had a thing about it, a soupy smog of feeling I can only describe as nostalgia. The catch is that it's nostalgia for a completely imaginary Thanksgiving, one dreamed up out of those old Norman Rockwell *Sateve Post* covers and pictures of the Colonial settlers in my grade school books. This Thanksgiving Day has everything—cold snow-grey air, bonfires, dogs, a Colonial house bursting at the seams with a rosy-cosy family and rosy-cosy relatives who frolic on hooked rugs, sniff the indescribably delicious spice smells in the air, and crack nuts and play something like whist while waiting for the summons to the Groaning Board.

I know. Poor Baby. Because naturally this Nostalgia Thanksgiving is a reaction to what my Real Thanksgivings were. The one thing that matched in both versions was the smells. By mid-morning the brick house in White Plains would start filling up with indescribably delicious smells. They would float upstairs to my room, where I, good, obedient child that I was, would be keeping myself amused, by painting with watercolors, reading Nancy Drew, rearranging my collection of playing cards, working on my scrapbook of Ginger Rogers and Fred Astaire. The day was always clear-skied, too warm for late November, and filled with that gelatinous bright yellow sunlight that makes you feel ineffably bored and depressed. It was always this sunshine, pouring through my windows, that woke me to an unnaturally quiet house. Daddy-Dads was off playing golf at the club, Mums was sleeping off the losses from last night's cards. The only sound was a faint closing of cabinet doors, or a muffled ringing of pots from down in the kitchen, where some poor maid was starting to cook our Thanksgiving meal, a meal that never remotely fulfilled the promise of those early smells.

Somehow, the day dragged along until three o'clock. At three o'clock on the dot (my mother used to say they waited at the gas station up the block), a grey sedan would pull into our driveway, the doors would burst open, and out would come a thin exhausted-looking woman in a grey caracul coat, a short and stocky man wearing a grey fedora at a slant made popular by Chicago gangsters, and a yellow toad of a little girl—my father's sister Jean, her husband, Murray, and their daughter, Grace. They came every year, driving all the way from Rockville Centre on Long Island. Since my father's other sister was dead, and my mother's only brother lived in Seattle, they were the only relatives who ever came. They were, in fact, the only relatives I ever saw. Once they were in the house there was a lot of air-kiss-

ing, after which Grace and I were told to go upstairs
and play, while the adults went into the living room to
have a drink and talk. As soon as this order was given,
tight little pains would start up behind my ears. Though
I never told anyone, dear Cousin Grace was a thief. Over
several years of Thanksgivings, during those interludes of
"play" in my room, Cousin Grace had managed to steal:
a bow-shaped barrette trimmed with rhinestones, an
enameled heart-shaped locket on a pure gold chain, four
Swiss handkerchiefs embroidered with Scotties, fifteen
playing cards, two blue china Scottie puppies, a silver
pen-and-pencil set, a tiny pillow stuffed with balsam and
embroidered "Welcome to Sunapee," a hand-tooled
leather bookmark I'd made at summer day camp, a cake
of soap shaped like Walt Disney's Snow White, and my
biggest treasure of all—an autographed picture of Herself (Ginger Rogers), inscribed "to dear Bettina Munvies
with fond regards," a prize I'd gotten by sending two
dollars and ten cereal box tops to her movie studio.
"Let's see all the new clothes you got," Cousin Grace
would say the minute we entered my room, sitting
down cross-legged on my bed. Anguishing—it *had* to be
the time she filched things—I'd dart into my closet and
bring things out. "That's kind of cute," she would say,
or, "That's a drippy-looking dress. I thought your
mother was supposed to have such good taste!" When
this ordeal was over, she would demand to see any new
additions to my various collections, collections of playing cards (naturally I had a superb one), china and glass
Scotties (I never had a dog), pictures of flowers cut out
of magazines, pictures of Rogers and Astaire. Fear for
my possessions—old Grace seemed like some fat yellow
amoeba who could absorb objects through her skin—
would finally make the pains behind my ears so bad that
I'd bring up the one thing I knew she would find irresistible. "Let's go down and see what they're eating with
their drinks," I'd say, and down we'd go to the living
room, thick with cigar smoke and the smell of Scotch,
where we'd eat any green olives or pieces of stuffed celery that were left, until a depressed-looking maid ap-

peared in the doorway and mumbled that dinner was served.

Though the maids varied from year to year, the meal was always the same: canned cream of mushroom soup, turkey, stuffing, canned cranberry jelly, string beans, sweet potatoes topped with marshmallows, salad, Parker House rolls, a huge ice cream mold of a turkey, and chocolate leaves. The turkey was always tough and stringy, the stuffing dry and mealy, the string beans underdone and a brilliant baking-soda green, the sweet potatoes too sweet and sticky with Karo. It was the charity meal, the poor relations invited once each year to share The Lord's Blessings and Give Thanks. Only I never heard anyone utter anything remotely resembling a word of thanks. What I heard was my Cousin Grace asking my father to save her "the-part-that-jumped-over-the-fence-last," my Uncle Murray talking about his ulcer, my Aunt Jean's nervous stomach rumbling, my mother's tinka-tinkle of the bell to summon the gloomy maid, my father's abortive attempts at bright conversation and his stifled belches. My father never seemed to belch at any other time during the year.

It was such an ordeal for one and all that poor Uncle Murray would forget his ulcer and drink or smoke anything put in front of him—Scotch, champagne, brandy, Havana cigars. After the meal we'd adjourn to the living room, where the windows looked out on a twenty-five-foot square of yellowed grass, a circular clothesline and the back of someone's garage. Belching uncontrollably, my father would put on the radio and twiddle the dial until he found something soothing, like André Kostelanetz. Uncle Murray would sit down on the couch and promptly fall asleep. Sending me and Grace out to play in the "garden," my mother would light her fortieth cigarette, and turning to Aunt Jean, would ask in a low discreet voice: ". . . And how is Jeremy?" Jeremy was the black sheep, the Renegade Son. Like his little sister, Jeremy was a thief, but a professional, and by the age of fifteen had been in and out of two reform schools. As soon as he was of age he joined the Merchant Marine, and when the war broke out he was on one of the first merchant vessels to be sunk. When the war broke out these Thanksgivings, like poor Jeremy, came to an end. By the time the war and gas rationing were over, we'd moved to the other, bigger house, but for some reason no one ever explained, those Thanksgivings were never resumed. Let us Give Thanks.

The noon siren just went off. George still hasn't called.

So much for Thanksgivings past. With that behind me, it's perfectly clear why I've made a small production out of Thanksgiving all the years I've been married. They call it Compensating. It began with my first little frozen-and-eviscerated turkey on West Ninth Street, and has been going on ever since. On the side of Norman Rockwell and The Pilgrims, Nostalgia, it's always been a classic American meal, but everyone's always loved it; no one's ever complained. This year, when Jonathan did, I pounced on his request for something different, and it worked: George vanished. I poured over cookbooks and Jonathan's old *Gourmet* magazines, and when I finally had an impressive menu mapped out, threw myself into the marketing and cooking. I ran around shopping by foot, picking everything out myself and lugging it home —the sixteen-pound bird, the vegetables and fruits. (I startled the hell out of them at the Nieuw Amsterdam Market, where, as Jonathan once informed me, "the clientele only orders by phone.") I even stood and watched the man in the fish store shuck the oysters for the stuffing, and walked all the way over to Schrafft's for the pumpkin pie, the one stand-by of the Nostalgia menu that intuition told me not to change this year. Then I cooked everything, from the soup, a *consommé double* which required two days of keeping a stock-pot bubbling on the stove, to the nuts, almonds I blanched, buttered, salted and roasted myself. Very Tabitha-Twitchit-Danvers.

Yesterday Thanksgiving Day finally dawned, cold and raw, the air smelling of snow. Good omen number one, I decided at 7:10 A.M. as I stood at our open bathroom window, breathing deeply: Nostalgia weather for sure. Feeling marvelous, I went quietly back to the kitchen, and once I'd made juice and coffee and had some of each, I set the table in the dining room and started the stuffing for the turkey. I had a lot to do.

At 8:20 I was sautéeing onions and parsley and celery and rosemary and thyme, when the door burst open and Sylvie came in. "Uk! Onions before breakfast. *Double* uk! Couldn't you wait until later?"

Sweet, as sweet as the pot of Irish honey I'd set at Jonathan's place, I said, "I purposely set the table in the dining room. You won't be able to smell anything in there."

Said Sylvie: "You can smell those bloody onions in our bedroom! That's what woke me up." She peered suspiciously at a bowl full of oysters. "What's in there?"

"Something for the stuffing," I said, weary of all this. "Fix yourself some breakfast, Sylvie, and carry it inside."

Later, after I'd finished stuffing the bird and it lay all trussed and ready to go, I decided to get dressed. There was something slatternly about cooking in a bathrobe and pajamas. Not Twitchit-Danvers at all. Very Aunt Tessie, in fact.

"What's that bloody smell?" croaked Jonathan as I was creeping towards the bathroom through the darkened room, clothes in hand.

"The stuffing for the turkey. Good morning, Jonathan."

"God," said Jonathan, a lump under the covers. "Turkey. Are you making a big production?"

"I'm making a Thanksgiving dinner, if that's what you mean. And rather special, like you asked— Why?"

"God," said Jonathan. "So I did. And here I am. I know it isn't possible, but it feels like I'm getting that goddamn Thing all over again."

"You're right. It isn't possible. You probably stayed too late and drank too much at Gaylord's last night . . . What time *did* you get in, by the way?"

"I don't know . . . Two. Three. But I certainly didn't drink too much."

I deliberately didn't ask if he had decided to invest in the show. "Well, there's your answer: you didn't get enough sleep. Don't forget, you were still sick last week, and we've been out every night since Saturday. You've simply overdone it. Go back to sleep for a few hours and you'll feel fine when you wake up."

"I doubt it," groaned Jonathan, and pulled the covers over his head.

I ought to have been warned, but of course I wasn't—I was too determined to have a nice day. By the time I'd finished dressing, some of my nutty high spirits had returned. The girls had been invited to go down to Seventy-second Street with the Jocelyns, to watch the Macy Parade. Once they were gone, I made their beds, did the breakfast dishes and put the chestnuts for the purée in the oven. It took me forever to shell three pounds of chestnuts. The recipe said to shell them while they were still hot, and by the time I was done my hands were covered with pricks and burns. But I stayed crazily cheerful —nothing fazed me, not even hearing Folly scratching at the kitchen door and remembering I hadn't walked her. I left the chestnuts simmering in some chicken stock, put on a coat and scarf and mittens and took her down. The air was raw and grey and Central Park West was completely deserted and still. Not a car, not a living soul. It was like the set of one of those movies where The Bomb has gone off, and the narrator of the movie is the only survivor left on earth. I stood there, bewildered, wondering if some terrible calamity *had* occurred, when I heard the faint oompah of drums and squee of trumpets floating, ghostly, on the wind. Swinging around, I saw the balloon figures bobbling, building-high, blocks down, and burst out laughing. I turned my back on the parade and slowly walked Folly, loving the bitter cold, the greyness, the random snowflakes that eddied down like bits of torn paper and melted on my sleeve. Nostalgia weather, clear and true.

"Tina? . . . Sylvie? Liz? . . . *Tina!*"

I let the front door slam behind me, unhooked Folly and went to the door of our room. Jonathan was sitting up in bed, looking confused and frightened. "*There* you are! Where the hell is everybody? I couldn't imagine what'd happened!"

Maybe it was something in the air. "The girls are at the parade with the Jocelyns, and I was down with Folly." I tugged the scarf off my head. "Have you been up long? Do you feel any better? You *look* better."

"I've been awake about ten minutes. So the girls are at the parade, are they? When will they get back?"

"Not till mid-afternoon. They're having lunch down at the Jocelyns'. Why?"

"Great," said Jonathan. "That gives us plenty of time."

"Time?" said Stupid, still wadded in camel's-hair and mittens.

"Time for a little ole roll in the hay."

". . . Now?"

"Of course now."

"But . . . you're not well."

"Well, I feel better now—feel pretty horny as a matter of fact. You can get awfully horny lying around in bed."

I stared at him. Terrible bands were tightening inside my head and my mittens were stuck to my wet palms. I knew I couldn't swing it. "Jonathan," I said slowly, "I can't. I'm sorry but . . . I mean I really don't feel like it myself. I mean *I* haven't been lying around, I've been *rushing* around, and I still have a tremendous amount to do. In fact, if I don't go and turn off the chestnuts this minute they'll get overcooked."

He stared at me with yellow eyes and gave me a frightening, twisted smile. "Okay, Ok*ay*. I get the idea." The smile fading, he said: "Do you think you could at least manage to bring me some breakfast on a tray? I think if I take it very easy all day I'll be all right. I *have* to be all right, since I have a big meeting tomorrow. I have to work all weekend, in fact."

"Of course I'll fix you a tray." I was so guilty I was near tears. "What would you like?"

"My usual Sunday breakfast. Juice and coffee, two four-minute eggs, two toasted scones—but without butter today—and some Damson Plum preserve."

By 3:30 everything was well in hand. I'd planned that we'd eat at 6:00, and at 3:30 the girls were still at the

Jocelyns' and Jonathan was back asleep. I set the table with the Porthault cloth and Baccarat crystal and Robinson silver (all bought by Jonathan in the last two years) and took Folly down again. It had gotten much colder and the fitful flurries had stopped. I was back in the kitchen slicing oranges and endive for the salad when the girls came in. After a breezy greeting they disappeared into the grocery closet and Liz came out, her hand jammed in a box of pretzel sticks.

"Darling, please don't eat those now," I said.

"But, Mudther, we're just *starved*," said Liz as Sylvie came out of the closet eating Cheese Doodles from the bag. "That stingy Mrs. Jocelyn only gave us peanut butter sandwiches for lunch," she added.

"She purposely did that. She knew I was fixing a big Thanksgiving dinner, and didn't want to spoil your appetites. Which is exactly why I don't want you eating that junk now, so please put those things away."

"What time is dinner?" asked Sylvie.

"Six."

"But that's two hours away! We'll die of starvation by then!"

I let them each take one more handful, and sent them into the den to watch *Great Expectations* on Channel Nine.

At 4:58 I went to our room to wash and put on some festive silk slacks and a silk shirt, changing in the bathroom because Jonathan was still asleep. Next on my agenda was a nice relaxing drink, and I was creeping through the darkened bedroom when Jonathan suddenly sat up in bed. "Hunhff. Hey, what time is it?"

"A quarter past five. You *scared* me, Jonathan."

"I was having this awful dream. It woke me right up."

"How do you feel?"

"I dunno." He snapped on the bedside lamp, wincing at the brightness. He looked terrible.

"I was just going for a drink. Would you like me to bring you one? A drink might be just what you need."

"It also might kill me."

". . . I hadn't thought of that. You might have something there, Jonathan."

I was already out in the little hallway when he called after me, "On second thought I'll take some sherry, Teen. Some Harvey's, not the Tio Pepe!"

I came back and gave him his sherry and sank wearily into the armchair with my bourbon. It was the first time I'd sat down all day.

As he sipped, Jonathan eyed me uneasily over the rim of his glass. "You look pretty tired, Teen. You've really knocked yourself out over this dinner, haven't you."

"I haven't minded. I've enjoyed it, it was something I wanted to do," I said truthfully.

Looking edgier by the minute, Jonathan drank silently. His pajamas were a wrinkled mess, his hair was standing up in wild tufts, he needed a shave.

I decided to get the bad news over with. "How do you feel now?"

"I guess better. But still a little woozy, a little weak."

"You really don't have to eat if you don't feel up to it, Jonathan. Or if you can eat something, but feel too weak to get up, I'll bring you a tray."

He blushed. "Oh, I feel up to eating, all right. The thing I *don't* feel up to is getting into a suit. If I sponged and shaved and put on some clean pajamas and a robe, would that be okay?"

"Of course that will be okay." I glanced at my watch and got up. "Excuse me, Jonathan, I have to go and baste the turkey. I don't want to rush you, but if you are going to do everything you said, maybe you'd better start soon—we're going to eat at six."

The dining room was silent, the tentative click-a-clack of silver on china the only sound. The soup had been finished, the bird had been carved, the accompanying dishes served, and everyone, faced with full plates, was slowly tasting things. That is, Jonathan was.

"My, this is delicious, Teen," he said, the only one who'd really begun to eat; the girls were still fiddling with rolls and salted almonds. "Isn't this just scrumptious, girls?"

"The stuffing looks different," Liz said warily, taking

up her fork. Sylvie had finally started. "Why didn't you make the old kind of stuffing we love?"

I took several sips of the beautiful Château Margaux Jonathan had opened. "It's nice to try something new for a change. Besides, Daddy specifically asked if we could have something different this year . . . didn't you, Jonathan?"

"I did," said Jonathan. "And I'm glad I did. It's great, just great, Teen. I've always said you had the makings of a superb cook."

Slowly, thoughtfully chewing, Sylvie finally said: "What's in the stuffing—those squoggly things?"

"You mustn't talk with your mouth full, Sylvie. Oysters. I suppose the oysters are what you mean."

In a spluttery explosion, Sylvie emptied her mouth onto her plate.

"*Sylvie!*" shouted Jonathan. "What do you *mean* by doing such a disgusting thing!"

Ashen, Sylvie gulped down ice water. I finished my glass of Château Margaux. Keeping her eyes lowered, Liz speared some dark meat with her fork, while Jonathan continued to glare at Sylvie.

"Sylvie. I am *talking* to you. What was the meaning of that outrage? Are you two years old?"

Sylvie put down her water goblet, tears in her eyes. "It was the oysters," she said faintly. "They made me sick."

"But you and Liz just love oysters," I said.

"On the half-shell with cocktail sauce, not in a bloody turkey, for God's sake!" Sylvie shouted hysterically.

Jonathan was as pale as Sylvie now. In a trembling voice he said, "Sylvie. You will apologize to your mother. To everyone at this table, in fact. You will then remain silent and eat this delicious dinner she's worked so hard to cook. If, after you've apologized, I hear one more word out of you, you'll go straight to your room and stay there until it's time for bed."

Sylvie stood up and burst into tears. "It isn't delicious. It's horrible!" she sobbed. "Those mooky chestnuts, those onions and celery in cream! Why, even the salad isn't normal . . . oranges and cut-up plants. I . . . I'm *happy* to go to my room!"

With that, she bolted. As her bedroom door slammed, Liz, eyes still cast down, poked her fork into the chestnut purée. Looking grim and ominously green, Jonathan pushed back his chair.

"Jonathan," I said softly, "leave her alone. She'll apologize after she cries it off. Sit down, your dinner will get cold."

"Actually," said Jonathan in an odd choked voice, "I'm not going after her. I seem to feel rather peculiar . . ."

With that, he too bolted. Using a boarding-house reach, I grabbed the neck of the bottle of Margaux and filled my glass with a rich red gurgle. After several sips I said to Liz, "It's all right, baby. You don't have to eat any more."

Her mouth was full. Unable to speak, her little throat working to swallow what she was chewing, she looked at me with brimming eyes. She broke my heart. "I'm not angry, darling, really I'm not. I just goofed this year. It's certainly nothing to cry about, so please don't *you* start."

She shook her head, finished swallowing what was in her mouth, said, "I'm sorry, Mommy, really I am," and burst into tears anyway.

Getting up, I went around to her chair and patted her. "Please don't, lamb. It's only food. Do stop, please. Come on and help me carry everything out to the kitchen, and after we're done, we'll each have a huge piece of Schrafft's pumpkin pie. That's one thing I didn't change this year."

We cleared the table, but before cutting the pie and sitting down to eat it at the kitchen table (the dining room was somehow not very appealing), I went up front to reconnoiter. Sylvie had locked the door and wouldn't answer, but I heard her blowing her nose, so I knew the worst was over and went away. Jonathan was stretched out on his bed, a wrung-out washcloth across his brow. He looked a lot like Garbo in *Camille*, just as Sylvie had a month ago, a bit of transmogrification that didn't bear thinking about. "God, I'm sorry, Teen," he mumbled, "but everything started spinning."

"Don't try to talk, just lie still and rest. Can I get you something? An Alka-Seltzer might help."

"I took a *double* Alki and the room's still going around. God. What a nightmare for you."

"It's not that bad," I said composedly. "The food was simply too rich and I made a mistake. Everybody makes mistakes," added Bettina the Wise.

I went back to the kitchen and was cutting the pie when Sylvie came in and apologized. I kissed her, cut three huge pieces of pie, and when we'd eaten them, shooed the girls out of the kitchen. I didn't give a damn how long it took me to clean up by myself; I had to be alone. Without my usual qualms about the starving populations of the world, I scraped plates full of food into the garbage. It was only when the water was slowly rising in the sink that a few lukewarm tears fell into the hot blue detergent foam. But that was all. I turned off the taps, wiped my eyes, and was briskly tying on an apron when the phone rang. I picked it up a few seconds after the first ring.

". . . Bruce Adderly here, Jonathan," a loud voice was saying. "I hope I'm not disturbing you. Awfully sorry to bother you on Thanksgiving Day, but it's important."

"Disturb me? Don't be silly, Bruce! How are you? You have a pleasant Thanksgiving?" The voice was loud and hearty and simply couldn't have belonged to the limp dishrag of a man I'd just left.

"A splendid Thanksgiving, Jonathan. And you?"

"Lovely, Bruce. Perfect. Couldn't've been better—Ah, what's this important thing you want to talk about, Bruce?"

". . . Actually, Jonathan, I think there's someone on this line."

"Is there? Is there someone on this line? Tina? Is that you?"

By way of answering, I hung up. I went to the counter where all the serving dishes sat, and picked up a lovely Meissen serving dish Jonathan had once found in a

Third Avenue antique shop. It was still full of puréed chestnuts. Taking careful aim, I hurled it with all my might at the fireproof steel back door; it broke with an enormously satisfying clacket and squoosh, leaving equally satisfying oozing streaks on the door as it slid to the floor.

Purged, I returned to the sink.

Sylvie poked her head in through the pantry door, from which point the mess was invisible. "What was *that?*"

"What was what, dear?"

"That awful crash."

"Just a plate. I accidentally dropped a plate."

She started to come in. "It didn't *sound* like just a plate dropping."

"Why are you still in your clothes, Sylvie? I thought I told you to start your bath."

Sylvie left to start her bath.

By 9:15 the kitchen was spotless, the back door included, and the girls were in bed. Ready to drop, I found Jonathan sitting up in bed reading *Country Life*. "Poor Teen," he said, glancing up. "What a rotten day you've had."

I was having none of that. "Who is Bruce Adderly?"

"I *thought* it was you on the line. Is that another new habit you've picked up? I certainly hope you enjoyed yourself."

"Who is Bruce Adderly?"

"A director. The one who's going to do Gaylord's show. A charming man . . . Had he known it was my wife eavesdropping, I'm sure he would've been more gallant."

"What did he want?"

His face was turning very red. "To know what I'd decided about the show."

"And what *have* you decided?"

His fingers were agitatedly rolling the magazine into a cylinder—or club. "To take a piece."

"For how much?"

"Not much."

"I thought you said they were only out for big game."

Raising the rolled-up magazine, he brought it down with a violent smack on the bed. "What the hell *is* this? Who do you think you are, cross-examining me? I don't like being cross-examined and I don't like your tone. At *all*. If you'd been more resourceful and had managed to find a sitter and come with me last night, you'd know that my judgment is sound. More than sound. So you can take that snide tone and do you-know-what with it, old girl. As always, I know exactly what I'm doing, so you'd just damned well better sit back and relax!"

Relax. Everybody's always telling me to relax. Well, I'm more relaxed now. It's 2:15 P.M. and I have a whopping case of writer's cramp, but George hasn't called. With three quarters of an hour left, I'll bathe and dress and get ready to go. Yes, I'm going. I guess I knew that all along. Of course I'm going— If after that Account I *didn't* go, I'd *know* I'd gone stark raving mad.

Snow was ticking on the windowpanes. Though he'd turned the radiator off long ago, the room was still too warm, was hot—hot, and filled with this feeling so thick you could cut it with a knife. We were lying and smoking on top of the blankets, both of us using the ashtray balanced on his chest. Hypnotized, I stared at the way a few black hairs curled up around the chunky glass. Everything about him, every movement he made, even the slow rise and fall of his chest as he breathed, seemed extraordinary to me. It was part of the spell that permeated the room. Suddenly he sighed, and to avoid getting burned through the glass, lifted the ashtray two inches off his skin while he stubbed out his cigarette. "Well, we're hooked. At least for a while."

"Um," I said, and with a kind of wonder watched him reach for the glass on the night table and drink. As I watched the liquid moving down his throat, I wanted to bend over and kiss the working muscles, kiss the hollow where his neck joined his chest.

"*He* didn't teach you all of that."

"Who?" I said dreamily, watching him wipe his lips on the back of his hand. He had broad, powerful, stubby-fingered hands, hardly what I'd once thought the hands of an Artist, a writer, should be. Marvelous hands. Incredible hands.

"Who. That goofed-up husband of yours."

The hypnotic spell broke. I stared at him, holding the ashtray out to me. What did he mean, "goofed-up"? I silently mashed out my cigarette.

"You screw around a lot before you married him?"

"Not a lot. Some."

"What's his problem, anyway?"

The room was hot as ever, but I was beginning to feel cold. "What do you mean?"

"I mean has he always been such a bird?"

To my astonishment, I was near tears: I suddenly realized that it was one thing for me to privately run down Jonathan, in my own thoughts, and quite another to hear somebody else make snide remarks about him, particularly somebody like George. "I gather you don't know it, but he's actually a very brilliant lawyer," I found myself saying, still unnerved by my discovery. "If he comes across as a little peculiar, it's because he's recently gotten involved in a lot of things that aren't his field, and he's . . . well, scattered."

Turned on by this rather surprising speech about Jonathan, I suddenly, overwhelmingly, wanted to talk about myself. I wanted to tell George everything, beginning way back with White Plains and working right up to now—but George had other ideas. Turning to look at him, I saw that he'd been thoroughly bored by even this preliminary explanation of Jonathan, and was yawning and scratching his chest while he stared at the ceiling. "He likely to get wise to this?"

"No. He doesn't watch me. He's much too involved with himself."

"Probably has a broad somewhere." Swallowing another yawn, he reached for a fresh cigarette.

"No. He isn't the type." I wondered how many packs a day he smoked.

George laughed. "They all say that. Though I'll admit I might not be so apt to stray with a piece like you around the house. Still, anything gets to be so much cold turkey after ten years. What I don't get is why it took *you* ten years."

Because. Because I loved Jonathan, that's why. Because I believed in all those square virtues—devotion, loyalty,

fidelity. Which weren't things I was about to say to
George Prager, so I said instead: "Sex isn't that important to me."

He began laughing.

"Well, it isn't."

"Baby, you don't act like a broad sex isn't important
to. The thing I'd really like to know is who broke you
in. Tell me about it . . . I particularly dig hearing about
that sort of thing. And don't give me any crap about
being a voyeur, I *am* a voyeur, it's one of my hang-ups
—we just haven't really gotten around to it yet. But for
now, tell me about it. What was he like? What did he
do, what did he have you do? I want a blow-by-blow
description." Predictably, he gave himself a couple of
laughs.

The only man I could describe would be the crazy
sculptor, my true Instructor, but now I wasn't in the
mood for telling George anything more about myself,
particularly that. "There really wasn't anybody like
that," I lied. "And you're wrong to think there has to
be. With certain women sex is instinctive; they're born
with it. It's like that thing Proust wrote about Albertine.
I've been rereading Proust and just came across it a week
or two ago, and I was so struck by it I read it over and
over. I think I know it by heart. Let's see . . . *'She re-
covered her dexterity only when making love, with that
touching prescience latent in women who love the male
body so intensely that they immediately guess what will
give most pleasure to that body, which is yet so different
from their own.'* "

Clapping his hand to his brow, George sat bolt up-
right in the bed and began to howl.

"You stop that, George. You stop laughing at me."

Gasping, choking on smoke, George wheezed: "God.
It's too *much*. Albertine. Albert— Don't you know, you
knucklehead, that Albertine was a goddamn *boy* and
that's why that bit says what it says. 'Latent prescience!'
My God."

I was shaking from head to toe. Through clenched
teeth I said: "I know all about it, so don't you *dare*
laugh at me. I know that Proust, as a homosexual, trans-

posed many of the sexes in the book, but in spite of all the current interpretations, I happen to think that the character of Albertine, like Odette de Crécy, was based on a real woman, not a man— I suppose you think Odette was a boy too?"

"What I think," said George, subsiding and shaking his head, "is that you'd better wash your brains of all that Sarah Lawrence crap."

"Smith," I said, slapping his face hard, and tried to climb out of bed.

But he grabbed the hand that had slapped him, grinning. "Sweetheart angel," he said, trying to pull me down on top of him, "you *ask* for it. Every goddamn time. You're really a pretty smart cookie, yet a lot of the time you act as though you had a shoebox full of immies for a brain. Why the hell is that? Is it your husband? Or was it a shrink? It's written all over you that you've been to a shrink."

Struggling to get free, I said breathlessly, "You're a cruel . . . sadistic bastard . . . and I hate your lousy guts. You always have to spoil everything . . . have to say or do something outrageous, say something you know is going to hurt me or get me furious."

Putting one hand on the back of my neck, he pulled my head down and shut me up with a long, violent kiss. When he finally let me go, he said to me, limp now, lying beside him and licking a badly bitten lower lip, "You don't hate me. And the shoe is on the other foot. *You* always spoil things by trying to dress them up. Why can't you take things as they are? Where the hell is your sense of humor? Why do you take everything so seriously?"

Oh, shut *up*, I thought. Shutup shutup and go back to doing what you were doing. "I hate being laughed at," I said flatly.

"You only get laughed at when you ask for it. Besides, you ought to learn to laugh at yourself."

Exasperated—it wasn't a lecture I was wanting—I touched him with Albertine-Albert hands.

He sharply inhaled, but then, sighing, shifted and pushed them away. "In fact," he continued smoothly, "you really ought to learn to be more tolerant of yourself."

I rolled on my back and stared at the ceiling. "You and your dictums. Do you practice what you preach?"

"I try. And I must succeed, since I don't go around all worked up like you. I try to keep things as simple and basic as possible."

"That shouldn't be hard, seeing you've only got yourself to think of and indulge," I said bitterly.

"You learn to do that sooner or later. Think only of yourself. And anybody who ever amounts to anything learns to do that. It's the secret of success, Pussycat." As he smiled pensively and reached for still another cigarette, I finally saw what was happening, and had the answer to his amazing lack of response. He'd had another, more powerful urge for the nonce, the same one I'd had before: he wanted to talk about himself. "Did you know I was married once?" he said now, lying back and blowing smoke at the ceiling.

"I'd heard," I said without enthusiasm. Shutting my eyes, I prepared for a long siege, even in anticipation feeling what he'd undoubtedly felt when I'd tried to launch *my* little tale: stale, crashing boredom. Nothing could have underlined more clearly the true nature of our feelings for each other, the staggering lack of interest each had in the other—one thing excepted, of course.

"Whatever you heard is nothing like the truth," he said. With that he was launched.

Actually, his story wasn't quite as dull as I'd expected, and was boring mainly because it's become a cliché: Poor Boy from Brooklyn Makes Good, Makes It Artistically. There were the immigrant parents, the father so mean and tight-fisted "he made Shylock look like a rose," who did things like make him and his sisters sleep in their underwear with "raincoats for bathrobes" all their childhood, and who terrorized the poor mother into an early grave. There was the escape from home into the Big War, the revelations of the Horrors of War in the Pacific, the malaria caught in the Philippines, the shrapnel burst that shattered his leg. (At this point in the story he lifted his left leg, and showed me some faint

scars I'd never noticed, explaining the miracles per-
formed by plastic surgery.) After he got out of the
Army, he went to college for two years on the GI Bill,
quit to join the Merchant Marine, and after six months
quit the Merchant Marine, jumping ship in Naples, and
naturally pushing north to Rome, where he settled down
and wrote a big trashy novel that had an enormous success. (I'd never heard of it, probably because at the time
it came out I was in the Smith College library, boning
up on Proust.) Hollywood. Money. Success which he
came back to this country to exploit and enjoy. A minor
celebrity, but still carrying enough weight to meet and
marry Millicent the Beautiful Socialite, a congenital liar
and nymphomaniac. Wrote his first play. A flop. Wrote
another which was a "sucks-egg *d'estime*," as Lawrence
Durrell has put it. Meanwhile Millie: it took him two
years of hell, during which they had a daughter, to discover she'd been hanging horns on him every time he'd
gone out the door. Didn't even know if the daughter was
his. All that. Big messy divorce (I vaguely remember
reading about it, so I must have come out of the college
library by then) which left him insanely bitter, vowing
he would Never Marry Again. (Though he didn't say as
much, it also obviously left him determined to become a
genius in bed, which he now is.) Writing for television
to make money, he started on his plays; success slowly
came, is coming still.

All through this I kept my mouth shut, realizing that
it was only natural that I would pick such a clear-cut
case. Because though he concluded by saying, "I'm a
man who loves women. Just that. Women. Plural," it's
just the reverse of course. But it takes me a while to
learn to keep my brilliant Insights to myself. When he
was done, more or less purged and ready for other
things, he rolled over and grabbed me. "But you, how do
you fit in? You're not like any of the broads I usually go
for, the kind I like to screw."

Now I was the one to push his hands away; it was
turning out to be quite an afternoon. "Maybe it's just
because I'm a married woman," I said, having to deliver

myself of that Insight. "Maybe you're still trying to get even with Millicent."

"Don't give me that stuff, baby. Not me."

"Why *not* you?" I persisted, trying without success to get away from those hands. "Some insight into your motivations could make a world of difference in your life."

He laughed. "My life is fine. And I think all that insight's what's got you so fucked up." Swift as a cat he slid over in the bed, moving in with dazzling deftness, and from above me said softly, exultantly, "Ah now that's what I call a reaction, Pussycat . . . ahyes, ahyes. Baby baby . . . have you *ever* had it like this?"

No. No. The answer is no. But now, two days later, I think I'm clear on why that is, and it couldn't be more obvious: George is the classic Heel, the Sadistic Rake whom certain kinds of women find irresistible—and I, by virtue of my current crazy condition, have become that kind of woman. The perfect Willing Victim, moth to the flame, all that old stuff. It couldn't be simpler. And it would follow that the sex would be fantastic; the violent pleasures to be derived from the sado-masochistic relationship have been adequately documented by experts. There are also probably some other Freudian explanations for this kind of sex and what gives it its powerful charge—something like saying that we're acting out The Death Wish or Cannibalism—we certainly go at each other as if we'd like to kill each other or eat each other up. The one thing that I really don't like is not any of the things we do, but his Professionalism. I can't think of a better word. The experience and practice implicit in everything he does, every move he makes, sometimes gets me so jealous I want to die. Cuckoo jealous. Cat jealous. Red jealous. Blue jealous. Green. Often *in medias res*. But knowing that there's no place for that, I try to put it down as best I can.

The point is, having made all these sobering observations, I've still decided to go on with him for a while. Why not? Why should I be disturbed by the sado-masochistic aspects of that relationship, when I have another one going? Why not face the truth: it's an enormous relief to have that sort of thing out in the open and act it out, instead of having to deal with it in a disguised form, all veiled and gussied up with domestic overlay as it is with Jonathan and me. The only thing I can't help wondering is how in hell I got to *be* such a goddamn masochist and Willing Victim? Is it the outcome of overdoing the Feminine Passive Role, of overplaying Limp Lady to Jonathan's Forceful Male? If so, I have, old Leonard Popkin, really been had . . . Christ, my head! A big bolt of pain shot right through it as I was writing that last sentence. I'll take it for a warning and back off from big questions like that. Judging from the pain—there it goes again!—they're dynamite.

Today happens to be Sunday and it's 4:07 P.M. Jonathan's health still isn't up to par, and he's napping in the bedroom with the phone turned off. The girls are in the den with the Jocelyn girls, playing Monopoly and making awful jewelry with the Make-a-Necklace set I bought them at Rachman's. I'm writing this in Lottie's room with an old William Powell movie (now *there's* a man) on the TV, and with Lottie's bureau drawer open and waiting in case I have to shove this in. No one has come back since I've been here, but the kitchen phone has rung four times. Each time it was someone accepting the invitation to our party . . . which I simply cannot bring myself to believe is only two weeks away. The dullness of Sunday must have frightened all those types into action, reminded them that there are still things like parties and that there's one only two weeks off they haven't even accepted yet. Two weeks. Dear God.

But no more pains in my head. I'll never question the validity of the Analytic Experience again. Now I'm off to walk Folly and make a vat of spaghetti sauce. The Jocelyn girls are staying to supper. The Jocelyn girls are staying to supper because one good turn deserves another, and where Mrs. Jocelyn's concerned, it's certainly my turn.

YESTERDAY AFTERNOON, on my way to a meeting about the Christmas Bazaar at the Bartlett School, I dropped into the Society Library and read a play of George's that was published last year. A terrible mistake. I could die for that idiotic crack at Charlotte Rady's: "I see you try to talk like the characters in your plays." I was either asleep or in coma the night I saw that earlier play. He doesn't talk anything like his characters and he's so good it doesn't bear thinking about. If I think about it, I'll have to try to reconcile George the Sadistic Rake, the deliberately coarse and vulgar Heel, with this other George (who *is* it?), this George the Playwright. Since that requires mental leaps over hurdles I know I can't clear, and since George the Swordsman, George the Heel, is the one I have to cope with, I'll simply bury the other George here and now, not praise him. Ever again.

The following letter also came yesterday. I'm putting it in here because I feel it adds a certain documentary tone; like footnotes, it supplements the facts in my little Account.

My dearest daughter:
I can't believe that another Thanksgiving has come and gone. With Thanksgiving so late this year it will be Christmas before we know it. I also can't believe we've been down here over two years and

haven't seen you or your dear ones in all that time.
I thought of you all day yesterday Thanksgiving
Day because we always had such lovely Thanksgivings when you were a child, real family get-
togethers. I hope you remember them with as much
fondness as I do. We had our Thanksgiving with
Lew and Grace Werber, I don't know if you remember them. They belonged to the club, he was in
woolens and had a stroke three years ago and came
down here to live. We see a lot of them. Speaking
of health, my own is wonderful knock wood. My
blood pressure is normal, my cardiogram likewise,
and my blood cholesterol level is low. I feel ten
years younger than I did three years ago. Also speaking of health, in the pictures you sent you look a
little thin and tired to me. I know you and Jonathan
have a busy exciting life nowadays but you should
take better care of yourself. Health is a precious gift,
don't abuse it. The girls on the other hand looked
wonderful. They are getting very beautiful and I
must tell you that when I looked at all the pictures,
yours included, I got a lump in my throat. I thought
back on all that terrible trouble you were in shortly
after college, and it seemed a miracle to me that
things worked out like this and you now have such
a wonderful husband and beautiful children and a rich
full life.

So far the weather has been very bad and too
chilly for swimming. However, that is just as well as
the pool developed a terrible crack in the bottom
and the contractor wants *four hundred* dollars to
patch it up. Of course we'll have to fix it but it burns
me up to have to deal with robbers. That's life, as
you will learn. In your letter you ask what we did
with ourselves. I go fishing a lot with some old
friends. I also go to the dog races and Hialeah and
have a standing poker game twice a week. Altho I
miss the golf badly, time never hangs heavy on my
hands. I'm sure it will surprise you to hear that your
mother has taken up racing too. Of course she has a
group of cronies who go in for bridge in a big way,
but I personally think they sometimes overdo it as
regards to stakes.

I know you get tired of hearing it, but now that we're really settled I wish you would come down. We have two extra rooms and I would have the pool fixed tomorrow if you wrote and said you would consider coming down over Christmas. Why don't you, is there anything to stop you? The girls would love it and you and Jonathan would have built-in baby-sitters and could go out every night to all the wonderful night spots. Over Christmas they get all the big names like Sinatra and Sammy Davis and such. To help sell you further on the idea I'm enclosing some pictures I took with a new color Polaroid I bought. The pictures were taken in September before the pool got cracked. I also want to add that the house is much bigger than it looks and has since been landscaped with some nice trees and bushes. Along with the pictures I'm enclosing a check for one hundred dollars which you and Jonathan should split and use for Christmas presents for yourselves. I'm going downtown to Lincoln Road next week and pick out the girls' presents myself. I get a big kick out of it, and if what I send doesn't fit them, mail it back and I'll get the right size.

I'll say goodbye now. Write soon and tell us the news and if you think you might come down over Christmas. Even though it's so near all you have to do is throw some things in a suitcase and get on a plane. Stay happy and healthy and remember you have everything a girl could ask for in life.

Your Loving Dad

P.S. Your mother's card game just broke up and she came in and sends her love.

P.S.S. I'm glad you liked the oranges and grapefruit. I'll send some more.

Daddy-Dads letter, written in a fine Cooper Union hand. The four soft-sell photographs are spread out in front of me. The first is a front view of a stucco house the color of a boiled shrimp, with a white roof and jalousies and a small lawn enclosed by a split-rail fence. The second is a view of what is in back of the house: practically all the space is taken by a huge glittery postcard-blue pool, with a small border of grass on three sides; on the fourth side, which has about six feet more of grass, there are some lounge chairs and an umbrellaed table, and beyond, behind a few palms, there is a sudden drop to Biscayne Bay. The third picture is of my mother, standing on a slate walk leading up to the house. She's smiling and, as always, is impeccably turned out in pale blue linen, but the shocker is her hair—almost white. Without the bleaches and rinses that kept it sandy for years, she suddenly looks her age—looks, in fact, as though she'd finally come to grips with something, but I find myself unwilling to even guess what that might be. The fourth picture is of my father standing by the split-rail fence, his bald head shining in the overhead beat of a noontime sun. There is a shocker here too: though his bald head and face and arms are a deep healthy brown, he looks shrunken, smaller than I ever remember him. He was never a tall man, but he was never *that* small. Also, though he's elegantly dressed, his dapper tattersall shirt seems to hang on him and his linen slacks indent sharply at the waist; while he's never been fat, he's always been a sturdy, stocky man, and for the last ten years he's had a decided paunch.

This picture upset me so much that I began to cry while I showed them all to Jonathan last night. "For God's sake, *now* what's the matter?" said Jonathan.

"I think he looks just *terrible*," I blubbered.

"He does not look 'terrible.' He had a heart attack and has been on a low saturated fat diet and has dropped some weight. *I* think he looks just great."

"He looks so small," I persisted, snuffling.

"He never was a big man," said Jonathan in his Patience-and-Fortitude voice. "But if you're so concerned about him, why don't you do what he suggests and go down for a visit."

"Go down when?"

"Over Christmas. Like he says. Even a week would do you and the girls a world of good, and from the sound of things it would make him happy as hell . . . I'm not sure *I* could get away, but I see no reason why you can't."

"Well, there is a reason and it's very simple. The girls

have made all sorts of plans for their vacation, and they'd be sick if I made them leave New York."

"Plans. What sort of plans could they have that would be more exciting than a trip to Florida?"

"Though you don't seem to realize it, they have a very busy social life of their own, Jonathan. So far they've got at least four parties to go to. Then there are quite a few things they wanted to see—the Royal Ballet, some ice show at the Garden, a puppet show from Vienna. I wrote away for tickets to all of them weeks ago, way back in October."

Jonathan stared at me. "Did you, now? How very organized." Then, swiftly, to try and counteract his rotten irony: "Well, I think it's too bad, I think a trip down there would be a great idea."

"Maybe I'll take them down over spring vacation."

"Spring is a long way away. *Any*thing could happen by spring."

"What does that mean?"

Jonathan shrugged.

"You mean my father could die by spring. Is that what you mean?"

"No, it isn't what I mean!" shouted Jonathan with such fury that I knew it was precisely what he *did* mean. "I didn't say it. Notice you did, old girl. What I meant was that you should do things when you have the chance, not put them off as you're so prone to do. I'm willing to bet that come springtime you'll have twenty other reasons for not going down."

I stared at his back—he was carefully hanging his jacket on the walnut valet stand—and decided to play it cool. He was quite right: anything could happen by spring. So I said nothing, and took a bath and got into bed and read one of the Rex Stout paperbacks I got at Rachman's for two hours before turning out my light. I have put all the other books, Proust included, back on the bookshelves in the den. Away. Away. *Away.*

"Kiss the hand which thou
  canst not bite"

"He who steals an egg
  will steal a camel"

"The end of gladness
  is the beginning of sadness"

"To know the road ahead
  ask those coming back"

"Do not peddle wood
  in the forest
  or fish by the lake shore"

"He who is drowned
  is not troubled by the rain"

    More messages from the fortune cookies
    that came with last night's dinner
    from The White Jade; Lao-tse is still
    locked up

ON TUESDAY NIGHT I was sitting peacefully in bed, started on my second Rex Stout, when Jonathan, fin-

ished with his evening of work in the den, came in and
laid two sheets of blue-lined yellow paper on my quilt.
Reluctantly leaving Nero Wolfe and Archie Goodwin,
who were about to sit down to Fritz's *tripe à la mode de
Caen*, I glanced down at the top sheet of paper. It appeared to be an elaborate sort of list. I raised my eyes
and looked quizzically at Jonathan, who was slowly un-
buttoning his shirt by his bed.

"That's the list of Christmas presents I have to give this
year," he explained. "Ones that can't be covered by gifts
of cash, or ones for instance like Miss Brekker, who require the personal touch of a little present *besides* the
cash. If you notice, I've put suggestions after each name,
with a sort of price ceiling after that. Of course you
don't have to follow my suggestions, or, needless to say,
spend as much as I put down. In some instances I've even
suggested stores for particular items, like Lord & Taylor
for Miss Brekker's boots. Lord & Taylor is great for
boots, and I happen to know she needs a pair. Fleece-
lined suede would be nice, as I suggested, and as you'll
see I even put down her size."

And I thought he'd been *working* in the den. "I take
it you want me to do all your shopping."

"Yes, I do," he said, going to the closet for pajamas. "I
haven't any time this year. Since you usually manage to
get your own shopping done by late November, I
thought you could manage to do mine this year . . .
You have done yours, haven't you?" he added slyly.

"Yes," I lied. I took up my mystery and the glossy
cover slid in my wet hands.

"Glad to hear it, because it's really much later than I
thought. I mean I suddenly realized our party is only
nine days away! I certainly hope you've arranged to have
the place done next week—the floors waxed and windows washed, et cetera—and you've called the florist and
ordered the flowers."

"Not yet." The print was crazily jumping around on
the page.

Restraining himself, oh, admirably, Jonathan stripped
down to his shorts and said, "Well, it's all you have to
do, you know. Beaumont takes care of every other little

thing, even *ice*, so you'd better get with it and make those arrangements tomorrow. Has everyone RSVP'd, by the way?"

"Everyone except seven or eight."

"What about Charlotte Rady? And Julie Hayes? And the Willards? They all accept?"

"Charlotte Rady and Julie Hayes did. Sally Willard called this morning and said they couldn't come."

Stricken, Jonathan paused on the last button of his pajama top. "Really? I'm very sorry to hear that. Very *very* sorry. Did she give any reason why?"

"They're off to one of those places to ski—Klosters or Kitzbühel or Gstaad—for a few weeks."

"Boy," said Jonathan, shaking his head and starting for the bathroom. "Some people really know how to live!"

As the door closed I stuck out my tongue. Then I finished lunch with Nero and Archie and followed Nero up to the orchid room.

In the morning, after a night of fitful sleep, I looked at the calendar first thing to see when I could do Jonathan's shopping: The next day, Thursday (today), Lottie was off and I was due at the Bartlett School for conferences with the girls' teachers; Friday I had an appointment at Jean Louis' to have my hair piled on top of my head (at Jonathan's Behest) for an opening at the Modern Museum. Which left that day, Wednesday, when I was supposed to go to George's in the afternoon. There was nothing for it, I had to call him and say I couldn't come. I called him at 8:03 A.M., the minute Jonathan and the girls were gone, hoping to catch him before he started working and took the phone off the hook. I woke him out of a sound sleep. After recovering from his fury over that, he listened, and then croaked, "What the hell have you got to do that's more important than coming here?"

I took a deep breath and shut my eyes. "I have to do some Christmas shopping for Jonathan. He gave me an enormous list last night. As it is, I haven't even started my own shopping yet, and it's crazy to make him suspicious by not getting it done."

There was a long sleepy silence during which he gathered himself up. Then: "You really do it up, don't you, doll? The whole schmear. I suppose you have a tree with a star and a crèche underneath?"

When I didn't answer, he said, "Ah shit," and hung up.

For several minutes I sat weeping on the bed. Spread out around me were Christmas catalogues from every store where we had a charge account, Jonathan's list, and an engraved card that had gotten mixed in with the catalogues: "Seasons Greetings from Your Garbage men, Anthony Ruzzo, Peter Snell, Joseph S. Doyle."

I finally got dressed and took Folly down. It was freezing cold and smelled like snow. Back upstairs, I put on some warmer clothes, and after making sure that all my Charg-a-plates and Jonathan's list were in my purse, left a note for Lottie explaining that I would be out all day. I also explained that the girls had dates at friends', and I'd pick them up on my way home, but asked her to please walk Folly (a rare request), and put the leg of lamb in the oven at 5:00.

In Lord & Taylor, Great for Boots, I bought Miss Brekker a pair of size 8½ mocha suede fleece-lined boots for $30.00, upping Jonathan's ante by $5.00. In Lord & Taylor I also had such a bad attack of vertigo that I had to sit down on the tiled floor of the ladies' room. I had to sit there because the nearest seats were behind doors which took a dime to unlock, and I didn't have a dime. The attendant (who also supplied change) finally came along and helped me to my feet, and after rejecting her offer to escort me to the store nurse, I fled out to the cold stinging air of the street. In Brooks Brothers, after I'd bought several of the ties and mufflers on Jonathan's list, I stood in front of a $50.00 blue Viyella flannel bathrobe for ten minutes. George. I would use the $50.00 my father had sent me. But then I remembered that morning's conversation and instead bought Jonathan a pair of silk pajamas and a cashmere sweater, paying for them with cash scraped from my weekly household allowance over a period of months. I was giving the clerk our address when I got a lump like a baseball in my throat. I had a vision of myself stretched on the floor between the counters, the snotty clerk doing a tracheotomy on me with his fountain pen. "And what apartment number?" he asked, but I turned and bolted down the aisle, out the door, and stood for five minutes gulping icy air on the street.

When I was certain I wasn't going to choke, I walked up a block to Abercrombie & Fitch and sent my father a fishing-tackle box with all sorts of compartments for lures and flies and spinners and reels. From there I walked to Saks and bought my mother a beautiful double-strand coral necklace. I deliberately chose Saks because they have a Miami branch, where she could exchange the necklace for something she "really needed"; everything I've ever given my mother has been taken back and exchanged for something she "really needed." On the jammed main floor of Bonwit Teller (Great for Umbrellas, according to Jonathan's list), I got another dizzy spell and broke out in a cold sweat. Since it was much too crowded to sit on the floor, I collapsed in one of the chairs at the glove counter, where I was forced to buy a $14.00 pair of kid gloves I didn't need; I couldn't just *sit* there in that mob. When the vertigo lifted, I got up and bought the three umbrellas and beaded evening bag on Jonathan's list, then went next door to Tiffany's and bought a gold tie pin and a bunch of small silver things that Jonathan had down. With the exception of Miss Brekker's, I didn't know a name on his list.

And so the day passed. The attacks of vertigo, suffocation and sweats came and went, but I kept going, and miraculously not only finished Jonathan's list, but did some shopping for the girls. By the time I'd collected the girls at their friends' and we got home, it was after six. I unlocked the door on a delirious Folly and an awful muttony smell of scorched lamb. In the kitchen I found a note from Lottie Scotch-taped to the icebox door: "My husband called at three very sick to say he was home from work and needed me. I feel just terrible but I have to go. I just took the dog down so that's all right, but I don't know about the lamb I just put it in

now at 275° and hope it will be O.K. I am sorry Mrs.
Balser and if you are angry I understand. It is twenty
past three now so you know how much to take out of
my pay. L.M."

I pulled the roasting pan out of the oven. The lamb
was a peculiar stringy-grey and gave off that awful smell
of mutton. "I like my lamb *saignant* like the French,"
Jonathan always gratuitously confides to people; "If
there's one thing I can't stand it's overcooked lamb." As
I stood there in my overcoat, looking at it and wondering whether I had enough time to cut it up and make a
curry, the phone rang.

"Tina?"

It was a man's voice, just familiar enough to put me
off my guard; for all I knew it could be anybody from
Peter Barr to Mr. Marks himself. "Yes?" I answered.

There was a hurried gulping sort of gasp at the other
end, then it came pouring out. The voice was now the
same as the other time, high, heavily disguised, distorted
with excitement, but the proposals were slightly different, wilder—a list of suggestions that might have
been compiled from the *Karma Sutra* and a Hammacher
Schlemmer catalogue. I stayed on, listening, because as
distorted and disguised as it was, the voice had a tantaliz-
ingly familiar ring.

"Hey whussay Tina?" it concluded moronically.

I said what I had to say and hung up, shaking with
fear and fury. I knew I'd done the wrong thing—you
aren't supposed to listen *or* talk to nuts like that—but I'd
desperately wanted to find out who it was. Though I
also knew enough to know that the sort of person who
made those calls wasn't dangerous, it made my blood run
cold to think that perhaps someone I knew socially was
doing this and getting away with it. It also made me furious.

Still shaking, I took off my coat and turned off the
oven. Suddenly remembering that the girls hate curry, I
threw the lamb in the garbage; I couldn't even cut it up
and give it to Folly, since I'd highly seasoned it with rosemary and garlic and grated lemon rind, the way Jonathan likes it.

I'd just finished checking the freezer, which had two frozen portions of *boeuf à la mode* and a frozen three-rib roast beef, when the phone rang again. I let it ring twice, then snatched it off the hook and put it to my ear but didn't say anything.

At the other end there was the faint clicking of a typewriter. "Hello?" said Jonathan. "Hel*lo*? Is anyone there?"

"Yes, Jonathan. I'm here."

"Tina? That you?"

"Yes, it's me."

"Why did you answer the phone that way? Is anything wrong?"

I let out a lot of air. "One of those telephone nuts just called here, and I thought it was him again. It's the second time he's called, Jonathan."

Jonathan sighed. "Tina, I came out of a meeting just to call you and tell you I'll be an hour late. I've only got a minute, so tell me about the crank call later. I just wanted to give you warning so that dinner wouldn't get spoiled."

"It's already spoiled."

". . . What?"

"I said dinner's already spoiled, it couldn't be helped. Can you pick up some sandwiches at Dillman's on your way home?"

There was just the background clacketing of the typewriter at the other end.

"Look, Jonathan," I said with what remained of my strength, "it really wasn't anybody's fault; it just couldn't be helped. I was out all day, and Lottie doesn't know about lamb, it's the one thing she really can't cook, and she put it in much too early because she had to leave."

"And why did she have to leave?"

"Her husband suddenly took sick."

"*I* see . . . And where were you?"

"Out doing your Christmas shopping, that's where. I thought you only had a minute, Jonathan."

After a slight pause he said, "All the lunch I had time for was a lousy corned-beef sandwich at my desk, so I certainly don't want any delicatessen dinner too. If I have to bring dinner, I'd rather get some Chinese food, but it's idiotic for me to take the time to stop off—just call The White Jade and have them send some stuff over. You can order me some of that soup they call Dow Foo Tong, a portion of Lung Har Gai Kew, a portion of Chow Foon Shee, and some fried rice. I'm too damned hungry to share portions, so if you want any of the same things, double the order. I won't get home till about twenty to eight, and if you want to start without me, go ahead."

I called The White Jade and ordered three Chicken Chow Meins, one portion each of Dow Foo Tong, Lung Har Gai Kew, Chow Foon Shee, fried rice, and all the fortune cookies they could spare. They must be in demand, because they could only spare six, but I managed to corner all six of them while Jonathan and the girls were eating peach pie. I read them before I did the dishes, and put the slips in my apron pocket to copy in here this morning.

About ten-thirty last night, I finally emerged from a long hot bath, facing the fact that hydrotherapy wasn't going to work. From the way I felt I also knew that all the Rex Stouts and Ngaio Marshes and Margery Allinghams in paperback couldn't put me to sleep without some reinforcement. I'd long ago hidden away my last Nembutal to be used in a crisis, but the situation at hand didn't quite qualify, so I stood by my bed, trying to get up the nerve to sneak into the pantry for a huge bolt of bourbon followed by a whole pack of Winterberry or Chinaberry chewing gum, when Jonathan came in. He'd been locked in the den since dinner. Now he came in and shut the door and then stood leaning against it, pale and Grave. In fact, one look at his face and stagey pose, and I knew that once again he hadn't really been working in the den at all, that, having locked himself in there to think things over, he'd decided we had to Have It Out. Again.

"Tina. We've got to have a talk," he said, still supported by the door.

"Talk about what?" I sat down on my bed and lit a cigarette. I felt stunningly calm.

"About everything. About, just for a starter, the way we live. The way we live is ridiculous."

"I couldn't agree more."

He gave a peculiar grimace, baring his teeth and squinting. "Don't start any of that heavy-handed irony with *me*, old girl. Not now. I warn you: I'm at my wits' end. I've been a very patient man. Fantastically patient. More patient than any other man I know would have been under the circumstances. But now my patience is just about used up. Oh, for a while a few weeks back there, I thought you were really beginning to pull yourself out of it, but I see now it's all been a deception, a careful scheme . . . Oh, I've *watched* you. You thought you were pulling some fast ones, didn't you, doing all sorts of little token things . . . like putting all those crazy books away. Well, I haven't been fooled, old girl. If anything, I think you're worse off than you were!"

As he paused for breath—why wouldn't he come off that door?—I thoughtfully blew out some smoke. "Would you like a divorce, Jonathan?"

He turned white and wet his lips. "Divorce. Divorce? Who said anything about *divorce?* That's part of what I mean is the matter with you. You over-react. Just because we're having a few disagreements, just because you have some problems, just because I don't like the way certain things happen or don't happen around here . . . doesn't mean I want to *divorce* you, for God's sake."

I was not impressed. If not, what then? But I by-passed the more obvious statements I could have made, and in search of something relatively simple and tangible to hang on to, said: "You said the way we live is ridiculous. Just what did you mean?"

"I meant the way things are around here."

"That's too vague. Things. What sort of things?"

"The arrangements we have with that goddamn maid, for instance. Why can't we have a normal maid like other people? Why can't she at least stay to serve the lousy dinners she cooks and wash up afterwards, the way every other maid does?"

"One of the reasons she doesn't is because I don't want her to, that's why. I don't want any tired Negro ladies standing on their feet until nine or ten every night in *my* kitchen, that's why."

"You and your muddle-headed liberalism!" he shouted. "That's what I mean. That sort of no-think. You never used to be like that. But if you insist on having such noodley scruples, then get a young, energetic *Swedish* maid. Or a Finnish or Irish or German maid. Only get somebody who can be properly trained, for God's sake. Trained to accommodate our needs. If one person can't do that, hire *two*. I certainly can afford it."

"I will not have two people working in this house, Jonathan. One is bad enough."

Suddenly Jonathan sagged, needed more support than the door. He crossed the room and collapsed in the armchair, where he sat for a few seconds shading his eyes with a hand, as if the light were too bright. Finally, peering out at me from under the shelf of fingers, he said hoarsely, "Tina. Tina, do you know how many times I've almost called Dr. Popkin in the last two months? Almost called to tell him about the shape you're in, and to beg him to call you?"

"What stopped you?"

"I knew it was against the Code."

I laughed. "Code. *What* Code? Go ahead and call him. Go in and see him, in fact. I'm sure he'd be delighted to meet you at long last—the model husband for the cured analysand. And after you're done telling him all about me, tell him all about yourself. I know he'd be just fascinated. And grateful. I mean after listening to all those poor sick slobs all day long, he would find it such a relief to listen to a really effective man. I mean how often does he get a chance to meet a lawyer, producer, stock market wizard and patron of the arts all rolled into one, a Renaissance Man? A completely masculine man who's absolutely clear on what a woman's role in marriage ought to be? Above all don't leave that out. You must give him your views of what *both* working roles in a successful marriage should be—he'll be thrilled by the brilliant simplicity of it all. You know—the Forceful Dominant Male, the Submissive Woman? The Breadwinner who has every right to expect the Obedient Wife to carry out all his orders? He'll lap it up."

Truly, I don't know where this speech came from. It just seemed to have pre-existed a long time, all ready for me to deliver when I found the courage and the right circumstances. It obviously struck home, because Jonathan just sat crumpled in the chair, peering out from under the shading hand with burning eyes. I was beginning to have some doubts and misgivings (Was I turning into a Castrating Woman? Was that all my sudden courage and strength meant?) when he finally said, very low, "If you want to know the truth, I'm more worried about the girls than anything else."

I stopped worrying about being a Castrating Woman. "The girls. Just what the hell do you mean by that crack?"

"I mean that girls look to their mothers to teach them about being women, to set examples of femininity for them—and you sure set one helluva horrible example."

I got off the bed. The steady calm that had supported me throughout this exchange was gone; I was shaking with rage. "You shut up, Jonathan Balser. You can take that kind of talk and shove it right up your ass. If there's any rotten example being set for those girls, it's not me. You say one more filthy word about it's being me, and I *will* divorce you, so help me God."

"Calm down. Calm *down*. Lower your voice and stop using such foul language. You'll wake the girls. And stop talking about divorce. If we work at it together, this marriage can be saved. It can be a damned good marriage if you'll only co-operate."

I giggled. No doubt hysterically.

Jonathan stared at me. "Oh Jesus. What are you *laughing* at?"

" 'Can This Marriage Be Saved?' We could always go on the program and find out."

"I don't happen to have your sick twisted sense of humor. I happen to believe that what I said is true. If we work together, and you're co-operative, we could have a good marriage, maybe even better than before. But I see now you won't do your part, won't acknowledge trouble and error where it exists—which means I have to try and be as strong as I can and carry on for both of us. I'm not going to talk about this ever again. I'm going to pretend you never said any of the bloody rotten things you said about me. I'm just going to pick up from here and carry on as best I can."

"That's very big of you, I must say."

Now Jonathan stood up. "I can't take any more tonight. I'm going down to sleep at the Harvard Club. When the girls ask where I am in the morning, say I was called out of town on an emergency during the night."

Thursday December 14

❧

IT'S ASTONISHING HOW married couples can live in a state of armed truce, yet, for appearances' sake, can go about acting as decorously and circumspectly as characters in a drawing-room comedy. Living it, I'm astonished by my capacity for deceit. Living it, I've discovered a latent talent for playing Margaret Leighton, both at home and at social functions—cool, urbane, airy, bright, gay. And Jonathan isn't any slouch either; Jonathan has been doing his bit too, playing early Michael Redgrave to my Leighton, and the two of us go around cuing each other in a bright snappy upbeat way that would do John C. Wilson proud. All this is for public consumption, of course. Privately we haven't exchanged a word since the night of the fight. Even so, each of us seems to have come to the same conclusion independently: now isn't the time for any big *putsch*. Why that is, I'm not sure. I can't speak for Jonathan, but I think it's mostly the girls. I think there are other things too—like the fact that up until a while ago we had so much, and neither of us wants to accept the idea that so much can simply vanish into thin air overnight; or, as sad proof to the contrary slowly piles up, neither of us wants to *let* it vanish without putting up a struggle. I don't know. I don't *know*. The truth is I don't like to think about it very much, I'm still too mad at Jonathan—but I think things like that are involved.

Anyway, having slept it off at the Harvard Club, Jonathan has been as good as his word: he is stoically Carrying On and leaving me alone. For example, on Sunday, instead of asking me to address the Christmas cards as he's always done, he did them himself. Or at least he started to. I'd been in the kitchen giving Sylvie and Liz and the Jocelyn girls a snack, and was on my way up front for some cigarettes, when I passed the den and saw Jonathan working on the stacks of cards. Naturally the door was wide open. It's called the Psychological Approach. They use it on children. I went in and helped him with the cards. The silence got so unnerving I had to put Beethoven's Sixth on the record player, but we finished the cards and got them out in the mail.

During this five-day period of adjustment that followed the fight, I never heard from George. I was dying to see him, but was too proud and ashamed to call. Then at noon on Tuesday the phone rang. Without even bothering to say hello, he said that if I wasn't planning to hang Christmas wreaths, why didn't I come over around three this afternoon? Though I was having trouble breathing, there was another reason it took me a minute to answer. I seemed to remember something scheduled for that afternoon, something besides finishing the damned Christmas shopping, but since I couldn't think what it was, I decided it couldn't be very important, and finally found enough breath to tell him I'd be there.

I was there, all right. Things were better than they'd ever been, though I wouldn't have thought it possible. Afterwards, as we lay smoking, not talking, I realized with a sinking feeling that I couldn't see him again until the following week. I finally tapped my cigarette off into the ashtray on his chest, and said, "Would you come to a party we're giving Saturday if I thought of a safe way of inviting you?"

"Not on your life."

"Why not?"

He turned his head on the pillow, curling his lips. "First of all, I hate parties. Second of all, I don't get my kicks from that sort of thing."

"What sort of thing?"

"That nobody-knows-but-us sort of crap. Poor baby, I might've known you would dig that kind of cheap thrill."

Because things had been so wonderful until then, I swallowed my anger and pride. "I only asked because it would be more bearable if you were there." As usual, in trying to make things better, I'd only made them worse, that being the sentimental sort of remark he loathed. Upset, I said acidly, "If you hate parties, what were you doing at the two where we met?"

"Checking up on a lying cunt."

"The tall skinny blonde?" That had been bothering me for weeks.

"What difference does it make who it was!"

"I only asked because it sounds as if you . . . cared . . . for her."

"Cared. Oh Christ. Are you going to start getting jealous and possessive on me?"

"Do you still see her?" I persisted, in the grip of the horrible thing that made my bones and teeth ache.

He glared at me with disgust.

"I suppose you never get jealous," I said.

"Not any more. I did once, but I made myself get over that. It's weak and sick— But you. You have no goddamn right to be jealous, and you'd better get that straight."

"I'm not jealous," I lied through my aching teeth. "Merely curious."

He gave me the snort I deserved.

"Exactly what did you mean when you said I have no 'right' to be jealous. Because I'm married? Is that it?"

For a minute he looked too exasperated to speak. Then he said wearily, "I mean that if we're having the straight sex thing we've agreed on, there's no place for jealousy. I also mean that you give me damned little of your time, too damned little for someone like me. What do you expect me to do while you're changing diapers and running errands for that husband of yours? And while we're on him, what about that? Or are you going to tell me you two never screw."

"No, I'm not." I felt idiotically happy: he could get jealous after all.

"*Well?* And supposing I don't like that."

"But you just finished saying you never get jealous any more." I was beginning to feel better than I had in years.

"I don't!" he snapped, furious at me and the way he'd gotten himself embroiled. "I'm just pointing out that if you wanted to get jealous on the grounds of what *I* do, you have no right, considering what you and old John-a-thing do . . . Ah, shit to all that. Come on, baby. We're wasting time!"

Later, he lay sprawled on the bed watching me comb my hair in the closet mirror. "What's today? Tuesday. How about Friday?"

My heart sank: here it was. Turning from the mirror, I said, "I know this will only prove your point, but the fact is I can't see you until next week. And next week will be the last time until after the holidays."

He just lay there, smiling.

"Don't you want to hear why?"

"I don't give a flying fart why."

"*One* of the reasons," I grimly proceeded, "is the damned party we're giving Saturday night. For the next few days I have to stick around and see that floors get waxed and windows get washed, things like that. On Friday I have to go to the dentist and the hairdresser . . ."

"Oh Christ . . ."

"But next week," I went on, "I can see you early in the week. It has to be early because I'm due to get the curse about the middle of the week."

"I don't mind that."

"I do."

"You would." Still smiling, he sat up and lit a cigarette. "And after the curse, what then? If only for sheer documentation this is beginning to be fascinating—in a hair-raising sort of way."

I made myself ignore this. "After that I have to be with the girls. They'll be out on their Christmas vacation, and I have to take them places."

From behind a dense cloud of smoke: "And you have the nerve to be jealous." A laugh.

"I'm *not* jealous," I said, near tears, yet still unable to move.

"Okay. You're not jealous. Grand . . . It's twenty past five. Hadn't you better move your ass?"

"What about Tuesday?" This was why I couldn't move. "Do you want to see me Tuesday afternoon or not?"

He stared at me with the marble-statue eyes, apparently as astonished as I was by the staggering amounts of what I would take.

"Sure, baby," he said softly. "Tuesday's fine. I'll even have some mistletoe hanging over the bed."

Once again I couldn't get a cab, and by the time Sven the drunken Swede had dropped me at our floor I felt calmer and less humiliated, but chilled to the bone. I unlocked the door on Mrs. Goodman standing alone in the middle of the hall, a snowsuit jacket in either hand. Beyond, in the living room, lamps were softly burning, and several magazines lay on the dented cushions of the wing chair by the fireplace.

For the second time in a half-hour I wanted to die. Mrs. Goodman and her girls, the thing I'd tried to remember when George had called that morning, the date I'd finally arranged to salve my conscience for the wheeling and dealing of three weeks ago. I'd not only forgotten her girls were coming and had therefore left all four children alone with Lottie—I'd also made a big fuss about her coming early to pick them up so that we could have a drink. How long had she been there?

Apologizing too profusely, I stammered something about unexpectedly having to rush downtown for some Christmas shopping, and about the terrible traffic. "Do you still have time for a drink?"

Considering the fact that she had on her coat and was holding those two jackets, I could have taken first prize for pure gall. She wanly smiled and shook her head, tweaking back some long lank blond hair. She was wearing a worn camel's-hair coat that was the twin of mine, thick ugly mustard wool stockings and high boots. "Actually, I was a bit late getting here myself," she said, trying to help me. "I'd love to stay, but I left Timmy with some neighbors, and I've got a roast in the oven that'll get burnt if I don't get back and yank it out."

I made a feeble try at a smile. "That sounds familiar."

Rightly, she was having none of that. It just happened that the apartment was spotless, the air was filled with the rich fizzy smell of the chicken Lottie was frying for dinner, and there I was, albeit upset, but radiating the afterglow of bed all the same. She smiled politely: "Your apartment is just beautiful." Then, raising her voice, she called Solange and Florence, and they came out with Sylvie and Liz.

"Where were *you?*" asked Sylvie as the Goodman girls buttoned and zipped with their mother's help.

The mysteries of infanticide were revealed to me. "Downtown, Christmas shopping."

Sylvie took in my packageless arms. "You should've told Lottie. She almost fainted when the four of us came in. And Mrs. Goodman's been here an hour waiting for you."

"Not an hour, Sylvie," Mrs. Goodman said gently, straightening up and catching the look on my face. Suddenly she grinned, a wry and self-mocking look in her bright blue eyes. "I know it's hard to believe, but life can be civilized at our house too. We're finally getting a girl from Sweden next week and it's going to change my life. Maybe Sylvie and Liz will come to our house over Christmas vacation, and when you come to get them we'll lock everybody upstairs with the Swedish girl and finally have our drink."

I laughed. She wasn't, as I'd so inspirationally put it, any *semblable* or *soeur* of mine—she was too damned healthy and too damned nice.

Having expertly provided this lighter note, she said goodbye and left with her girls. And her simple, direct personality had such a positive effect on me that I snapped right out of my need to wallow in guilt. From then on, things were all right, better than they'd been in a week—until around eleven, when Jonathan came out

of the bathroom and said, "Hey, Teen. How about a little ole roll in the hay."

They were the first words he'd spoken to me in private
in a week.

I blinked at the Margery Allingham I was reading;
marvelous Albert Campion, so deft, so debonair, swam
in his paragraph of print. Here it was, what I'd been
dreading ever since I'd been going to bed with George.
It made me wild. Why *now?* Why when things were so
horrible? The answer, of course, was that this was another one of his ways of trying to Carry On, and I'd
damned well better co-operate if I didn't want to bring
on another knock-down drag-out fight. So I climbed out
of bed and went in the bathroom, thinking of the Mary
McCarthy character who'd gotten her kicks from sleeping with her husband and lover in the same day, laughing
Wicked Inner Laughter while she did it; I couldn't *be*
like that, I told myself.

It seemed I could. Surprise surprise. Just minus the
kicks and Wicked Inner Laughter, that's all. "It's been a
long time, we both needed that," said Jonathan afterwards, and climbing into his bed, turned off his light and
fell right asleep.

Today is Thursday, Lottie's day off, and I'm here all
alone waiting for a man to come and wax the floors for
the party Saturday night. I'm here all alone, I repeat, yet
the way I feel I don't give a damn if I get raped, stabbed
sixty times, dragged to the basement in a laundry cart
and stuffed in the incinerator with my feet hanging out.

THE PARTY
Saturday, December 16

AT 7:35, TOO KEYED-UP about the party to sleep, Jonathan got up and took a shower, waking us all with the noise of gurgling drains.

By 8:30 we were all in the kitchen eating breakfast. Reaching for the pepper mill, Jonathan ground it squeakily over his four-minute egg and said to me as if Sylvie and Liz weren't there, "I forgot to ask where the girls are spending the night."

The girls stopped eating their Maple Crispies-and-cream.

"They're spending the night here, of course. Why?"

Jonathan dropped a nugget of butter into his egg cup and reached for the salt. "Why? Because with the party going on, I assumed you'd arrange for them to stay overnight with friends."

Stunned, the girls watched their father beat up his egg, violently whirling and clacketing the spoon around in the delicate Wedgwood egg cup.

"And why did you assume that?" I said when the racket died down.

Jonathan tasted some of the mucked-up egg, which apparently was all right since he didn't reach for any-

216

thing else. "I assumed that because of the problem, a problem of simple logistics, that their being here will create. For one thing, how d'you expect them to get any sleep with all the racket? For another, where are they going to be before their bedtime? I can't stand it when kids show up at grown-up parties. I know some people think it's cute, but it just isn't *done*. I mean I personally think it's offensive as hell when people dress up their kids and send them out to bow and curtsey and pass around canapés, and I certainly hope you or the girls didn't have anything like that in mind."

Finally looking in their direction, he saw they'd not only had that in mind, but had been looking forward to it for weeks.

Though it took a lot of doing, he got them to the point where they understood that this sort of thing wasn't Done, and even got them to agree to stay in their room, where he promised one of Beaumont's lackeys would bring them some canapés. While this was going on I began to shake so badly with pure rage that I couldn't pick up my coffee cup. His brainwash accomplished, Jonathan pushed back his chair and lit up one of his rotten little cigars. Expansively blowing out smoke, he said, "Now, girls, soon's I finish this cigar, I'm going out to buy some Christmas decorations. How would you like to come along?"

"Christmas decorations?" I gave up on the coffee; I'd reheat it and drink it when I was alone.

"Greens," said Jonathan. "We completely overlooked any kind of festive seasonal touch. I mean do you realize that Christmas is only nine days away?"

The girls, who'd begun to eat again, stolidly went on spooning up soggy Maple Crispies.

"Somehow it slipped my mind," I said faintly. "But since I've ordered flowers as you asked, why not just call the florist and have him send some greens along with them? Why on earth bother to go out for them?"

"Because I don't feel like paying an arm and a leg for them, that's why. It makes sense with flowers. You *have* to pay to get quality with flowers, but not with something like greens. I discovered a terrific place over on

Ninth Avenue last year—that's where I got that gorgeous spruce we had."

"Are you going to buy a tree now?" Liz burst out.

"Not today, sweetheart. We'll do that next week. There isn't time to trim a big tree before the party. Besides, it would take up too much room . . . Well, how about it? You girls with me?"

It seemed they were.

By 11:45, when they returned, I'd cleaned the kitchen and made the beds and walked Folly and calmed down. Since Lottie was staying overnight to help out at the party, I'd told her not to bother to come in until 1:00 so that her day wouldn't be too long. They trooped in, Dickensian, rosy-cheeked, arms piled with boughs of evergreens, which they carried into the pantry. The smell was delicious, like a forest in Maine. There were swags of spruce, ropes of longleaf pine, loose branches of dense and burry fir, and a huge Della Robbia-style wreath thick with berries and cones. While they hung up their coats I stood sniffing, finding myself smiling without knowing why. George, I thought for the first time that day—for the first time in days—and then knew why I was smiling. Oh, George.

Jonathan got the stepladder and a hammer and some nails, and followed by the girls (who seemed happy again), went to work. While they decorated, I started to make some lunch. I'd found half a cold chicken in the icebox and decided to make some club sandwiches which everybody liked. I was frying the bacon when Jonathan burst through the pantry door, hammer in hand. "For God's sake, Tina! The whole place stinks of bacon!"

"It's a perfectly respectable smell." I calmly went on turning the slices in the pan with a pair of tongs; I'd sworn that no matter what he did or said, I wasn't going to let him get to me again that day. I had to conserve my strength for bigger things.

"It's a smell that takes hours to go away. It'll be just like the Bronx when our guests arrive! Couldn't you use your head?"

"They don't eat bacon in the Bronx you mean. And at least it's not mushroom-and-barley soup." But this was said to the pantry door, swinging back and forth. He'd already gone.

At 12:20 I followed a dense trail of pine needles from the pantry into the living room, where they were all busily looping swags of spruce over the valances and tiebacks of the drapes. A pine rope decorated the frame of the doorway, and the mantel was piled with boughs of balsam.

"Doesn't it look nice?" asked Sylvie.

"Lovely," I said, wanting to give credit where it was due. "It really does look very festive."

"You sound surprised," said Jonathan, coming down off the ladder just in time to catch me staring at the millions of pine needles covering the pale living-room rug.

"Lottie'll be able to get that up in ten minutes with the vacuum," he said brightly, making for the pile of spruce on the floor. ". . . Where *is* Lottie, by the way?"

"She's not coming in till one today."

"Ah, *I* see," he said and started back up the ladder.

So did I see. See that he was just loaded for bears today, and that I was going to have to be made of iron not to let him get through to me again. "You'd better not start that new rope now. Lunch is ready." Turning to go, I saw the mistletoe, a lavish bunch with fat waxy white berries, tied to the hall chandelier with a red satin bow. Kiss kiss, I thought, looking up. And just who in that bunch will be kissing who? George, I thought for the second time that day. Oh, *George.*

At 12:30 we were all in the kitchen eating, when the back doorbell rang. I opened the door on two huge men, each carrying a stack of gold bamboo-and-red-velvet chairs. "Balser?" said one, and when I nodded, they marched in and dumped the chairs in the dining room with Folly wildly yapping at their heels. Making seven trips, they deposited in the dining room fifteen crates holding glasses and gold-rimmed white china decorated with gold crested B (for Beaumont, not Balser), thirty gold bamboo-and-red-velvet chairs, two mahogany bars,

two coat racks with hangers, a huge crate marked
CHAFERS & COOKERS, a stack of silver trays and plat-
ters engraved with the crested B and covered with Saran
Wrap.

Jonathan signed the chit and tipped them and we tried
to resume our lunch.

"I'm too excited to eat," said Sylvie, pushing away her
sandwich.

"It's snowing!" shouted Liz, who sat facing the window.

Jonathan yanked back the checked curtain obscuring
his view. "Oh, *no*."

"What's the matter, Daddy?" asked Liz.

"The snow will keep a lot of people away from our
party. That's what's the matter."

Since nobody was eating, I got up to clear. As I
passed in front of the window I saw a few thin snowflakes floating down. "It doesn't look like anything
more than a light flurry, Jonathan."

"That's because we're looking out on a courtyard, and
courtyards create *up*draughts. It must be snowing like
hell if even this much manages to come down back
here."

I'd forgotten he was an authority on courtyards. It
seemed to be Aunt Tessie's day.

I set some plates on the sink counter and tried again.
"Well, even if it is snowing hard, this is New York City,
which has taxis and snowplows. I never heard of a little
snow keeping anyone from a party in this city."

"You seem to forget all the people who go to their
places in the country for the weekend, and were planning to come back in just for the party. Like Graham
Tilson from Bucks County, or Iris Puderis from New
City, just to name two."

"Iris Puderis? *Who* is Iris Puderis from New City?"

"Iris Puderis just happens to be one of the hottest
sculptors in this country— But the point is, do you
think any of those people are going to want to risk driving on the parkways in a *blizzard?*"

Made of iron, like I said. However, I was spared the
necessity of putting myself to the test of an answer, be-

cause at that moment Lottie let herself in the back door, and this seemed to be a signal for adjournment. Nobody, thank God, wanted dessert.

At 3:00 the apartment was deathly still. After vacuuming up the pine needles and cleaning the kitchen, Lottie was sitting in her room sewing. The girls were downstairs at the Jocelyns', which I found a trifle embarrassing, since Jonathan hadn't let me invite the Jocelyns to the party, and Jonathan was taking a nap. I suddenly found myself wild with nerves. Jonathan hadn't told me what time Beaumont was coming, and it had finally occurred to me that since the party was scheduled to start at six, he ought to have been there by now. To distract myself, I went around checking the flowers and putting cigarettes in boxes and urns. Then, unnerved by the shining expectant silence that filled the apartment, I decided to walk Folly. It was snowing again—it had been stopping and starting since noon—so I bundled up and put Folly's sweater on.

By the time I got back upstairs I felt much better. I left my boots outside the front door, and still wearing the two old sweaters and baggy flannel slacks and thick sweat socks I'd put on for warmth, I padded to the kitchen to make myself some tea. The back doorbell rang just as the kettle started to whistle.

Five people good on the grubby back landing amidst the garbage pails and empty milk bottles, looking about them with the faintly dazed air of deposed nobility. They all seemed to be dressed in black, and each of them carried two huge natty rattan hampers. The tallest, a pale sepulchral man in a black coat and homburg, with lines like dueling scars seaming his face, stepped forward and removed his hat. The hair under the hat, obviously dyed, was like patent leather, and was worn in the style favored by T. S. Eliot in his middle years. "Madame Balser?"

"Yes."

"Beaumont Service, Madame." Giving a little bow from the waist, he stared down at my old white sweat socks.

"Oh yes. *Do* come in."

Stony-faced, they filed past me into the kitchen, where they put down their hampers and stood blinking about them. Besides the somber man, there were two husky blond young men and two gaunt older women with flinty faces and tightly crimped grey hair. As they stood in the middle of the kitchen, looking like mourners at a wake, Jonathan came in. Awakened by the doorbell, he was sleepy and dazed, and his hair stood up in tufts all over his head. "Ah, Monsieur Beaumont!" he said, confusedly smiling and heading with an outstretched hand for the tall man. "What a pleasure to meet you in person at last!"

The man left Jonathan's hand flapping in the air. "I am not Monsieur Beaumont, Monsieur Balser. I am Monsieur Henri."

Wide awake now, Jonathan jammed his hand in his pocket. The others, watching this with great boredom, exchanged smirks. "How d'you do, Henri," said Jonathan. "And what times does Monsieur arrive?"

"Monsieur Beaumont does not arrive, Monsieur Balser. Please. Is there somewhere my people can change their clothes?"

"Doesn't arrive? You mean not come at *all?* I'm afraid I don't understand."

Half-shutting his eyes, Monsieur Henri sighed. "Monsieur Balser. Monsieur Beaumont only appears at those parties where it has been . . . ah, specifically indicated and the necessary arrangements have been made. I am Monsieur Beaumont's head man. I have been with Monsieur Beaumont eleven years. I assure you, Monsieur Balser, all will be taken care of just as if Monsieur Beaumont himself were here."

During this exchange, Monsieur Henri's People had reached the end of their patience. Glaring glassily at each other, they unbuttoned their overcoats and mutinously began to shuffle their feet and cough. I still stood by the back door, my feet sweating in the sweat socks.

Jonathan looked horribly close to tears. "I'm quite sure that what you say is true, but it should have been made clear to me. I wasn't told that one had to make

. . . ah, special arrangements to have Monsieur Beaumont appear." Flushed, he turned to me. "Tina, will you please show these people where they can change their clothes—I've something to attend to up front." He bolted.

Which left me holding the bag with a little problem I'd never taken into account. Where *were* all those damn People going to change? The only really available place was Lottie's room, so I muttered something to all those furious faces, knocked on her door and went in and shut the door behind me. Lottie was sitting in her armchair, shortening a tartan skirt of Sylvie's and watching TV. She assured me she didn't mind at all, turned off the set, gathered up her sewing and purse and followed me back out in the kitchen, where the five of them were unpacking the hampers in their overcoats. The two young men rushed off to change, slamming the door behind them. I introduced Lottie to the remaining three and said to Monsieur Henri, "Mrs. Masters will be happy to show you where things are, and give you any help you need."

"We do not require any assistance, Madame. We always bring all our own equipment and prefer to use our own staff."

"Ah, yes," I said, and breathlessly asked Lottie to come with me. In the front hall I began apologizing, and told her to go in the den and make herself comfortable.

For a minute she just stood there, clutching the skirt and sewing box and purse. Then, greatly embarrassed, she said, "Would you like me to just go on home, Mrs. Balser? There's no need for me to go, I 'ranged for my husband to stay overnight with my sister and all, but I don't want to be in the way."

I wanted the floor to open up and let me fall down into Mr. Joel Mossbach's apartment. Taking a deep breath, my face on fire, I laboriously explained that even though she wouldn't be helping out with the actual party itself, I needed her badly. "You see, Mr. Balser wants the girls to stay in their room while the party's going on, and I thought you might keep them company and fix them some supper."

"Well, that's different. I be glad to keep them company—but don't you think that man'll get annoyed if I go in the kitchen to fix them some supper?"

Annoyed. I burst out laughing and our awkwardness vanished. I told her that she indeed had a point; I'd send out for sandwiches for all of them.

In our room Jonathan was standing at the window, staring out at the slowly falling snow. Jonathan is not given to watching the scenery. When he heard me shut the door, he turned. His face was white and strained. "I'm really terribly upset," he said superfluously.

"Oh, Jonathan, does it really matter whether Beaumont's here or not?"

"Yes, it matters. You're goddamn right it matters! I'm certainly paying enough for him to come and show his bloody face. He at least could have *told* me. I mean if it was just a question of more money, which I'm sure it is, I would've paid. Gladly."

"Well, next time you'll know," I said and picked up the phone and called Dillman's Delicatessen.

By 5:20 Jonathan was completely restored. All pink and freshly showered and shaved, wearing his silk robe from Knize, he was sitting in the armchair vigorously buffing his Peal shoes when the girls burst into the room. Liz was in tears. It seemed that she and Sylvie had been hungry, and drawn by the delicious smells, had gone into the pantry, where they'd found several finished platters of canapés set out on the counter. They'd carefully lifted the plastic wrap covering one of the trays, and were about to take one canapé apiece, when Monsieur Henri had appeared.

I listened to only half of what Monsieur Henri had said to them, and started for the door wearing only a robe and slippers.

"Tina!" shouted Jonathan. "Don't you *dare* to go out there looking like that, Tina! This is just the sort of thing I wanted to avoid by having the girls stay overnight with friends. But everyone thought I was such a monster for even suggesting it. *Now.* You stop that blubbering, Elizabeth. Monsieur Henri was right. It isn't like when those other ladies come and cook dinner for company.

These people are professionals. These people are perfectionists. These people do things in a highly organized way, and we have to respect their way of doing things. If he doesn't want you or your sister underfoot or spoiling his hard work, then you listen to him. You go to your room, both of you, and stay there. I'm really too embarrassed to even ask him to send anything in to you."

As they both wordlessly turned and left the room, Jonathan calmly began to buff his shoes again. He knew that I was standing there staring at him, but he refused to look up, so I finally went into the bathroom and shut the door. I stood at the sink, shaking, distractedly picking things up—a bottle of make-up base, a box of face powder, a cake of soap, a jar of deodorant—and putting them down again. Though I faced the mirror, I couldn't see my face. *George*, I thought for the first time in hours and the third time that day. Oh, horrible terrible marvelous George.

At 5:35 the front doorbell rang. Jonathan was in his shorts, fitting his gold cuff links into his monogrammed shirt, and I was in my slip, brushing my hair at the mirror. We looked at each other; nobody in the crowd arriving later would be caught dead arriving a half-hour early to *any*thing, so who could it be? There were loud voices in the hall, and a second later a discreet knock on our door. I put on a robe and opened the door two inches on one of the blond young men in a starchy white coat: there was a man in the hall, he said, who claimed to be our neighbor and who demanded to see either Jonathan or myself.

Being more presentable, I went. Mr. Meyer, our next-door neighbor, stood glowering under the mistletoe. Kiss kiss. There he was: my prize. "I just wanted to say you've got your helluva goddamn nerve!" Mr. Meyer began shouting while I was still a good eight feet away. "How the hell are me and my wife supposed to get in and out've our front door with those lousy coat racks in the way? Not to mention the friends who're dropping in to see us later."

Oh, I loved it. Loved it all: the mistletoe dangling over

Mr. Meyer's bald head, which matched the color of the mistletoe's ribbon; Monsieur Henri's nose poking through the pantry door; one of the crimpy ladies gaping from the dining room; one of the blond young men gaping from the living room. And Mr. Meyer's cigar, five times the size of one of Jonathan's, drifting ash onto the hall rug, giving off a smell of burning rope which quite eclipsed the smells of herbs and baking puff-pastry and spruce and pine. I loved it all so much, was so grateful to him for appearing, that I hated having to set the record straight. But sweetly and very gently, I finally reminded Mr. Meyer of his daughter's engagement party a little over a year ago, an evening when there'd not only been two coat racks out in the hall, but an accordion-violin combo playing far far into the night. Looking oddly puzzled, poor Mr. Meyer opened his mouth, shut it, opened it again and said: "Two wrongs don't maka right. And I tell you something. I wouldn't've come over to make this fuss if it hadn'ta been for that husband of yours. If that husband of yours hadn'ta rung my bell one night last week and ast me, no *told* me, to get a new doormat and to take in our umbrella stand. Said the umbrella stand was an eyesore. That's the word he used. *Eyesore.* I mean he's got his goddamn nerve, that husband of yours. Just who the hell does he think he *is?*"

It was a good question. And since it was one I was unable to answer, Mr. Meyer gave himself a sort of general shake all over and went banging out the door.

At 5:52 I came out of our room, dressed and ready for the fray. Finished long before me, wearing a brand-new suit he'd gotten from a tailor named Spiff and which he'd coolly confessed had cost two hundred and fifty dollars, Jonathan was already prowling around the apartment. When I reached the front hall I saw that he'd made his peace with Monsieur Henri; the two of them were having an intense conference in the living room, which seemed to be overflowing with gilt bamboo-and-red-velvet chairs (were we giving a cotillion or a cocktail party?), coasters and extra ashtrays. In the dining room one of the blond young men was busily checking the equipment on one of the mahogany bars, so I promptly asked him to fix me a drink. Congratulating myself on having held off that long, everything considered, I took a big bracing sip and carried it to the girls' room. The door was closed and a huge sign written with red Magic Markers was Scotch-taped across the top: PRIVATE! NO ADMITTANCE! PROCEED AT YOUR OWN RISK!

I risked it and went in. Lottie had brought in her portable television set, and the three of them sat eating their delicatessen supper off of paper plates, watching the Million Dollar Movie. Folly sat hopefully begging at Lottie's feet. The room smelled of pickles and mustard and hot pastrami on rye. All mouths were full and working, all eyes were glued to the screen. Without taking their eyes from the set, the girls assured me that I looked "just marvy, Mudther," but Lottie did look away long enough to assure me they had everything they wanted. I could well believe it. The Million Dollar Movie was *The Philadelphia Story*, and I'd have given anything to be able to stay in that room with them, eating a rare roast beef sandwich and watching those two beauties, early Hepburn, early Grant.

At 6:10 the doorbell rang, and one of the flinty ladies showed in the first guests, Jonathan's broker (or one of them, anyway), "Hank" McCustin and his wife Mildred. I'd met them once before at a big rowdy party at their house and liked her. He was a big slick blond, a real operator, but she was a thin, nervous, overdressed and—at least when tight—extremely funny woman. I greeted them warmly, but Jonathan was less enthusiastic. He'd invited them because he'd felt obliged to, hoping they'd get lost in the crowd, but as we stood with them in the hall, I could see that in his book they'd committed an unforgivably depressing gaffe by arriving so promptly and showing themselves to be so overeager. I also saw that he was furious at the way Mildred looked—poor Mildred, our missing Christmas tree in her tinselly beaded dress.

By 7:20 the hall, living room, den and dining room

were filled with about a hundred people milling about. Or rather a hundred people were milling about in those rooms; they didn't seem filled. I've always thought we were lucky to have such large-scaled, high-ceilinged rooms, but I'd never had a chance to see how they seemed to swallow people up. One hundred seemed like fifty, and the result was not Felicitous. Oh, there was a lot of smoke and heat and movement and noise, and Jonathan rushed around keeping things moving, or so he thought, but in spite of it all I saw that things never jelled and the party never really got off the ground.

I also saw a lot of things I could have done without seeing. I saw a Well-Known and I thought solvent young actor pick a tiny Vermeil fish up off an end table in the living room, and jam it in the pocket of his suit—a suit that was a dead ringer for Jonathan's $250.00 job from Spiff. I saw Carter Livingston hanging moonily around one of the young blond bartenders, until finally, thinking nobody was looking, he slipped a note in the boy's pocket and got a big blush and the big nod as a reward before he slunk off. I saw Graham Tilson deliberately drop his cigarette on the dining-room rug and grind it out with his heel; while I was getting up the courage to go over and slap his face, he took the arm of the woman he'd brought (all the way from Bucks County on the parkway in the snow?) and steer her out the front door without saying goodbye to anybody. I saw the owner of the gallery where Jonathan buys most of our paintings make a pass at Charlotte Rady, who subsequently bent over and whispered something that made the poor little man go green; a minute later *he* went out the door without saying goodbye to anybody. I saw a Well-Known director stand alone in a corner and watch Jonathan try to charm a Well-Known actress just four feet away, and the director's face was the most frightening study of sheer loathing I've ever had the privilege to behold. I saw the McCustins, alone and deserted for the twentieth time in an hour, finally go desperately barging up to the Barrs and Franklins, and five minutes later saw them, alone and deserted for the twenty-first time, go creeping out the door also without saying

goodbye to anybody. I saw Frank Gaylord taking down
the phone number of the Well-Known actress Jonathan
had been fawning over, while just three feet away
Margo watched with smoldering eyes, ignoring Jonathan's gallant attempt to divert her. And to top it all, I
saw the Markses and old Hoddison (his wife has leuke-
mia) standing in a closed threesome by the fireplace,
watching but not joining the action, taking in everything
from Jonathan's eclectic room to his eclectic collection
of friends. Though two of the other younger partners
and their wives were there, and though Jonathan
brought over only the choicest celebrities to be introduced, the three of them kept to themselves. Since the
firm handles celebrities from all the worlds Jonathan had
drawn on, and then some, I knew their attitude couldn't
be snobbery or shyness, so I watched them until I realized that it was only bewilderment—Is this Jonathan?
Our Jonathan? Our brilliant Jonathan *Balser?*—and it
was all I could do to keep from rushing over and saying,
But didn't you know? That's *just* who it is.

I also saw, I might add, the crimpy ladies and blond
boys continually weaving in and out of all this with
loaded silver trays, but I never did see Henri. He was saving himself for his big walk-on later.

I also never did see Iris Puderis. Iris Puderis didn't
make it.

No one stood under the mistletoe.

At 8:03 I found myself trapped against a bookcase in the
den, the Modern Library *Brothers Karamazov* pressing
against my spine, Frank Gaylord pressing against my
front. He was leaning forward, supported by arms outstretched to the bookcase, a hand on either side of my
head. I was like the prisoner in London Bridge. He was
telling me about my Secret Potential. He said: "You
may fool a lot of people with that shy and quiet put-on
of yours, but not old Franko. I'm willing to bet you're a
regular little *mad*woman in the sack." Something about
the voice set up sympathetic vibrations in my auditory
canals. I said: "Do you like to talk on the phone, Old
Franko?" Franko said: "Whah?" I looked him in the eye

and said: "I said do you like to talk on the phone?" He turned a distinct shade paler. "What kind of a stupid question is that?" I laughed—by now he'd turned very pale indeed—and pretty certain I'd drawn a bead on old Mr. Telephone Pervert himself, I ducked under his right arm like the prisoner in London Bridge, and walked off. I felt fine.

I walked down the hall. The girls were in bed, and Lottie was adjusting the picture on the TV. *The Philadelphia Story* had ended and now they were watching a Mexican horror movie about vampires. I kissed the girls goodnight and told Lottie there was no sense in her staying; I'd go get her cabfare and she could go home. With some embarrassment Lottie said that no cab driver would take her uptown that late, and since she was terrified of the subways at that hour, she'd prefer to stay the night if it was all right with me. I said it was fine with me, but where would she stay until Beaumont's People had cleared out of her room? "I'll just stay in here," she said. "When the girls turn out the light, I'll sit in the chair and take a little nap. The girls say they don't mind longs I don't snore. When the party's over you just come and shake me and I'll go on back to my room."

As I came out of their door, I almost collided with Charlotte Rady, who'd been in our bedroom fixing her face. "Marvelous party, angel," she murmured, detaining me with a heavily jeweled hand. "But I've really been terribly worried about you all evening . . . In spite of that heaven dress, you don't look well. Is something wrong?" Dear Charlotte. A bit thrown off by all this sudden personal interest, I stammered something about the strain of being a hostess and tried to escape, but she wouldn't let go of me. In fact, as she bent over to peer at me more closely, she began squeezing my hand, and I wondered if I'd been wrong about her not liking women. "But where on earth's the strain when you've got Beaumont?" she asked. "I'll admit he's trying, but he's also such a bore. I do wish Jonathan had called me. I'd have told him about this other new person who's simply marvelous. Everybody in the *world's* had Beaumont do those omelettes and crêpes and nobody's going to use him any more—he's about to get the comeuppance he deserves." Dear, *dear* Charlotte. She blinked at me: "Whatever are you laughing at?" I said: "We're having omelettes." She laughed and let go my hand, thank God. "You're utterly mad, but all the same I've begun to grow rather fond of you." Then an odd sneaky look came into those eyes with their pinpoints of pupils (goofballs? horse?) and she added, "So fond, in fact, I'm going to give you a word of advice. As Iago said to the Moor, 'Look to your wife, observe her well'—only of course you must switch the sexes around, Bettina dear." For a few seconds I just stood there. We were still in front of the girls' door. PRIVATE! NO ADMITTANCE! PROCEED AT YOUR OWN RISK! I looked at her dead-white face, swollen with the importance of what she thought she knew, and I began to laugh again. "Why, Charlotte, I didn't know you'd done Shakespeare! I mean here all this time I've been doing you a terrible injustice, thinking you'd just been one of those white fox-and-lamé movie queens. I certainly owe you an apology."

I hadn't thought it possible, but she grew even whiter. "I take it back. You're not mad, not mad atall, just horribly vulgar and *sick!*" she hissed and rushed off. I went into our bathroom, where I calmly powdered my nose, and came back out to find Jonathan, Frank Gaylord and Margo at the front door. "But we're having this marvelous food," Jonathan was saying. "Can't you skip your date and stay?" Frank Gaylord said, "Sorry, old chap, we've had this date for months and months," and grabbed Margo by her white string-bean arm and yanked her out the door.

At 8:33 Henri began serving omelettes. He'd set up shop in the dining room, where a long table had mysteriously replaced the bar. The table was covered with plates, silver, napkins and bowls of truffles, mushrooms, chives, caviar, sour cream and Westphalian ham. Presiding over intricate spirit lamps, Henri served up omelettes to order . . . only there were very few orders. Appalled—any life left in that party was going to be extinguished immediately—I went and hunted up Jonathan and found him talking to the Markses in the living room. Old Hoddison had left long ago. I apologized and drew him aside to tell him what Henri had done. "I know you made a point of telling me that you think you have to give people something more than just canapés and cocktails, but some of these people have only just gotten *started*. This is a drinking crowd, Jonathan, and it's too early for most of them to even *think* of food." Looking quite wretched, Jonathan nodded. "I know. I told Henri the same thing when I saw him setting up, but he said they had another party to do, that if I wanted food at all, it had to be now, and that if I didn't want it I had to pay for it anyway."

By 9:15 there were thirteen people left at the party. Seven of them sat around the living room, somber and sober, drinking coffee and eating petits fours. The other six were in the den, crowded around the bar that Jonathan had finally ordered Henri to reopen; both bars had closed down as soon as he'd started to serve the omelettes. The crowd around the bar were all what Jonathan once called Theater Folk, and were having a loud argument about where they would go for dinner. "Let's go to Gino's, I'm starved," said one. "No, let's go some place we can dance," said another. "Let's go some place we can get some chow and *then* let's go some place to dance," said still another. Said speaker Number 2, "Whyn't we have a fast omelette here and then go some place to dance?" "Because I don't want any crap omelettes!" said speaker Number 1; "I want some Ginny food!"

At 9:50 Jonathan saw The Beaumont Service out the front door, handing out lavish compliments and tips. I went into the girls' darkened room and gently shook Lottie awake, and after she'd shuffled stiffly off to her room, I went into the pantry and poured myself a huge snifter of Jonathan's best Napoleon brandy. I'd stopped drinking hours ago. I carried it to the living room, which was so immaculate it was impossible to tell that a party had just taken place there. Which was a point: had a party taken place?

After shutting the door on The Beaumont Service, Jonathan joined me, sinking down on the other end of the couch. He was smoking one of his little cigars and looking very pleased with himself. "Well, what do you think?" he said after a few thoughtful puffs. "I myself thought it went very well."

I warmed my brandy between my two palms. "It was all right. I just think he ruined things by starting those damn omelettes so early."

Apparently forgetting that we'd been in complete agreement on this an hour earlier, Jonathan said angrily, "A lot of people were hungry, as it turned out. Of course you'll always get a bunch of deadbeats who never want to eat, who'll only stay to soak up the booze and leave the second you shut down the bar, but I think most people were damned happy to see those omelettes."

I bent and slowly inhaled the lovely rich fumes. "Jonathan. How much did it cost?"

"What difference does it make!" Jonathan exploded. "Why in hell should you care how much it cost? *You* didn't have to lift a finger—isn't that enough?"

Be Still, My Heart. "I'll bet it cost close to a thousand dollars."

"Oh God," said Jonathan and stood up. "I might've known. You always have to spoil things, don't you—you have to put the kibosh on everything. You're not happy unless you're giving something the axe . . . Which reminds me. Just what the hell did you say to Charlotte Rady, anyway? I saw the two of you deep in conversation outside the girls' room, and next thing I know she's charging out the front door, giving me a pat on the arm as she goes, saying, 'You poor dear boy!' "

I laughed. "What makes you think *I* said something? What makes you think it had anything to do with me? Maybe she was bored. Maybe there weren't enough celebrities. Maybe she felt *déclassé*—she made a great point of telling me that people in the know aren't using Beaumont any more. Or maybe she just needed another fix."

Jonathan opened his mouth, thought better of it, and shut it again. Turning on his heel, he went out, slamming our bedroom door. I stayed in the living room until midnight, drinking brandy until I was anesthetized. When I went into our room, Jonathan was lying on his back, his mouth open, snoring to beat the band. At least he hadn't asked me what I'd said to make Frank Gaylord leave the party.

ᴏᴏᴋɪɴɢ ᴀɴɴᴏʏᴇᴅ and embarrassed, George tore the
rappings off the box—annoyed, I thought, because I'd
ought him a present, embarrassed because he hadn't
otten me one. In the box was the blue Viyella flannel
obe I'd seen in Brooks two weeks before; I'd gone
own late Monday afternoon, after the Christmas pag-
ant at the Bartlett School. Yesterday, with the girls
ut for Christmas vacation as of Monday, my big prob-
m had been how to get the box out of the house with-
ut their seeing it. I solved it by smuggling it out in a big
hopping bag, which was part of the alibi I'd thought up
o cover my leaving for two hours: I had some last min-
te Christmas shopping to finish up. The wheeling and
ealing never ends.

George took out the robe and held it up. "I've never
wned a bathrobe in my life, believe it or not."

"I believe it. I remembered."

His eyes narrowed. "Remembered *what?*"

I'd done it again. As always. I sat blushing, detesting
yself.

"You mean that bit about my wearing a raincoat for a
athrobe when I was a kid?"

As I attempted a shrug, he laughed and tossed the
obe back into the box. "Would you be sore if I took it
ack and got some shirts? I'm pretty low on shirts."

For once, I didn't rise to the bait. Calmly, I said, "Just

235

because you're embarrassed about not getting me a pres
ent doesn't mean you have to get tough." I laughed. "I'o
die if I ever got a present from you."

"You would, huh?"

"I would."

"Then get ready to die." He left the living room and a
minute later came back with a package, which he
roughly dumped in my lap.

Now I was the one who was embarrassed, and he
laughed. "Since you're still alive, open it."

With clumsy fingers, I did. Inside was a pale blue silk
chemise printed with pale green butterflies. French and
very expensive. I knew because I'd always wanted one
like it, but had never had the nerve to buy one for myself. I looked from it to him, a bit stunned—and wary.

"The minute I got it home yesterday, I realized what
a goddamn corrupting influence you are. I was going to
take it back until that crack of yours changed my mind
. . . Well, don't just sit there. Try it on."

"Now? Here?"

"Now. Here." He smiled. "You suddenly modest or
something?"

While he stood, arms crossed, watching from the window, I took off every stitch. The living room was freezing and I *was* suddenly modest and self-conscious under
his cool, critical eyes. Shivering, I slipped on the chemise; it fit me perfectly.

"Just as I thought," he said, laughing, from the window.

"What's just as you thought?"

"You don't look at all sexy. But still it's an improvement on that Best & Company Lady Lingerie you always wear. Come here."

"Why can't you just shut up for once?"

"*You* shut up. And come *here*."

"You're right by the window. I'm freezing as it is."

Swearing, he came at me, Playing the game—a silly
innocent one for a change—I ran laughing, breathless
inside to the warmer room.

Later he got up off the bed and went back into the

iving room, and soon reappeared belted into the blue
wool robe. For the first time since I'd known him he
ooked really handsome, unbearably handsome, and
knew it. Preening, swaggering, he opened his closet door
and studied himself in the full-length mirror inside: his
hair was tousled, his face relaxed and flushed and as
young as a boy's. "Not bad," he said, grinning at his
reflection. "Not bad at all. I just may keep it. It's certainly a lot classier than walking around in underwear
shorts."

As he stood, a male peacock, admiring himself, I
smiled, but two ugly thoughts crept in: Who else will
see him in that robe? And did he really buy that chemise
for *me?* It fit me, true, but it also would fit a tall skinny
blonde.

Now, even before I got so loony last summer, I'd seen
how a thought could precede by seconds or minutes an
event that dramatized the very essence of that thought.
Depending on the circumstances, I'd either chalk it up
to coincidence or to a combination of telepathy and
ESP. Today it was telepathy-ESP.

No sooner had those two unpleasant thoughts crossed
my mind (one thought really) than George's bedside
phone began to ring. Every other time I'd been there,
this bedside extension had been carefully unplugged
ahead of time, and the one or two times the kitchen extension had rung he'd ignored it as if he were deaf.
Today for some reason he'd forgotten this methodical
bit of preparation (the chilling implications of which I'd
always tried to ignore), and had left the bedside extension plugged in. It rang and rang and rang.

George went on preening at the mirror.

My heart was racing. "Answer it," I finally said.

Turning from the mirror, George stared at me coldly,
his eyebrows going up.

The phone continued to ring. Whoever it was knew
George and his habits, and was determined to see if they
could smoke him out.

"*Answer* it, goddamn it!"

George smiled and slowly walked over and picked up
the phone.

Closing his eyes, he turned his back to me as I lay rigid on the bed. "No," he said. "No, in the can." He listened awhile, holding the phone jammed up against his ear so that it was impossible for me to hear anything. "You never said who else was going to be there." Again, he listened. Though I was under two blankets I was shivering. ". . . Yeah, yeah. Ok*ay*. Will you get off that stupid kick, for God's sake!"

The sheets rustled as I threw back the covers and got out of bed.

Turning, he glared at me as I went out. The living room was freezing, and my teeth were chattering from the cold and rage, but my clothes were in there and I didn't want to hear any more. I could still hear him, talking low; then he suddenly raised his voice and shouted, "I told you to knock it off! I'll be there at eight!" and slammed the receiver down.

He came into the living room, where I was frantically pulling on clothes. "I thought we had an agreement."

I yanked on my turtleneck sweater.

"I thought it was agreed that jealousy was out. That you had no damn right to be jealous."

"I'm not jealous. I just feel sick."

"Why? You asked for that, begged for that. You ask for it all the time, as I told you. What are you trying to prove—that I'm a rat, a bastard? You know that. In fact, that's what sends you."

"Sometimes," I admitted, with an honesty that startled even me. "At others it makes me want to throw up."

"Everything has its price."

"I know. I just can't pay it sometimes."

"Then you damned well better get straight on that once and for all—can you or can't you? If you can't, get off the pot. You're trying to confuse things, as I knew you would. All this jazz with the *presents*. As I said, you're even corrupting me. I must be out of my mind."

Finished dressing, I raked my fingers through my hair. I didn't want to stay there long enough to comb it. "Any time anybody shows signs of being human, you think they're out of their mind," I said, putting on my coat.

"Not human. Sentimental. Trying to dress things up. We happen to be lucky enough to have a fantastic sex thing. Don't ask me why, but we do. Just that. *Sex*. Sex is sex. A lay is a lay is a lay. You want to get laid, come here and get laid. Royally laid. You want a lot of *schmalz* and trimmings along with getting laid—find yourself a nice guilty-type Adulterous Husband in that brilliant social set you travel in. They're past masters at that sort of shit."

My hand on the doorknob, I said: "You don't need a woman. You need a sex machine."

He laughed. "It sure would save one helluva lot of trouble." And as I went out the door he shouted, "Merry Christmas! 'God bless us every one!' "

THE GIRLS WENT BACK to school today. Though they saved me, really, these last two weeks, I'm looking forward to some silence and solitude soon. I don't quite have either at the moment, because Lottie is just outside this closed door, vacuuming two inches of pine needles off the hall rug. They came off by the millions when we lugged the tree (a nine-foot spruce) and wreath and garlands and ropes out to the garbage twenty minutes ago. I had promised the girls to leave everything up until they were back in school. Well, they're back, and we're in The New Year. Today, the third day of our New Year, finds me not filled with bright resolutions, but deeply depressed. This time, for a change, it's not my dear nerves, or even a post-holiday letdown, but just an overwhelming sense of waste about the last two weeks.

I did have a wonderful time with the girls, taking them to their parties, taking them places with friends, etc. Aside from three visits to the dentist, where in a crash program I got everything finished up, the days were spent with them. The nights were atrocious, party-party all the time. Except for New Year's Eve, I won't go into them. Christmas, thank God, came and went. Jonathan gave me a gold pin and an alligator bag. I gave him the silk pajamas and cashmere sweater and some ties. The original Gold Dust Twins. The girls got almost everything they wanted and said it was the best

hristmas they'd ever had. I think they meant it. I don't
nderstand it, but that's not required.

New Year's Eve. I'd like to write about that because it
icks in my mind.

his year we had only two invitations, one from the
rockmans, one of Jonathan's partners, and another
rom a couple Jonathan had met at the backers' audition
t Gaylord's. For the last two years we'd had four or
ve New Year's Eve invitations to pick and choose from,
nd had only gone to the party Jonathan had thought
Vorthwhile. This year, upset by the slim pickings and
eeling wallflowerish, Jonathan said he wanted to go to
oth, so of course we did. The Brockmans' party was
tuffy and deadly, with everybody dressed to kill and sit-
ing around like statues, sipping champagne. Since the
Markses were there we stayed an hour; when they left,
ve went on to the other party. The couple, whose name
vas Payne or Pyne, lived in a brownstone in the East
eventies. The house had five floors and the bottom three
vere all going, with canned music blaring from hidden
peakers on each floor, and people doing all the new
lances, Wiggle Woggle Wump. The people were unbe-
ievable, ranging from swarms of those young girls with
Mad Ophelia hair that show up everywhere, to delegates
rom the U.N. Ever world was represented, and there
vere just enough celebrities to make people go around
eering hopefully at each other with that "And who are
ou?" look.

The noise was deafening, the crush alarming. Even
onathan seemed a little overwhelmed by it all, and once
e'd found our host and hostess and introduced me, he
teered me to a relatively quiet corner on the second
loor. We stood there God knows how long, drinking
nd watching the crazy people do the crazy dancing,
leither of us aware of the hour or how close to mid-
light it was. I'd even forgotten it was New Year's Eve.
'or one thing, though I kept a calm face on things, I
vas secretly fighting my usual battle with my two pet
ears, agoraphobia and pyrophobia. I was also fighting
he conviction that this was just the sort of party George

might show up at, and though I knew it would crea
certain problems, I was hoping he would. After tw
weeks of terrible conflict, of thinking about him in tl
wildest places at the wildest times—watching Cinderel
perform a series of *entrechats* at the Royal Ballet wit
the girls, sitting in the dentist chair, helping Liz off th
ice at Wollman's, etc.—I'd decided to keep on playin
and to try to play it his way. A lay is a lay is a lay. I'
finally realized that no matter how rotten he seems, l
isn't as rotten as he seems, and at this time in my life l
helps me keep going. He saves me, does George. Th
fact that at the other extreme it's the girls who save n
too, is something I don't even want to *try* and under
stand. When you're in this condition you just grab a
any straws.

Anyway, I was standing in the corner with Jonathan
wondering what I'd do if someone shrieked "Fire!
(break the window to my left with one of those Bieder
meier chairs, and chance the one-story drop to th
street?), wondering what I'd do if George suddenly ap
peared ("And this is my husband, Jonathan, Mr. . . . al
I'm sorry, I've forgotten your name"??), when Jonatha
suddenly said, "I've got to find a can, I don't feel well."

He didn't look well, either. Pale, tense, his forehea
beaded with sweat. "Do you want me to come wit
you?" I said.

"No, you stay here. I'll be back." Pushing through th
crowd, he stopped to ask directions and then bolted fo
the stairs.

After almost fifteen minutes I was alarmed. Had h
passed out on the bathroom floor? He'd been beltin
down drinks, which was completely unlike him. Was h
stretched out, sick, on some bed upstairs? I finally de
cided to investigate, and had almost reached the othe
side of the room when all the lights went out. "*Happ
New Year!*" someone shouted, while at the same instar
the canned music stopped with an ear-splitting elec
tronic scratch, and "Auld Lang Syne" began boomin
through the speakers.

Terrified by what I heard happening around me,
flattened myself against the wall: from the darkne

came grunts, squeals, shrieks, laughter, curses and the sounds of shattering glass. My God, it's turned into one of those Circus things, I told myself. Cowering against the wall, I tried to calculate the distance to the door and stairs in the dark, and was just starting to edge my way, crabwise, out of there, when I was brushed by a pair of groping hands. Before I knew what was happening, the hands closed on my shoulders and pried me off the wall, dragging me forward, and while one hand gripped me like a vise, I was set upon by the other, and by a mouth with a tongue like a fist. In the violent scuffle that followed, my glass fell to the floor and smashed, explaining the sounds of breaking glass I'd heard all around me. Struggling, clawing, I tried to get away from that maniac, but I couldn't even scream because of the mouth sealing mine. At last, in a burst of strength, I broke free, and as I bolted I heard low laughter. He *was* a maniac! I pushed my way past two tightly locked people and finally reached the stairs, where I put a guiding hand on the rail and started down, almost stepping on another couple halfway down. I was groping my way across the entrance hall to the front door, to icy night air and sanity, when the lights went on.

There were about six couples in that elegant little foyer where I stood clutching the newel post. One of them was on the black-and-white parquet floor. All of them separated violently as the lights came on—some embarrassed, some sheepish, some brazenly amused. The return of the lights made no difference to the couple on the floor. Near me, a very young girl with dazed white face and torn dress was shrinking against the wall. "Are you all right? Can I help you?" I asked, but she shook her head. Suddenly I felt very weak and in need of help myself. I pushed past two young men who were staring, rapt, into each other's eyes, and went into the large ground-floor room and sank into the first empty chair against the wall. As the music resumed on the speakers, I sat blinking at men wiping off lipstick, at women straightening disheveled dresses and hair. When Jonathan finally appeared, looking quite all right again, I jumped to my feet. "Jonathan! What *took* you so long? I was so worried! Are you all right? Where *were* you?"

Jonathan stared at me coldly. "Where was I? I was in the bathroom. I told you I felt sick, didn't I? I was so damned dizzy I took some Dramamine I found in the medicine cabinet—that'll give you an idea of how rotten I felt."

"Were you in the bathroom when the lights went out?"

"I just told you I was, didn't I?" snapped Jonathan so irritably and so emphatically that I felt my skin begin to crawl: My God, could it . . . could it possibly have been *Jonathan?*

As I was considering this really terrifying possibility, Jonathan bent down and chastely kissed me on the cheek. "Happy New Year. Come on, let's go and get some more to drink."

If he'd been so sick why was he going to drink again? "Jonathan, I'd like to go home. These people are out of their minds."

"Oh my God." Jonathan shut his eyes, and when he opened them they were frightening. "On New Year's Eve. Even on New Year's Eve. What is it *this* time?"

Something kept me from saying, "I almost got raped, that's what it is this time." Instead, I said, "I told you what it is. I just don't like these people."

"And what people *do* you like?" he said softly. Then he gave a little chuckle and shook his head. "Boy, that's rich. Just because you can't function socially, you expect me to go creeping home at twenty past twelve on a New Year's Eve. Well, I've got news for you: I'm not going. If you feel so threatened, *you* go, but I'm staying. I'm going back upstairs and get a drink and talk to Whatshisname—the one who got the Pulitzer Prize for poetry last year."

For a minute I stood shaking and thinking of how it would be, wandering the streets alone on New Year's Eve, trying to find a cab. Then I went upstairs to talk to Whatshisname.

I've put all this down for what it's worth, and now that

it's down, I'll forget it. Just the thought of those hands and that mouth is enough to make me sick.

I called George before I sat down to write this and arranged to go there this afternoon. Just before New Year's Eve, when I was finally straight on the fact that I'd play it his way, I'd called him twice to tell him so, but he'd either been talking to someone or had the phone off the hook. I didn't let myself think about what he might have had it off the hook for. When I called just a while ago, he seemed pleased, in his inimitable way, to hear from me, but was as casual as if I'd last spoken to him yesterday instead of two weeks ago. I didn't tell him about the other times I'd called.

Now, with two hours before I'm due there, I'm off to do a few chores. First I have to drag all the boxes of Christmas tree ornaments back down to the basement storeroom, taking Lottie along as a bodyguard, of course. Then I have to go through the stack of Christmas cards we received this year, and make a list of who sent them before I throw them out. Jonathan asked me to do that this morning, before he left for work. He said: "We sent out three hundred cards this year. We received two hundred and twenty-eight cards. I see no point in sending cards next year to any of the people who couldn't be bothered to send us one, so make a list and we'll know who to cross off next year."

No. No. It *couldn't* have been Jonathan on New Year's Eve.

THE CITY IS IN THE GRIP of what they call a Snow Emergency, which means there's been a blizzard, and schools and most offices are closed. Hoddison and Marks is open, but the Bartlett School is closed, and the girls are inside painting with their new Christmas watercolors as I write this. Since Liz has a cold, I would have kept her home from school anyway. How she *got* the cold is another story, which I'll tell later in today's Account.

The snow started Friday morning and by mid-afternoon had gotten so bad I only stayed at George's for an hour. (Yes, I was back again after only two days.) But he didn't mind my rushing off. In fact, he doesn't mind anything these days. Since that last meeting just before Christmas he's become very agreeable and nice. It has nothing to do with my falling into line. Sex is Sex is et cetera, because he took that as a matter of course. I think the explanation is that he's working hard on something that's going well, but with him you never know; he'd die before he talked about his work. Whatever it is, I'm not sure I like it. He's much *too* nice.

The snow kept up all through Saturday, stopping sometime before dawn Sunday. The Barrs gave a huge party Saturday night, and snow and all of course we went; since there weren't any cabs Jonathan hired a limousine. It was still snowing when we got home at three, but at seven I was awakened by blinding light: the snow

246

had stopped and the sun was refracting so powerfully off all the whiteness that it seeped through the shut blinds. I lay there, wide awake and staring at the bars of light on the ceiling, fighting a wild and childish urge to get up and go out in the snow. I reminded myself that I'd only had four hours' sleep, a lot to drink, and that Sunday was a long day—but it did no good; I *had* to get up. I crept into the living room, where the light was so blinding I couldn't see for several seconds. I went to a window and looked out. For two days snowplows had worked around the clock, pushing huge drifts to either side of the street where cars were trapped. In the hours since the last plow had passed, new snow had covered these cars-in-drifts, making huge white hills on both sides of Central Park West, while the street itself, covered again, was without a mark or track. There wasn't a sign of human life. Nothing moved or stirred except an occasional tuft of snow fluttering down from a branch, where it had been dislodged by huddling pigeons.

I simply had to go out there to breathe that clean sparkling air and make first tracks in all that untouched whiteness. I padded back inside, and after dressing in the bathroom, was tiptoeing back past Jonathan's bed when he opened one bloodshot eye. "What time is it?"

"Seven-thirty," I whispered. "Go back to sleep."

Thrashing and muttering, he covered his head with the pillow.

I was pulling on my boots in the front hall when I thought of all those pigeons. So I went to the kitchen and grabbed an unopened loaf of white bread and a large cellophane bagful of filberts, and left.

The sidewalk in front of our building had been shoveled clean, which I found astonishing, considering the hour and the help in our building. But the drifts at the curb were impassable, and I stood there a minute wondering how I was going to get across to the park without snowshoes, then plunged in, sinking up to my knees.

Puffing, I finally stood on the opposite sidewalk with a sense of victory. At the entrance to the park I stopped, not from any fear, but because of the impact of the scene in front of me. It was what I'd come for. All was

still, still, until a pigeon or the growing warmth of the
sun would send a tatter of snow drifting down. I jus
stood there, smiling, until I saw about ten pigeons squat
ting in a tree, peering hopefully down at me, and I go
to work.

The problem was the soft snow on the path, inche
deep; any bread or nuts I scattered would sink down
lost. I'd simply have to tamp down the snow. Using the
sole of my size 9½ boots, I stomped and hopped around
packing down all the snow within a radius of five feet.
was out of breath by the time I'd finished, but I begar
tearing up slices of bread and scattering the pieces or
the flattened snow. The minute the first two pieces hi
the ground they were there, with a great draughty flap
and whir, about forty of them. Summoned by some pi
geon supersonic communications system, they came
from trees deep in the park, and within seconds the
ground in front of me was a mass of scrabbling, jabbing
lurching birds. I kept on tossing out bits of bread until
two or three pigeons, hungrier and bolder than the rest.
began to hover in the air around my head. Annoyed,
then frightened, I started to wave my arms and jump
around like a mad animated scarecrow, shouting, "Shoo!
Shoo! Get away, you damned vultures!" and they finally
flew off.

Suddenly three squirrels appeared, pushing coolly
through the gabbling gobbling pigeons, coming to sit up
and beg within inches of my boots. I tore open the cellophane bag and began scattering nuts. Again, within
seconds some animal telegraphic system went into action, and before I knew what had happened there were
about ten squirrels. Some sat on their haunches at my
feet, and clutching the nuts in their paws, scrapily
gnawed through the shells. Others grabbed their nuts
and went bounding over the snow in great kangaroo-
leaps that kept them from sinking in, finally scuttering
up a tree, where they began the same noisy gnawing.

I stayed there for about fifteen minutes, feeling crazily
lightheaded and happy, having the nicest time I'd had in
years. A couple of times I caught myself thinking that I
was like one of those loony old ladies who go to the

park with shopping bags full of goodies for their Little
Friends, that there I was, Saint Bettina of Central Park
West—but I squelched these self-destructive little sor-
ties: I told myself that I was out there doing something
I'd really wanted to do, for a change, and as a result I
felt so marvelous that all my stupid dreary problems had
vanished . . . like that rat had vanished down the hole
that long-ago autumn day.

When I started for home I was absolutely starved, and
as I walked out of the park I began planning the enormous breakfast I would have. Three squirrels and several
pigeons followed me all the way to the curb.

I was taking off my dripping boots and setting them
neatly on our doormat, when Sylvie, who had heard the
elevator, opened the door for me.

"Good morning," I said, somewhat startled, kissing her
on the cheek. "What are you doing up so early? You
been up long?"

"No, I just got up."

It was said with such elaborate nonchalance that I
stopped unzipping my old ski parka and stared at her.
She was wearing the new wool challis robe she'd gotten
for Christmas, a matching hair ribbon, and was dazzlingly neat and clean. From the kitchen came the smell of
frying bacon.

"If you just got up, who's frying the bacon?"

"Daddy is."

"What on earth is he doing up?"

"I don't know, but he's the one who woke *us* up."

"Whatever for? Why did he want to wake you so
early on a Sunday? What's going on?"

Sylvie stood blushing. "He didn't do it on purpose.
We just heard him laughing and got up to see what was
so funny."

"And what was?"

Turning scarlet in her struggle not to laugh, Sylvie
burst out, "Mudther . . . what were you *doing* out
there?"

"Doing?"

"Yes. Out in the park. We all watched you from the
window, hopping around, waving your arms, and it was,

oh . . ." Frantically trying to swallow her laughter, she ended in a snort.

"I was getting a little exercise, working up an appetite for breakfast." I marched down the hall to the kitchen.

Liz was at the counter, shaking up chocolate milk in a large old mayonnaise jar, Jonathan was peering into the empty breadbox, a package of English muffins in his hand.

"Good morning," I said in a voice that would have done Dame Sybil Thorndike proud.

Jonathan looked up from the breadbox. "Good morning . . . Tina, what happened to the bread? There was a whole unopened loaf of white bread in here yesterday afternoon. I saw it with my own eyes."

"I fed it to the pigeons. Surely you saw that with your own eyes. Sylvie just told me you did."

Suddenly they were all watching me, all three of them; Sylvie had come skulking in after me.

In a dangerously sweet voice I said, "Why do you need white bread? Every single Sunday for the last two years you've had toasted muffins or scones with two four-minute eggs for breakfast. And the girls have eaten waffles or pancakes. No one in this house except Lottie ever eats white bread. I buy it specially for her."

They were all blinking. Finally Jonathan sighed and said, "Well, that's true. I certainly admit that what you say is true. But as long as I was up today, I decided to make the girls some Sunlets as a special treat. We *do* eat white bread with Sunlets."

Sunlets. Jonathan learned how to make Sunlets at some boys' camp in Maine when he was twelve. To make a Sunlet one takes a slice of white bread, tears a round hole in the middle, drops the holey bread into a panful of hot bacon drippings, breaks an egg so that the yolk fits into the hole—and then fries up the whole mucky mess.

"You haven't had Sunlets in three or four years. If I remember correctly, you said that because of the cholesterol thing, because they were so unhealthy, you weren't going to make Sunlets ever again."

"I didn't say ever," said Jonathan. "A little bit of

bacon fat every once in a while couldn't hurt anyone."
He looked at the girls, who were standing very still,
watching and listening to their Loving Parents. With a
tremendous visible effort Jonathan pulled himself together and transformed himself into that old stand-by,
Daddy-Dads, Popsy-Poo. "Well, no Sunlets today, girls.
Instead, I'll make you that other Balser special—super-
dee-dooper scrambled eggs." He paused, looking at me.
"How about you, Tina? Will you join us in some su-
per-dee-dooper scrambled eggs?"

"Thank you," I said faintly, "but I don't seem to be
very hungry. If you'll excuse me, I think I'll go get out
of these hot slacks."

When I shut the bedroom door, I was shaking from
head to toe. I also seemed to be running a fever. To calm
myself, I pulled the armchair to one of the windows
overlooking the park. The blinds were already drawn up;
it was, without a doubt, the window they'd watched me
from. Pushing up the window and letting in some cool
dry air, I sat down, lit a cigarette and looked out at the
view. The perfect pristine scene of an hour ago had vanished. The snow was melting, a truck was scattering a
filthy-looking mixture of salt-and-cinders on the street,
and mobs of children were racing over the paths and
hills, dragging sleds over the unmarked expanses of white
and throwing snowballs at the pigeons and squirrels.

I'd been sitting there about a half-hour when Jonathan
came in and shut the door behind him, then stood leaning against it. *That* old pose. "You don't care what you
do or say in front of them, do you?"

Craning around in the chair, I blinked at him through
the smoke of my fourth chain-smoked cigarette. "You
lousy bastard," I said hoarsely. "Making my own daughters laugh at me."

"Ah, so that's what it is. I might have known you'd
get everything twisted."

"You lousy bastard, you sadistic prick. Don't you *dare*
take that line with me, don't you dare try and Angel
Street *me*. You let my daughters see that you find me
ridiculous, encourage them to laugh at me too—what
have I got twisted?"

"Ah, that's what I like. Nice ladylike talk."

"What have I got *twisted?*" I shouted. "Sylvie told me you woke them up, you were laughing so hard at me, and then all three of you stood looking out, laughing. I repeat: what have I got twisted in that?"

"Lower your voice, for God's sake. And stop over-re*a*cting. You're almost hysterical. It wasn't like that at all. What happened was that you woke me up going out of here, and I couldn't get back to sleep. Also, that damned dog was whining because you'd gone off without her. I got up to pee, and on my way back to bed, stopped at the window to see what had happened to the snow, and there you were. You were unbelievable—hopping and leaping around—unbelievably funny. I laughed, and the girls, who were up *any*way—I think the damned dog woke them up too—came in. That's all. I repeat, you looked unbelievably funny. There's no crime in laughing at something funny . . . What the hell were you doing out there in the first place? Since when have you become such an animal-lover? Or maybe I shouldn't ask. After all, it's a well-known fact that most animal-lovers are profound people-haters, misanthropists. Which is what you've turned into."

In a whisper, I delivered myself of a few obscenities I hadn't even known I knew.

"You're not well," said Jonathan, also in a whisper.

"On the contrary. I'm fine. In fact, I'm beginning to think what I said is right—there *is* a lot of Angel Street going on around here."

"Angel Street." Then, as he now did so often at a certain point in our hostilities, Jonathan crumpled. He gave himself a sort of shuddery shake, rubbed his eyes and said, "Tina, I'll tell you something. It just so happens I'm not in any shape for this. A lot of complicated things have been going on at the office. I've got a lot on my mind, I've been under all sorts of pressures, and I just can't take being under them at home too. Can we call off this kind of thing for a while? You can think of it as an armed truce if you want, only for God's sake let's call a halt to the hostilities."

I longed to say, taunting: Can't you bear the truth?

But at this point I sort of crumpled myself. So I just said, "What complicated things have been going on at the office?"

He shrugged. "I'd rather not go into it . . . I promised to take the girls out for lunch and then go sledding in the park with them. Would you come along? It would help smooth over the rotten little scene you and I pulled in the kitchen—all of us being together."

"I'm sorry, but I'm just not up to it, Jonathan." Which was the truth: my four hours of sleep, the drinking I'd done to get through the Barrs' party and my rage were all suddenly taking their toll. I felt about two hundred years old, and only wanted to crawl back into bed and go to sleep.

"What should I tell them?"

"Tell them I don't feel well. It's the truth. The truth carries a lot of weight."

And so I went back to bed, and Sylvie and Liz did that rare thing—spent almost a whole day with their father. They had lunch at Dillman's, then came back and got the sleds out of the basement storeroom and stayed out until it was dark. When they finally came in, Liz's boots were sloshing inside with melted snow, and her nose was running. I suppose it was simply that Jonathan, throwing himself into his Popsy-Poo role, got carried away for a variety of reasons. Whatever, he kept them out far too long, without checking on things like their boots or the temperature—which had dropped to 18° by five o'clock. As a result, Liz has started a cold. But there's nothing to do about it except wait and see. It would hardly help to take the Gerber stainless-steel carving knife to Jonathan.

I SHOULD HAVE taken the Gerber stainless-steel carving knife to Jonathan after all. Liz's cold turned into a monster and ended up in her ear. Though she finally went back to school yesterday, she's still on one of those mycins, and now Sylvie has it. When Sylvie first came down with it, it looked as if it was going to be a light case. Yesterday, though her head was suddenly afloat, her temperature was normal, but she was bored and cranky beyond belief. Because Liz had stayed in bed, she insisted on staying in bed too; turning into Jonathan, she sat there, the quilt covered with wads of Kleenex, giving me and Lottie orders for crackers, ginger ale, tea, magazines, Lottie's TV set, etc.

By noon I knew I had to get out of there for a while. Aside from one or two evening parties, I hadn't been out of the house for a week. When Liz's cold had been at its peak, I'd had to break a date with George, and had had to do it by telegram since he wouldn't pick up his phone. I'd realized he'd be furious, but since Liz's fever had been 105° at the time, I hadn't cared. By yesterday I cared again: was he still furious? In fact, by noon yesterday I suddenly needed to see him so badly that I didn't want to waste time by going to a pay booth, where I couldn't be overheard. Since it was noon, I knew he might be taking a break for lunch and pick up the phone. I turned up the sound on the TV in Sylvie's room, locked the door to my room, and carried the phone on its extension cord into Jonathan's closet. All those suits made it stuffy as hell, but they also made it soundproof. And my hunch was right—he answered. But he wasn't furious at all; he was the way he's been since Christmas, maddeningly amiable and as casual as if we'd last talked yesterday. He listened to what I had to say, and after a horribly unpleasant pause, told me to come over at 2:00. He said: "I don't mean to sound ah brusque, baby, but you can't stay long." I should have hung up and not gone, then or ever again, but being me I said sharply, "I wasn't *planning* to stay long," and hung up. And went at 2:00.

It was absolutely incredible, and I'd thought it had already gotten as incredible as it was ever going to be. But afterwards, though I felt rather overwhelmed, I also felt unbelievably depressed. And it wasn't any of that *omne animal post coitum triste* business, either. It was just terrible, and I was lying there, pretty close to tears, when George said, "Since you're on the outside, how about getting up and fixing our drinks." Since I was on the outside, I did.

"You've got a pimple on your ass," he said as I came back through the door.

"I know." I handed him his glass and sat down on the edge of the bed, relieved: this at least was the old George.

"You're also getting too goddamn skinny," he said, jabbing me with a finger; "I can see your ribs."

I took a big swallow of my drink. "Stop picking on me, George. I told you the girls have been home sick and I've been taking care of them. In fact, Sylvie is still home sick and I really shouldn't have even left her to come here today . . ." To my horror, I began to cry, the big hot tears spilling out of my eyes and running down my cheeks.

For a minute George just sat there staring at me, his face expressionless, sipping his drink. Then he said quietly, "What the hell are you crying about? Or don't you know."

"I *don't* know," I sobbed. "All I know is that I feel

just t-t-terrible. Maybe it's guilt about leaving Sylvie. Maybe it's because when I mentioned Sylvie's name I realized that you don't even know the names of my children, or care what they are. Maybe I'm crying because you never want to know a thing about my life, because you clearly don't give a damn about anything that happens to me . . ."

George, who had been jiggling the ice in his glass and eying me in a cool, utterly detached way, said: "If you can turn off the waterworks and listen, I have something to say which I think might cheer you up. And hand me those cigarettes while you're at it."

I stopped crying, handed him the cigarettes and blew my nose in a Kleenex.

Making an elaborate ceremony out of it, George lit a cigarette, leisurely blowing out smoke. "One of the reasons I let" (*let!*) "you come here today was because I wanted to say in person what I had to say. Knowing you, you'd have gotten it all wrong if I had said it on the phone. I wanted to tell you that I thought we ought to cool this for a while."

He's tired of me, I thought with a wild lurch of something like hope.

"It's not because I'm tired of you," he continued calmly, "though I do get goddamn tired of these little obligatory agony-scenes you work up. It's because *I'm* tired. Period. Exhausted, really. I had three hours' sleep last night. I've been working like a sonofabitch, day *and* night. When I work, I work like a madman. I never do things by halves, as you know. The thing is, I can't work like that and do other things." He laughed. "At least I can't and do them justice. I've tried to swing it, but I realize I can't. Contrary to what I like to think, I'm not Superman."

I looked at him, really looked at him, for the first time since I'd come in. (And I'd accused him of not taking an interest in me!) He did look exhausted, his eyes sunken and bloodshot, his color vile. "Is it a new play?"

He smiled ironically.

"You must . . . believe in it, if you're going all out this

way. Did you start it over Christmas? I'm curious—it would help explain a few things."

The smile grew worse.

I sighed. "All right, George. And just what is your idea? 'Cool this.' What does that mean? Does that mean we don't see each other for a couple of months, until your play is finished, and then pick up where we left off?"

"Who's talking about months? All I thought was that we'd let things ride for a few weeks, maybe even less—and that when things let up a bit here, I'd call you."

"But what about the times you get Writer's Block? Wouldn't you want me to come over and help diddle away the time until the Block passed? Or don't you ever *have* Writer's Block?"

Glaring, stony, he watched me get up and begin to put on my clothes. The silence made my skin crawl. Finally he said softly, "Do you know how many times you've done this Angry-Exit scene?"

"I'm not a playwright," I said, zipping my skirt. "I'm just a dumb crazy housewife who's in water way over her head."

George laughed. "You're a housewife, all right—but you're not dumb and you're not crazy. Just a little bit mixed up. And you'll stop being mixed up as soon as you learn one or two things. One of them is to settle for one thing, and then stick with it. I'm not saying what you ought to settle for—that's your problem—but you've got to decide what it is, and then stick with it. As soon as you do that you'll straighten right out. The other thing you've got to learn to do is what I told you once before—take things as they come, calmly. So far you can't. For instance, look at what you're doing now. I take the pains to explain something to you, ask you to understand—and whammy, suddenly we've got a big Renunciation Scene going on, suddenly you're mad as hell."

I checked myself in the mirror. "I'm not mad. I have to go home. I told you I left a sick child to come here."

George sighed. "Okay, you're not angry. When I call you, will you come?"

"Of course," I lied, turning from the mirror with a smile.

George laughed. "I'm not sure you mean it, but come here and give me a nice big feely kiss before you go."

When I got home Sylvie had a fever of one hundred and four, and Lottie was almost hysterical. She had looked in the address book and called Doctor Miller's office, but the answering service had told her it was his afternoon at the clinic. They had not suggested that she try Young Doctor Bookman. Desperate, she had called Jonathan at his office, and was on the line with him when I walked in the door.

"Where the hell have you *been?*" he shouted when I'd taken the phone from Lottie, who quickly vanished.

"I was out doing some errands."

"Errands? What mother leaves a sick child to go out and do some *errands?*"

"Stop shouting at me, Jonathan. Sylvie was fine when I left, and she'll be on the way to being fine again if you'll get off this line and let me call the doctor."

"Lottie says she couldn't get the doctor!"

"I'm hanging up, Jonathan," I said, and did. I called Young Doctor Bookman, who miraculously was not only in, but said he was just finishing up for the day and would stop by in about twenty minutes.

It turned out that Sylvie had contracted a "secondary infection." She was put on the same mycin wonder drug as Liz, and by nine o'clock her fever had dropped to 99.3° and she fell into a relatively peaceful sleep. Meanwhile Jonathan had come home and we'd had dinner. It was, however, a very peculiar Jonathan who arrived home at six o'clock: pale, subdued, he apologized for his ranting on the phone (almost making me faint) and made himself a whopping drink, which he refurbished and carried to the table, where he sat morosely sipping it, barely eating his dinner, barely talking to Liz and me. Afterwards he closeted himself in the den, and passing to and fro with things for Sylvie, I heard him talking endlessly on the phone.

At 10:30 I was in bed happily reading a Josephine Tey when Jonathan came in. After shutting the door he went and sank heavily into the armchair. Steeling myself, I finally looked up over the edge of my book: Oh God, I thought, here we go again. The whole works. Only this time I don't think I can stand it.

As always, there was the Portentous clearing of the throat. "Teen," he then said. "Teen, I want to apologize again for shouting at you over the phone before. The truth is, my nerves haven't been all they should be, I've been a bit on edge. I was frightened as hell about Sylvie, but after you hung up I realized that you've had your hands full these last ten days with both girls sick, that you hadn't been out of the house . . . You certainly deserved a breather, a few hours out of here."

I put the Josephine Tey face-down on my quilt. Contrition? Solicitude? What the *hell* was going on?

I had even greater cause for astonishment when he fumbled in his breast pocket, and pulled out a pack of cigarettes and lit one. As far as I knew he hadn't smoked a cigarette in almost a year and a half. Fascinated, but on guard, I watched and listened carefully as he blew out smoke and then continued.

"In fact, while I was in the den I thought about that a lot—how the girls, being sick, have gotten so run down, and how you've worn yourself out taking care of them —and I had what I think is an inspired idea. I think that just as soon as Sylvie is well enough to travel, all three of you ought to get on a plane and go down and stay with your folks for a week or so. As your father said in his letter, they'd be built-in sitters. You'd not only get some sun and rest, but some time to yourself."

When Jonathan calls my mother and father "your folks" I *know* something's up. "Why do you think we should go now?" I asked. "The girls don't have any sort of vacation coming up."

"I think you should go now because, as I said, the girls' resistance is lowered, they're run down. In their weakened state they'll only catch something else at school. A week of sunshine would build them up and carry them through the rest of the rotten weather. And it would do you a world of good too, Teen. You look all tuckered out."

"For that matter, so do you," I said. "Maybe you're the one who ought to take a trip."

Violently blinking, Jonathan finally gave me the thin ghost of his Patience-and-Indulgence smile. "I don't think old Hoddison would ah appreciate that . . . there's enough tension around the office as is. But just because I can't get away doesn't mean you can't. And your folks would be tickled to death."

"Your folks," "world of good," "tuckered out," "tickled to death"—all bromides that Jonathan really goes out of his way to avoid. Plus this Concern. I was finally growing alarmed. I stared at his drawn face and said gently but firmly, "It's simply impossible, Jonathan. The girls have already missed too much school. They're already way behind in their work, and letting them fall behind any further is out of the question. I might consider taking them down later, during spring vacation, but not now."

"And when *is* their spring vacation?"

"I don't know exactly. Sometime around the end of March, beginning of April."

With a defeated sigh, Jonathan put out his cigarette.

"Why are your nerves on edge, as you said before? Just what *is* all this 'tension' at the office?"

"Oh, the usual sort of intramural rivalries and squabbles," he said vaguely, and stood up. "It isn't only that . . . the market has been lousy the last week or two; in fact, for a couple of days there it looked like the bottom was going to drop right out of it." He began to undress.

"I see," I said, picking up Josephine Tey, not really seeing at all. "I'm sorry to hear it."

Without success I tried to withdraw into my mystery again. Jonathan puttered about, undressing. Without looking up, I could tell that he'd come to a stop in front of the bureau, and was standing there in a state of indecision. Finally, very swift, very matter-of-fact, he said, "Teen, could you let me have one of your sleeping pills?"

"*Sleeping* pills?"

He gave me a good old Ironic smile full-force. "Yes, sleeping pills. Those pills you started taking the end of the summer and have been taking ever since."

Unnerved—he was only half right, but if he'd noticed I was taking pills, what else had he noticed?—I decided to use the old ploy of counter-attack. "Why do *you* need a sleeping pill? You can always fall asleep, no matter what."

"There's always a first time. I have the feeling that if I don't take something, I'll be up all night. And I can't be up all night; I have a crucial day coming up tomorrow."

I wordlessly got out of bed, opened the top bureau drawer and took out my glove box; lifting six pairs of gloves, I picked up the small plastic phial hidden beneath them and gave Jonathan my last Nembutal—the one I'd been saving for A Crisis. Though this was hardly A Crisis, I felt, looking at him, that he needed it more than I ever would; besides, being an old hand at this, I had other ways of coping with insomnia. Jonathan took the pill, quietly thanked me and went into the bathroom. After a minute the shower started running. Perhaps the gravitation of troubled humans to water—hydrotherapy—is instinctive. He stayed in the shower fifteen minutes, the water pouring and pouring down. When he came out, billows of steam trailed after him, but his flushed face was relaxed. As he passed by, he bent to kiss me goodnight, then climbed into his bed and was asleep within five minutes.

Needless to say, I did not follow suit. Around three, helped by a little bourbon and leaving Tabitha-Twitch-it-Danvers in the broom closet, I finally fell asleep.

THIS AFTERNOON I WALKED Folly, then stayed downstairs to wait for the school bus—something I haven't done in a year. Though they'd both been back at school all this week, I haven't let them make any after-school dates; Florida may be out, but there are other ways of looking after their health, conserving their strength. Because they'd been bored with their late afternoons, today I'd planned to take them to Indian Walk on Broadway for some new waterproof fleece-lined boots, both as a diversion and part of my new Health Insurance plan. They were surprised and clearly not overjoyed to find me waiting for them, and I decided not to mention our destination until after they'd had some cookies and milk upstairs.

"A Mister Prager called while you were downstairs, Mrs. Balser," Lottie said, completely matter-of-fact, as we came into the kitchen where she was ironing Jonathan's shorts and handkerchiefs.

"Didn't you buy any Oreos, Mudther?" asked Sylvie, already rummaging in the grocery closet. "I don't see any Oreos. Did you forget to order them again?"

"He says you should call him right back," continued Lottie, folding a monogrammed handkerchief into a neat square. "I wrote the number on the pad by the phone in your room. I was up there putting some of Mr. Balser's shorts away in his chiffonier when the phone rang."

"You'll find the Oreos on the second shelf, behind the

262

box of Minute Rice," I said to Sylvie. "Thank you, Lottie, I'll call in a while." Trembling, I went to the icebox
for the milk. Why had he risked calling and leaving his
name? Why had he called at all? It had only been a
week. Writer's Block, I thought with venom, my hands
shaking so badly I spilled some milk as I poured.

"Mudther," said Liz. "Can we put our milk and cookies on a tray and have them in the den in front of TV?"

I'd already set their milk on the table, where my shaking hands had made both glasses slosh over. I got a dishrag, "Not today," I said, mopping up the spilt milk.
"Come sit down. After you're finished we're going to
walk over to Broadway to buy you both some new
boots."

Groaning, they came to the table. "Why boots?" said
Liz.

"Because your old ones leak. That's how you got
sick."

"Why do we have to *walk?*" asked Sylvie. "We just
got over being sick. We'll get sick all over again."

"Nobody takes a cab for five blocks. You won't get
sick again, and the air will do you good."

"What's so good about New York air? Since when
does New York air do anybody good?"

Though she had a point, it was all I could do to keep
from slapping her, hard. "Don't start being fresh, or
you'll regret it, Sylvie. You'll be very sorry indeed. You
eat up those cookies and drink your milk without one
more word."

"All right, all *right,*" said Sylvie. "Only don't get so
bloody excited, for God's sake!"

In two steps I'd crossed the room and smacked her so
hard that bits of chocolate cookie flew out of her
mouth. Scrambling to her feet and knocking over her
chair in the process, she convulsively swallowed what
was left in her mouth. "Oh, I hate you. *Hate* you!" She
ran from the kitchen up to her room, where the door
loudly slammed.

In the silence that followed, the other two looked at
me, Lottie clearly shocked and disapproving, Liz licking
her lips, clearly terrified.

"That child has gotten entirely too fresh," I remarked in a general sort of way. "Someone has to draw the line . . . Drink up your milk, Liz, and we'll go to Indian Walk. If Sylvie apologizes before we leave, she can come too."

Now Liz pushed back her chair. "I don't want to go to Indian Walk. I don't *want* to go out. I don't *want* any boots. I don't want *any*thing from you." With that, she hurled herself across the room at Lottie, almost toppling the ironing board, throwing her arms around Lottie's waist and burying her face in the broad blue chest. Over her head, Lottie and I stared at each other, both of us at a loss, both acutely embarrassed. Then Lottie put a hand on Liz's hair. "Elizabeth. Apologize to your mother. That's no way to talk to your mother."

"*Ont*," said Liz, muffled by blue cambric.

"It's all right, Lottie," I said, not knowing what on earth I could mean, and walked out.

Sylvie was lying face-down on her bed, not weeping, in fact, not making a sound, her face buried in the pillow, her hands clenched on either side of her head. As I sat down, the mattress sloped, rolling her gently towards me. When her legs touched my hips she violently heaved herself away.

"Please sit up, Sylvie. I want to talk to you."

". . . nothing to talk about," she said into the pillow.

"Sit *up*, Sylvie."

She sat up. Her face was frighteningly pale, and the faint pink ridges left by my fingers stood out on her right cheek. She stared at me with the yellow phase of those yellow-brown eyes, mercilessly taking in my wind-blown hair, my old slacks and sweater, my hastily powdered face.

Disconcerted, I lapsed into Faculty Advisor prose. "Surely you realize," I began, falling back on some faintly remembered figure of authority, "that you and you alone are at fault. Surely you must see that it is your own basic *att*itude that brings on these terrible scenes and quarrels we seem to have so often nowadays."

Seeing nothing of the sort, she continued to stare at me.

"Have you nothing to say, Sylvie? Not one word of apology?"

Swallowing hard, she suddenly hung her head and began to pick at the tufts on the candlewick spread. "You always have it in for me."

"That's not true!" I said fiercely. "If at times I've seemed excessively . . . harsh, it's only because you've been impossibly fresh or arrogant. I don't understand why you've gotten that way. I've tried, and I think I have some idea, but I don't understand it all yet. The thing *you've* got to understand is that I have no intention of putting up with that sort of behavior any longer. Why, you've even got your sister acting that way! As you know, she imitates every little thing you do or say. And it simply has to stop. Do you hear me, Sylvie?"

"You don't love us," she said flatly.

"Sylvie. How can you *say* such a thing!"

"I can because it's true. You don't. You don't seem to care about what happens to us . . . you don't seem to care about *any*thing. I mean you used to be so different, so sort of bright and gay and pretty and well-dressed and nice and we were proud to have you as our mother. Now . . . oh, *I* don't know . . ."

As she finally began to weep, throwing herself face-down on the pillow again, I was relieved. I put a hand on her arm; when she shook it off, I decided to wait out the storm and lit a cigarette. My hands were completely steady now. Calm, but by no means unfeeling, I smoked and waited while the weeping reached its climax, leaving faint gaspy sobs in its wake.

I handed her a Kleenex from the box on the bedside table. "Sylvie. What you said just before was terribly wrong, and hurt me badly. I love you and Liz more than I can say. If I don't always show it it's because I don't ever want to smother you. As for the changes you think you see in me, you must understand that there are certain times in women's lives when things become . . . well, difficult."

Sylvie sniffed. "You're too young for the menopause."

I burst out laughing, and as always, laughter immediately cleared the air. "I didn't mean that. I meant more complicated and . . . subtle things."

"You mean like you and Daddy always having fights, like his always picking on you?"

Appalled, I knew I'd had enough for one afternoon. Nevertheless I managed to say lightly, "Whatever put such an idea in your head? I don't mean anything like that at *all*. I meant, speaking in a very general way, that when you're grown up, life is full of stresses and can get rather complex and painful at times."

"I know that," Sylvie said with disdain.

I stood up. "Well, if you know that, you must be more tolerant. You must use your mind—you've a very fine mind—and not be so quick to pass judgments. You must try to be more understanding and courteous. Now go and splash some cold water on your face. After that you can go in the den and watch TV. It's too late to get the boots; we'll get them tomorrow. Besides, it's begun to snow."

Reluctantly, I headed back for the kitchen; I had things to clear up there too. Liz was at the table, finishing her milk and cookies, Lottie had resumed her ironing. When I came in, Liz glanced up at Lottie, and then, lowering her eyes, said, "I'm sorry about before, Mother. Sorry for everything I said. I'm ready to go for the boots whenever you are."

Every bone in my body ached. "It's all right, Liz. We'll just forget the whole thing. We won't go for boots today; it's snowing now. You can go in the den and watch TV with Sylvie."

With a look of immeasurable relief, she fled. As the door swung shut, I looked at Lottie, painstakingly nosing the tip of the iron between the embroidered letters of Jonathan's monogram. There was so much I wanted to say, beset as I was by the need to justify myself, justify my behavior, which I knew she had thought unnecessarily harsh. But I also knew, perhaps once and for all, that she didn't want to hear it, didn't want to be dragged in, so I only said, "Thank you, Lottie," and started for the door.

"Mrs. Balser?" she called after me. "With the roast of ef, you want mashed or pan potatoes?"

"Pan, please," I said, and went up front to our room. osing the door, I sat down on the edge of Jonathan's d and stared at the message pad where Lottie had ritten George's number and name heavily in pencil. As aid, it had only been a week. I hadn't expected to hear om him, if ever, for weeks and weeks. If I didn't return e call, it would be over, done. He was not a man to ursue. I tore the sheet of paper off the pad. Then, re-embering a novel I'd read years ago, in which a crisis d been brought about by the same circumstances, I ered at the page underneath the one I'd torn off. Sure ough, there was George's name and number deeply in-ented, plain as day. God bless you, Elizabeth Bowen, I ought, suddenly remembering exactly which novel it d been, and tearing off the next five pages, I carried em into the bathroom, ripped them into tiny bits and ushed them down the toilet with a savage sort of glee: erything in its place.

In the pantry I got a drink and brought it back to our om. Slowly sipping, I stood at the window, staring out the snow. The flakes were hard and coated and went ck-a-pick on the glass—nagging, insistent—just like the oughts in my head. I'd tried for three days to suppress em, but now they were at me, pick-a-pick, pick-a-ck, pick-a-*pick*: the curse is now five days overdue; ou have never, except when pregnant, been as much as e day late; you have not gone to bed with Jonathan in er a month.

TWELVE DAYS LATE the curse is, counting today. I'v
been so frantic I couldn't even write in here. I'm doing i
now simply to try and pass the time until a noon ap
pointment, and to try my damndest to write mysel
calm. Five or six nights ago I made, literally *made*, Jona
than make love to me—the worst sex experience I've eve
been through in my life. Since he wasn't at all in th
mood, I had to seduce him. At first I thought he wa
going to be impotent; desperate, knowing I was takin
risks ("Where'd you learn *that?*"), I began to work o
him like a professional, but luckily he only thought
was sex-starved after the long Hiatus and finally seeme
to respond to the novelty of the whole thing. As soon a
it was over I realized that in spite of all my rotten effor
it wasn't going to work; he isn't going to be foole
Whatever else he may have become, Jonathan hasn't be
come moronic, he can still count. Ever since the days w
had such trouble Starting Liz, he's known that my "fe
tile period" comes smack in the middle, on the fou
teenth day of a twenty-eight-day cycle . . . and befo
that night we hadn't been to bed in *any* of the twenty
eight days he would count from.

So I'm frantic. I'm frantic because unless I see
abortionist, Jonathan will discover I'm pregnant b
somebody else and divorce me. And (this is the shocke
the very idea of my divorcing Jonathan or of Jonath

vorcing me fills me with terror, puts me on the brink
f the abyss. *Why?* I've asked myself a thousand times.
Vhy, when life with Jonathan has been such hell,
10uld the idea of losing him or that life throw me into
1ch a panic? Though I haven't been in the best shape
)r thinking things through, I've made a few stabs at it:

Is it because you still Care for Jonathan, and therefore
1n't bear the thought of losing him? I asked myself for
starter. Working on that for a few days, I've often
)und myself staring at Jonathan when he was going
1rough the mail, or carving a roast, or turning his pock-
:s out onto the bureau—and the damndest thing hap-
ens sometimes. I'll be looking at him in a bewildered
)rt of soft-focus way, not seeing him so much as the
ict of him (Is this somebody I still Care about?) and
ondering how the hell everything got to this awful
)int. All the details like the peevish set of his mouth, his
ew $7.00 haircut and his new $200.00 suit are blurred,
nd I only see things like the shape of his head or the
olor of the hair or the way his shoulders move—and
1ddenly I get a funny kick in the middle, yes, that old
hestnut, the Shock of Recognition: It's still him all
ight, he's still in there *some*where, the Jonathan I still
are about.

Which is hardly the signal for crescendo violins.
hough he may still be in there, getting him out is a
hole other story—if it can be done at all. But I did love
im once, and think I can salvage some of that feeling if
can be done. And if it can be done, and if the present
orrors can be resolved, we could all be spared a lot of
ain and could all go on living the life we've been living.
Vhich brings us to what I finally saw as one of the big
)urces of the panic. With this "shoebox full of immies"
have for a brain, I've finally begun to perceive that the
fe I've been living is right for me, that I'm in the right
iche. That if I divorce Jonathan or Jonathan divorces
1e, I'll never find the right niche again. That if Jonathan
adn't changed so, I could stay in this niche. That if, as
:eorge put it, I have to learn to settle for one thing, this
fe with Jonathan could have been it if only things
adn't gotten so out of hand. Iffy ifs. How typical of

Alice the Goon. Who, I might add, I look like all the
time now.

Well, it won't be long before I know for sure what
has to be done, and then take steps, one way or the
other, which will be a relief. It's the waiting that's been
hell, and a couple of times I've even thought of suicide.
Yesterday morning I stood at the bedroom window
trying to get the nerve to open the window and jump,
but Tina the Comedienne won out: I had this vision of
myself soaring, like Mary Poppins, out over Central Park
West, tweed skirt and Lady Lingerie from Best's belling
out, and stayed inside. But by yesterday morning, I also
knew that, suicide failing, I had to talk to someone or
really go stark foaming frothing mad. The only possible
Someones were George or Doctor Popkin, and since it's
a trifle late for Popkin at this point, it was George.

I kept on getting a busy signal, which of course meant
the phone was off the hook. I decided I wouldn't give up
until it was past the time he might take a break for
lunch, so I sat by the phone two hours, chain-smoking,
trying his number from time to time. At ten past twelve
the line was open. After about the tenth ring he
snatched it up and shouted "Yeff?"—his mouth full of
food. When I identified myself, he wetly swallowed and
said, "What's on your mind?"

"I have to talk to you, George."

"Not today." He took another bite of something and
started chewing noisily.

"I *have* to talk to you, George. *Today.*"

"I'm busy today. And tomorrow too. I called when I
wasn't. You're a week too late."

How almost true. A week plus four days. Taking
what was left of my pride, I said, "George, *please.* I
won't stay long."

"Come at four," he said, and hung up.

Looking grim, he held the door wide like a movie butler. Without taking off my coat, I walked in and sat
down on one of the chairs flanking the couch, slowly
looking around.

What had I expected? Balls of crumpled paper? Glue

l ashtrays? A three-day growth of beard? As always,
e room was excessively neat. The only sign of work
is a thick stack of paper on the card table, weighted
wn by a clean ashtray and unopened pack of ciga-
ttes. Just so, George himself, though pale and worn-
oking, was combed and clean-shaven and convention-
y dressed in slacks and shirt, except for a pair of those
bber Japanese thong-sandals from the 5&10 on his feet.
Hands in pockets, he strolled to the middle of the
om and cryptically smiled. "So. You think you're
ocked up. That it?"

I just sat there.

He laughed. "Why are you surprised? It figured that
ould be the pitch— And if you are knocked up, so
hat?"

Slowly I said, "I think I'm pregnant by *you*."

He laughed again. "You're absolutely nuts. You al-
ys wear that thing."

"They're not infallible. They've been known not to
ork."

"Even if you *are* knocked up, you sleep with old Big
ddy."

"I haven't in over a month. Oh, I did a few nights ago,
t he won't be fooled. He can count."

For a minute George just stood and gave me the most
illing look I've ever received—and I've received some
auties from Jonathan. Then he went to the card table
d opened the pack of cigarettes. "Just how late are
u, anyway?" he asked, lighting one.

"Eleven days."

He blew out smoke in a spluttering whoosh. "For
rissakes," he said, coughing. "And that's what you're
orrying about? I've known some broads to be as late as
ree weeks, but they always came around."

"I don't give a damn about 'some broads'! I've never
en late. Not one day."

"Have you seen a plumber?"

"No. It's too early for any kind of test."

He smiled, the full-force George smile. "So *you* say.
his is something I happen to know a lot about. Those
umbers can often tell something right off. I suggest

you go and let one have a look before you get yours
all worked up . . . Why, incidentally, *are* you
worked up?"

"I told you. Jonathan will know it's not his child."

"Can't you ever use those scrambled eggs you've g
for brains? If you are knocked up—and I don't thi
you are—didn't you ever hear of an abortionist?"

By now I was so breathless with rage I couldn't spea

"Or maybe," George said softly, "maybe that's wl
you're here. Maybe you're here to try to make me po
up the dough for an abortionist. *Is* that why you'
here?"

I stared at him, paralyzed. Yes, that's why I was ther
Though I'd hidden it from myself with the lie that I ha
to "talk" to someone, that was exactly why I was ther
Without a cent of my own, without a checking accoun
with the weekly household dole the only cash I ever sav
the only other way I could have paid for an abortic
would have been to try and get the money secretly fro
my father, and even I shied away from all the filthy in
plications of that. So there I was. "I hate you," I sa
hoarsely. "I hate you and always have. And the real re
son I'm so worked up is I can't bear to think of any pa
of you growing in my body . . . my womb!"

Laughing, he clapped his hand to his head. "Ohbo
the works. Baby, won't you ever learn to leave anythir
out?"

I got up out of the chair and hit him as hard as
could, letting my nails rake down his cheek. I heard h
startled gasp, saw his boiling eyes. Then he swun
open-handed, and hit me back so hard I saw stars. Y
do, I discovered. See stars, that is. I was so stunned I ju
stayed where I was, dangerously close, while he gave
soft puff of a laugh in my face and said: "Madan
Ovary. That's you."

As he stood there, chuckling, enchanted by his ov
wit as always, I backed off to the door. I knew it wou
take very little to make him hit me again, but with n
hand on the knob, I couldn't resist: "You're sick. *Sic*
A latent homosexual like all Don Juans."

He stopped laughing. "Girl, if you're not out th

or in one second flat you're going to be a basket
se."

I was out the door and halfway down the stairs in
ree, too frightened to even wait for the elevator.

By the time I got home the right side of my face was
vollen and red. Luckily the girls were out visiting
iends, and Lottie was picking them up. Cold water
ily made the swelling worse, so I gave that up, sat
wn on the bed and thought hard until I had a passable
ory for how my face had gotten that way. Then I
ced the next problem. Monster George had been right
ain: before making any other plans, I had to see a
umber. But which one? I could hardly use my own
ostetrician. The yellow pages didn't list doctors by
eir specialties. I couldn't go to any of my friends'
ostetricians. How was I going to find a plumber? I'd
st begun to wonder how one went about getting a
ime from a hospital, when in a lightning flashback I re-
embered the dermatologist I'd once gone to for my
zema. His office had been in an old Park Avenue build-
g, right next to the office of an obstetrician named Dr.
eter Kupferman. It had made an impression on me be-
use the door to Dr. Kupferman's waiting room was al-
ays left wide open, and in passing, one was treated to
ud blasts of Musak and the sight of huge-bellied girls
inking sleepily at magazines. My dermatologist hated
upferman.

I got out the phone book. A Dr. Peter Kupferman
as still listed, but in the fourteen years that had passed,
r. Peter Kupferman had fallen on hard times, and had
oved from Park Avenue to Columbus, right near here.
nce this was a break—I hardly wanted or needed a
ooming success for this job—I called immediately, and
Mrs. Marvin Stanley was given an appointment for the
ext day (today). He *had* fallen on hard times.

After that I was so tired I just stretched out on my
ed without turning on the lamps. When the front door
immed, I thought it was Lottie and the girls and didn't
ove. Then the door opened and Jonathan came in.

It was not my lucky day. It was just five o'clock, an
most unheard-of hour for Jonathan to be arriving home.

He'd clearly gone straight to the pantry when he'd cor
in, for he held a drink in one hand and the stack of m
from the hall table in the other.

"Why are you lying down in the dark? Why are y
lying *down*?" Snapping on one of the bureau lamps,
peered at me. Since I lay with my right cheek on t
pillow, he couldn't see anything wrong with me, but
could see something wrong with him: he looked terrib

"I'm just tired," I said. "But you're home awfully ea
ly—are *you* all right?"

"Just tired like you. Bushed," he said. He turned
the other bureau lamp and started opening the mail.
he tore open envelopes, I steeled myself and sat up;
could hardly lie on my right cheek all night. Finishe
he tossed the letters aside with a mutter of disgust—th
were mostly bills—and turned around. "For God's sak
Tina, what happened to your face?"

"I got hit in the face with a shopping bag."

"Say that again."

I did. Then I told him my little tale: I'd been dow
town late and couldn't get a cab; I'd finally gotten on
crowded bus where a woman, rushing for the door, ha
side-swiped me in the face with her shopping bag.

I knew he was really Bushed when he bought it. F
was more than Bushed. He was, as they say in Shak
speare, passing strange. Wearily, he rubbed his eyes. "
must have been filled with rocks. Jesus Christ, she cou
have put out your eye. Did you get her name?"

"She was out the door before I'd stopped seein
stars." Something made me add: "Did you know th
you really do see them? Stars, I mean."

"Yeah. I learned that back in my high school scrir
mage days." In one gulp he finished his drink, then stoc
staring at me in the most unnerving and peculiar wa
Finally, almost gently, he said, "I wonder why the
things keep on happening to you."

I'd had the answer to that one ready and waiting f
months. "Why? I'm the Perfect Victim. Didn't y
know?"

Then came the shocker. The real shocker. Jonath
shook his head and said sweetly, sweeter than he's be

in years: "I wouldn't say that, Teen. Wouldn't say that at all. The thing you are, and shouldn't be, is much too hard on yourself."

And with that astonishing line, he went back to the pantry for another drink.

As always, I've put it down for what it's worth. As always, putting it down has helped. I'm calmer than I've been for twelve days. Now it's time to go see the plumber, Dr. Peter Kupferman.

IN THOSE SADISTIC CARTOONS the girls watch on TV, Bugs
Bunny, or Heckle and Jeckle, or Mighty Mouse, there's
always a wild chase-and-fight scene; during this mad im-
broglio, one of the participants, pursued or pursuer, in-
evitably gets smashed by some heavy object—a steam-
roller, a falling safe, a Mack truck, a piano—which leaves
them a flattened, one-dimensional pancake version of
themselves, which picks itself up, dusts itself off, and
feeling no pain, resumes the chase, Carries On. Well.
That's me. Flattened. A pancake version of myself. But,
strangely, feeling no pain, and Carrying On.

What happened? We'll take it good and slow:

Yesterday I went to Dr. Peter Kupferman. "Fallen on
hard times" is putting it mildly. An obscenity of a little
man. A small fat pink piggy-man with a bad nose job
and pornographic hands, one of those plumbers who like
their work. He was on to me and my game right off,
and put quotation marks around Mrs. Stanley every
time he said it. After a horribly prolonged examination,
during which the nurse remained absent (he is not concerned about ethics, is Dr. Peter Kupferman), he said:
"It is impossible to be certain on the grounds of a physical examination alone. The condition of the cervix and
uterus could indicate imminent menstruation, but they
could also indicate pregnancy. With the old tests it is
too early to determine anything, but a new test has been

iscovered, and though it is still in the experimental
tage, it may help answer your questions." Giving me a
ignificant look, he then wrote out the name of a labora-
ory on Sixth Avenue where I was to drop off a speci-
nen this morning. Paying cash, I left, convinced that old
Peter Kuperman was a pipeline to an abortionist, if not
ne himself.

At 6:45 this morning I slipped quietly out of bed,
urned the lock on the bathroom door, and obtained the
pecimen. I wrapped the specimen bottle in several layers
f Saran Wrap, put it in a flowered Bonwit Teller bag,
nd hid the whole prize package in the bottom of the
hamper, under layers of Jonathan's shirts and shorts and
ocks and handkerchiefs. I then washed and washed,
Tina Macbeth again, and went into the kitchen to start
breakfast. I got everybody out in record time, and by
9:00 was all dressed and putting on lipstick in the bathroom, rushing to get the specimen to the lab, when the
bells began to ring. Now. In the three years I've been living in this building I've never heard those bells before,
but the minute I heard them this morning I knew what
they were. I looked at Alice the Goon in the mirror and
giggled: Death-by-fire—one of your sweet dreams about
to come true, dear girl.

Though I knew it probably meant I'd really finally
gone crackers, I felt almost cheerful. I calmly picked
Folly up off my bed and went to the front closet for her
leash. There I smelled smoke, and when I opened the
front door I saw black clouds of it pouring from the
cracks around the elevator door. It was such thick, tarry
smoke I could barely make out the Meyers' door, where
the morning paper still lay on the mat. Coughing, I
stood in our doorway: were they still asleep? Should I
let poor Lily and Harry Meyer be "burned to a crisp"?
Putting our door on the latch, I dashed across the hall
and frantically rang their bell. Then, since I could neither see nor breathe, I suddenly decided I wanted to live
after all—very much—and giving their bell a last jab,
bolted back inside our apartment, coughing and gasping.
The smell of the smoke had made Folly as hysterical as I
should have been; she was howling like a seal. When I

could breathe again, I calmly picked her up and walked through the apartment to the back stairwell, which I remembered was supposedly fireproof.

It apparently was, because there wasn't any smoke out there, but from above and below came the sounds of doors slamming, running feet and women hysterically gabbling. Over all this those bells went on clanging. Still loonily calm, I patted Folly soothingly on the head and started decorously down the stairs. "Walk, Do Not Run, to the Nearest Exit," I said to myself as I went clip, clap, clop down, until I realized that the Nearest Exit—the ground-floor landing which led to the lobby—had a grillwork gate which was kept locked against prowlers at all times. Had the super unlocked it, I wondered idly, or would the bodies of forty-odd housewives be found heaped against it, "charred beyond recognition" as they so cheerily put it in the tabloids?

I'd gotten down two flights, when a back door on the landing I'd reached was yanked open by an enormous brassy-haired woman. "For God's sake!" she shouted as I sailed past. "Where the hell are you going? Where's everybody *running* to? There's been a regular stompede past this door—is everybody out of their weak minds?"

"Not really," I called airily over my shoulder. "The building seems to be on fire. You'd better come along too."

"But it's only one of the front elevator cables, for chrissakes. One of the front elevator cables caught fire, but they've got it under control now."

I stopped and turned four steps below her. At a level with my eyes ten carefully painted toes were sticking out of a pair of gold mules. Letting my eyes travel upwards along astonishingly good legs, considering the rest of her, I recognized her as another one of the building's so-called celebrities Jonathan had pointed out—an ex-Ziegfeld Girl named something like Carrie O'Harrigan or Sally Mulligan, who had probably once been beautiful, but now looked like an Irish Sophie Tucker. "How do you know it's under control?" I asked, watching her stoop and pick up the two bottles of milk the milkman had left by her garbage pail. She had on one of those

hort puffy-quilted nylon housecoats, and was as care-
ully made up as any Ziegfeld girl about to step on the
unway.

"How do I know? I phoned that drunken nogoodnick
prick of a super, that's how I know. A regular panic
could start in this building and they'd never tell you a
thing to stop it."

Laughing—I loved her—I said, "A regular panic *has*
tarted," just as four terrified women, in various states of
undress, and three children came barreling down the
tairs. As they blindly tried to bolt past us, Mrs. Mulligan, still clutching her milk bottles, bellowed, "For
God's sake stop! *Stop*, d'you hear? There's no danger!
STOP!"

They stopped. Keeping her voice at a roar they could
hear above the bells, she explained what had happened.
While she shouted two more women in bathrobes
rounded the bend in the stairs, and the bells suddenly
topped. ". . . reported to the Housing Authority!"
houted Mrs. Mulligan and then, like the bells, subsided.
Stunned by the silence, the eleven of us were just standing there, deployed at various points on the landing and
tairs like figures in a high school pageant, when from
below came a man's voice and the clomp of heavy booted
feet on the stairs. A second later, rounding the corner
below us, a six-foot fireman came into view. Overwhelmingly young, husky, smiling and Irish, wearing rubbery
clothes that made a swishing sound, carrying a hatchet
—there he was, the hero of the pageant.

"*Good* morning, ladies!" he said, giving off a smell like
a bathing cap as he brushed past me and doffed his
long-tailed hat. He came to a stop on the landing next to
Mrs. Mulligan and said, beaming, "It's all over now. It
was only an elevator cable and we've got it under control. You can all go back to your kitchens and have a
econd cup of coffee."

"If it's under control what's that hatchet for?" asked a
suspicious girl in a Black Watch bathrobe, clutching a
child with either hand.

"To open the skylight atop the main shaft and let out
all the smoke. Terrible stuff, that smoke. Could spoil yer

carpets and draperies." Putting his hat back on, he
started making his way through the women to the next
flight of stairs.

"How about a cupuv for yourself, dear boy," called
Mrs. Mulligan, who'd been raptly drinking in this broth
of a lad all the while.

"Not today, luv," said the Dear Boy, and with a wink
and another tip of his hat he disappeared up the stairs.

Sighing, still hugging the milk bottles to her giant
breasts, Mrs. Mulligan extended the invitation to all ten
of us. She had a "wizard" coffee-maker that could make
twenty cups of the best coffee you ever had in six minutes, she said proudly.

The two women with children declined, but the rest
of us accepted. Carrie O'Sullivan (her real name) had a
huge, glorious buttercup-yellow kitchen gleaming with
brass and copper pots, and fitted out with every new
electrical appliance on the market. Within ten minutes
we were seated at her large white-marble table, drinking
the best coffee I've ever had, eating Mrs. Herbst's strudel,
and smoking away. Though she'd been put off by Folly
at first—she hated dogs, she said—Carrie O'Sullivan had
ended up giving her a whole raw kosher hot dog, and
Folly sat adoringly at her feet. After we'd exhausted the
topic of the way the building was run, our hostess took
over. She had just finished telling us all about "Flo," and
was describing the booming Ladies' Gymnasium she ran
on Broadway (which explained all the present com-
forts), when I finally became aware of the physical sensations I was having and what they meant. I'd been so
absorbed I'd forgotten all the things that *not* having
them had meant; I had completely forgotten that morning's important errand. Refusing to get excited—it could
be just a false alarm—I finished my coffee and strudel
and reluctantly rose to go. I'd been having a marvelous
time. I dragged Folly away from Carrie, said goodbye to
all the ladies in rollers and slacks and Brunch Coats, and
after thanking Carrie and promising I'd come ride the
exercycles at her gymnasium, walked back up the two
flights to our apartment and confirmed the good news.

When I'd taken care of necessities, I took the Bonwit bag out of the bottom of the hamper, emptied the specimen bottle into the toilet and flushed and flushed. I put the bottle out back in the garbage can, and came up front and washed and washed. Tina Macbeth for a last time. Then Folly began whining, and I realized that the poor thing had never been walked, so I put her on the leash again and took her down in the back elevator, which smelled of rotten apple cores, orange peels, coffee grounds, garlic salad dressing and old lamb-chop bones.

Once out on the street, the last traces of the zombie-trance I'd been in all morning vanished. It was a freakish February First—balmy, mild as May, windless, with a strong sun beating down. All yesterday's snow had melted. Without a thought for muggers, rapists, Uncle Pee-Pees or gangs of toughs, I turned into the park and walked and walked and walked, stopping only twice for Folly. I was deep in the park when a terrible exhaustion suddenly hit me, and I sat down on the nearest bench. Lighting a cigarette, I listlessly watched a rat, not more than four feet away, eat some bread put out for the pigeons.

It's over, I told myself. It's really over. You're free to pick up the pieces and start again. But I felt nothing, nothing, nothing, no elation or emotion at all, nothing but the cramps and the warmth of the sun on my head and back. Free to pick up the pieces and start *what* again? I didn't know. George had said I'd be all right as soon as I learned to settle for one thing, but what *was* that thing? I didn't know, I didn't know, so I finally got up and came home and sat down to write in here. Now, having written myself to this point, I know at last what I'm going to settle for and who I'm going to be. Who? Who is that? Why, Tabitha-Twitchit-Danvers, of course. The lady with the apron. And check-lists. And keys. It's me. Oh, it's *very* me, and I can't for the life of me see why I didn't realize that before. I suppose, for one thing, Jonathan wouldn't let me. It hardly fits his image of what the wife of a Renaissance Man should be.

Well, I've tried to be his image, tried to be a lot of things, but now I know. That's who I'm going to be, and if Jonathan doesn't like it he can lump it. Tabitha-Twitchit-Danvers-Me.

Friday February 2

'HOUGH I HADN'T SAID as much, I'd thought of yesteray's entry as perhaps being the last. But we're not done et, it seems I have another Account:

ast night, needless to say, I was exhausted; I was in bed y 10:00 and asleep by 10:15, in spite of really terrible ramps. At 3:00 I woke up with a jump, but it was othing like the old jumps which started the insomnia ycle. (Though I haven't reported it in here, my insomia has slowly receded over the last two months, with nly an occasional bad night here and there.) This was ifferent—it was as though someone had called my name r shouted—and I rolled over, startled, and saw that Jonthan's bed was empty, with the covers thrown all the vay down to the foot of the bed. For some reason the mpty bed and ringing silence terrified me. Where was e? Not in the bathroom, because its door stood ajar and ae lights were out. My heart began to hammer away, nd I threw on a robe. The living room and den were ark, but the pantry door stood open, and at its end I w the light from the kitchen coming under the door.

He was sitting huddled at the kitchen table, bundled ato his flannel bathrobe, holding a mug of something so ghtly with both hands that his knuckles were white. At ae *whoosh* of the swinging door, he jumped and almost pset the mug, turning to stare at me with puffy bloodshot eyes. "God! You *scared* me, Teen. What are you doing up?"

"That's what I came in here to ask you. I woke up and saw your empty bed and got worried— Are you all right?"

"Yeah, I'm all right. Go on back to bed, Teen."

I tried not to stare at his swollen eyes. "But why are you up?"

"I couldn't sleep, so I finally got up and came in here for some hot milk and honey. My mother used to give it to me sometimes when I was a kid, when bad dreams woke me up. It used to work like a charm."

Mother. Bad dreams. Hot milk and honey. It was too much. Gentle, more gentle than I've ever been in my whole life, I said, "You've been crying, haven't you, Jonathan?"

"And what if I have?" he snapped.

I took a deep breath. "Well. If you have . . . it's a little unusual. I mean it's not something you go around doing."

He made a horrible noise that was a cross between a laugh and a grunt.

"Jonathan, please. Won't you tell me what's wrong?"

Now he gave a smile that matched that noise. "Just about everything you can think of. That's what's wrong."

Suddenly I had to sit down. As I went to the kitchen table and pulled out a chair, I saw the cigarettes—six stubs in the ashtray and a hastily torn-open pack next to it. Jonathan watched me take this in. Trying to hide my dismay, I nonchalantly reached for the pack and lit myself one, wondering how long he had been back on them: had he started that night two weeks ago, when he'd asked me for the sleeping pill, or had he been back on them longer than that? Finally I saw that he had his hand out for the pack, and pushed it across the table. Number seven. As he lit it, his hand shook so badly that I couldn't watch.

After looking down at the white formica table top a few seconds, I said, "When you say everything I could think of is wrong, what do you mean? The way things are here—the way things are between us?"

Again that laugh. "I wish I did mean that."

I looked up. "Well, what *is* it then? Won't you tell me *any*thing?"

"You really want to hear?"

"I think it might be a good idea."

Taking a deep shaggy breath, Jonathan jammed out the barely smoked cigarette in the ashtray. Then he pushed his chair away from the table, and crossed his legs and shifted his position, so that he was facing the counter wall and cabinets instead of me. What I could see of his face in profile was so frightening—it seemed to be dissolving, falling apart in front of my eyes—that I looked away and found myself staring at his feet, an even more disturbing sight: one long bony foot was twitching and jerking with such a violent life of its own that the deerskin slipper from Abercrombie & Fitch flew off. I looked up again.

"Well, *first* of all," he began in a low breathless voice. "First of all, I've lost more money in the last few days than I ever can or will tell you about. Our stocks are not only just about cleaned out, but there's also a staggering debit."

Despite the first-of-all, I was overwhelmingly relieved. "Oh dear, Jonathan," I said inappropriately. "How did that happen?"

"*How.* It would take an hour to tell you. I suppose it all started with what you called my 'wild spec-u-lating.' Then, when the market took a dive a couple of weeks back, I was really in hot water. I was called for margin and had to sell in that putrid market, sell all sorts of things, and even then I still couldn't cover . . . Do you get the general idea?"

I nodded. "So now we're in a new tax bracket. Is that why you were crying? Is that why you look like that?"

Turning full-face, he gave me that horrible smile. "Remember I said *first* of all, old girl."

I nodded again. I remembered.

He took another deep breath. "Second of all, things aren't very rosy at Hoddison and Marks. It seems old

Hoddison has been very displeased with me this last month or two or three or four. 'Displeased' is putting it mildly, of course. It seems he hasn't liked my 'attitude' for a long time, hasn't felt I've really been with it—and a motion that I tried for in a suit about a month ago, and lost, finally really capped it. I think he thinks he's Sydney Greenstreet, for God's sake, the way he carried on in the two long talks we had. Talks. After nine years, nine *years* with that goddamn outfit, I get called down like a bloody office boy! Told, or rather, warned, to start getting with it."

"Well, you can and you will," I finally said in a Girl Scout voice that revolted even me. "I mean after you pull yourself together about the beating you've taken on the stock market, and swing some loans to start paying your debts, you'll be able to concentrate on your work again. You'll be your old self again in no time."

"No," he said. "No. That's one thing I'm never gonna be."

"Oh, Jonathan. Now what does *that* mean?"

Once again he reached for a cigarette and went through the grueling business of trying to light it. This time I didn't take my eyes off him, though he practically disappeared in a cloud of smoke.

"What that means," he finally said, "is that I've got to go through a complete character change, a rehabilitation, as my analyst puts it, of my character, or face the consequences and snap."

"Analyst."

"Yah, that's right. Analyst. Wig-picker. Shrink."

". . . How long have you been going to an *analyst?*"

"Well, let's see. About three weeks. Counting the three sessions with Popkin, maybe four."

In the silence the refrigerator motor started with a loud whir, and we heard Folly scratching at the door. Like me, the poor dog had been disturbed by the empty beds, and had come to see what was going on. Needing time to absorb what I'd just heard, I got up and opened the door. Wiggling, poodle-foolish, Folly came bouncing in and joyously headed for Jonathan. She might just as well have jumped on a corpse. Giving up, she crawled dejectedly over to me, and after a few reassuring pats, disappeared under the table.

"So. You went to Doctor Popkin," I prompted, as ready as I'd ever be to resume this conversation.

"I went to Doctor Popkin."

"When? And what finally made you go?"

"I went the day after we had that fight—the one about my making the girls laugh at you while you were feeding the birds. I went because I couldn't stand it any more. I was convinced you were losing your mind. *You* wouldn't go, so I finally went to tell tales on you and see if there wasn't some way you could be *made* to go. *Ha.* You know what happened?"

"No. What happened?"

"Old Popkin pinned the rose on *me*."

Understanding everything I'd understood for God knows how long, I said, "I don't understand."

"It's me, old girl. Not you. *Me.* You yourself said as much a couple of times. Me. Me. Not you. Oh, you've got your problems, all right, but Doctor Popkin said they were the usual problems of the average middle-class girl who's been brought up to expect all sorts of gratifications and glory, and has one helluva time adjusting to the demands and frustrations and disappointments of reality. He said that even though you'd been successfully analyzed, had most of that analyzed out of you, mild flare-ups from any residual problems were to be expected from time to time. He said that normally you could have coped with that sort of thing, worked it out on a subconscious level, but what was clearly one of those ah . . . resurgences had been aggravated by my attitudes and demands, and consequently had been blown up into a sort of state of crisis which will subside as soon as I lay off you and get to work on myself."

Stunned by this long-winded spiel, this technical recitation and explanation of all my poor symptoms, I just sat there. It certainly hadn't taken him very long to learn the lingo; it usually takes new analysands a few months. Then, of course, you can't shut them up.

Already calmer, Jonathan smiled, a real smile at last. "He even said your refusal to come and see him was a

good sign, a sign of your inner resources and strength.
Deep down you knew it wasn't you, and yet your pride
—after all, you'd chosen to love and marry me—and
your integrity—you didn't want to hurt me—kept you
from letting yourself face who it was. He said, and I
quote: 'Bettina is a very good person, a fine human
being.'"

This was too much to take. All the other bouquets
had made me feel bad enough, but now I felt positively
rotten. *Who* was a fine human being? But awful as I
felt, I wasn't about to contradict him or to start any
confessional spiels of my own. I took a deep breath and
slowly let it out. "Why isn't Popkin analyzing you?
And who is this other analyst you've been going to for
three weeks?"

"Popkin said that though some analysts do it, he
doesn't believe a husband and wife ought to be treated
by the same person, even when there's a time lapse as in
this case. So he sent me to this other guy."

"Is he—the other analyst—any good?"

Jonathan shrugged. "How the hell do you know?
Popkin gave me a long list of his credentials, and he was
trained at all the right places and belongs to all the right
institutions. I even had him checked by Max Simon. But
who knows? All I know is that he *talks* an awful lot.
Christ, I didn't think they talked, I thought they just listened. But I gather there are two kinds—the kind who
talk, and the kind who listen. I've got the kind who talks.
He listens to me talk, then *he* talks. And not only does
he talk, but Christ, the things he tells me that are wrong
wih me! It's enough to make me want to get up off the
couch and take a dive out of his office window onto Fifth
Avenue."

"It can't be that bad. It just seems that way. I mean
maybe I shouldn't stick my two cents in, but it seems to
me that whatever's gone wrong has just come up in the
last few years. I mean you were really quite different
when we first met and when I married you. You only
changed a few years ago, and whatever it is that made
you change is the problem."

"I didn't change. I was always what I am now—

greedy, aggressive, hostile, dishonest, and ambitious beyond belief. It was just that I managed to hide it better
at one time."

For a minute I just sat shivering and staring at the
floor. The kitchen was warm, but I was freezing. Also,
my cramps were back, and unbelievably bad. "You aren't
really like that," I said at last. "Some analysts, the talking
kind, pile it on pretty thick in the beginning—all the
bad news at once. They can make you feel pretty shitty
about yourself. It's part of the technique. But when you
get further on into it, things will lighten up. Things will
get better, you'll feel much better about yourself—
you'll see. I mean what I'm really trying to say is that
bad as they seem at the moment, things aren't really that
bad."

Swallowing, he dropped his eyes. "I haven't finished."

"You mean there's a fourth-of-all?"

He nodded, grim.

Knowing, really, what was coming, I waited.

He licked his lips and suddenly said, very loud, almost
defiant: "I've been having an affair."

Yes, I thought. "Yes," I said.

"*Yes?*"

"Yes. With Margo Whoosis. Gaylord's . . . ah . . .
girl."

His colorless face turned bright red. "Did she call
you? Is that how you know? She threatened to call you
a month or so ago. *Did* she call you, Teen? I'll kill her if
she did!"

"No. She didn't call me. I knew it all along without
really knowing, if you know what I mean. Even without
Charlotte Rady's delicate hints."

"Charlotte Rady? My God, that means half of New
York must know."

Does it really matter? I thought. I said: "Your tense
confuses me. 'Been having.' Does that mean it's over, or is
it still going on?"

"It's over. I broke it off a few weeks ago. I wanted to
sooner, but didn't have the nerve. Christ, she's crazy,
really out of her mind! I had no idea of what I was getting into until it was too late. I mean there was this ah

powerful physical attraction I still can't explain. Things weren't so hot between you and me that way, and I figured it was your fault, so why not? Why make such a big deal out of it, everybody else does it now, it's taken for granted—why shouldn't I swing too? . . . Only thing is I'm not cut out for all that jazz. I can't swing. All the lies and all those arrangements. And the guilt. It was tearing me apart."

I was having a terrible battle with myself. Finally, to keep myself from blurting out *my* little tale, I said, "When you wanted me to go to Florida with the girls a few weeks ago . . . was that when you were trying to break things up and she was threatening to call?"

"Partly that. All hell was breaking loose on every front around that time, and I didn't want you looking at me too closely— You know, if I may say so, you're pretty damned cool."

"How would you like me to be?"

He blinked. "Hell, *I* don't know. I guess I expected tears, recriminations, a big scene. But then I guess I don't know anything any more. All I do know is that I feel like a rat. I think I just about hit bottom that night you wanted to make love, and had to work on me. I realized how I'd been neglecting you in that way, and Jesus, how I hated myself!"

Well, that made two of us. Remembering that awful night and my motives, I stared at him, near tears, my heart racing. I stared and stared at his face, abject, haggard, full of self-hate and self-pity, until a voice in my head shouted, *No!* No, dammit you *won't!* And then, knowing I wouldn't, I immediately felt release. It was a giant step for me. Though I knew it might help him, might make him feel better about himself if I too Confessed, I decided I would never tell him about George. What for? I had nothing to gain, and everything to lose, once his brief spell of feeling better about himself was over. In deciding this, I wasn't trying to "punish" him by letting him wallow alone in guilt because I felt he was to blame for so much, my going to George included. No. It was more simply that for the first time in my life I was being completely realistic, without any gratuitous masochism thrown in: I'd had *enough* of mucky messes; I knew what I meant to have and be, and I was going to go after it.

"Do you want a divorce, Teen?" asked Jonathan, breaking the silence, apparently having thought along the same lines. "I'll understand if you do."

"No, Jonathan. I don't want a divorce."

He let out a sigh of relief. "My doctor said you wouldn't. He said that in thinking that you would, I was being emotional as usual. He said that you sounded far too intelligent for such 'dramatic clap-trap.' In fact, he said that if you had the patience and understanding he suspected you had, we could pick up the pieces and probably work out a far better relationship than we had before. Thing is . . . *do* you have the patience and understanding, do you think we *can* pick up the pieces and go on?"

I was gritting my teeth. Why were all those noble virtues and qualities being attributed to me? It was almost more than I could bear. To set the record straight, would I have to Confess after all? "Yes. I do," I said quietly.

"It may sound funny, but I think so too. I mean we're suited to each other in a very basic way, Teen. And I also think that underneath all this . . . we still really love each other . . . Don't you think that's true, Teen?"

It wasn't a word I wanted to hear just then, so I nodded, hoping that he'd shut up and go to bed.

But manic with the release of the Confessional, he rattled on. "Maybe we ought to move out of this damned city, to the country somewhere."

"What? *Why?*"

"Because. For one thing it would be a fresh start. For another, it would be simpler values, simpler things. No more rat race."

I finally saw that he'd reached the point of exhaustion where he couldn't think straight. "They have rat races in the country too, Jonathan. And I don't want to live in the country. I want to go on living here."

"But don't you see that life here will be different? I

mean what with my debts and paying for the shrink and the girls' school, God knows how we'll get along."

"Jonathan," I said gently. "Life in the country isn't cheap. And Thoreau is dead. And your debts aside, you have a splendid income . . . But these are all things we can go into later. I really think you ought to go to bed. You look just terrible and you're not making sense."

"You're right," said Jonathan, and stood up, swaying. "I'm suddenly so punchy I don't know if I can make it from here to our room. Aren't you coming too?"

"Soon," I said. "You go on ahead. I'm not very sleepy, so I think I'll try some of your hot milk and honey."

"Don't bother," he said with the ghost of a smile. "It doesn't work." He stumbled out.

I sat there at the kitchen table for half an hour before I looked at the electric clock above the sink, and saw that it was twenty to five and that there was a cockroach trapped in the face of the clock. It had probably crawled in through the opening for the wires at the back of the clock, and come out through the small hole where the hands were attached to the face. The cockroach was huddled down between the 2 and the 3, and as the second-hand moved around, I stared: a miniature "Pit and the Pendulum" was going on right in my kitchen, right in my Westinghouse clock! As the second-hand neared the 2, the cockroach sort of quivered and flattened itself down, but not quite far enough, for the long needly brass tip gave the roach a grazing pick as it passed over its back. I pushed back my chair and in one step was at the sink and yanked the clock's plug from the wall. Was it dead? I lifted the clock off its hook and shook it and the roach began to run. Obviously not even badly wounded from its bout with the second-hand, it ran crazily round and round the numbers, too frantic to get out the same way it had got in. I laid the clock on the sink counter, got a hammer out of the tool box in the broom closet, and went back and gave the face one smart rap, which made a neat pie-shaped crack in the glass. Placing my index finger on the apex of the wedge, I gently pushed; the tip went down, the flat base came up, and I gingerly lifted out the whole piece. The roach ran crazily round the numbers one last time. Then, with a little jump, it climbed out onto the glass, getting itself over the sharp edge without injury. From there it ran down the clock's side and across the counter to the wall, where it vanished down a hole in the plaster between the tiles—damaged but undaunted—home to wifey and the kids.

ABOUT THE AUTHOR

SUE KAUFMAN was born in New York City, attended school on Long Island and was graduated from Vassar. She is married to a doctor and they have a ten-year-old son, James, and an eccentric dachshund, Poppy. *DIARY OF A MAD HOUSEWIFE* is Miss Kaufman's third novel.

BANTAM BESTSELLERS

OUTSTANDING BOOKS NOW AVAILABLE
AT A FRACTION
OF THEIR ORIGINAL COST!

Wait 'til you see what *else* we've got in store for you!

Send for your FREE catalog of Bantam Bestsellers today!

This money-saving catalog lists hundreds of best-sellers originally priced from $3.75 to $15.00—yours now in Bantam paperback editions for just 50¢ to $1.95! Here is a great opportunity to read the good books you've missed and add to your private library at huge savings! The catalog is FREE! So don't delay—send for yours today!